The Devil's Tune

Mihaela,

Merry Christmas,

The Devil's Tune

Iain Duncan Smith

IAIN DUNCAN SMITH

16" December 2003

ROBSON BOOKS

First published in Great Britain in 2003 by Robson Books, The Chrysalis Building, Bramley Road, London, W10 6SP

An imprint of **Chrysalis** Books Group plc

British Library Cataloguing in Publication Data
A catalogue record for this title is available from the British Library.

ISBN 1 86105 666 4

Typeset by SX Composing DTP, Rayleigh, Essex
Printed by Butler & Tanner Ltd, Frome and London

For Betsy, Edward, Alicia, Harry and Rosie, without whose love and support nothing would be possible.

Prologue

Silence. That earth-scented and damp-edged stillness, just before the dawn. Starless, moonless, the edge of transition, a gap in time before the sun beyond the Apennines slowly undims the landscape. Then, with first light, the sounds. An edgy, cautious, discordant orchestra of birds, whose growing volume tracks the dawn from a surround of olive trees which, like old forgotten sentinels, stand stiff-limbed among the rocks.

In this growing light an outcrop of land rises from the shadows and on its edge, slowly uncovered, man's thumbprint in stone. Four old walls roofed in terracotta tiles form a hollow square. Against the outside of these walls, the sun-picked bougainvillea and inside, jasmine leaves scent the cool morning air as a gentle breeze stirs the dew-heavy flowers in the courtyard.

As the sun touches the horizon, its light bursting over the hill above, distant footsteps can be heard echoing along a passage. A black-clad maid walks slowly from her living quarters, through cloisters, up solid stone steps, past an anteroom and into a kitchen. In the kitchen her low-toned singing begins. Softly, it catches the light breeze and drifts across the courtyard and through open windows, it hangs in the spaces. Not words, just lilting rhythms, reaching out, stretching, drifting as they slide through heavy shutters closed against the night.

Half awake and covered by a sheet, John Grande stares at the ceiling. For hours, he has listened to the noises of the night, counted their rhythms and measured their volume before sensing the heavy silence at the edge of dawn. He lies still, for sleep has become such a stranger that he doesn't even toss and turn any more. He is used to these hollow moments. It's not the dark but the first flicker of light he fears – the light which brings the whispering rush of cluttered memories spinning round him like a vortex. He reaches for the side of the bed and grips tight, like a man on a rollercoaster who aches for the ride to stop. Then, as always, his memory roars at him, dragging him back – back to those mornings as a boy, so far away, when this room marked the same beginning, acted then as now as the starter's gun. He can see that wiry boy, burned brown, half wild and salt stiff – a pressure cooker of anticipation. That boy – him, alive with a sense that night was just another shade of day – is now gone. Then the years tumble across his memory, casting images then flicking them aside to be lost as others are made. These dreams, this place, always the same, created and defined by these old walls – the stone, the colour, the heat, they frame his memory like a picture.

Now his eyes are open, darting around the room in the dying gloom. He can't be sure where the dreaming stops for everywhere his mother's face smiles back at him, beckoning, saying something. Then, just as it seems he will hear her words, she is gone, replaced by the dark-haired Julia, his wife, with their small boy. He fears the sight of her, yet yearns for it. He knows what always comes next – the screams and the broken bodies. Policeman and death, and the violence, always the violence. Then they too are gone, snatched from him as they were in life – no goodbyes, just the laughter, hanging in the thick air. Somewhere always that taunting laughter echoing as the churning tide of memory crashes against him and leaves his face wet to mark its passage. He is awake, the vision gone, the moment has passed and slowly, carefully, he releases the side of the bed and closes his eyes again.

Coffee. The insistent aroma intrudes and pulls his heavy eyes open again on thin strands. He sits up, and listens to the disembodied singing. Then with fixed expression, he slides out of bed and dresses. Minutes later, walking quickly and quietly out of the villa through a back door, he descends down a track to the bay below. Once there, casting his shirt aside, he runs into the sea and swims, burying himself beneath the water until he feels his lungs must burst and then, only then, he surfaces, sucking in the fresh morning air.

1

Il Lupo de Mare

It was nine o'clock when John Grande emerged from his swim.

The small cove was well secluded and John knew that it could only be reached from a couple of villas some distance away, and it was hardly ever used by anyone else. He waded out of the water and over to where his towel lay. He dried himself, then picked up his book. He found a rock, large enough to provide some shade, sank down gratefully against it and started to read. There was only the thinnest of breezes which licked across him from time to time and, apart from the gentle sound of the small waves lapping against the rocks of the cove, all was quiet. As time passed, the peace of his surroundings and the warmth of the sun made his eyelids heavy and his head dropped lower and lower until finally it was still. The book lay open on his lap, its pages occasionally flicking over, as though turned by some unseen hand.

As the sun rose higher and the shadows slid away, Grande's breathing became slow and even – deep sleep, finally deeper than anything he had known for two years, had finally claimed him.

Some small rocks and pebbles clattered down the other side of the cove behind him, as two women walked down an old path onto the beach. They were both tall and slim and dressed in loose-fitting T-shirts. One was blonde with a classically beautiful face, the sort seen on glossy magazine covers all over the world. The other, her sunglasses pushed back off her face and her dark hair fastened behind her head in a no-nonsense way, had a handsome face with strong, clear features and wide, dark eyes, which drew the observer in.

'Where do you want to go?' the dark-haired woman asked.

'Anywhere, Laura,' the blonde replied, 'anywhere.' She looked towards a large rock at the far side and pointed. 'I can't get over,' she began, 'the way your father never had you to stay here before.'

'Well, I guess we both just got used to it,' Laura replied. 'My mother didn't want me to have any contact and we lost touch.' She paused. 'They never spoke after the divorce. She wasn't bothered, but I was. As I got older, I wanted a father. Yet she junked every reminder of him. I had to piece it all back together myself. But he can't have cared either,' she glanced back towards the villa. 'After all, he could have written,' she shrugged.

'You know, Alice, I never had any letters, cards or presents; he made no contact at all except for the cheques. And he didn't invite us this time; I invited us.' She smiled, 'It took me a while to find him after my mother died, but . . .' she stopped beside the rock, 'my mother told me he just wanted to be alone. Thing is, there was never another woman. It's funny really, she seemed to find that tougher – to lose out to nothing.' She stared out to sea, then shrugged. 'I'm, well, we're here, that's all that matters.' Throwing her towel across the rock, she pulled off her T-shirt and walked to the sea, closely followed by her friend.

Twenty minutes later, the dark-haired girl walked back to the rock, still wet from her swim, picked up her towel and started to dry herself. At that moment, on the other side of the rock, John Grande woke up. He stretched slowly, easing his stiff neck, while glancing at his watch. Standing up, he looked up at the villa, his back to the sea.

'Jesus!' Laura exclaimed, staring at his back.

Turning around quickly, he found himself facing an attractive dark-haired woman. 'I'm sorry . . .' he spluttered.

'No – well . . .' she half smiled. 'Don't worry,' she said, as she slowly slipped a towel around herself. 'You startled me, that's all.'

'I was reading,' John glanced down at the book now lying in the sand. 'I must have dozed off.' Dark hair, he thought, then took in her dark brown eyes and large mouth, which seemed to smile easily. 'Anyway, I'm John Grande,' he smiled faintly.

'Laura Buckley,' she replied, pointing behind her, 'I'm up there with my father.'

'And I'm up there,' he replied, pointing up towards the villa, part of which was just visible from the beach.

'Ah, I was wondering who lived there,' she replied. 'My father said it was some sort of love nest for a king, said some guy known as "Il Lupo . . ."'

'Il lupo de Mare, the Sea Wolf,' cut in John. 'An old Italian fairy tale. It's what the locals call him.'

'Sea Wolf?'

John smiled, 'He has a white beard, so does the man in the fairy tale.'

'Oh, I see.'

At that moment her friend walked up. Unlike Laura, she made no effort to cover her nakedness, but dried herself in a lazy and distracted way, her eyes never leaving his.

'This is Alice van Buren. Alice meet . . .' Laura Buckley turned. 'I'm sorry, I forgot your name.'

'John Grande,' he replied, glancing at his watch.

'We've disturbed you . . .' Laura said.

'No, no – I have to get going for a meeting. I was about to go anyway.' He bent down to pick up his towel and book.

3

'What? On vacation?' Alice van Buren cut in.

'Well, I'm not really on holiday, I'm here to see some paintings. I'm an art dealer.'

'He's in that villa,' Laura said, turning to Alice, pointing, 'the one with the white walls and terracotta tiles on the ridge.'

'The one we saw on our way down?'

Laura nodded.

'Looks gorgeous,' Alice continued. 'How old is it?' she asked, drying her hair, her eyes still never leaving his.

'It was built for Murat in 1813,' John replied, 'when he was king of Naples.' He slipped his sandals on before continuing. 'During the summer he moved to a small palace in Positano, the one that's a hotel now. You might have seen it. But he wanted somewhere he could . . .' he turned back towards them 'entertain his mistress.' He threw a towel over his shoulder. 'As you say, his love nest,' he said, glancing at Laura, 'so he came to Ithaca.'

'Ithaca?' Alice asked.

'The house's name is taken from the Cavafy poem – you know, it's the journey not the arrival that's important. My uncle has always believed life is about the journey, the next challenge. Anyway,' he shrugged, 'my grandfather said everyone in our family would come back here.' He hesitated as he looked at the dark-haired woman.

'How long are you here for?' Alice asked.

'Not long. I have to leave tonight, I'm afraid.' He smiled, 'Well . . . good to meet you,' and turning, he walked across the beach and up the path.

'Pity,' Alice van Buren said absent-mindedly, now combing her hair. 'Pity.'

'Yeah,' Laura Buckley replied. She continued to watch John as he climbed up the track, 'You know, Alice, he looks kind of sad, don't you think?'

'I don't know about that; he's good-looking anyway.' Alice van Buren laughed, then laid her towel out. 'Even if he was a bit skinny.' She took a magazine out from her bag and put on her dark glasses and lay down.

Laura continued watching John as he walked up the path and over the ridge. 'A sad-looking guy . . .' she muttered, her voice trailing away as she sat down.

It was mid-morning when John Grande reached the hill above the cove. Following a narrow path, he climbed a small ridge directly above the villa. From this point, he had a clear view of the villa and the small cove to the east. It had always been a favourite spot of his; he remembered how often he had hidden there, able to watch his uncle and his mother moving around the villa while they shouted for him. It all seemed so long ago.

With the olive trees behind him, he gazed out over the sea. His thoughts turned back to his decision to come to the villa and stay with his uncle. The irony was that he had not come on a social visit at all; the villa held too many memories for him and he felt it was still too soon to return. This visit, he insisted, was all about business: his business. He kept telling himself it had been a coincidence, just a strange coincidence. Four weeks before, an American had walked into his gallery in London searching for pictures by a prewar Italian painter named Licatta. John could picture the man now, as clearly as the day he had stood before him. Short and heavy-set, he had a pugnacious face, broken only by a thick, drooping moustache, the kind that was fashionable in the seventies but was now, in 1995, as dated as flares and flowered shirts. Most memorable of all, however, were his eyes. They were small like a ferret's.

'I'm lookin' for six Licattas,' the man had said bluntly, his eyes boring into John. He could remember how surprised he had been. Usually, he might expect a request for one painting by Licatta, or even a few paintings, but a specific demand for six had struck him as bizarre.

As an art dealer specialising in twentieth-century European art, John had sold some Licattas before. There was a small demand for his paintings; he was not a major artist and his had always been a specialist market. The strange thing was that the short, stocky man, Jason F Peach, didn't seem like any dealer or collector he had ever known. But Peach wanted the pictures and was prepared to pay well over the going rate.

John made some inquiries but hadn't found any more Licattas, so he put it down to a lost opportunity and forgot about it. Then, a week later, his uncle had telephoned with the news that a neighbour of his was selling part of his collection. His uncle had been given two or three very significant names from the collection. John had hesitated; he'd feared a return to the villa, a place of so many memories. Yet, with the prospect of what sounded like a dealer's dream sale, he agreed. He promised himself that the visit would be short and focused and, most importantly, the gallery needed the money.

Sitting on the ridge above the villa, the events seemed a million miles away, yet he knew he was due to see the collection in an hour's time. He'd leave, he told himself, immediately afterwards.

He turned his head towards the villa, so beautiful in the morning light. He stood up, about to walk towards it, when a sharp glint of light caught his attention. He looked towards a small, raised area of ground just behind the olive trees, to the east of the villa. He could see nothing at first. Then the glint caught his eye again and, as he looked back, this time something moved. Staring hard, he became sure that someone was standing on a ridge just behind the villa. He scanned the ridge, his hands shading his eyes; through the heat haze he could see a man staring at the house. Another glint – binoculars. John was puzzled. He couldn't recall seeing anyone up there before. Looking around for a way to get up to the ridge, he saw a path through the olive trees a few paces from him. Once in the olive trees he would be out of sight. From where he stood, the path ran through the olive trees and up to a point just below the ridge line.

He moved quickly along the track, as it took him deeper into the grove. Stopping at the bottom of the ridge, his position still screened by the trees, he became aware of the smell of strong cigarette smoke. There was a thick, chesty cough from the top of the ridge. Inching his way cautiously up the small bank in front, he was just drawing level with the edge of the ridge when his foot slipped, sending a shower of stones down the incline into the trees.

He tried to climb quickly, aware he must have given his position away. With a last effort, he hauled himself up, just in time to hear a car door slamming behind the trees, then an engine starting up. Running towards the noise, he arrived in time to see a car disappearing down a track, which he knew must head to the road beyond.

The dust from the car obscured his view and he cursed his own clumsiness. He retraced his steps to the spot where the stranger had stood. From there, someone could see into the villa; any comings and goings would have been watched with ease. John frowned and turned to go, when something on the ground caught his attention. A small, half-finished cigarette was still smouldering. He turned it over in his hands and found that he could make out the beginning of a name, 'Sip . . .'

'Sip . . . Sip,' he muttered, before knocking the tip off and dropping the cigarette into his pocket.

With the sun on his face, he gazed across to the villa. The morning sun on its walls picked out the sharp colours of the flowers in the courtyard as, from across the ridge, faint laughter carried on the slight breeze, disembodied and distant. At the mouth of the bay, John could see a fishing boat, not full of fishermen, but of tourists, nosing its way through a mirrored surface, on its slow journey back to Positano.

As he walked towards the house, watching it absorb the dull heat of the sun, John thought about his uncle. Despite the dull ache and the memories, he knew that no matter how much he tried to forget his past and the villa, he couldn't; it was a part of him. The smells, the sights and the sounds were drawing him closer. Yet, as much as it drew him, he instinctively resisted. His journey back to it was far from complete; he needed time – much, much more time.

An hour later, John was staring at an Art Deco villa as his uncle climbed out of his car. Built on two levels, the front was large and rounded, with matching, curving steps leading to the grand front door, above which stood a large balcony. On either side of the steps were two nude, female figures, holding glass orbs in their outstretched arms. Two sides were set back into the hill, with the other two sides facing onto the bay. The reflection from the rounded windows by the steps was quite dazzling.

'Built by one of Mussolini's relations in the early thirties,' John's uncle Ralph said. 'Whoever it was who built it, they must have spent a fortune. Look how it's cut back into the rock so that the villa is at right angles to the bay.'

John nodded, fascinated by the sight.

Then a tall, rather gaunt-looking man started down the steps. He walked slowly, leaning heavily on his walking stick, breathing with difficulty.

'Mike D'Ostia,' he said, as he stopped in front of John, his hand outstretched. He had dark, sunken eyes, a pronounced hook nose and thin lips. John shook his hand slowly, noticing the man's skin had an unhealthy, translucent look to it, like the sheen of an old waxwork. He led them back to the house.

Once inside the hall, it was as if they had stepped back sixty years. Everything was Art Deco: the lamps, the tables, even the chairs. They walked through into another room to be greeted with more Art Deco furniture.

As they moved about, John listened to D'Ostia talking about the villa. He spoke fast, pausing only to inhale from a cigarette which seemed permanently clamped between the yellowed fingers of his shaking left hand. His accent was unmistakably New York, yet every now and then there was an Italian twang at the edges. John became aware of women's voices behind them in the hall. As he listened to his host, D'Ostia noticed John's distracted look and, inhaling deeply on his cigarette, he glanced at the door. 'Wait here, I've got to see . . .' his voice trailed away as he walked through the door towards the hall.

John walked over to a large picture window facing south east. It was an immense view. He could see the large sweep of the gulf stretching away towards Sorrento. Below the window the rock fell away very steeply down to the water's edge, two hundred feet below.

Hearing more voices to his right, he walked over to a side window. From there he overlooked the front steps and he could see the same two women who had been on the beach that morning climbing into a car. He watched as the car disappeared up the drive. The dark-haired woman's face seemed to hover in front of him, her soft eyes holding his.

'Mr Grande.'

John turned to see D'Ostia standing beside him as the maid held out a glass of white wine. He watched D'Ostia limp towards his uncle.

John left the window reluctantly.

'Now, come and see the pictures,' D'Ostia said over his shoulder, as he took John's uncle by the arm and led him gently but firmly towards the back of the long room. John spotted a small pen-and-ink sketch in the corner of the room.

'Do you mind if I have a look?' he asked.

'Sure, go ahead,' D'Ostia replied.

John could feel D'Ostia's eyes boring into him as he walked towards the sketch.

'It looks like it could be . . . a Picasso?' John glanced back in surprise at D'Ostia, in time to see him nodding. 'And,' John continued, raising his eyebrows, 'it looks like . . . you?'

'Your nephew has a good eye,' D'Ostia's face cracked into a faint smile, 'He's right – Picasso did that in less than one minute on the back of an old scrap of paper.' For the first time his hollow face seemed to crack around the edges into a thin smile.

'Come over here,' D'Ostia continued, 'you'll find this even more interesting.' D'Ostia turned and walked towards a panel in the wall. From his pocket he produced a set of keys, unlocked the panel and pulled it open. Standing behind him, John could make out some numbered buttons. He watched as D'Ostia pressed a combination and shut the panel, locking it again after him. D'Ostia turned to his left and pushed what appeared to John to be just another section of the wall, but to his amazement, it gave way and swung open. 'Follow me,' D'Ostia wheezed as he walked through.

John was quite unprepared for the sight that greeted him. In front of him was an oblong room, painted white, the walls of which were hung with a number of paintings.

He followed D'Ostia down three steps. Above him was a large glass dome, through which a gentle, indirect light filtered to fill the whole room. The room was not large but because it was divided into two sections, it felt even smaller. John counted fifteen paintings, nine in one section and six in the other. In the first section they all had one thing in common: every one seemed to have a religious theme. However, in the second section, the six were all by the same artist. And, as he looked at them more closely, he realised they were by Licatta. He frowned as he turned to find D'Ostia staring at him. 'So,' D'Ostia broke the silence, 'what do you think?'

'Very impressive,' John said, choosing his words carefully. He pointed towards the nine paintings. 'I'd hesitate before putting a price tag on that section over there. You've got some wonderful paintings. There's a couple from the Perugino School, one there by Brueghel, another by Caravaggio . . . Over there – well,' he paused, turning to face D'Ostia, 'let me be frank, this is very strange. A few weeks ago a man walked into my gallery and asked to buy six Licattas. I couldn't lay my hands on any and I forgot about it. Then out of the blue came a call from my uncle saying you have a collection to sell, and here I am, and look, it just so happens you have six Licattas on your walls . . . Coincidence?'

'Perhaps,' D'Ostia replied flatly. He lit a second cigarette from the first, which was now smouldering in his left hand, then walked over to a small table and stubbed the first one out in an ashtray. 'I want you to sell these six in London.' He pointed at the Licattas as he spoke, 'Once you've done that – if you do it successfully,' he looked John in the eyes before continuing, 'I plan to sell the others as well,' he drew on the cigarette, 'through you.'

These last words puzzled John. While a possible sale of the nine pictures in the first section would be any dealer's dream, there were too many unanswered questions.

'Let me get this right. You knew about this request for Licattas?'

'Perhaps,' D'Ostia said, 'but you shouldn't trouble yourself over that. Just think of it as a deal – like any other.'

'Why me?'

'Why not you?' D'Ostia replied. 'You're a dealer, you know all about early twentieth-century painting – and these,' he pointed at the section containing the Brueghel and the Caravaggio, 'well, I'm sure you could deal them out through others. And, if I'm not mistaken, you could use the money.'

The first section was just what his gallery needed: a collection of masters worth many millions with a handsome percentage. D'Ostia had made it clear that it all hinged on the Licattas. What would he be getting involved in? There must surely be a link, he thought, between D'Ostia and that man, Peach. He walked towards the Licattas and stared at each one in turn. He was only too well aware of his gallery's growing financial difficulties. This sort of deal could change all that. But still he hesitated; there was something wrong. Common sense surely demanded that he walk away, he reasoned, but . . .

'Well, Mr Grande?' D'Ostia interrupted his thoughts.

'It's a very strange proposal – all I have to do, you say, is sell these six paintings with the promise of more to come – those nine . . .'

'Only if you agree to sell these,' D'Ostia interrupted, pointing at the six Licattas. 'Those or nothing.'

'That would depend on the price and commission.'

'Don't worry about that. You'll find me very generous.'

John looked at his uncle, who frowned as their eyes met.

'I'd want to know how much,' he continued, turning to D'Ostia. 'There's also the chance that I won't be able to find a buyer – so it'll need to be worthwhile.'

'Triple your usual commission for the Licattas – easy money, Mr Grande, if, as you said, you already have a buyer,' he smiled.

'That's very generous – yet, why me? You could do it more easily for a lot less here in Naples.'

'Look, Mr Grande, *I'm* not worried about the money – *you* are! I give no explanation, I only make deals. You'll have to take it or leave it.' He stubbed out his second cigarette. 'I didn't take you for a fool, though – it's easy money. Remember, the art of a good deal is that both parties feel they get something.' He lit another cigarette. 'The choice is yours.'

John's lips tightened. He didn't like being referred to as a fool. It had all the features of a setup, he knew, but it was also a lot of money.

'If I agree,' he began, 'will you guarantee that these nine

paintings will be sold by my gallery after these . . .' he flicked his hand at the Licattas 'are sold?'

'Sure.' D'Ostia paused and reached into his jacket. 'Here are some photographs of the Licattas.'

John took the envelope and opened it.

'You've taken a lot for granted,' he said.

'No, like I said, Mr Grande, I never took you for a fool.' D'Ostia smiled. 'It's a deal?'

John glanced at the photographs, feeling uneasy. It was a strange proposition, yet it was simple; all he had to do was to sell a few Licattas to someone who wanted to buy them – there was a market place ready and waiting for them. It should, at most, he mused, be relatively easy – a quick sale – but that was the problem: it was too easy. Yet the gallery did need the money.

'OK, it's a deal,' John replied, looking at D'Ostia as his lips parted into a smile. Behind D'Ostia he could see his uncle was frowning, clearly concerned.

When they arrived back at the villa, John walked into the drawing room, took off his jacket and sat down at the piano. He was worried about the deal and dissatisfied with himself. Uncomfortable and angry, he started to play. The music didn't help; it conjured up haunting images of his wife and child. Their presence made him tense and he dropped his stiff hands down onto the keys in a crescendo of noise. He sat still, head bowed as the noise faded away.

'The car will be here in five minutes,' Ralph said as John emerged onto the terrace. 'Strange deal, John,' he continued hesitantly, 'I wish I'd never got you to come here. It worries me; it doesn't make sense. Are you sure? You don't have to go ahead.'

'Well, you know him – was I right to accept?'

'I'm not sure,' he answered, 'and I don't really know him. Oh, we've met on a number of occasions, but he's always kept himself to himself. What concerns me is the way he's planned everything, set it up, the way he assumed you'd agree.' Ralph paused. 'Are the paintings genuine? Are they worth anything?'

'Too genuine – that's what worries me.'

'Not too late to cancel,' Ralph looked at John and frowned. 'The real reason I agreed to call you – I confess, John – was to see you again. I used the sale as an excuse. I wish I hadn't now.'

'You're right. There are potential problems but there always are over deals like this. I'd be mad to turn this down. After all, what should I care? At the end of it all, it's just a deal. Anyone else would jump at the offer.'

'John, if it's just the money, I . . .'

'No. It's not just the money – of course I could do with it, but it's the reputation which comes with a deal like this. Anyway, it's been a dark time for me – I must get back into all of this. A dealer needs a deal and I need to put my life together again.'

A car horn sounded on the other side of the villa.

'I'll get my bags.'

Ralph followed him to the front door and watched him hand the baggage to the driver.

'Take care of yourself,' he said. 'Keep in touch.'

'And you,' John replied. There was a moment's hesitation. 'I've not been the best of guests. Perhaps we could have talked, it's just that it's difficult . . . You know, I'm sorry,' he dropped his head, 'she's everywhere in this house and I can still see him running, his little feet . . .'

Ralph laid his hand on John's shoulder, 'I know, John, I know.'

John took a deep breath, 'I must go.' He slid into the front seat and the car pulled away.

'You'll be back, John, that much I do know. You'll be back,' Ralph muttered, as he watched the car disappear up the drive.

2

The Deal

It was Friday lunchtime in the gallery. Outside, the rain was falling heavily, bringing the Indian summer, which had filled London with hot, dusty days and sultry evenings, to an end.

John Grande gazed out, his head pressed against the gallery window. It had been a month since he had returned from Italy and there had been no word, no letter, nothing from D'Ostia. He had tried endlessly to telephone him, but without success, and he'd even asked his uncle to try to find out what was going on. The only answer was that the villa was locked and shuttered, with only the housekeeper in residence. She knew nothing about her employer.

Perplexed, John watched the rain fall, his emotions mixed. He had known from the outset that it was stretching coincidence to the limit for an unknown American to visit the gallery looking to buy Licattas and then, out of the blue, for him to be offered six to sell. Yet, despite the absurdity, once he'd agreed with D'Ostia, he found himself more and more excited by the prospect. For the first time in three years there had been an edge – a sense of purpose to his life. Now, all the excitement slipping away, he was left with that old, empty feeling, made worse by the heightened expectation. The strangest part was that Peach, the man who had

15

wanted the Licattas in the first place, had not returned to the gallery.

John knew only too well that the last two years had been terrible for the gallery and that their credit was now non-existent. Another bad year and they would be forced to sell. His partner had doubted the Italian deal from the outset; at best, he had said it was a set-up, or a hoax. Their relationship had been deteriorating for some time and the deal apparently falling through had aggravated the problem. He knew he should have been relieved, in the sure knowledge that the suspicious deal would trouble him no more; yet he couldn't help but think of the money, the excitement, the sense of purpose, which had now all gone, leaving him looking foolish.

The clicking of the computer keyboard in the background and the rain pattering against a plate-glass window seemed to blend together as he shut his eyes.

'John – your uncle – line one.' The receptionist's soft voice cut into his thoughts and he picked up the telephone.

'I hoped I'd catch you. Look, there've been some strange developments.'

John smiled. His uncle sounded breathless, like an excited schoolboy.

'You're already aware that D'Ostia left about a week after your visit?'

'Yes, but . . .'

'Well, it now appears there was an attempted break-in at his villa at about the same time.'

'Same time as what?'

'The same time as D'Ostia left.'

'How do you know? After all, he's gone.'

'The police found a body on the rocks below the villa. Apparently fell to his death – the housekeeper reported a smashed window.'

'So where's D'Ostia?'

'No one knows – or at least no one's saying, anyway.'

'Who was the man?'

'A part-time fisherman, though locals say he was more of a part-time crook. Petty theft, you know. He lived in Sorrento.'

'Murder?'

'No, the police are treating it as an accident – a sort of death by misadventure.' He paused, 'Oh yes, I found out something else, another little twist – seems the man had been hired by an American.'

'To break in? Who was it?'

'I don't think anyone knows. I understand his wife told the police about him. He was someone who came and went – seems the police have got nowhere and I think they've stopped any further work on it.'

John laughed gently.

'Why are you laughing?'

'Nothing, I was just thinking that both our first impressions were correct. At least, I suppose I've been spared any further dodgy decisions. One way or the other, this will just make me look even more foolish.'

'Look, I'm really sorry, John – I knew all along I shouldn't have brought you over here – it's my fault.'

'No, it's not your fault. I came readily enough – after all there was a demand here, it seemed too good to be true. What else could you have done? No, it's not your fault.'

'What's happened to the man who wanted the Licattas?'

'Oh yes, I'd almost forgotten about him. He must have gone. Anyway, he hasn't bothered to contact us. Strange . . . all these coincidences.' He sighed. 'The main thing is at least the waiting has stopped and I now know that it's over.'

The call ended and John walked back up to the front of the gallery as his partner, Richard Patrick, entered. His clothes and hair were wet. He stared hard at John, as he took his coat off at the door.

It is seldom matters of great importance that break relation-ships; they create the environment, set the scene, but it is invariably the little things that form the focus of seething resentment. As Richard returned, the sight of John Grande, dry, relaxed, and gazing out of the window, his back turned to an empty gallery, was too much for him to bear. He had just been told that an exhibition he had planned for months at the gallery had been cancelled. He was frustrated and angry and, with all his hard work gone to waste, he was ready to explode. He glared at John.

Sensing the tension, the receptionist muttered something about lunch and, quickly grabbing her coat, dashed out of the gallery. John Grande's partner snorted and swept past him, disappearing into the storeroom at the back. When he re-emerged, John was with a customer, and it was ten minutes before they could talk.

'I doubt he'll be back,' John muttered as he walked towards his desk. 'Probably just sheltering from the rain.'

'Ah, well, he should have felt fairly comfortable with you then,' Richard replied.

'Very droll, Richard, very droll,' John said casually as he flopped down into his chair.

'Maybe, but you can tell me what else, if anything, you've achieved in the last year except gazing out of the bloody window.'

'Come on, Richard, what's the point? It's a matter of record, you already know – it's not great, it could have been better but there's little point trying to blame each other. After all, if my deal with the Licattas had gone through . . .'

'Oh yes,' Richard interrupted, 'I wondered how long before we'd hear about that – and if your fairy godmother had also granted you three bloody wishes . . .'

'Rubbish! It's not like that and you know it, it could have been an excellent deal.'

'Could have been!' Richard mocked, 'You've changed your tune. When you came back from Italy there was big talk about a big deal. A dead cert, you said. Pah!' he flicked his hand dismissively, 'I suppose next you'll say the deal is definitely off!'

'I've no idea. It was all set up.' John leaned back in his chair. 'The problem is, the man has disappeared.'

'Ah!' John's partner muttered, 'what you mean to say is that it was just another excuse to get away from here and leave me to do all the work. We've only your say so the deal ever existed.'

'No! You know well enough. I'm not in the habit of lying . . .' John's voice trailed away, 'Oh, what's the bloody point, you've clearly made your mind up.'

'There, you're wrong – you made it up for me. This whole damn gallery is collapsing around us and we've no more money. There is no better reason to make my mind up than a lack of money.' He shook his head slowly, 'Look, there's little or no reason to go on, we both know and if you can't see it, you're more of a fool than I think you are. I want out! I don't want any more fairy tales, I've had enough of working with you!'

'For Christ's sake! That's a bloody mad solution,' John exploded. 'What about our investment?'

'Mad? I'm not mad! Far from it,' Richard said coldly. 'If anyone is mad, it's you! God! Why don't you ask all your friends? That is, if you can find any. For the past two years it's been impossible here. God knows I was sorry when Julia and your son were killed, but *two years*, John, I ask you! All I could ever get out of you were "maybes" or the occasional "perhaps" – I've had to carry the whole damn thing and frankly, I've had enough. It's been like dealing with a corpse. Even that was bearable but when you're meant to be back here getting on with it full time, you swan off to Italy with some nonsense about Licatta paintings.' He shook his head, 'Never here, never – and when you are, you might as well not be.'

'Look,' John began quietly, 'don't do anything hasty.' Even before he had said it, he knew his choice of words was wrong.

'Hasty? Hasty!' Richard stood up and walked towards the front of the gallery, talking over his shoulder as he went. 'The only damn thing I haven't been is bloody hasty! Two long years!' He turned to face John, who had followed him. 'There's no money coming in so I want out. I couldn't care less about what happens to this place after that.'

'Don't you realise that would finish the gallery off? All that we've worked for!' John's voice was raised as they stood face to face, both flushed and angry, John's finger jabbing at his partner. 'Well, I'm just not going to let you – what you're proposing is commercial death. I can't buy you out.'

John gazed at his partner, shaking his head, despair in his eyes. 'It's all I have – we have. Without this place, I would have gone under . . .' He rubbed his temples as they began to throb.

'I'm sorry, I really am, but I'm not the social services. It's over,' Richard replied curtly, 'Just accept it.'

'That's the most selfish thing I ever heard. I carried you all those years ago when you couldn't raise the stake. You'll be killing me . . . I'm not going to take this lying down.'

'What will you do?' Richard asked with a sneer.

'I'll make sure you're finished in this business as well.'

'Really? I don't think so – just more rantings from someone whose grip on reality has slipped,' Richard retorted.

'Maybe, maybe, but I'll make sure you're dead in this business,' he blustered. They both knew it was an idle threat.

With perfect timing the front door swung open and the receptionist walked in. She stopped as John finished speaking; then, as she walked to the rear of the gallery, she looked from one to the other. Richard just shrugged, shook his head and walked past John, back to his desk.

With a quick glance over his shoulder at the receptionist, John stormed out into the street.

He didn't care where he walked, he just walked. What hurt was that he knew that much of what his partner had said was true. He had become obsessed and isolated and Richard had carried the gallery for the past two years. But he also knew that the gallery was all he had and he wanted it to succeed; he didn't want to end it. The rain fell, and still he walked, going over and over his nightmare. There seemed no other way; without a substantial deal, the gallery was finished. All his partner had done had been to tell him so bluntly. As he took shelter in the entrance to Kensington High Street station and watched people rushing past, all of them with their heads down, he realised that his partner had been right. He was clutching at straws, hoping for something to take him away from his constant nightmare.

The last two years had sucked the heart out of him. Richard was only saying what everyone else must have been saying. Perhaps he was right, there was no point. It was over.

Seeing that the rain had stopped, he turned down his collar. He shrugged, 'Accept it, just accept it.' And then he turned and walked slowly down the street.

It was half an hour before he returned to the gallery. 'John,' the receptionist began, 'you've had a call from a Mr Spellman of Rutman and Rogers.'

'Who?' John asked, his wet jacket and trousers hanging limply around him.

'He's a lawyer with one of those corporate firms.'

'Oh,' John glanced at the note. 'What do they want with me?'

'They wouldn't say. But you've an appointment for two-thirty.'

John glanced at his watch and back at her, perplexed.

'I know, John, but he wouldn't take "no" for an answer, said it was urgent.'

'But that's in half an hour,' he objected. 'Look at me, I'm a sight.' He glanced at the back of the gallery and saw his partner with a customer. 'I suppose I'd better go. God! It's probably someone suing us for unpaid bills.'

Half an hour later, John was standing outside an office just off Bond Street, glaring at the crumpled piece of paper in his hand. He pushed through the glass doors and took the elevator to the fourth floor.

At first the receptionist, and then Mr Spellman's secretary, refused to let him see the lawyer, saying that they knew nothing about the appointment. He tried to explain that Mr Spellman had made the arrangement personally. They looked disdainfully at him, clearly unhappy about dealing with someone in such a dishevelled state. Finally, after some pressure, the secretary agreed to go and ask the lawyer. She reappeared quickly, a scornful look on her face, to usher John into his office.

John was greeted by a tall, slim, dapper man in his early fifties, with a large head and thick, swept-back hair. He took a seat in front of a mahogany desk while Mr Spellman walked slowly to his chair on the other side. The desk was clear except for a few papers on the far right-hand side and an unopened letter in the middle of the blotting pad.

'I'm sorry that I had to be so vague on the telephone, Mr Grande,' Spellman began, 'I realise I owe you an explanation.' The lawyer leaned forward in his chair and put his elbows on his desk, his light-blue eyes never leaving John's. 'I am retained by a Signor D'Ostia and he has placed in my hands some instructions that he wishes to pass on to you.' As he glanced down at the letter in the middle of his desk, John sat upright, his mouth dropping open.

'Did you say D'Ostia – that is, D'Ostia of Positano?' he demanded.

'Indeed,' Spellman looked up and held out the letter, 'I believe that he's already spoken to you. You will under-stand, therefore, that this letter is simply confirmation of arrangements already agreed. He was particularly concerned that this letter of instruction should not leave my office.'

'Can you tell me where Mr D'Ostia is now?' John asked, as he took the letter from Spellman.

'I'm sorry but I'm not at liberty to divulge any other information about my client, except of course to offer any assistance you require as a consequence of the letter.'

As the solicitor finished speaking, John looked down at the letter and slowly turned it over in his hands. The back of it had been sealed with wax. With one movement of his hand, he broke the seal.

Dear Mr Grande,

This letter is a confirmation of our agreement and arrangements. By the time you receive this, you will already know I am no longer at the villa. There is no reason for you to contact me directly. If you wish to contact me at any time, you should do this through Spellman.

The minimum price of the six Licattas is £25,000 each. Your standard commission is as agreed. Pass the remainder to Mr Spellman in the form of a cheque.

Further arrangements concerning the other pictures will be passed to you as soon as this sale is successfully completed.

D'Ostia

John looked up at the lawyer. 'But there aren't any pictures, and he's asked me to sell at a price over double the usual value.' He tapped the letter as he spoke, 'That's just not possible, I don't think anyone would pay . . .'

'I'm sure,' interrupted the lawyer, 'my client has taken that into account. I don't know what you discussed before but I assume his instructions are clear.' Spellman's even tones were beginning to aggravate John.

'That's all well and good, but I'm the art dealer and I can tell you that those paintings are not worth this.'

'I know nothing about any art deal,' began Spellman, without expression, 'however, if you wish to decline his offer, I will inform my client without delay, if that is your wish.'

'Well . . .' John began as he looked down at the letter. He could see the gallery in Positano as clearly as if he were still standing in it. 'Don't worry,' D'Ostia had said, 'you'll get a lot more for these than you think.' John thought of his gallery and the need for money. The real prize, he knew, was to sell the other paintings. Now that was a prize worth having. 'No,' John conceded, 'that won't be necessary.'

'Good,' Spellman said, getting out of his chair. 'Now, if you could pass me the letter?' he asked as he walked around the desk. John handed the letter to him.

'What about delivery?' John asked, 'There's nothing . . .'

'Not something I'm aware of, I'm sorry,' Spellman replied, as he placed the letter on his desk. 'I expect someone will contact you.'

For an experienced and senior solicitor, used to dealing with business clients, this was an unusual meeting. However, Spellman knew that D'Ostia paid well for his services and chose, as a consequence, not to question his rather theatrical way of proceeding. Today he knew he was to pass over a letter, not to involve himself in what was being transacted or why. He had fulfilled his client's request precisely and had been as discreet as ever. Emotion never strayed into his arrangements; he knew that a clear mind was required on all occasions and that he was paid for no less. He had long learned to execute the instructions and not go beyond this. However, as he brought the meeting to a close and watched the dishevelled man get up from his seat opposite him, something in the back of his mind nudged him, something more was required. He hesitated. It was not a requirement placed on him by D'Ostia, yet he felt he needed to offer the man in front of him some advice.

'Mr Grande,' he said carefully, 'I don't know how well you know my client . . .'

'Not well,' John replied as he stood up. 'Not well at all. I shouldn't think anyone does.'

'Quite so, quite so. However, in that case, I hope you won't mind if I offer you a thought for the future,' Spellman paused as John stared at him in surprise. 'Whilst I know nothing about this deal, I have dealt on behalf of my client for a number of years, and I have come to know him as a very competitive man, a meticulous planner but, most of all, a man with a tremendous grasp of detail. As you embark on this enterprise you would do well to understand that he is also a man who, once having made a deal, is always determined to see it through to a successful conclusion. Successful, of course, from his standpoint.' As he spoke, he folded the letter in his hands and tapped it on the desk as he finished. 'Now, if you'll forgive me, Mr Grande, I have, I believe, another appointment.' He walked towards the door. 'I should also tell you that I do not think there is any need for any further contact between us – you just have to send me the cheque. To that end, once you have gone, I shall, of course, destroy this letter. Good day, Mr Grande.'

With these words he ushered John out.

Two minutes later his secretary returned to his office.

'Your next appointment is here,' she said briskly.

'Good,' he said, picking up the letter from D'Ostia and handing it over to her, 'I don't think I'll be needing this any more; shred it immediately and make no copies.'

Outside the half-lit gallery, one slow Sunday evening in late October the wind gusted, swirling the forgotten litter and early leaves in a lazy tarantella. The few people moving through the square did so with their heads set, coats buttoned up, walking quickly, their heads down to avoid the wind and the swirling showers of rain.

John Grande looked at the street outside and involuntarily shivered. He absent-mindedly picked up the letters lying on the mat and quickly flicked through them to see if there was anything for him, without really taking them in, his mind elsewhere. He tossed them onto the receptionist's desk and anxiously checked his watch. Then he turned off the overhead light, but kept a light on at the far end of the gallery. While he waited he planned to catch up on some work, but he knew his sense of foreboding would not let him. With D'Ostia's first delivery of paintings due, he knew he would get nothing done. He sat down at his desk and shuffled through the papers, occasionally glancing at the door.

An hour later, there was a short buzz at the door. John looked up, startled. Framed by the front window, a man in a shiny bomber jacket peered in, his breath misting up the glass. His face was partially obscured, hidden in the shadows, but John could see he carried some papers in one hand.

'You Mr Grande?' the man asked as John opened the door.

'Yes,' John replied.

'Got a special delivery,' the man muttered as he turned to look at a van behind him.

John followed the man's gaze and could just make out a second person, sitting in the passenger seat. He looked from the van to the man in front of him. The man's eyes were just slits in a very fat face. John stepped back, recoiling at the stale smell of the man's breath and his powerful body odour. The man was sweating and breathing heavily.

'In here,' John said, as he opened the door wide.

It didn't take the two men long to unload. John finished checking the pictures against the inventory as they laid them out in the storeroom. Then he saw the men to the door and locked up behind them. Once back in the storeroom, he unscrewed each box to carry out a much closer inspection before putting the boxes onto shelves.

As he came to the last box, he rubbed his tired eyes and yawned. Placing it on the chair in the centre of the storeroom, he looked at it carefully and was about to turn away, when something in the bottom right-hand corner caught his eye. A closer look revealed that some paint had cracked. Cursing, he fetched an anglepoise lamp and positioned it over the corner of the picture. Under its sharper light, he could see that an area of about two square inches had been affected and that, while some paint had cracked, a smaller section was in a worse state, with some parts already flaking away. He took out his handkerchief and very gently brushed away some loose pieces of paint. Instead of seeing a primed canvas below as expected, he was surprised to see more paint, most of which seemed to be intact. Slightly puzzled, he searched through his desk until he found a large magnifying glass and a paper knife.

Through the magnifying glass, he could see that the remaining paint underneath was quite different and that it appeared to be darker. He peeled back some more of the flaking paint, then put his magnifying glass down slowly and walked back to a seat in the corner of the storeroom. He sat down heavily, the realisation of what was in front of him hitting him hard. There was no doubt about it: the Licatta had been painted over another painting.

John Grande sat still for some time, his heart pounding, trying to come to terms with the enormity of the discovery. He stared at the picture from across the room, his mind awash with the hows, the whys, the wheres and the whos. They were quite empty and pointless questions, he knew, yet they kept coming back and remained unanswered. He thought about D'Ostia and kept asking himself why he should want to involve him in what was obviously a fraud. He thought about the approach from the man, Peach, and the highly inflated price tag that D'Ostia had set on each of the Licattas. As his mind churned, one thing was glaringly obvious: he was being used as a middleman between D'Ostia and Peach, both of whom must surely know what lay beneath the Licatta. D'Ostia had promised him the sale of the masters only if he sold the Licattas. Now it was different. The more he thought about it, the more tangled the whole thing became. What, for example, about the others? Could they all be the same? He shook his head. He even began to doubt his first assessment and tried to persuade himself that perhaps he had been wrong. He checked the cracked canvas again; it didn't take long, he had been right the first time.

His thoughts turned to the police – perhaps he should speak to them. His hand moved towards the telephone, but he hesitated. He realised that no one knew where D'Ostia was, and the only existing evidence was that he, John Grande, held the pictures without any explanation. 'No paperwork, Mr Grande,' the man had said. There was no way of linking D'Ostia even if he could be found. No paperwork from the lawyers either. Spellman made it clear he knew nothing about the transaction. And anyway, the letter would be destroyed by now. The last thing he wanted to do was to involve his uncle. He was the only one who could possibly have explained why the pictures were in his possession. D'Ostia's lawyers would deny all knowledge, he was sure.

He tipped his head into his hands as he remembered the last words of the lawyer. Strange as they had seemed at the time, he now realised that they had meant something, a warning.

'I need help,' he murmured as he walked over to his desk and pulled out an address book from the drawer.

'Jack Maguire speaking.' The voice at the other end of the telephone had a slurred Dublin accent.

'Jack, it's John Grande.'

'What's that? Who d'you say?'

'John Grande,' John spoke louder, 'don't you remember Jack – The Grande–Patrick Gallery, for God's sake?'

'Sure, sure I do – Jesus! No need to shout for pity's sake!'

'Jack,' John continued, ignoring his complaints, 'I need your help.'

'At your service, Johnny boy.' The voice was all charm again, 'I'll come round tomorrow . . .'

'No, not tomorrow. Can you come to the gallery tonight, Jack? Tonight means now, Jack.'

'I like that,' Maguire began, 'it's been months since we last spoke, you weren't desperate over those months – eh? Now all of a sudden it's got to be right this minute, regardless of what I may think. How do you know I am not busy?'

'At half past ten? If you are . . .' he paused, 'I'll make it worth your while.'

'Well,' Maguire paused, 'then again, perhaps I'm not that busy. Only for a short time, mind.'

The gallery was perfectly still. John was asleep, his head resting on his arms, when the buzzer at the door sounded. He sat up quickly and rubbed his eyes then glanced at his watch: midnight. Through the glass he could see the familiar broad face of Jack Maguire leering at him. His ruddy complexion and thick, dark, swept-back greasy hair were unmistakable. He was smiling.

'Johnny,' he said, as John Grande opened the door, 'as you can see, I came as soon as I could.' He walked slowly into the gallery and stood waiting for John to close the door, his breath thick with drink.

John led Maguire into the storeroom at the back, talking about the damaged painting. Once in the room Maguire sat down facing the picture. He reached into his jacket pocket, pulled out his glasses and put them on, then leaned forward.

'Looks like you've got yourself a bit of a problem here,' he said as he looked up at John. 'So what do you expect me to do?'

'First, I thought you could at least use your experience to confirm whether you think this is a fraud,' John said, offering him the magnifying glass.

'Is that all?' Maguire shook his head. 'Now, you've done as much already. Why else am I here?' He examined the picture again. 'I don't know much about the one on top . . .'

'Licatta.'

'Well, whatever his bloody name is, I'll bet a pound to a pinch of shit, his picture is covering up a better one.' Maguire lifted some of the pieces of flaking paint. There was silence for the next few minutes broken only by Maguire's laboured breathing as he crouched, studying the picture: then he muttered something and sat back in his seat.

'Yes? What is it?' John looked in expectation at him.

'These late nights, they give a man a terrible thirst.' Maguire looked up. 'Nothing a whisky wouldn't . . .'

John shook his head, smiled and left the room, returning moments later with the drink.

'Well, what do you think?' he asked as he pulled up a seat and sat down.

'Sure as God made little green apples, this is a fake. I've seen this a few times before, it's usually done to get past Customs. Nice work if you can get it, I say.' He gulped his drink. 'There's money in this.' He took another sip. 'Well, you called me Johnny, what else do you want?'

'When I called you, I wasn't sure. I suppose I rather hoped you would tell me I was wrong. Now you confirm it all, Jack, I just don't know. I suppose I really ought to explain to you.'

'No, thanks,' interrupted Maguire, raising his hand. 'No, thanks. I have a feeling about this – the less I know, the better it will be for me.'

'So what?'

'Look, I can do one of two things for you: I can either clean it up and you can have a look at what is underneath, or I can patch it up. It's your choice.' Maguire finished the last of his drink. 'Or I can do nothing. But I don't want to know anything about any of it.'

'Perhaps I should talk to the police.'

'The police? Bollocks! There is no "should" about it. Take a little advice from me, Johnny: in this world, do what leaves you safest and richest.' He laughed. 'There must be money either way. The thing is, where is the least danger?' He lit a cigarette. 'Now, take me, I used to do things for the *craic*, the sheer hell of it. Not any longer; when you get older, you need something more, more substantial. If I were you, I'd take the money and sleep easy. You have to decide how to do that.'

John got up and walked to the back of the storeroom. He needed to think.

He knew the right thing would be to go to the police and tell them everything, but there was the gallery to consider. A deal like this, with the other pictures as well, didn't come a gallery's way normally, and it was good money. Then he remembered the dead man in Positano; the stakes, to someone, were very high.

'Come over here, Johnny,' Maguire's voice broke in on his thoughts. He was crouching over the picture again with a magnifying glass and a thin paper knife.

'Something else, what d'you think caused that picture to crack?' He tapped the paper knife in his hand as he spoke, puffing smoke across it.

'Someone must have dropped it, I suppose,' John replied, but Maguire shook his head.

'Here, have another look and tell me what you see.'

John leaned forward and looked through the magnifying glass again. 'What I saw before: flaking paint and another picture definitely behind the one that is on top.'

'No, have a look at the frame – go on.'

John bent forward again and stared at the cracked area. 'Nothing I didn't see before . . .'

'Any damage to the frame or canvas?' Maguire asked.

'No,' John replied, 'none that I can see, I . . .' He stared at Maguire.

'Ah, at last – you've noticed. No damage to the frame.'

'Yes, it's as though something has just lifted the paint off the canvas. Perhaps something dropped onto it when it . . .'

'I doubt it – the case would have protected it,' Maguire interrupted. 'Besides, it would have to have been something pretty special to lift one layer of paint and not the other. Divine intervention perhaps,' Maguire laughed.

Why would D'Ostia, John wondered, ask him to sell pictures and then damage one deliberately? The only explanation was that the shipping company somehow damaged it in transit, nothing else made any sense. Yes, he thought, that must be right.

'Safest and richest, Johnny, always the best policy,' Maguire interrupted. 'The question is, which course fulfils your plan? Patch it up, sell it on and no one's the wiser.'

John stared at the painting again. 'Look,' he began, 'I don't want you to do anything. For the moment, I just want you to take the picture, if you could, back to your workshop. I'll call you tomorrow, once I've had a chance to think through the implications.'

Maguire wrinkled his face.

'Look, Jack,' said John holding his arm tightly, 'you'll have to bear with me. I know it seems ridiculous but I don't want that picture here in the gallery in this state. But I'm not asking you to do anything to it until we talk tomorrow.'

'That might be no problem at all, Johnny boy, but then it could be difficult . . .' he began pulling his pocket inside out,

'The only problem is that I seem to be temporarily embarrassed by a shortage of funds.'

'Five hundred pounds now and the rest when I have decided what to do – suit you?' John replied.

'Fine. It depends what you want me to do tomorrow, but I can wait – not long, though.' Maguire smiled. 'How do you know you can trust me, Johnny?'

'I'll have to,' John smiled back, 'but then again, I've got nothing to lose and I don't think there is very much point in you speaking to the police.'

'Right enough, now that would be a criminal thing, Johnny. Safest and richest, just remember it, that's my motto.' He stood up to go. 'Oh yes, I'll need three or four days to do a good job, so let's have some notice,' he said over his shoulder as he picked the picture up.

Together, they put the picture back in its box and took it to the back door. He bundled Maguire and the picture into a taxi. 'Don't forget, call me when you get home!' John shouted after Maguire.

He inhaled deeply as the taxi drove off. Before he re-entered the gallery, he glanced across the road into the dark shadow below the shop doorway. For a moment, he thought he saw someone move but, when he looked again, all was quiet and the street was empty. He shivered. Twenty minutes later the phone rang. It was Maguire – the picture was safe.

Following a sleepless night, John Grande was still uncertain about the right course of action. He was in the middle of something, whether he wanted to be or not. It was while he was shaving that he made his decision. He smiled into the mirror: as Maguire said, the safest option was to pretend that nothing had happened and patch the picture up. It was also the most profitable.

One telephone call was all it took, and Maguire moved into action.

John had known Maguire for years; he was a man with a wealth of knowledge about the art industry and, more importantly now, a one-time restorer of paintings. He had also painted a few fake pictures himself.

By midday, John felt more confident about his decision. After all, he reasoned, the note in the solicitor's office said nothing about the strange American. It just told him to sell them, and that was what he would do.

Even his partner seemed surprised by the presence of the Licattas. Their argument of a few days before had been put aside, although, John was sure, not forgotten.

By 5 p.m. John was beginning to relax. It was all going well, all they needed was a few days, he thought. He was verging on the complacent when, an hour later, alone in the gallery, his peace of mind was shattered.

Advancing towards him was the same short, stout, ferret-eyed American he had thought had gone for good – Jason F Peach. John felt his heart race as they shook hands.

'I hear you might have some Licattas?' Peach began.

'Maybe,' John answered.

'So,' he said looking around, 'which ones are they?'

'Why?' John began.

'No games, Mr Grande, I'd like to see them.'

John frowned. This was not what he had expected. The man knew all about them; perhaps he even knew how many there were. John tensed.

'They're not here – I have them inside,' John said, turning away to the storeroom. 'I'll just get them out.' Carefully, he took the pictures down from the shelves, carrying the first one through to the gallery. As he placed it down behind his desk, he was struck by a strong smell of tobacco. Not the usual kind, but much thicker, stronger, Turkish-smelling. The smell seemed redolent of some other place, which he couldn't quite recall. By the time he'd brought out the fifth painting, Peach was stubbing a cigarette out in the ashtray.

'That it?' he asked.

'Yes,' John replied.

As Peach fiddled with his mobile phone, John walked towards his desk. The cigarette was still smouldering and he reached to put it out by stubbing it harder into the ashtray.

'Turkish?' John muttered to himself as he crushed out the last ember. 'Where, where?'

'What? Sure,' Peach muttered, mobile phone clamped to his ear. 'They're here – yeah – now.'

John froze. Clearly visible on the cigarette was the word, 'Sipahi'. The smell and the word were the same as the one he had found on the ridge in Positano. They were like twins; one was smoked further down but that was the only difference.

He studied Peach – it must be him, the man on the ridge that day. He felt a shiver running down his spine. And the dead man on the rocks? John turned away. He needed to get control of himself; everything was racing away from him. It was then that the door opened.

'Mr Grande, this is Mr Wessells,' Peach announced.

John turned and found himself staring at a small man, much older than Peach. He was bald with a sharp nose and heavy spectacles. John thought he must have been in his late sixties or early seventies.

'So, these are the Licattas,' the man said, walking past John. He stood, looking from one to the other. 'Where is the sixth?' he demanded, turning to face John.

'The sixth?' John began trying to fight back waves of panic. 'The sixth isn't here,' he said lamely.

'I can see that.'

'No, I mean, I am expecting it,' John stuttered. 'Mix-up at customs – four days,' he said quickly.

'A delay?' The little man asked, shaking his head and looking intently into John's eyes.

'But, we were told . . .' Peach began before the other cut him short with a wave of his hand.

'OK. But we're here to get all six,' Wessells continued, 'I'll pay you for all six now, I wouldn't want any more mix-ups.' He watched John carefully, 'So how much do you want, Mr Grande?'

John took a deep breath and answered, half expecting a complaint. To his surprise, a briefcase was laid on his desk and a chequebook taken out: £150,000. Wessells wrote out the exact amount and signed the cheque.

'I'm going to be expecting the sixth on time, Mr Grande,' began Wessells. 'Just don't forget. You have two days to produce the other picture or I'll see it as a breach of contract and take the required action. I'd been expecting this last picture and it's vital you get it – two days, Mr Grande – two days.'

John could only stare in silence as the men left the gallery.

'I owe you an apology . . .' John jumped as his partner spoke. He hadn't heard him come in. 'Is this the deal?'

'What?'

'The deal?'

'Oh yes . . . or at least part of it.'

'What's the matter? You look like you've seen a ghost.'

'Yes,' John replied, 'probably mine.'

3

The Race for the White House

President Carson watched the Secretary of State's retreating back as he walked slowly out of the Oval Office. As he left, the President's secretary bustled in. She swept up the file on the desk and turned to go.

'Mati, can you get Frank to come in,' he said, his smooth Southern voice hardly more than a whisper.

'But Mr President, you've a 10.30 with Senator Black.'

'Stall him. I want to see Frank for a few minutes.'

'Of course,' she said, shaking her head slightly and closing the office door behind her.

The President stood up slowly, walked to the window, and gazed at the Rose Garden. He was looking at the roses but he didn't see them. His thoughts were elsewhere.

For many, President Carson was considered the most formidable politician of his generation. An even better communicator than President Reagan, he had come from behind to win the Democratic nomination and then the election, two and a half years before. In doing so, he had ended a fallow period for the Democratic party. He had torn it from its obsession with the old principles of redistribution and had broadened its appeal. Now he was seen as a common-sense man, the 'guy next door'. But he had used this image ruthlessly in his dealings with the Republican-controlled Congress. Power was President Carson's driving ethos. He had always believed that simply by his being there, things would be better – as long as the public liked it, that was enough. And he had quite brilliantly positioned the Republican-dominated Congress as too ideological when it imposed a new budget on him. By persuading the public that he had made the best of it, he had positioned himself as the 'anti-politician' defending them against Washington politicians. He fostered the appearance of an outsider, but he knew how to play the political game with the best of them. The deals, the federal contracts, they were what he was brilliant at.

While Washington looked at him and bit its lip, middle America looked at him and smiled. It was the political equivalent of the three-card trick. And yet . . .

He heard the door open and turned around.

'Good morning, Mr President,' Frank Parry said crisply.

President Carson didn't answer, but turned back to gaze at the roses.

'Strange, don't you think, Frank?' he said slowly, softly, 'these roses go on blooming despite the heat, all through the summer, and yet they still look so delicate.'

Frank Parry frowned as he walked towards his boss. He was the President's chief of staff and most trusted confidant. It was he who had believed in Carson's eventual victory, when most had written him off after he had lost the race for the governorship of Kentucky ten years before. He'd helped him become Governor one more time and that success had been the springboard into the White House. There wasn't a thing Frank Parry couldn't discuss with the President: it was his judgement the President trusted and on which he leaned.

A stocky, balding man who never raised his voice, and whose icy calm in all situations was legendary, Parry was the opposite of his boss. They made a strange duo – the tall, handsome, volatile politician and his short, quiet adviser.

'They're tougher than they look – just try grabbing hold of the stem,' Parry said as he reached the President.

'Maybe, though someone could always cut them down,' President Carson replied slowly, his voice flat.

'They'd have to come through me first,' Parry said quickly, shaking his head.

'Maybe,' Carson said, smiling faintly as he turned from the window. 'Maybe.' He walked over to his desk and sat down. 'What is it, Ted?'

'Did you see what Douglas wrote in the *Post* today – and they're meant to be on our side! He's calling for an investigation into the land deal, you know the one when I was Governor first time?'

'Sure, I remember,' Parry shrugged, 'You were accused of clearing the sale of that State Guard depot and then banking the purchase by that company. But you were cleared.'

'But the Republicans want to reopen the investigation and now Douglas . . .'

'Relax. It's just pre-election bullshit. You told me yourself that woman . . .'

'Julia Haskins,' Carson said softly.

'That's her. She testified that you had nothing to do with it – it was her company, for Christ's sake!' Carson nodded slowly as Parry continued, 'they had nothing then and they got nothing now.'

'There's her business partner.'

'Big deal, so he's now saying you put money in it. He's got no proof – it's his word against hers and she died five years ago.'

Carson swivelled his chair around to face the window and took a deep breath before replying. 'There's more to it than that, Frank. Collins, you know Congressman Collins, tells me that the Republicans have persuaded Julia Haskins' sister to speak out.'

'Why should that matter?'

'Because she will say I was sleeping with her sister at the time of the Guendo depot purchase and the subsequent investigation.'

'OK,' Parry replied, 'OK, I agree that's not great but it's only her word again. That shouldn't be enough to reopen the enquiry.' Parry walked around the desk so that he could make eye contact with the President. 'Ted, you've never said much about this before but I've got to ask you, is it true, did you have an affair?' There was a long pause. Carson stared back at Parry for what seemed to him to be an age before slowly nodding. 'So, Ted,' Parry continued nervously, 'did you . . . did you have any investment in her company?'

'It's not quite that simple, Frank,' Carson said evasively as Parry felt his heart sink, 'It was a long time ago and our marriage was going through a rocky patch. We wanted kids, couldn't have them. We were thinking about divorce. None of this will probably make much sense to you, it was long before I knew you. Anyway, I guess you're thinking all that's irrelevant, but you know it's not. We had a child, a girl.'

'*We?*' Parry gulped, '*we* means who?'

'Julia Haskins,' Carson quickly replied, 'and me.'

Parry's eyes widened as he took an involuntary step back. His mind was churning, the bright day had now been replaced by the horror story that was unfolding in front of him.

'Pretty little thing,' Carson continued, now strangely relaxed as though finally, after all these years, he felt released. 'Couldn't keep her, of course – Julia knew that – so she put her up for adoption. Broke her heart, wouldn't speak to me again, except for one thing . . .'

'What was that, Ted?' Parry croaked, his throat dry, already guessing the answer.

'Well, that's the point. I agreed to put money into the land purchase so that Julia could set up a fund for our daughter with whoever adopted her.'

'Oh, my God!' Parry covered his eyes. 'So you did put money in?'

'I had no other choice – she was my daughter. Besides, Julia would have told the whole story.'

Parry walked slowly round to the chair in front of the desk and sat down. He needed to pull himself together.

'Does her sister know?' he asked, frowning.

'I don't believe she does,' Carson swivelled round to face Parry. 'No, we agreed no one should know.'

'What about the hospital? Where did she have the child?'

'New York – an old Convent maternity hospital that also helped arrange adoption. I think it's closed now.'

'OK, OK,' Parry stated slowly, deliberately groping his way forward. He took a deep breath. 'This is enough to screw us all up, but if you say no one knows, we'll have to close down all the ways anyone could find out. First, we'll have to discover what happened to the girl. At the same time, we'll have to get Congressman Collins and our other Supporters in the House to delay any decision about reopening the enquiry. They can hold on to the fact that it's the sister's word against ours. We'll have to get something on her – discredit her, something from her past. You know, bitter jealous sister getting her own back. We can do this.' He stood up and, frowning, leaned on Carson's desk. 'But you have to put this out of your mind, tell no one.'

'You're the only one.'

'Good. I'll get onto it right away. We've got to find the girl.'

The door opened and Mati, Carson's secretary walked in.

'It's nearly 11 o'clock,' she began, glaring at Parry, 'and Senator Black's waiting. You can't keep him any longer.'

'OK,' Parry looked back at the President, 'I'll be a couple more minutes, I've something else.'

'No, the Senator's getting annoyed,' Mati responded abruptly.

'We've nearly finished. Tell him in a couple of minutes.'

Mati snorted and left the room.

'You ought to know,' Parry began, 'that Kelp's now looking and sounding unhelpful.'

'But he's already said he would back me,' Carson frowned.

'No, not quite, we assumed he would.'

'Are you saying he's withdrawing his support?'

'It might be worse.'

'Support someone else?'

'Well, he may run himself.'

'You're kiddin' me,' Carson snorted, 'Run against me?'

'Yes.'

'But I thought you said last month the nomination was sewn up.'

'It was.'

'A Democratic Senator running against a Democratic President for the nomination?' Carson stared at Parry.

'It's happened before,' Parry let it sink in. 'And I hear he's not the only one.'

'Who?' asked Carson, starting to panic.

'Only rumours at the moment but the significance of Kelp is the fact that he supported you last time. After all, most people thought he'd run himself then.'

'But he's too old now.'

'It isn't that simple. There's a group of people out there who see this as the last throw for the wartime generation. He's pretty fit. Look at Bob Dole.'

'Has Kelp decided?'

'I don't think so, but who knows?'

'I'd better call him . . .' Carson began.

'No, wait,' Parry said emphatically. 'You'd only sound worried. It could tip him over.'

'Sure. Good point. Work off strength. You'd better talk to him, for God's sake, stop him!'

Parry walked towards the door and hesitated, looking awkward, 'That might be difficult. I'll level with you – I hear rumours that he's going to announce it tonight.'

Carson slumped back into his chair. 'It's over then, that and the enquiry, I can't stop him.'

'Sure you can. It just got tougher, that's all. Now we've got a fight on our hands.' Parry turned and left the room.

A cold November evening in the windswept town of Waterloo, Iowa – the final stop on a four-day tour by Senator Ewan J Kelp. It was in the fast-filling hall of Waterloo's high school that Ewan Kelp was expected to make the announcement that he would run against President Carson for the Democratic nomination.

As he sat in the car bringing him from the airport, he was trying, not too successfully, to put the meeting that he had just come from in perspective. It had been a difficult visit to a steelworks, ending with a union meeting with a group of the workers. In the warmth of the car, the anger they had shown seemed a million miles away but he knew he could not minimise its significance. They had been let down, they said, by President Carson. A President who was more concerned with his friends in the service sector and Wall Street than with them. A Democrat, they complained, shouldn't stand idly by as thousands lost their jobs in the manufacturing industry. They wanted a change of policy – more security. Kelp reassured them and pointed the finger carefully at Carson.

Now, in the comfort of his car, he reflected on the complicated four-tier caucus system in Iowa, which he hoped to swing his way after his whistle-stop tour. Tonight was to be the moment. He had planned to go on the offensive in Iowa and Michigan because they were the earliest states to declare; a strong showing, he knew, in these states in early February would help to start the momentum that he hoped would roll him into Super Tuesday and the Democratic Convention and then onto the White House.

Ewan Kelp looked up from the text of his speech and, taking his glasses off, gazed out of the window, through the mist covering the glass, and watched the dirty snow on the side of the road. Next to him was Dick Mason, his campaign manager, who'd known Kelp for thirty years. He also sat in silence. He knew that Kelp liked to compose himself before he made a speech and always demanded absolute quiet.

Both knew that this was the last chance for Kelp. A fit 72-year-old, tipped as the 'most likely man' for so long, a successful businessman and scion of an old and established New England family, he had a record in the Senate that made him respected, even feared politically, but never loved.

The car pulled into the front of the school. Television cameras moved in towards the car, their powerful lights dazzling the occupants. As Kelp stepped out, his wife Mary-Lou, who had gone ahead, moved forward and hugged him.

Questions were fired at him from all directions – he answered none. This made the press shout even louder.

'Hey, Senator – over here!'

'This way!'

'Goin' to declare?'

However, instead of walking past them and into the school as planned, he stopped at the entrance and looked at them.

'I have a statement . . .'

They fell silent, but the clicks and flashes of the cameras continued.

'I am tonight,' he began, 'officially declaring my campaign to become the Democratic candidate for the Presidency. And I hope,' he continued, 'when you have heard my address, you will concentrate on the real issues that face us. Let's keep this, the most important democratic election in the world, about the issues. I make only that appeal.' He paused as the questions surged. 'There is only one issue: this race is about a President's strength of character, even more, it's about leadership not gimmicks.' He looked carefully at each of the cameras, 'It's about whether the President is fit to be in office.' Then turning slowly, he walked towards the door. There was uproar behind him.

Inside the hall, supporters waved little flags as he entered, some cheered, and all stood and applauded as he made his way to the platform and took his seat. After a swift introduction by the local congressman, Kelp began. His deep resonant tones carried clearly to all in the hall. He was acknowledged by friend and foe alike to be a fine orator. Not given to exaggeration and hyperbole, he made sure his simple words carried a clear meaning. Through a balance of fact and humour and a delivery that improved as he worked his way through his speech, he soon had a very willing audience applauding, laughing and, on occasion, cheering. However, he knew this speech was not for the audience in the hall, but for the press, and through them the general public. The audience in front of him was important only for its timely responses, which would convey public support for his message to the country at large. People in America liked a winner and the more the audience responded to him, the more he would seem to be one.

He finished his speech and sat down to noisy applause, the platform and hall rising to him. He stood again and smiled at the cameras while raising his arm in acknowledgement. At that point, on script, his wife of thirty years walked from her seat behind him and embraced him. Together they stood waving at the crowd and then they walked slowly into it. Always smiling, shaking hands furiously, nodding as he caught people's eyes, it became an almost regal procession moving slowly towards the door. The high school band played with gusto and the cameras flashed as the arc lights blazed.

Fifteen minutes later, outside the school, their two large Lincoln continentals were waiting, with polished black paintwork and dimmed windows. Surrounded by cameras, Kelp and his wife slid into one of them. Inside, the quiet contrasted with the noise and pressing bodies outside the school. Both Kelp and his wife sat without speaking as the seconds ticked by, gazing out of the windows as the car moved through the town.

'Well?' Kelp turned to her, 'what do you think?'

'You were good, Ewan, but then you always are,' she replied tersely.

'Is that it?' he snorted. 'Just good?'

'Well, what else do you want?'

'Some support, I guess.'

'You've always had my support. You always knew that.' She looked out of the window, her face flushed. 'Why now? That's what bothers me. Last time when you pulled out you said it was over, you'd never think of running again. After all the attacks from the Press, you were so hurt. I believed you and I thanked God,' she shook her head, 'I guess that's the kind of fool I am.'

'I meant it. I really did.'

'Then why . . .' she turned and looked at him, 'did you decide to go ahead now? You didn't even ask me – you just told me.'

'What was I to do?' He turned away in exasperation. 'Carson's betrayed the American people, he . . .'

'That's nonsense, Ewan – this is your wife you're talking to. You want to be President and this is an opportunity, that's all. I've never known why you didn't run before but I had a right to expect that you'd retire like anyone else – I mean, my God, you're 72!'

'You're impossible. You've always hated politics, and me in politics, now when the opportunity arises . . .'

'I support you,' she interrupted, 'I always have. God knows, I've followed you around dutifully enough over the years, but don't ask me to like it – I don't hate politics, I hate what it's done to you over the years. It's twisted you, eaten you up. Perhaps now, one way or another, this will end it.' She grasped his hand, 'I just don't want you to be hurt, that's all.

I'm tired of picking up the pieces.' He pulled his hand away and gazed out of the window.

They sat in silence as the car drove into the airport and pulled up alongside the waiting aircraft. Mason followed Kelp and his wife onto the plane. She took her seat behind Kelp. Next to her sat Carol Newman, who was tasked to look after her and handle any press.

'It was good, Ewan, very good,' Mason started talking as soon as they were in their seats. He was smiling, his face flushed, 'We hit the button. The Press hadn't expected your declaration then.' He sat back and looked at Kelp. Just enough flattery, it was necessary to keep his man's spirits up, but not too high. The Senator was resting his head on the back of the seat, eyes closed, as the aircraft took off.

'I think we've done it,' continued Mason, 'the newsrooms are buzzing. Even Marriott is going to rerun the last part in his show tonight.'

'Marriott? Aren't I seeing him on Tuesday on that link-up?' Kelp said as he opened his eyes.

'Yes, just after the Harvard speech.'

'What else have we got on the schedule?' Kelp looked up at Mason as he reached into his briefcase and pulled out a sheaf of papers. Mason handed a file over to Kelp.

'Only a few changes since we last spoke, Ewan. Eight o'clock in the morning, New York.' Mason reached into his briefcase and pulled out another file. 'At noon you've got the UN lunch with the secretary-general – that's a great coup. I don't know how you swung that. Everyone knows that Carson hasn't been there for a year.'

'What's friendship for, Dick? I've known him since the early days. He owes me.' For the first time that evening, Mason saw Kelp's face crease, not so much into a smile, just a faint flicker and he knew it wasn't for his benefit.

'Anyway, Ewan,' he continued, 'your address at Harvard

at 8 p.m. on foreign policy will look great.' He opened the file, 'I've got the draft of your speech here.' He passed it across to Kelp, who flicked through it while he listened. 'Tuesday, you're in Washington for the debate and on Thursday evening there's an address to the veterans. Just one change Wednesday morning, you're due to visit that urban renewal project, you know . . .'

'Is that all fixed now?'

'Yes, I guess so.'

'Is Benjamin Clay going to be there?' Kelp asked. The very mention of the man's name made Mason shudder. For some months the black preacher had been criticising Kelp for his lack of commitment to the underclass. He was unpredictable and potentially dangerous. They both knew he was already in with Carson, too.

'Yeah, but it's the sort of project that could give you great credibility. You know, Carson's been making a real effort over Clay.'

Kelp nodded, 'Good coverage?'

'Yeah, so that's all fixed.' Mason laid the file back on his knee and looked again at Kelp. 'And as we agreed, our agenda – economy, foreign policy and social issues. At last we're getting some momentum.'

Kelp looked out of the aircraft window while he spoke. Lights twinkled below. 'Thinking about it, you may be right, Dick, you may be. That visit to the project is important – we'll be taking Carson on in his own backyard.' He paused and looked at Mason. 'Funny how things change – once upon a time an Ivy League background was enough to guarantee you the route to the top. Now look at us.'

'I could fix up a private meeting for you with Clay on Tuesday night,' Mason said. 'It might be worth it – he destroyed O'Keene's hopes of making it to the Senate.' Mason shook his head. 'And Carson won't . . .'

'Yes, OK, we do need him but don't let him get too close –

it's up to you, Dick, don't blow it. Just make sure he stamps my ticket, that's all I want.'

Over the next two hours Kelp settled down to work on his speech for the UN lunch, then fell into a deep sleep. Mason wandered to the back of the aircraft to speak to the rest of Kelp's team.

The touchdown at La Guardia was smooth. Kelp stared thoughtfully out of the window and watched as his car drew up beside the steps of the plane. He walked to the aircraft door where his wife joined him. 'Where's Levinson?' he asked. Sol Levinson was the treasurer of the campaign team. He also worked as vice president, in charge of finance, for Victor Acquilan, Kelp's business partner and long-time friend.

'He's with Victor – you know they're going over the figures – again.' Mason replied, shaking his head despairingly.

'Oh,' Kelp nodded. 'Money problems?'

'Levinson says we're spending too much, Ewan,' Mason sneered, 'no control, he says.'

'Maybe,' Kelp answered over his shoulder as he started down the steps, 'but what does he know? If you want to win you've got to go hard and fast and build a lead.'

'Well, you'd better square it with Victor.'

'Sure, sure . . .' Kelp's voice trailed away. 'What about Douglas at the *Post*? That son-of-a-bitch had better get off my back.' He looked at Mason as they reached the car. 'What are you doing about him?'

'I don't know. Trouble is the man is too highly thought of – he's an institution. But if it's any consolation, he's going for Carson as well. He's been calling for an enquiry into some land deal Carson got caught up in twenty years ago.'

'I don't give a shit about Carson – just keep him off my back!'

Laura Buckley had spent most of her life since leaving college putting her career first. Inheriting her father's determination, she had set her sights on making a success of her career in television. She approached it with such single-minded determination and devotion that, at the age of 34, she was producing the number one discussion/news show on network TV, the *Jack Marriott Hour*, three times a week. She now had a formidable reputation for securing the right interviews for the show and, while to the public the success was due to Jack Marriott's urbane laid-back style, those in the business knew that it was down to the combination of the two of them. Now people queued up to be on the show and instead of having to fight for success, it came easily. The show's format was copied everywhere. The problem was, she was bored.

There was a heavy clunk as Laura's New York apartment door shut behind her. She locked it with meticulous care and, hanging her overcoat in the hall, walked through to the living room and switched on the light. She stopped in the middle of the room and kicked off her shoes – the carpet felt soft through her stockinged feet as she wriggled her toes. Walking over to the answering machine, she played her messages while she untied her hair and then poured herself a glass of wine. To her disappointment, there were no messages from her father's Italian lawyer in Rome, only one from Pat – 'Where the hell were you for lunch, honey?' She screwed up her face as she recalled that she'd had lunch with two of Kelp's team, arranging the time for the link-up with Kelp in Boston. Laura sighed and made a mental note to call him tomorrow and apologise.

Billy Joel's 'Piano Man' filled the room as she flopped down in an armchair to gaze at the ceiling – still no word from her father. Her brow furrowed. It seemed so long since she had stayed with him in Positano. She realised he was an ill man and God only knew what had happened to him. Perhaps she should take some time off and try to find him? But she had no information. She had asked the lawyer but he claimed her father didn't want her to know his whereabouts. Perhaps, she mused, if she were there, in his office . . . Her thoughts rolled on, always returning to the same conclusion: her father had planned it from the start, no final farewells, no sitting by the bedside of a man who no longer recognised anyone. 'No one will watch me die,' he'd said before she left in the summer, 'no one.'

Laura walked through to her bathroom and started the shower. She glanced in the mirror; she looked tired and there were shadows around her big brown eyes. She turned away and shrugged. For years she had played down her good looks. To get on in what was still a man's world she wanted to take them all on and beat them. As she threw off her clothes, she remembered with a half-smile how she even took to wearing glasses with plain lenses with her hair pulled back and only a little make-up. As the years had gone on, through drive and determination she had achieved what she wanted. Yet now she couldn't help feeling empty, almost unfulfilled; there was the recognition that something was missing. Playing her looks down had become too much of a habit to break – men were either friends or partners in bed, and there were precious few of those. She never allowed a friend and a lover to become one, she didn't want any man that close. She was guarded and reserved and, while she had some women friends, she was considered aloof by most of them and a dangerous loner.

She stood under the shower and let the hot water pour down over her head and back. Bored as she was becoming, normally she enjoyed getting the show out and on those evenings she always went through the same routine. Home by herself, shower, light supper and bed. She made a point of shutting out the show. Yet tonight she cast her mind back to the programme and smiled. Who would have thought, she mused, that Kelp was capable of creating such a storm? Not only did he attack Carson, he put down a sizeable economic marker with his speech. The link-up with him now looked like a master stroke. Monday would be very interesting – she smiled to herself. Once the election was over she would speak to Walter Harvey, her director; she knew it was time she moved on. Turning off the shower, she reached for a towel.

Once dried she pulled on a bathrobe and walked back into the living room. Sitting down in an armchair she picked up the telephone and dialled a number. After a few tones, the telephone was answered. 'Alice, it's Laura,' she said.

'Hi, Laura, where are you?'

'Home, I just got back.' Laura tucked her legs up under her as she talked.

'I saw the show, Laura. Marriott was . . .'

'. . . an oil slick?' Laura laughed.

'God, yes!'

'But the public love him.'

Laura Buckley had known Alice van Buren ever since she had come to work in New York. Alice's looks and composure turned men's heads wherever she went. She enjoyed the attention and played them along. She partied at every occasion and was seen in all the most fashionable haunts, invariably with a different man. Yet behind the social merry-go-round lay a sharp business mind which, at the age of 30, had taken her to a full market listing for her interior design company. It had grown from a one-woman operation six years before to a multimillion dollar concern. Once there she sold her shares and, because she said she needed the challenge, started a design magazine which was making a profit after a year and a half, and all the signs pointed to further success.

'I kicked him out,' Alice said emphatically.

'When?'

'An hour ago. Would you believe his nerve, Laura, he was sleeping here and at least three other places!' Laura smiled. 'He was banging everything in sight!'

'But, Alice, you were going to kick him out anyway – I thought you were bored of him.'

'I was, but that's not the point. I mean, two-timing me. I can understand the odd one, but he'd become a Manhattan exercise bike!'

Laura smiled again and then started to laugh.

'But what am I saying – you call me and I waste time talking to you about that bum, I'm sorry.'

'No, I only rang to talk . . .' Laura's voice trailed away.

'Any news about your father?'

'No, nothing.'

'But he must have left some forwarding address.'

'He did, but not with me, with his lawyer in Rome.'

'Well, why can't . . .'

'Because he has been given strict instructions not to reveal his new address or telephone number. I've left another message but there's been no response so far.'

'It seems like only yesterday we were in Positano on vacation. I knew he wasn't well then but I . . .'

'No, it was all planned. As far as he was concerned, we had said our goodbyes.'

'Maybe someone else saw – wait a minute, what about that English guy we saw as we were leaving the house – you know, wasn't he the one we ran into on the beach?'

'Oh yes, I forgot,' Laura smiled as the encounter on the beach swam into her memory. 'The sad-looking one. Had a look like a lost boy – yes, I remember now.'

'Who was the old guy with him in the car?'

'I think my father said it was his uncle,' Laura sat back in her chair. 'What's the use? I don't even know who he was.' There was silence for a few seconds.

'Maybe your father mentioned it.'

'Maybe, maybe . . .' Laura quickly changed the subject.

Minutes later Laura finished the call. She sat still, thinking about what Alice had said, trying to remember a name, without success.

Across town the lights still shone from an office in the top quarter of the Empire State Building. Victor R Acquilan sat in his shirtsleeves, cigar in hand, reading through spreadsheets on his conference table. He was a big man with broad shoulders and a large head. He had a Roman nose, on which was balanced a pair of half-moon spectacles.

Across from him sat another man – thin, with grey hair, pallid complexion and wearing a round pair of glasses. His jacket was hanging on the back of his chair and he was watching Acquilan intently, his nervous eyes never leaving his face.

'OK, Sol,' Acquilan said, 'move the contingency money forward. That should cover the next month.'

'Fine, Victor, but you and I both know they're spending too much too soon. Once this is gone, what will happen when another crisis erupts later?' Sol Levinson spoke quickly and without any expression.

'I know, Sol, I know. But the plan was to start fast and get on a roll early.' Acquilan looked up. 'You remember, before Carson realises what's happening.'

'Oh, I can see that, but when is all this expenditure going to give them lift-off? It hasn't happened yet, that's for sure, and now we're already into the contingency.' He shook his head. 'They're spending faster than we planned; we're gonna be back on your money before long.'

Acquilan trusted the sharp brain and deadpan style of the accountant. He had been with him for years and had kept Acquilan's business empire surging ahead – he was, in Acquilan's eyes, a tax genius. When it came to money, he was normally right.

'OK, Sol, I agree. I'll speak to Mason. But you should remember we've got three major fund-raisers coming up and that should improve cash flow.'

'If you say so, Victor. But I would be happier if someone kept a closer eye on Mason.'

'Sure, it's going to be that way from now on. Pichowski's just got this deal in London to complete, then he'll be with you – trust me. And from what I hear in Waterloo . . .' The buzzer on his desk interrupted him and he picked up the phone. 'Acquilan,' he said slowly.

'Victor, it's Ewan.'

'Hi, Ewan – what do you say, the news is great.' Acquilan paused and cupped his hand over the mouthpiece. 'It's OK, Sol, you can go now. I'll talk to you tomorrow.' He watched Levinson pick up his papers and leave the room before continuing. 'Sorry, Ewan, just saying goodbye to Sol. Anyway, looks like you gave it to them. I watched Marriott tonight, even he said you've set the pace.'

'For the first time I really feel that we are on the move.'

'See, I told you, Dick was right. Waterloo, Iowa – a great touch. That bit at the start about the press lowering the quality of the debate – that really knocked them off balance.'

'Dick's idea. The other good news is that Marriott's producer has confirmed the link-up in Boston. It'll be coast to coast.'

'Good news, good news.' He paused. 'And I've got some more news about the other deal. Weitz took delivery of the items. We're just waiting for the last one.' There was silence at the other end. 'You there, Ewan?'

'Yes, that's good then, it looks like you were right, Victor – I can run. I'm all clear . . . but what about the diaries?'

'No, not yet . . . still, soon . . . and then Cosmo . . .'

'Cosmo, Cosmo . . .' Kelp's voice trailed away in exasperation.

'Not long, Ewan,' Acquilan interrupted, 'first the pictures and then the diaries, we're nearly there – I'll speak to you tomorrow.' He put the phone down.

Acquilan sat on the edge of his desk looking out through his window. The shadowy shapes of buildings across Manhattan, pockmarked by lights, seemed close enough to touch. Below and to the left there was that dark, almost menacing smudge that was Central Park. Acquilan wondered how many screams could be heard at that moment from this very small island. People, he thought, shouldn't rely on others, not the police, not anyone. You had to fight on your own. No one should be allowed to stand in the way of the successful. Getting to the top wasn't easy and staying there even harder. 'Always pay off old debts,' his father had said and, at long last, the one remaining debt was soon to be paid – to Cosmo.

He smiled as he reached for the telephone. It rang for some time before being answered.

'Acquilan,' he barked. 'What kept you?'

'Oh, hello Mr . . .' Pichowski began. 'It's 4.45 in the morning and . . .'

'Have you got the sixth picture and the diaries?' Acquilan cut him short as he looked at his watch.

'Not yet, we . . .' Pichowski stuttered.

'You told me it would be with you today. I even sent Weitz to help. If you've blown it . . .'

'No, Mr Acquilan. This guy Grande said it hadn't arrived yet when we took the other five. He said . . .'

'Today – so?'

'We'll get down there first thing. Anyway, me and Bernie think he's holding out – knows something and he's not telling.'

'Jesus, Pichowski! Get me Weitz,' Acquilan snarled.

There was a pause as Weitz came to the telephone.

'Victor, it's Bernie.'

'Bernie, what the hell's going on? I sent you to identify the paintings and you still haven't got the last one.'

'It's this guy Grande, he's screwing us around.'

'So do something.'

'That's what we're going to do. Today is his last day.'

'What about the diaries?'

'I'm not sure, he hasn't said anything yet.'

'You and I both know they were part of the deal, Bernie. They were meant to be handed over at the same time – so where are they? Cosmo said, "Pictures and books".'

Weitz had been with Acquilan for a long time and, unlike Pichowski, Acquilan appreciated his advice and listened. The plan had always been for Pichowski to do the legwork and then call in Weitz as soon as the pictures were found. After all, Weitz was the man who had been with Acquilan right from the beginning. 'Cosmo could be playing games, Victor. Just look at how he's worked it so far.'

'What do you mean?' Acquilan's voice was harsh.

'Well, we both knew he'd do an exchange through a third party, yet he left enough clues for even Pichowski to follow all the way to Positano.'

'So?'

'Think back, Victor. Why'd he take the pictures? Money? Perhaps. Yet he kept the ones he knew you wanted more than any others. All the rest were sold. Ewan's diaries went missing. We've always assumed they were burned in the fire – now he says he took them. Why? All those years, not a trace, nothing. He never made contact, no threats – even when you built the corporation – no demands. Remember, we always wondered. We even thought he'd died. Pichowski never turned up anything. Then Ewan looks like declaring and all of a sudden, he makes contact. He wants to do a deal, to sell. Just a few words and for the first time in years, he's got us going again.'

'Yes,' Acquilan murmured. There was something in what Weitz was saying.

'You there, Victor?'

'I'm here – go ahead.'

'This English guy, Grande's his name. I think he knows more than he's letting on. Could be he's part of it. After all, why delay the sixth painting? All six were on the shipment, we checked. It's too much of a coincidence, and his uncle lives next door to Cosmo . . .'

'You mean this guy knows who he really is?' Acquilan interrupted. 'That he's Cosmo?'

'No, probably not. He is known as D'Ostia – that's who Grande thinks he is. Still, I don't believe in coincidences like that. I mean, why pick this guy to make the transfer – it could have been done in New York – anywhere.'

'Well, if he knows as much as you say, does he know who you are?'

'No, he knows me as Wessells, not Weitz, and Pichowski as Peach.'

'OK, Bernie. But remember, no slip-ups or the three of us – Ewan, me and you – are in deep shit. Just sort it and get the hell back here, pronto!'

'Sure, I'll . . .' Weitz began but the telephone had already gone dead.

4

A Trap from the Past

Sitting behind his desk at the *Washington Post*, Jack Douglas felt content, his eyes fixed to the screen of his computer as he typed in a few corrections. All around was controlled bedlam as last-minute changes were made to the layout of the newspaper before it went to press.

Jack Douglas was known throughout the newspaper world as one of the most astute of commentators. He worked freelance with a series of papers syndicating his articles on a regular basis. He had spent a large part of his career working for the *Post* and had ended up as editor there in 1970, a position he didn't much like. He preferred to write and had returned to the *Post* as a syndicated columnist. Finally, at the age of 70, he had decided to retire. Then, two years later, the *Post* had persuaded him to write a regular feature on politics and his 'Letter from the Capital' became widely read across America. Regardless of high days or holidays he produced his column for eight more years. Then, just when he had been about to call it a day, Gene Meyer, the editor of the *Post*, asked him to stay and help cover the forthcoming election. It meant an extra column each week. He pretended to his wife and friends that he was doing it to help the paper out but secretly he relished the work. He disliked growing old and hated the idea of retiring. Growing old gracefully was not what he had ever intended. He knew he shouldn't be but he was more and more irked by the glib young college graduates who came straight on to the paper. They were still wet behind the ears and what was worse, they couldn't write like he did. He would say to anyone prepared to listen that they should have worked an apprenticeship.

The irony, he knew, was that he'd never intended to go into the newspaper business but the Second World War had changed everything. He'd enlisted well under age and saw service in the Pacific in the last year of the war. It was there that he had started writing for an army paper and found he'd got a talent for it. When the war was over, one of the correspondents remembered his work and he found himself being offered a job on the *Courier*, an upstate New York paper. Then he'd gone to Korea as a war correspondent and when he came back he soon became editor. By the 1960s, he was at the *New York Times* and from there the *Washington Post*.

'Hey, Jack,' a slow southern voice broke into his thoughts, 'you got a minute?'

Douglas looked up to see a thickset man of fifty, with a cigarette clamped in the corner of his mouth, the smoke climbing up the side of his heavy face obscuring the no-smoking signs all around the office.

Jack Douglas smiled as the editor, Gene Meyer, turned and shuffled away back to his office. Meyer was the one achievement from his time on the paper that he was really proud of. As editor, he'd brought him in, straight from the army. Echoes of his own past. A Vietnam veteran at the age of 21, Meyer had written to him with copies of some of his work. Douglas hired him on his gut instinct, against the advice of everyone else. He never regretted it for a moment. Meyer had developed fast; his languid, almost sleepy, style belied a sharp brain with a real sense for a story. Douglas picked up his papers and followed Meyer into his office. As he sat down, he nodded to the deputy editor standing by the window.

'I'm on a different line this week,' Douglas began.

'Personal?' Meyer frowned.

'That's right. You remember the piece about this being a dirty election. One of the networks said our political system had sunk to an all-time low. So I thought I'd disagree . . . After all, it doesn't even compare to President Jackson's campaign,' he leaned forward as he spoke and tossed his article on Meyer's desk.

'President who?' Meyer glanced across at his deputy editor, Don Grover.

'– you know, 1828, General Jackson's campaign for the Presidency.'

'That Jackson! Christ, Jack,' Meyer chortled. 'For a minute there I thought you were referring to Jesse!'

'Spinning's always been around. His people put it out that his opponent Quincy Adams had sent American girls to the tsar when he was a diplomat in Russia.' He glanced at Meyer, who was smiling. 'And in response, Quincy Adams said that Jackson had murdered six soldiers under his command in the 1812 war and . . .' he paused, 'that he was a bigamist and an adulterer.' Douglas sat back in his seat as Meyer laughed. 'Makes Carson's problems look pretty tame.'

'Gene, Jack,' the deputy editor interrupted, 'I hate to break in on this historical debate but we've only got a couple of minutes.'

'Sure,' Meyer said, nodding. 'Jack, look, I've had an idea: I'd like to run some personal features on all the candidates.'

'What kind of an angle?'

'I was thinking more of your personal view of what each stands for; you know, the public out there half the time doesn't know what these guys believe in. A bit of their background; you might even find they believed in something after all.'

'Go easy though, Jack,' Grover said quickly. 'Kelp's none too happy about us, and particularly you.'

'He never is,' Meyer cut in dryly. 'No complaints from this department.'

'I hear you, but Don's got a point. They didn't like the piece I did before he declared – you know, "The Nearly Man".' Douglas stood up, 'I'll need to give some thought to the idea, though.' He turned and walked to the door, where he hesitated, 'When do you want to have it?'

'Just before the Iowa caucus – anyway, let me know what you think. This is additional to your normal column. I still want that when you . . .'

'You mean, if I can,' he interrupted, 'after all, I'm nearly eighty.'

'No,' Meyer looked uncomfortable as he frowned. 'Well, I know, it's a lot of extra work . . .'

'Yeah, yeah,' Douglas smiled broadly as he stood up, 'as we used to say during the war, "Go tell it to the marines."' He waved his hand at the editor. 'No problem,' he said as he left the office.

Forty-five minutes later, arriving home, Douglas remembered his wife was out for the evening and, without bothering to turn on the lights, he carried his bag up the stairs to the bedroom. He was tired and intended to go to bed after his shower. Although he would never admit it to anyone on the paper, he felt every day of his age.

As he put his bag down, he knocked a magazine his wife had been reading off the bed. Splayed out on the floor he could see it was the *Spectator*, a British weekly magazine. His wife, still a British citizen after all the years of marriage to him, always bought it, mostly she said for the book reviews. He smiled as he picked it up. Its opinions were a little too conservative for his own taste but he knew the writing was normally pretty good. He flicked through the pages and was just about to put it down when a headline caught his eye: NEVER MIND THE HYPE WATCH THE BACK-GROUND. He caught sight of the name 'Kelp' and turned back. Fishing his glasses out of his pocket, he started to read. It was a well-written article by one of the British foreign correspondents based in Washington.

The author compared the candidates' different backgrounds, which Douglas thought was an interesting angle. Yet it was the last part that caught his attention. The careful summary of the business activities of Senator Ewan Kelp acted as a catalyst, nudging his own memory. The article reminded Douglas of Kelp's father's prewar bankruptcy, how the Kelp family had been forced to sell their house in Newport, Rhode Island, and their large town house in Manhattan. Yet within two years of the end of the war, Kelp had restored and revived the family fortunes to such an extent that he had even bought another large house in Newport and the family had re-established itself in the same New York society from which it had been so ignominiously ejected.

Leaning against the headboard of the bed, he took his glasses off and lay them on his lap. This was the almost classic story of the rise and fall of an old New England family that had almost by some miracle reversed itself. He was reminded how, as a young New York reporter, he had often wondered about Kelp's meteoric return. But there had always been too much to chase and report and he'd put the story behind him. When he'd edited the same paper a few years later, Kelp had stood for the state legislature, but he'd only dealt with his policies, never the man himself.

It had been well known in New York that Kelp's father had ruined the family. Like so many of those old families – the Vanderbilts and others – the decline was fast. Nothing new in that. The history of the USA was littered with old family names that ended up on Skid Row. People were always interested in such tales but that alone wasn't enough. Show them there was new money and they'd read on. He smiled slowly – old name, new money – it might even make a good article for the *Post*, just what Gene was looking for, he thought.

He switched the light off and turned over. Downstairs, the front door opened as his wife returned but he did not hear her; still fully dressed, he was already asleep.

In London, it was a dull, overcast and damp morning as John Grande walked out of High Street Kensington tube station towards the gallery. Wrapped up in a heavy blue coat, he still felt cold. His hands were thrust deep in his pockets and his collar turned up as he walked towards the square.

He had a sense of relief, after all the pressure of the past few days, that the last picture was now ready and could be sold to the two Americans. He had seen it and was pleased with the completed job. Needless to say, it had taken more than the four days that Maguire had forecast. Today was day five, and for the last two days Peach had never seemed to be off the phone to the gallery. Yet, strangely enough, he mused, Peach hadn't telephoned for a whole day – he even began to wonder vaguely if he was still interested in the painting. He hadn't had a chance to ring Peach but he knew that it was the first thing he would do as soon as he reached the gallery. He glanced at his watch nervously – 8.45 a.m.

Outside the gallery, two police cars and an ambulance were parked, their lights flashing in an unsynchronised and hypnotic pattern, as two men carried a folded stretcher from the ambulance in through the gallery doors. John stared, his heart racing. He ran the rest of the way until he was stopped by a policeman.

'I'm sorry, sir, but you can't go in.' John peered inside, only half aware of the policeman's arm restraining him.

'I must, I'm John Grande,' he protested, turning to the policeman as he spoke, yet the man's arm remained.

'I don't care who you are, you can't . . .'

'What's the matter, son?' The voice was Glaswegian and came from a short, dark-haired man wearing a tweed jacket. He was standing behind the young policeman, looking at John.

'It's this man . . .'

'Grande, John Grande, that's who I am,' John gabbled. 'I own the gallery.'

The older man led John inside. All was chaos and devastation. Some paintings were missing off the walls, most of the bronzes and other statues had been knocked off their podiums, some lay broken in heaps. Through the half-opened door into the storeroom, John could just make out flashes of light as someone took photographs. Deep in the shadows at the back of the gallery sat the receptionist, her head clasped between her hands. John felt numb, overwhelmed by the sight. As he looked around he could see the detective's lips moving, yet no words. He shook his head.

'. . . Detective Sergeant Mackie, Regional Crime Squad.' He peered at John. 'As you can see there's been a break in.'

John looked at the detective's face for the first time. He was clean-shaven with a strong jaw, dark brown eyes and thinning hair. John thought he must be in his fifties but the bags under his eyes made him look tired and even older. John looked away; the receptionist walked towards him. 'Are you all right, Ursula?' he asked gently, laying a hand on her shoulder.

'Oh, John,' she choked, 'it's awful.' Her head went down and she started to cry. John stepped forward and gave her a hug. 'I found him, it's horrible – he was in there.' He looked towards the storeroom and then turned to the detective sergeant.

'Who, who's in there?'

'Your receptionist identified . . .'

At that moment the ambulance crew came out, carrying

the stretcher with John's partner on it. As they went past, John could see his face; it was as pale as a waxwork exhibit. His mouth was half open and around the top half of his head was a gauze net holding a large dressing in place. 'Is he still alive?' John whispered, as he watched him pass.

'Just, only just,' was the reply from one of the ambulance crew as they rushed him outside. Sirens blaring, lights flashing, the ambulance pulled away.

Detective Sergeant Mackie was talking to another police-man and John took the opportunity to question Ursula.

'I thought he was dead when I came in, John.' Her voice sounded relieved and she even managed a pathetic smile. 'He looked so lifeless – it was awful.' She bent her head down.

'What time was that?' John asked softly, his head on her shoulder.

'I can't remember exactly, around 8 a.m. or so.'

'That's a bit early, why were you here then?'

'Richard asked me to put his exhibition list together. I hadn't finished last night and he was in such a bad mood he stormed out, saying that it had to be ready by 10 a.m. today so I thought I'd better get in early and finish it.' She paused to wipe her eyes.

'I rang the police as soon as I found . . .' She looked nervously towards the storeroom door. 'They were very quick.' She stopped talking as Detective Sergeant Mackie walked over to them.

'Miss Corey, you've been a great help. The officer over there needs to take a few more details from you and then you are free to go. She will also arrange transport if you need it.' He smiled at Ursula and pointed towards the policewoman by the desk at the rear of the room. 'Mr Grande, I'll have to ask you to stay for a little while so that you can give me an idea of what was stolen or damaged.'

'Of course . . .' John started to walk towards the storeroom.

'No, Mr Grande, not yet. We will need to give them a few

more minutes in there. Perhaps we could talk over here.' He pointed to the receptionist's desk. 'I've a few questions to ask you to clear up some points of detail.'

By the time they had sat down, John's mind was calmer. He thought back to the last conversation he had had with the two Americans, Peach and his colleague, Wessells. He could see Wessells standing by his desk staring at him, those dead eyes behind the thick lenses and that flat menacing monotone.

'So, Mr Grande, it's day four and still no picture. It's time to talk.' He had paused and looked around before continuing. 'Let's stop the bullshitting and the games – we both know that you've got it and there's no late delivery.'

'Wait, you . . .' John had begun.

'No, Mr Grande, no more bullshit – we know, OK?' He had waited as Peach had lit up a Turkish cigarette and exhaled. Wessells had turned sharply and given Peach a cold, hard look. He had stubbed out the cigarette.

'So,' Wessells had continued, 'if you're waiting for a better deal, don't bother. We'll pay more if you get the painting – ten grand on top, if the picture is here tonight; if not,' he had paused again as he put on his raincoat, 'I guess we'll have to terminate the deal.'

John had wondered as he listened to Wessells how much he knew. Yet he still needed more time. He remembered how he decided to go along with them and most of all how difficult it had been to keep his voice from shaking as he spoke. 'I'll do my best,' was all he'd said.

'Until tomorrow – I'll wait for your call,' Wessells had said as he reached the door. Peach waited behind, then reached out to brush something from John's shoulder.

'Tomorrow,' he had snarled, 'could be pay day, Mr Grande.' His voice was low, almost a whisper. John had stepped back. 'One way or the other, tomorrow we'll be back.'

John could still see in his mind's eye their retreating backs. Now he realised there was no doubt about the who or the why. His heart was racing and a cold feeling was spreading over him – what had he done? If only Maguire had . . . Perhaps they would even have got away with it. He shook his head.

'Mr Grande . . .' Somewhere he could hear a voice . . . a Scottish accent . . . strange, nothing to do . . .

'Mr Grande, are you . . .' He found himself looking up into the eyes of Detective Sergeant Mackie, who was now leaning over him, '. . . OK?'

'Yes, sorry, I . . . I . . .' He flushed red.

'I thought you had gone into a trance,' Mackie spoke as he walked around the desk. 'Would you like a coffee?'

John nodded. 'Thanks, yes.'

'Seddon!' Mackie called to a young policeman by the door. 'Nip out, lad, and get us two coffees – I think there's a place on the corner.' He turned to John, who nodded in response and after giving the policeman some loose change, he walked back to his seat. 'Been a bit of a shock I dare say, Mr Grande – I won't keep you long, just some routine questions.'

'Before you start, could I ask you what exactly happened here?'

'Aye, but I can only give you an outline, mind. We're still figuring out the details.' John nodded. 'Well, it would appear that a person or persons broke in here disabling your alarm, probably through the back door. You'll be able to tell me later what they took – then either your partner disturbed them or they disturbed him; either way, there was a struggle and someone struck him on the side of the head with a crowbar.' John glanced across at the transparent plastic bag by the door, holding a matt-black crowbar. He shuddered.

'That looks like ours – we keep it in the storeroom to unpack cases.'

'That's all I'm able to tell you right now,' Mackie continued. 'Now I need to know a few things from you, if you don't mind. Your partner, can you give me his full details and as much background as you can – we know his father is a politician.'

Questions continued but it was all John could do to concentrate enough to answer them. He sipped his coffee intermittently, responding when required and, as though magnetically pulled, occasionally turning round to look towards the storeroom.

'I think that'll do for the moment, Mr Grande.' Mackie was shutting his notebook. He slid it into his inside breast pocket and leant forward as if to get up and go. 'Oh yes,' he said as he sat back, 'I must ask you, where were you last night? As a formality, you understand.' He smiled.

'What, sorry, I . . .' John had allowed his mind to drift back to the night with Maguire.

'Last night, I was asking if you could account for your whereabouts . . .'

'Last night? I . . . I, didn't do anything, I was . . . at home.'

'Presumably your wife could . . .'

'No. My wife is dead.' The tone of John's voice changed and he stiffened in his seat. Mackie watched this change with interest.

'It's just a formality, but we have to confirm the whereabouts of those nearest to the victim, you understand.' He smiled again but as John watched, he was left in no doubt that nothing was ever a formality with this man. Men like Mackie do not carry out formalities, they dig and sift. 'Only,' Mackie continued, 'it would help if someone could confirm.'

'I'm sorry, no one would be able to. I was working on the accounts from the gallery.'

'You see,' Mackie said, staring straight at John and ignoring his last reply, 'everyone is ruled in during my investigations until they rule themselves out – everyone.' A photographer interrupted him.

'I'm done, Sarge.'

'Did you get some of the back door?' Mackie asked.

'Oh, yes, covered everything.'

Mackie turned back to John, 'Mr Grande, I wonder whether you would be able to carry out an inventory, see what's missing. Would that be possible in the next 24 hours?'

'Certainly.' Then it occurred to him that this might further delay the sale of the last Licatta. What if they watched him? He couldn't start doing deals away from the gallery. 'When do you think we will be able to reopen?'

'Well,' Mackie looked at him, startled, 'if you give us the inventory first, it should allow me some time to decide if we have enough from here and then you can clear up. However, whether you would want to open up so soon is a different question.'

Aware that the question had sounded callous, John shifted uneasily in his seat. 'It was just a general question,' John stammered. 'Just a general . . .' His voice trailed away.

Mackie gave him a strange look, as though he wanted to ask him another question, but slipping his notebook into his pocket, he excused himself, walking outside to talk to one of the other detectives.

John looked around. Ursula had gone home and the forensic people seemed to have disappeared. An eerie stillness had descended on the gallery. John felt himself drawn, as though by some strange force, to the storeroom. He hesitated in front of the door, then stretching out his hand, he pushed it open.

The light was still on, illuminating a chaotic scene. Some pictures lay across the floor and, in the corner, the remains of a marble bust. The racks at the back were in a mess. It wasn't until he looked at the left-hand rack that he became aware of a large dark stain on the carpet. The sight of the blood made him feel dizzy and he leaned against the door frame for support. Was all this because of Peach or just a coincidence? A crude robbery that went wrong or a warning to him? But if it was a warning, why Richard? Why not him? It all made no sense. He knew he was overdue with the picture but surely this was not necessary? Why? Why? he asked himself. But in the quiet of the gallery, he knew there was only one answer and his head bowed as the heavy blanket of responsibility settled around his shoulders and made his knees buckle. There was no need to go on questioning, he knew that it was him: he was the only answer to all the questions.

'Kelp's last chance,' the headlines said. Senator Kelp settled into the seat of his campaign aircraft smiling smugly, a glass of Scotch in his right hand. He knew his political skill lay in his record as an uncomplicated old-fashioned politician who would be compared with the White House incumbent accused of corruption and incompetence.

This chance, he knew, had been a long time coming – from the day he volunteered for war and lied about his age. As a young man, he'd vowed to succeed whatever it cost – nothing would or could be allowed to block him. His father's fall from grace and social ostracism had scarred him. He had to watch his father's kindness and trust being thrown back in his face. The traits he had been brought up to believe good and worthy had become badges of weakness in Kelp's eyes. They were the reasons for the family's misfortune and Kelp quietly grew to hate the easy-come, easy-go approach of his father. He developed a single-mindedness and a sense of purpose that bordered on the obsessive. To a young Kelp, selfishness became a virtue, not a vice. No one, he decided, gave favours; everything achieved would be done regardless of others. His first objective was to raise his family back up to its rightful place and, when that was done, he'd set his sight on the Presidency.

For years he'd waited, forced to watch while lesser men had scrabbled for the post – watched and hoped. Wishing for the day when his past couldn't hurt him any more. Only one man, some paintings and a few diaries stood in his way. His smile faded as he remembered that the spectre at his feast was a man called Cosmo, armed with the knowledge of the events of 1944 and 1946. Ewan Kelp knew that this one man had the power to destroy him and his lifelong ambitions. Remembering this was, even now, all these years later, enough to send a shiver of panic through him and he gripped his glass tightly. If the public knew what had happened they would be unforgiving. Kelp's fear was made worse when he recalled the two things that held the key to his exposure: Acquilan's obsession with the six paintings and a set of diaries written by him, containing a faithful account of all that had happened.

As he closed his eyes he calmed himself with the thought that, despite Acquilan's desire to repossess the six paintings, he had taken charge and was determined to work it all out. Kelp's confidence in Acquilan was supreme, going back to the war when he was the very young officer in charge of the platoon of which Acquilan was a sergeant. Kelp knew that what he lacked in experience then was more than made up for by Acquilan's drive. It was Acquilan who had recognised the possibilities in him and who had shaped Kelp from day one. It was a case of the kid from the Bronx meets Ivy League, a partnership that worked by serving the purposes of two selfish men in equal parts.

'Yes,' Kelp tried to reassure himself, 'Victor will fix it, he always does.' The self-satisfied smile didn't return but the worried look fell away.

Three thousand miles away events were unfolding at a rate and in a way that would have further disturbed the Senator's thoughts, had he but known about them.

Inside a London pub called The Australian, at a table in one corner, sat John Grande. It was two days since the robbery at the gallery and his partner was still in a coma at St Mary's

Hospital. He knew the police suspected not only his partner's boyfriend, who had conveniently disappeared, but also himself. There had been two further interrogations at the police station and even fingerprints to check against those on the crowbar. He knew the investigating officer, Mackie, was sceptical. The man's calm bank-clerk image disguised a very sharp mind and each of his questions seemed to be saying, 'I don't believe you'.

As John sat in the pub, he tried to understand what he had become involved in and how. He was certain that Peach and Wessells were responsible for the attack. He felt sure the man's real name wasn't Wessells any more than the name Peach was genuine. Certainly, they were both dangerous, but what he couldn't figure out was why they would bother to raid the gallery. After all, he'd assured them that they would get the picture. Why try and kill a man? He shook his head and checked his watch.

'I wonder,' he said to himself, 'where Wessells is . . .' Then he felt a hand on his shoulder.

'Mr Grande.'

John turned quickly and looked up to find himself staring into Wessells' thick lenses.

'So, Mr Grande,' Wessells said in his flat monotone as he sat down, 'you called?'

'You heard what happened?'

'Some.'

'Look – were you anything to do . . .'

Wessells cut him short. 'I'm a businessman, Mr Grande. You and me, we got a deal. The way I see it you were going to deliver the last picture, so it wouldn't be necessary, would it?' Wessells raised his eyebrows as he finished speaking.

'No,' John replied, hesitantly. 'Well, whoever did it has just delayed things. I can't get into the gallery until tomorrow. The police won't let me. So the deal can't be completed until tomorrow afternoon at the earliest.'

Wessells gazed at him intently while he spoke, his eyes never leaving John's. When he finished, Wessells continued to sit in silence. After what seemed an age, he took off his glasses and started polishing them.

'Mr Grande, I already know the cops have given the gallery back to you, so why are we playing games?' He slipped the glasses back on his nose. 'You're not in high school any more,' Wessells smiled faintly, 'so no bullshit. I just want what I came for and what I know you've got.'

'Have it your way, Mr Wessells,' John began, hoping his voice didn't betray his nerves, 'but I'm not going to produce this for you until tomorrow – mid-morning at the earliest.'

'OK, Mr Grande, if you say so,' Wessells demurred. 'Noon?' John nodded.

'And there's a package of books, they'd better be ready by Friday. You'll have them there for us as well. I understand the other party sent them to you.'

'What books? I don't know anything about any books,' John spluttered, his composure completely gone.

Wessells stared at him, his face hard, his eyes cold. 'Don't worry, you'll be paid as agreed, fifty grand . . .'

'What?' John stared back at Wessells. 'I know nothing about that, no one told me about books. Besides, I'm an art dealer not a bookseller. Why . . .?'

'Bullshit, Mr Grande! You've been chosen, so just take the money and smile,' Wessells hissed. 'Unless of course you plan to hold out for more again.' He tapped the table. 'But I'm a reasonable man, so I've given you an extra day for the books.' Again, the clipped smile. 'So let's say . . . noon tomorrow, I'll take the last picture. And noon Friday I'll pick up the other package. Take my advice, Mr Grande, deliver and don't ask questions.' He paused and moved towards the door. As he did so, a man at the bar stood up and walked out. It was Peach.

John Grande stared at his beer. A cold sweat trickled down the nape of his neck and his heart pounded.

He'd always suspected and dismissed it but now there was no denying – he'd been set up. The trip to Positano, the damaged picture and now those books, all the way along. The two Americans didn't believe a word he was saying and, after the delayed picture, they'd be certain John was lying. He also knew that D'Ostia had never mentioned any books. But unless he could deliver, Wessells would assume he was holding out. John thought of his partner, shook his head and returned to the gallery.

Half an hour later, after two attempts, he finally got through to Mr Spellman, D'Ostia's solicitor, on the telephone. After a short and rather tense call, during which time Spellman denied all knowledge of any books, John put the phone down.

'All business between us is concluded, Mr Grande,' the lawyer had said in his precise, clipped tones.

John stared out of the window of the gallery, an idea slowly taking shape in his despair. He walked back quickly to his desk and rang Maguire.

5

The Chase

An early fall of snow lay across all the familiar landmarks in Washington. The air was cold and there was a strong north-west wind swirling snow against the sides of the buildings. Ronald Reagan National Airport seemed less busy than usual, although the occasional aircraft could be heard, drifting in along the Potomac.

On arrival at the *Post* building, Jack Douglas went straight to the editor's office, where a meeting was just breaking up.

Gene Meyer greeted him with a big smile. The bulky, heavy-featured man always seemed to have two cigarettes lit at any one time, and this morning was no exception. He was just stubbing one out and inhaling another as Jack walked in.

'Grab a coffee,' Meyer said.

'I only wanted to give you that article on the Reverend Benjamin Clay,' Jack replied, as he put a set of typed pages on the desk.

'I keep getting calls from Jim Donald, Jack – you know, Kelp's press secretary.' Meyer waved his hand towards a stack of papers on a table in the corner of his office.

'You mean spin doctor. So?'

'Well, anyway, some gripe about how you're not telling it as it is.'

'What they mean, as you know, is they want me to tell it as they see it.'

'He maintains,' continued Meyer, 'that Carson's people have been packing all the caucus meetings in Iowa with his supporters.'

'Sounds like Carson's got them scared,' Jack interrupted and pointed to his article sitting on Meyer's desk. 'Don't worry, Gene, I've covered it, here.' His voice was flat.

'What?' Meyer stubbed out his cigarette.

'Just that no one really knows just how many of Carson's supporters have infiltrated these meetings. But for once Kelp's right – the system in Iowa always did lend itself to that kind of tactic. It's not that new or illegal.'

'Who do you think it's gonna be?' Meyer perched on the edge of his desk as he spoke. He was always amazed at Jack's ability to sniff out news where others failed.

'For what it's worth, it should be Carson – he's in the lead by five points . . .' Jack Douglas got up and strolled over to the coffee machine and poured himself a cup as he spoke.

'Do you think Kelp will lose so bad he'll pull? I mean, after all, it's a big gap,' Meyer asked.

'I didn't say anything about Kelp losing that bad – anyway, it's not important who wins, the size of the victory here matters. Carson still faces the possibility of an enquiry into his land deal. That'll have an effect – it's all too unpredictable. Besides, you've got to be careful about the polls in Iowa, Gene, they can be misleading. Remember how they missed Gary Hart's support in 1984 and overestimated John Glenn's? They only take the views of those who go to the meetings – they don't get the level of commitment across the state. Carson's people, when they attend the meetings, deliberately won't say whom they are supporting. It is all part of the campaign, only let the other candidates know how strong they are just before the February vote, when it will be too late.' He walked back to his seat. 'It's going to be a tight one.'

'Good,' Meyer chuckled. 'Now look . . .'

Jack Douglas watched Meyer as he laid out his plans for the paper over the election. He thought about the old days when Meyer had been one of his deputy editors, when he, Jack, had been in charge. He remembered how, when he'd decided to step down, he'd fought very hard to get Meyer made editor after him and, as he knew it would, it had done wonders for the paper. Meyer was a better editor than Jack ever was, and Jack was the first to admit it. Jack stood up as Meyer finished.

'Hey, one minute, Jack,' Meyer said quickly, 'have you thought about my idea on the features?'

'Sure, I've had some thoughts.' Jack watched Meyer light up another cigarette. 'But, I'd like to work on an angle that might take me away from this place for a couple of weeks – I need a little more time.'

'Not too long, I hope.'

'It's to do with something round about the end of the war. I can't say exactly what, but I will get back to you before I finish.'

'Fine, fine. Just keep in touch, OK?'

Jack nodded in reply and picked up his briefcase. Ten minutes later he was in the library.

The rectangular room in front of Jack housed a small office. As soon as he stepped in, his face broke into a big smile.

'Joe Schwartz! What in God's name are you doing here?' Jack Douglas exclaimed, his voice full of surprise. He shook hands with a slim, white-haired man, whose angular, wrinkled face had also broken into a broad grin.

'I just came back, Mr Douglas. I couldn't stand being retired. Mr Meyer called, said he couldn't get anyone good and asked me to come back.' He paused, 'plus a sidekick.'

'You son of a gun. I retired you ten years ago. You must be 74 or 75 if you're a day!'

'Hey, so who's counting?' They both laughed. 'Anyway, the way I hear it, you've been brought back as well.'

'True,' Jack Douglas smiled. 'I guess they did just that.'

'It's sad, Mr Douglas, all these kids today, no commitment,' Joe Schwartz looked around and then lowered his voice, 'You know, this guy here, he don't even read the papers – I ask you, Mr Douglas, work for a newspaper and not read the news!' He gestured over his shoulder with his thumb.

Joe Schwartz had worked for the paper since leaving school, first as a cub reporter and then, years later, almost by accident, he'd ended up in the library and never left. His brain was the most well-stocked computer Jack had ever encountered; the man never forgot an article or where it could be found. He remembered what was in all the major papers and had kept track of them daily. Jack now realised it was a stroke of luck that Joe was back, as he was sure only someone with his skills could help him.

For a few minutes they sat down and talked of old times and the people they had known. Then Schwartz changed the conversation.

'You ain't down here, Mr Douglas, just to chew the fat with an old-timer like me. You're after something, so tell me.'

Jack grinned. 'I've got a small problem, Joe,' he began. 'I need some information on a couple of the candidates in this election around the end of the war – I am particularly interested in Senator Kelp. I've made a few notes. We'll need to look through his war records and anything written about him around that time. I guess it's a tall order so just tell me if I'm looking down a dead end . . .' His voice trailed away.

'Hell no!' Schwartz shuffled through the notes. 'If you give me some specific dates, I can do this.'

'I can give you this . . .' Jack Douglas handed Schwartz the typed summary. 'The main dates and Kelp's general activities are there.' Jack watched while Schwartz, placing his half-moon spectacles on his nose, skimmed over the page. He took his glasses off and looked up.

'I can't promise anything on the army records, Mr Douglas, but I might get what you want from the articles – something in *Life*, perhaps *Time*. I'll have to check. Can you give me a couple of days?'

'Sure. If it's a real problem, Joe, I'll take whatever you can get.'

'Mr Douglas, have I ever let you down before?'

'No,' Jack Douglas shook his head, 'you never did,' he paused, 'but we've both moved on,' he smiled gently. 'You know, seeing you, well, it's a real shot to the system.' He smiled again.

'Well, Mr Douglas, if it wasn't for these old bodies, I'd almost believe it was them old times again.'

Detective Sergeant Mackie was contemplating his cup of tea while sitting at his battered old desk in a room full of grey-metal filing cabinets. Apart from the distant sound of telephones and the occasional shadow sliding past his frosted door, he was alone. He stirred his tea slowly without taking his eyes off the cup, his thoughts on the file in front of him – The Gallery Attack. For the first time in ages he was feeling the pressure – no real leads, the son of a cabinet minister in a coma, close to death. The Chief Superintendent and the Press were asking questions and he had no real answers. There was a knock at the door.

'Come in,' Mackie looked up as the door opened. 'Sit down, laddie,' he said as a young detective walked in. The new arrival felt he had stepped into a time warp from the early sixties: the paint was so faded it was difficult to tell what colour it once would have been.

'Sorry I got delayed, Sarge.'

The detective shuffled the papers in his hands. Mackie leaned back in his chair and sipped his tea. He held the cup in both hands. 'So have you got all the files this time?'

'Oh, yes.'

'Good.' Mackie paused and put the cup down. 'Let's go over it once again.' He leaned back in his seat. 'We've got a man in a coma as a result of sustaining a heavy blow to his head. From what forensics confirmed, it was the crowbar we found in the gallery. We've got three sets of prints on the crowbar, two identified and one not yet.'

'The prints of the victim and those of John Grande.'

Mackie nodded. 'Aye, now, time of attack?'

'Between midnight and one o'clock.'

'Witnesses?'

'Well, not any that saw it happening, but that bloke across the way, I spoke to him, and he said he noticed someone who fits the description of the victim go in and, at about one o'clock, someone else, who seems to fit the general descriptions of both Grande and his partner's boyfriend, Havers.' The detective shifted his feet uneasily, 'You know, he was going to have an exhibition at the gallery?'

Mackie smiled. 'Aye.'

'Quite a good description really. Anyway, both Grande and Havers look similar in build.'

Mackie held up his hand. 'What floor did this witness see it all from?'

'Second, just in front of the gallery.'

'Seems remarkably sure of himself.'

'Says he thought he heard a car alarm go off, woke him up.'

Mackie made a note on a piece of paper. 'And the receptionist?'

'Well, she said there was going to be an exhibition in a week's time and they had all been busy moving stuff around that afternoon. The storeroom had a fair amount in it when they closed up. Oh, yes, she also said that Patrick and Havers were going to call back later that evening to finish it off.'

'Just the two of them?'

'She didn't think Grande was, but she couldn't be sure. She did say he often came back to the gallery late, though.'

Mackie nodded again. 'You'd better bring Havers in. There's a few questions we need to ask him – and fast!'

'I was going to do that . . .'

'Good,' interrupted Mackie, 'So when's he due in?'

'Well, um, ahem!' The detective glanced down, 'Thing is, Sarge, he's not there.'

'Where?'

'At home – he's disappeared.'

Mackie sighed and shook his head. 'When?' he asked wearily.

'Just after we checked his fingerprints.'

'Well, you'll just have to find him then, won't you.'

'We've a couple of addresses which are being checked now.'

Mackie made a few more notes, then stood up and reached inside his pocket for a pipe, filled and lit it as he walked over to the window. While the detective carried on running through his notes, he blew a cloud of smoke at the window.

'So, what do you think about it?' Mackie asked.

The detective smiled and sat up. 'Well, the way I see it – I mean, the only ones who could have done it were either Grande or Havers – after all, their fingerprints are all over the crowbar.' He stopped as Mackie turned round.

Mackie raised an eyebrow and looked back at the detective, 'Go on.'

'Take Grande. The receptionist said there had been a lot of arguments between Patrick and him. On one occasion, Grande is even said to have threatened to kill Patrick.'

'When was the last argument between them that she knew of?' Mackie cut in.

'She didn't say precisely, it was about the exhibition. She

said Grande didn't think they ought to go ahead. At least that's what she thought – she couldn't say for certain, she'd just come into the gallery and caught the end of it.'

'Aye,' replied Mackie. 'But she also said they argued a lot.' He puffed at his pipe again.

'Well, yes, maybe this makes a difference.' The detective reached into the file and pulled out some papers. 'They have been trading at a loss all year, and last year was the same – they have a lot of debts.' He passed the papers over to Mackie. 'The receptionist said they used to argue about whose end of the business was doing better – gives us a motive for the crime, doesn't it, Sarge?'

'It certainly helps your theory,' Mackie laid his pipe on the desk, 'though it hardly makes a case.' He put the papers down.

'That's the problem, that's why it's difficult. Nothing clear either way. We need to speak to Havers. You've got to find him,' Mackie paused, looking down at the detective, 'meanwhile, we'd better keep an eye on Grande too. What's he up to?'

'Strange, he seems genuinely cut up about his partner,' the detective paused, 'he's an odd bloke though. Wife and child killed by a hit-and-run driver and all the friends we've talked to think he's half off his trolley. He's quite a loner.'

Mackie's years of experience gave him a strange feeling about this gallery case. Things didn't seem to fit together and that troubled him.

'The boyfriend,' Mackie mused, 'why would he run?'

'Guilt perhaps; anyway he's disappeared into thin air.'

'What about fear?' Mackie said slowly and, without waiting for an answer, continued, 'Never rule out blind panic. Anyway, Grande's all we've got for the moment.'

Mackie picked up his pipe and stared out of the window.

'Something tells me Mr Grande knows more than he's letting on. Watch him carefully.'

'So you think he did it, Sarge?'

'What?' Mackie turned and looked at the detective as if surprised he was still there. 'Oh, that's irrelevant, laddie – we'd better make sure we watch him well, though.' He started to light his pipe again. 'And find Havers,' he added.

'It's done, the pictures are all on their way,' Pichowski said as he lit a cigarette and sat down.

'You're certain – no chance . . .?' Weitz replied.

'They'll arrive Thursday next week, 2.30 p.m. at JFK,' Peach interrupted. 'It's all here.' He handed a wallet of documents to Weitz. 'There's no chance of . . .'

'Don't count on it yet – wait until they confirm that they've gone,' Weitz muttered as he glanced through the papers. 'No diaries?' he asked, looking up in time to see the smile fall from Pichowski's face.

'He said he didn't know anything about them – insisted there were no other books or papers.'

Weitz sat in silence for the next few minutes, staring through him as though he wasn't there.

'Either Grande knows nothing,' he said slowly, 'in which case we're being worked over by Cosmo, or he's holding out – perhaps for more money, like the pictures, or,' he paused, screwing his face up, 'they're in cahoots and both trying to work us over.' He took his glasses off and wiped them. 'Any news on who did the job on his gallery?'

'No, Bernie. But whoever did has left Grande as a prime suspect, along with his partner's boyfriend and I hear he's run.'

'Well, Grande clearly thinks we did it – he said as much at the meeting yet scared as he was, he still delayed giving us the picture. You'd think the guy would hand it over if he thought we had done it. I just can't figure him out. He must know something or why string us along like this?' Images of the strange, haunted-looking Englishman flashed in front of him.

'Time you paid him a call. Let's find out what he knows.

You'd better move fast – pay him a visit tonight. Not too much, just a warning – we need the diaries.' Weitz finished polishing his glasses and put them on. 'You know what I think, Pichowski?', his voice hardly a whisper, 'I think we've just stepped into a trap, like a mouse that's being played with, and the trap's about to be sprung – there's something about this guy Grande, don't ask me what. I just wish Ewan had never decided to run for President. The minute he did that he fucked us all – Cosmo's been waiting all these years. He won't let go now.'

'I don't understand, Bernie . . .' Pichowski began, 'Why would the guy go to all this trouble? He's loaded! What's driving him?'

'Revenge, pure and simple. Morrow was his greatest friend – they grew up together. Cosmo believes we murdered Morrow and tried to kill him as well.'

Weitz shrugged in resignation. 'Don't worry, just get to Grande – and don't forget my name's Wessells, you slipped up yesterday.'

'Sure, leave it to me.'

'I've got a bad feeling about Grande,' Weitz muttered.

A worried Ralph Grande sat at his desk in Positano, reading and re-reading a letter that had just arrived. It was from a lawyer in Rome. Not any lawyer, he thought, with a small sense of relief but the lawyer representing D'Ostia. In the clearest, grammatically perfect English, it asked him to pass on the enclosed letter to his nephew, John Grande. The letter to his nephew was not sealed.

For some time, since D'Ostia's sudden departure, Ralph had been trying to find out where he had gone. The house-keeper was either the most perfect keeper of secrets, or she genuinely did not know. He was inclined to think the latter but he did manage to prise out of her that she received her instructions from a lawyer in Rome – a Signore Soletti. Ralph tried to make contact but to no avail. All his letters remained unanswered and he had more or less given up in despair. Then John's partner was attacked.

As he watched events unfold in London, he felt a growing sense of guilt. He had brought John to Positano; it was he who had acted as a willing dupe, dragging John into the dangerous course of events which had followed. He had done so for selfish reasons. He had simply wanted to see him again and the peculiar proposition seemed like the only way to get him to return to Positano. It was his fault that John was now in so much trouble. The worst of it was that all of this was crashing in on John after two years of depression following the terrible death of his wife and child. Ralph shook his head at the enormity of what his own selfish desire had done to the one person he valued above all others.

He stared down at the unopened letter. It was strange, he thought, to send an unsealed letter, unless he was meant to read it. He shrugged and, pushing back the flap, pulled the letter out of the envelope, his heart beating faster. He hadn't expected much but the letter even managed to fall below his expectations. All it contained was a blank sheet of paper on which was written, in a heavy, neat hand:

Dear Mr Grande,
   I understand from your uncle, Ralph Grande, that you want to speak to me. If that is still your desire then I can be reached on my direct line.

At the bottom of the letter was a Rome telephone number, the same bar the last digit as the office number on the headed paper accompanying the note.

'Well,' he muttered, 'At least we've made contact. God knows, that's something. And I suppose he wouldn't have written if he had nothing to say.' He flattened the letter out on the desk and reached for the telephone.

John Grande walked back to the gallery from the Underground. His collar was turned up against the cold wind that cut across the square. It numbed his cheeks but helped to clear his head after the morning he'd endured.

His interview with the police had not gone well. Mackie had sat in silence to one side of the table, his eyes boring into one side of John's face – it was the young detective who asked questions. Claustrophobic and intense, the interview made it clear to John that they didn't believe any of his alibis. He had been at home, in bed, no witnesses. Someone, it appeared, had said they'd seen him go into the gallery late that night. It was a lie, yet it gave the police cause to doubt him. What bothered him most was the way Detective Sergeant Mackie just sat at the table watching him without comment. He shuddered as he thought about it. His only hope lay in his plan to get away. It'd better be now or it would be too late. He knew that Wessells and Peach were still after the books – the diaries, whatever they were. They didn't believe he knew nothing about them. The net was closing in but he needed more time.

Inside the gallery all was clean and tidy. The damaged stock had been put away and the place looked more or less back to normal.

John had made up his mind, his resolve now strengthened by his interview with the police. He didn't know what was going on but he knew he was being used, even set up, a pawn in someone's dangerous game. Everything around him was on the brink – his business, his partner's life and now his freedom, perhaps even his own life. Yet, despite his fear, a thrill of excitement coursed through him when he thought of his plan, a plan made much easier by his uncle's telephone call that lunch time.

As he opened the desk drawer and took out his passports, he felt as though a weight had been lifted from him. He had purpose again, a sense of direction.

His thoughts were interrupted by a tap on the door and Maguire's face peering in.

'So where did it all happen, Johnny?' Maguire glanced around as he walked in.

'In the storeroom,' John said over his shoulder as he locked the door.

'How's he doing?'

'Stable, no improvement.'

Maguire walked to the storeroom, pushed the door open and peered in. 'Poor bastard,' he muttered, as he turned to look at John. 'So the police think it's a burglary?'

'Maybe – maybe not. They didn't take anything, perhaps they weren't after anything at all.'

'What about the last picture?'

'I don't know – they've got it now anyway – maybe it was them – strange, because it wouldn't make much sense,' he paused. 'They knew they were going to get it.'

'But maybe just to hurry you up?'

'Could be,' John said quietly.

'Strange doings, Johnny boy,' Maguire murmured.

'Well,' John faced Maguire, 'that's why I asked you to come, Jack.'

'Nothing to do with me now,' Maguire said, turning to face John. 'Don't you remember, the less I know the better.'

'Relax, relax. I don't want you involved in that way, at least not the way you think – I just want you to do me a favour.'

'Ah! So that's it, favours now, is it? If I remember the last time I did you a favour . . .' Maguire gestured over his shoulder, 'your partner ends up in hospital.' He smiled. 'Favours to you at the moment seem to pay back permanently, Johnny boy.' He pulled out a tin of tobacco and rolled a cigarette.

'That's the point, I'm certain it's all to do with me, not Richard – he just got in the way.' John shrugged. 'It's obvious.'

'That so, Sherlock? You'll be calling me Watson next.' He lit his cigarette. 'But what's all this got to do with me?'

'Well,' John stared at Maguire, searching for some clue to his thoughts in his craggy features. 'I'm going to have to trust you some more.'

'Are you now – well, you would be the first but what makes you think I want to be trusted?'

'It's quite simple,' John began. 'I'm leaving tonight. I've got to sort this all out and the only way to do that is to get the hell out of here.'

'Sounds sensible to me,' Maguire drew on the cigarette. 'I agree, the best thing is to piss off before the police get to you.'

'I'm not running, Jack, I'm going to find out what the hell's going on and I need you to help me.'

'How the hell can I . . .' Maguire began, standing up.

'Hear me out,' John answered quickly, holding up his hand. 'I want you to look after the gallery while I'm away.'

'Jesus!' Maguire shook his head violently. 'You must be stark staring mad. Me, run this?' he spluttered, stubbing out his cigarette, 'A Maguire in respectable work – nine to five – with the police all over me like lice on a kid's head. Oh no, you're asking too much, Johnny, too much.'

'Look, before you say no . . .'

'I think you misheard me – I just did.'

'Let me first explain. There will be two other people here – Ursula and an assistant, a young guy, who has worked off and on here over the past year. I've arranged for him to come in for a while to help. They'll do the day-to-day stuff, all you have to do is be here and make sure it runs smoothly.'

'Bollocks! You don't need me to do that. There's another reason, come on, out with it,' Maguire considered. 'You know, you're a clever bastard – you don't need me to run this. You want me for something else.'

'OK. Look, Jack, I need someone to keep an eye on the police and, for that matter, anyone else who takes an interest. I'll need to know who is after me and why, you know . . .'

'I do, I certainly do! Are you mad?'

Maguire shook his head slowly, 'Why should I, why, when the first thing that'll happen is the police will be down my neck the moment I move in and you move out? They won't buy it.'

'Doesn't matter, they'll have to. I've made the papers over, giving you power of attorney.' He held out a sheaf of papers. 'Besides, you'll take a percentage of everything, Jack – that'll at least make it worth your while.'

Maguire waved his hand angrily at John and cut him short.

'I'm surprised at you, not much point in having a fat wallet when you're dead. If anyone else had asked me to do this I'd have been out that door ten minutes ago – Jesus! Don't know why I don't go now.' Maguire looked at John, his eyes narrowing. 'You still haven't made it clear why I should put my neck on the line for you.'

'For the reason I've given. I'm in deep trouble. I'm sure the police now think it was me. There's too much circumstantial evidence. The gallery is doing badly, Richard wanted to sell, I didn't. Then there's the arguments and they even think I threatened to kill him.' He looked carefully at Maguire, who was nodding slowly, thoughtfully.

'You're the only one I know who could pull it off.' He laid the papers on the desk. 'To be honest, there's no reason at all – except I suppose,' again he paused, 'for the *craic*.'

'But you know you haven't a hope. You don't even know where to start.'

'With D'Ostia's Italian lawyer. My uncle has been trying to make contact with D'Ostia and has found out he has a lawyer in Rome.'

Maguire shrugged. 'Don't know who he is but I do know about lawyers – they charge their mothers when they ring home.'

'Better than nothing.'

'I'll take nothing – they're all bastards who've got cash tills for brains.'

'Well, if you won't help, I'll have to do it alone. It just means I'll be blind to what the police here are doing and those two Americans.'

'They won't stick around once you've gone – they want you,' Maguire answered softly as he rolled another cigarette, 'and the police will take some time before they decide what to do.'

'Look, it was a long shot, too much to ask – I just hoped.'

'You know, Johnny,' Maguire lit the cigarette and inhaled, 'I haven't seen you so fired up since . . .'

'Since she was killed?' John cut in, his face flushed.

'Sure,' Maguire nodded. John turned away. The memory of that day was still painful. The deep emptiness inside him welled up at the mention of Julia. But he was also guilty – guilty because with all that was going on, he hadn't thought about her, or his son.

Maguire watched John and then, picking up the papers, he spread them out.

'Where do I sign?' he asked emphatically.

'What?' John responded in astonishment.

'Well,' Maguire continued, glancing at his watch, 'we've got a lot of work to do. Where . . .?'

John put his finger on the document.

'There.'

'So when're you off?' Maguire asked, dropping the pen onto the desk.

'Now, tonight, in two hours' time.'

'What if I'd said no?'

'You did, remember?' John smiled.

'You bastard,' Maguire laughed. 'Ah, well, as the late great Brendan Behan said, "You pull the chain and in a jiffy your shit is floatin' down the Liffey."'

In New York, Laura Buckley finished reading the morning's papers. She picked them up, then dropped them onto the floor, making sure she kept the *Washington Post*. She folded it so that only half of one page was visible and then pressed her intercom. 'Sally, clear these papers away and get Joe in.'

Two sides of Laura's office were glass, with a couple of pillars breaking up the view. Normally the Manhattan skyline was visible with the Chrysler Building and the Empire State Building dominant and, in the distance, the Hudson River. Today, however, she could just make out the Chrysler Building, the Empire State was only a shadow and the rest was wrapped in a shroud. The air was thick with swirling snow. From her nineteenth-floor office, New York in winter was a cold, grey place.

Laura was beginning to feel stale. December in New York and everyone was already winding down for Christmas. Endless invitations. She knew she was the perfect 'spare girl', the perfect match to be made. She could almost see them competing with each other to find the right type who would bond with her. At first she had found it amusing, later she tolerated it, but now she had become so bored that she had taken to refusing invitations out of hand. Most men in the city, she found, were so caught up in themselves they didn't need anyone else. They just wanted looking-glass partners – those whose attractiveness complemented theirs and made them look good twice. Big as the city was, she found the society she moved in small and incestuous. She also realised that the more she refused the invitations, the sharper the comments behind her back – reclusive, obsessive, selfish, on and on. What she had come to believe was that none of it had any point any more. Fashion shows, dinners, parties, clubs – she was bored by it all. The shallow bonhomie, the money, the false friendships and the character assassination.

All of this was exacerbated by her failure to contact her father since the summer. Time and again she had tried but each time she had drawn a blank. At first, after the holiday, she'd been able to immerse herself in her work – there was always another news story to follow. But even at the height of this activity, she found herself increasingly wondering whether her father was dead, and if not, then what condition he was in. She sat down in her chair and leaned her head back.

'Laura . . .' she looked up. An overweight man in shirt-sleeves and braces was standing at the door.

'Hi, Joe!' she said, 'take a seat.' She pulled the copy of the *Post* off her desk and tossed it over to him as he sat down. 'Did you read the Douglas piece today?'

'Not yet, why?'

'Because he's writing about corruption in politics and giving it an historic angle. But, because most of all, I hear that Kelp won't have him near his campaign headquarters any more, says he is deliberately going for him.'

'I heard that a few days ago. So?'

'So, it's a coded message,' she replied, leaning forward, her chin jutting out. 'Let's get Douglas on the programme, give him a run on Kelp.'

Joe laughed. 'Wow, you're all fired up today. I'll speak with Jack.'

'No. Just do it.'

'But, you know how he hates it when we don't consult . . .' he said hesitating. 'OK, OK. You're the boss.'

Laura watched him walk out of the door. She had no intention of revealing her plans to her presenter, Jack Marriott, until it was all fixed up. He was becoming more and more puffed up, kept on trying to get involved in everything, blocking good ideas and interfering. But, she thought, this was one item he would have on his plate before he knew it. She smiled in satisfaction.

'Only one person can be in charge, Jack, and it's not going to be a handsome talking head, full of air,' she muttered.

At that moment her secretary put her head round the door. 'You're wanted upstairs, Laura.'

'Who? I'm busy, tell them . . .'

93

'Mr Philips,' her secretary cut in.

Laura smiled. 'OK, I guess he's one I have to break my schedule for,' she said as she reached for her jacket. 'Tell him I'm on my way.'

'I already did,' her secretary replied confidently.

'I should know,' Laura muttered sarcastically, 'you would always have my best interests at heart, even if I didn't see it.'

Sam Philips was chief executive of ABS Broadcasting. Her first thought was to wonder why he wanted to see her, but there was no point in speculating – his little game was to spring surprises. It made him feel in control.

'Sit down, Laura, sit down,' Philips said as she entered his large office.

Laura looked across the room at the avuncular figure of Philips, advancing towards her. They shook hands and she made her way to a chair, nodding at the other person in the room – Walter Harvey, her mentor. He smiled at her as she sat down but said nothing.

'Laura, I am sorry to bother you,' Philips began, 'I know you're busy.'

'Don't mention it,' she replied – as if he cared, she thought.

'I've got some things I want to discuss with you,' he continued.

Laura smiled to herself. The same old story. She knew he didn't mean discuss, he meant to tell her. Still, she thought, small gestures pleased him.

'What I am about to tell you is a little sensitive, so I'd like you to treat it as confidential.' He glanced at Harvey and then back at Laura.

'Yes, of course,' she replied, certain it probably wasn't that important. He believed it was clever leadership to create a little conspiracy, to make an employee feel on the team – and she also knew the tactic worked. He'd taken over a small, failing network and turned it into the most successful against all the odds.

'Well, Laura, Walter here is moving . . .' Philips paused and glanced back to Harvey, 'he is moving to become my deputy with a place on the board.'

'That's great,' Laura said, sitting forward in her seat and smiling broadly; she was genuinely pleased.

'Just a minute, Laura,' Philips motioned her to stay seated. 'That, of course, leaves a vacancy at the news and current affairs section which, after consultation with Walter, I've decided to offer to you.' Now it was his turn to sit back and smile.

At first Laura didn't register what he had said and just looked blankly at him, 'I'm sorry I don't understand.'

'I'm offering the job at news and current affairs, the one that Walter is leaving, to you.'

'The same – to me,' she repeated, genuinely surprised – she knew there were many more senior executives in line for the job. 'But, I wasn't expecting . . .'

'I thought you hadn't picked up on any of my hints the last time I saw you,' Harvey got up out of his seat as he spoke and walked towards her. She looked bewildered.

'What hints?' she replied. 'All I was aware of was that you were trying to change the way your job worked – now this.' She turned and looked back at Philips, who was smiling again.

'Well, what do you say?' Philips asked.

Harvey was standing in front of her and grinning.

'I'm happy where I am,' she replied, 'I mean, what about the programme? We've got . . .'

'Don't worry, we thought you might want to continue to run it until you find a successor. You can manage both for a little while.' Sam Philips smiled. 'No one knows better than you what the job requires – it'll be your first executive decision.'

Laura looked from one to the other. Maybe they were right, maybe it was what she desired? Here was a golden opportunity – the promotion that anyone in the media world would give their right arm for and yet she hesitated.

'Yes, of course I accept. Thank you,' she said as she shook hands with them both – but with an empty feeling. This was everything she'd been working for – a step away from the board, in control. Yet, yet . . . She smiled as they congratulated her. It's what I want, she told herself, it's what I need.

6

The Trail

Saturday evening at Camp David. In the fireplace, a log fire was blazing. In front of it, in a circle of armchairs, sat four people, each in slightly preppy casual clothes. In the middle was President Carson, to his right, Dan Petrone, the chairman of the committee to re-elect the President – in effect his campaign manager – and, on his left, his chief of staff, Frank Parry. Beside Petrone sat a rather nervous, bald-headed small man clutching a sheaf of papers. Each page was covered in bar charts and figures in graphs. Seth Gold, the resident pollster, fidgeted, waiting his turn.

'So, Seth, are you sure it's not a blip and that he's really closing?'

'He's definitely closing, sir,' the small man said quietly. 'There's been a shift and it's going for Kelp – you're still ahead by five points though.'

'That's a fall of five since Kelp declared, isn't it?' Carson interrupted, his voice heavy.

'Yes, but he's unlikely to sustain it. This is – ah – the result of his initial publicity, it might flatten out. Well, it often does.'

Carson nodded slowly and gazed at the fire.

'OK,' Parry said quietly, leaning across to the man. 'You can go now, Seth, thank you.'

Gold nodded and, picking up his papers, left the room.

The remaining two exchanged glances before Petrone spoke, 'Kelp was always bound to start up fast . . .'

'Not that fast,' growled Carson. 'A couple of points, you said.' He snorted and walked over to the fireplace to throw another log on the fire and pour himself a drink.

'So far,' Petrone began, 'it's only Kelp. We've worked the others and, providing we all stay on top of it, it'll be OK.'

'Well, that depends . . .' began Parry.

'On what?' Carson demanded as he slumped back in his chair.

'On whether they can reopen the enquiry.'

'I thought we had that blocked in the House,' Petrone responded quickly.

'We did . . .' Parry began.

'So?'

'Someone is feeding the Republicans with details of your involvement with Haskins.'

'That's not new. We all know that her sister's doing the talking. They can't prove anything, it's just her word . . .'

'No, someone else tells me that they suspect Haskins had a kid, *your* kid – it wasn't the sister.'

Carson didn't reply, he just stared at the fire. He felt his stomach tightening. Was it going to end here? Twenty-five years in politics with one aim – he'd achieved it all – but here, within sight of a second term, it was starting to crumble. He knew the Republicans wanted to get him on the land deal. Now it was all down to Julia Haskins' testimony. They wanted to prove she had lied under oath all those years ago. His relationship with Julia had been denied during that testimony, now they were trying to show that he had committed perjury over her as well.

The fire crackled and spat as Petrone turned to Parry.

'What do they want?' he asked.

'To reopen the enquiry. That's got to be their aim. After all, it would be perfect, particularly now we face a challenge from Kelp and none of their candidates outscores you. They need to split us, it's their best chance. Even if they fail, some dirt will stick.'

'They'll never get that. They won't even get into the House on that – they'll look stupid trying,' Petrone said, shaking his head.

'Sure . . .' Carson muttered absent-mindedly. 'Sure.'

'Julia Haskins stated in her original testimony that you didn't have a relationship with her,' Parry continued, 'and her testimony cleared you in the original investigation into the investment.'

'Well, that's pretty watertight,' Petrone smiled, anxious to move on, 'I think it's under control. Do you want to go over the remaining schedule?'

'Can we have a break, Dan? I just want to have a few words with Frank.'

Petrone nodded and left the room.

'Well?' Carson asked as the door closed. 'You said you have something for me?'

'I do and I don't,' Parry began. 'You covered your tracks well.'

'Had to – I was finished if anyone found out.'

'Well, no records exist – we tried everywhere.'

'What about the Mother Superior?'

'Lives in Rome – she's in the Vatican. Anyway, we contacted her by phone. Says she can't remember, said thousands came through the home for adoption,' Parry paused, 'Apparently the records were destroyed in a fire.'

Carson raised an eyebrow and nodded slowly. 'So that's it?' he asked, sighing.

'No, there's the money.'

'What money?'

'The money you put in trust.'

'That's a different matter.'

'But it's still traceable. I'll need your financial records and we'll have to get Haskins' too. That's going to be where they'll go if they reopen the enquiry.'

'I thought we were blocking that in the House.'

'We won't hold it if they force it to a vote. They'll probably get it. That means a special Prosecutor.'

'What, on the word of her sister and business partner?'

'This is politics, Ted. It has nothing to do with the nature of the charge. All they need to do is leave a sense of guilt in the mind of the public – no smoke without fire.' Carson nodded. 'Besides, we know where the trail leads and we've got to block them.'

Parry stood up and walked over to the fireplace.

'Kelp will use this as well,' Carson grunted, 'Mr Squeaky Clean – it pisses me off!'

'We'll just have to find something on him,' Parry replied. 'Look, I suggest we get Dan in. He needs to be in on this.'

'But we keep the rest away from him?'

'Sure.'

Petrone was brought back in. 'Sorry, Dan. I just wanted to talk to Frank about this attempt to reopen the enquiry into the land deal. We both agree that we need to create a distraction, something on Kelp, to stop him using it.'

Parry watched his boss throughout the exchange. How like him, he thought, to place them all in trouble through his own actions and then to act as though he was the wounded party. His single-minded and utterly selfish behaviour was, he knew, both his strength and his weakness. When applied to key political decisions it was what made him so formidable, devastating on the rebound when others wrote him off. Yet when it came to his private life it was more often than not a death wish. Now, not for the first time, Parry knew he had to pull him out of trouble. It was a roller-coaster ride with what he felt was an amoral child. They had always, in the past, been able to distance him from the worst of his decisions, to keep him clean. Someone else took the drop. Parry knew that this time it was different, there was no going back. He shrugged.

'We're already trying,' Petrone replied, 'but it's pretty tough.'

'What about his past, isn't there anything?' Parry asked.

'Squeaky clean – and I mean squeaky,' Petrone replied. He saw how his reply caused Carson to slump in his chair. 'But we're trying to run the line that this is a Republican extremist attack and the witch-hunt of a successful President for short-term political reasons. Makes you the underdog against the brutal Congress.'

'That's a start, I guess,' Carson intoned.

'What about his past? We should do some work there,' Parry muttered.

'Problem is, the guy's a war hero – Purple Heart. It's not easy, but we'll try,' Petrone replied.

'Well, keep me informed,' Parry said, kicking at one of the burning logs. 'We'll need something to take the shine off Kelp.'

'In the meantime, Mr President, you should get out there and start campaigning – show everyone some of the magic we know gets them going. You're at your best out there – they love it,' Petrone perched on the edge of his seat.

'And it'll put pressure on Congress,' Parry continued, developing the theme, 'you'll be able to play the Washington outsider unfairly attacked by Congress.'

'Sure, but while Kelp plays squeaky clean, we've got a problem,' Carson said. 'We've just been told that he's closing, halved my lead, so this won't be enough.' Carson looked from one to the other, 'So there's nothing on him?'

'As I said,' Petrone grimaced, 'we looked at that. He seems to be clean as a whistle.'

'There's got to be something,' Carson finished his drink and stood up. 'Put some more people on it – Frank, get Pete Neal at the NSA to take a look.'

'Are you sure?' Parry asked.

'Yeah, and Dan,' Carson laid a hand on Petrone's shoulder, 'we'll start campaigning – you're right, it's the best way to kick Kelp's butt!' He grinned at Petrone and then looked beyond him into a large mirror hanging on the wall. He stroked his face before turning to Parry, 'And you, Frank, you've got some work to do – don't leave me out there hangin' by my balls! I'm relying on you.' Parry smiled faintly. It was his balls that had put him there in the first place, he thought.

'We'll do our best,' he replied.

John Grande checked his watch. It was five o'clock. Rome in December, wet but not cold. The cab driver had pulled up a block away from the Via Veneto and across the street from the office of Soletti, D'Ostia's Italian lawyer.

John sprang from the back of the cab and rubbed his eyes. He felt he'd already made some progress and he was only a few days out from London. A few days and a lifetime away, with Maguire taking on the gallery, while he tried to piece it all together. The lawyer was, as his uncle reminded him, crucial. He was at Soletti's office so quickly only because of the hard work his uncle had put in, piecing some of the jigsaw together. It was his uncle who had found out who D'Ostia's lawyer was and had made contact.

Yet despite all that work, the lawyer wouldn't take his calls for the first two days. Then, to his surprise, on the third day there was a call to fix the time and date for an appointment. While it raised John's hopes that the whole matter would be explained, he carried a nagging doubt at the back of his head. Now, as he sat in the car, his optimism was fading. Could D'Ostia be drawing him further along? Yet he knew he had no choice. To return to England meant the police or the Americans – he had to go on, but to what?

At six o'clock he walked into a waiting area to be greeted by a short, dark-haired man in his late forties, wearing a beautifully-cut pinstripe suit. He introduced himself before ushering John into his office. As John waited for Soletti to sit down, he looked around the room. The walls were covered with paintings and prints of English country houses and there was even a watercolour of the Houses of Parliament.

'Mr Grande,' Soletti began, as he sat down at his desk, 'how good of you to come.' John noticed his English was almost too perfect, like a 1930s BBC announcer. Soletti took out a silver case and offered a cigarette to John before taking one himself. 'When first your uncle wrote,' he exhaled a cloud of smoke as he continued, 'I was alas unable to assist him. I would so much like to have helped, but . . .' he shrugged. 'However, since then my client's situation has changed and I am instructed to pass some information on to you.'

'At last!' John exclaimed.

'I'm sorry?' Soletti responded, drawing heavily on his cigarette.

'Nothing,' replied John, 'it was just that I'd been hoping for so long to get word from him and . . .'

'Of course, Mr Grande,' Soletti paused and reached into his desk drawer. 'Here, I have a letter for you, which I hope answers your questions.' He passed John a letter with a wax seal. 'If you like, you can read it here.'

John looked at it, turning it around in his fingers. He had a strong feeling of foreboding. Always letters, he thought, and letters with wax seals – another game? More theatrics?

John opened the letter. On a single piece of paper the following was typed:

You should go to Goldstein and Davidoff, 570 West 42nd Street, New York. There see Mr Goldstein. I have given him instructions to clear everything up and finish what you have started. He knows about the diaries.

The letter was unsigned. John looked up. A deep sense of disappointment filled him. 'What's all this melodrama about?' he asked. 'Another lawyer? Why?'

'Just what it says,' Soletti replied. 'I'm sorry but I haven't read it. I'm simply passing it on. There is nothing else to say about it. I hope, however, that the contents are clear enough.'

'Yes, they're clear. But what I don't understand is there's no mention of any of the other paintings he said he wanted to sell originally. What happened to all of these?'

'I'm sorry, Mr Grande, truly very sorry. I'm his lawyer but not privy to all his plans. All I know,' Soletti said, lighting another cigarette, 'is that I was to give you the letter,' he exhaled slowly and paused, 'I also have some unfortunate news to give you.'

'What's that?'

'I'm afraid Signore D'Ostia is dead. He died in Switzerland in a clinic near Bern some days ago,' Soletti replied, reaching into his drawer. 'I have the death certificate here to show you.'

'D'Ostia dead? I can't believe it!'

John leaned forward on his seat, angry that the man who had done so much to endanger his life had escaped from him and was now unaccountable. 'What about this,' he said waving the note, 'surely he just gave you this?'

'Ah yes, the note. He gave me that two months ago – he said it wouldn't be long before he died. I was to give it to you then.'

'But,' John spluttered, 'that was before I knew anything about the diaries!'

'I'm sorry,' Soletti smiled weakly, 'I know nothing about any diaries. I am simply relaying a message.' He opened a buff-coloured file and pulled out a piece of paper. 'The death certificate, if you would like to see it?' he said, holding it out towards John.

John took it – only a week before D'Ostia had died of cancer. He handed it back. John read his note again. So, he thought, the chase was beginning. No pictures, although part of him knew and always expected as much, but what about the diaries? John had no idea where it would end or how. Yet the note spoke for the first time of the diaries and he knew he had no option but to follow the instruction – either that or return to the UK.

'Mr Grande,' Soletti's voice pushed its way into his thoughts, 'I am very sorry but there is little I can do to help. I am simply relaying instructions. Also, if you would like, I'm to give you these.' He opened his drawer and took another envelope out. He passed it across to John, 'Air tickets – first class, open, Rome to New York.'

'So he expected me to go then?'

'All I can say is I was instructed that once you had seen the note I was to give you these. If you didn't wish to go, then I was to take them back.'

John stared first at the tickets, then at Soletti – no choice – no choice kept pounding through his head. He reached out and picked them up reluctantly.

'Good,' Soletti smiled, 'that I believe concludes our business unless there are any more questions?'

'Not much point, is there? You can only give the same answer.'

'That is so,' Soletti bowed his head. 'I'm sorry. But you should not feel you are too late – the certificate says a week ago. You know,' Soletti continued, 'he would not have seen you before he died. He left strict instructions about that.'

Soletti stood up. 'Have you anywhere to stay tonight?' he asked.

'No, I'll call . . .'

'I won't hear of it. My secretary will arrange it immediately.'

'Thank you,' John replied, then he stopped at the door and

105

turned to Soletti, 'I wonder, could she also book me a flight to New York for tomorrow?'

'Of course.'

Soletti led John down the hall to the reception desk and issued instructions. Then they said their farewells and Soletti turned back to his office.

John re-read the note as he sat down beside the secretary's desk. He dropped the letter onto it, shaking his head slowly.

'New York, tomorrow, first flight,' he said, in reply to her question. He pushed his chair back, went over to the window and gazed out, his thoughts adrift in a chain of inexplicable events. Behind him the secretary, the receiver clamped to her left ear, looked at him casually, then slowly, carefully, she reached across the desk and turned his letter around. After she had finished responding to the booking agent's questions, she surreptitiously read the letter and jotted down some details. Turning it back, she put the receiver down.

Soletti sat in silence after John had left his office. He'd never enjoyed working for D'Ostia but for a man with expensive tastes like himself, money talked, and in D'Ostia's case, very loudly.

The Englishman, lost, angry and even a little scared, bothered him. It wasn't as though he was, or ever had been, a believer in conscience – a fatal thing in a good lawyer, his father had once wryly remarked. No, it was having to move beyond the written page to glimpse the results of his client's scheme. It had been like looking through a window and seeing a murder take place and then turning up your collar and crossing over the street to go home. There was a moment when he'd been tempted, almost, to greater explanation but he had resisted.

Lawyers, he mused, would always be able to excuse themselves because they are simply the hewers of wood and the drawers of water – obeying instructions. He need now only read the will to D'Ostia's daughter and his job would be complete. He locked his office door. Yes, simple work for very good money. An expensive way to pass messages on, but why should he care? There was nothing illegal in it.

The following morning, as his aircraft took off, John Grande gazed out over Leonardo Da Vinci Airport as it slipped below him, with Rome on the horizon. He studied his two passports, one British, one American, carefully. He was lucky, he knew. Having an American mother allowed him dual nationality, which was useful because it meant fewer checks and less delay. He slipped them into his pocket and then, leaning back in his seat, he closed his eyes.

Laura Buckley marched into Soletti's office in Rome. His matter-of-fact phone call with the news of her father's death had driven all thoughts of her new job completely from her mind.

'Again, please accept my greatest sympathy for your loss. I am sorry it should be me who is the bearer of such bad news.' He reached into his drawer and pulled some papers out.

'When did it happen?' Laura asked. 'And where?'

'Exactly eight days ago. I informed you as soon as I knew. The place of death is on the certificate, a copy of which I have here.' He tapped the bundle of papers in front of him.

'It was a clinic near Bern, the Boltigan Clinic, I believe.' He pushed the paper towards her. 'Specialists in the treatment of advanced cancer.'

As she reached for the papers Laura felt tired. She had flown from New York as soon as she heard from the lawyer. It was the morning after her appointment as the head of news and current affairs.

'Do I get to see him? Where is his body?' she asked.

'I'm sorry, Miss Buckley, but in the will, which I am about to read, he insisted his body be cremated and his ashes scattered on the cliffs by his villa in Positano before you were informed.'

'But couldn't you have waited? I could have at least attended . . .' Laura's face flushed as she spoke, clearly hurt that her father had excluded her this one last time.

'I'm sorry but you see they were explicit instructions. He wanted no one there but his housekeeper and it had to be done within two days of his death. They were his wishes.'

Laura felt angry and sad and, despite herself, her eyes welled up with tears.

'Are you all right?' Soletti asked. Laura nodded but kept her head down.

'If you would like some time alone . . .'

'No,' she looked up, regaining control. 'Please get on with it.'

Soletti read the will, which was fairly simple. All her father's estate had been made over to her, including the house in Positano and a very sizeable sum of money, amounting to close to $50 million, most of it in investments and some valuable paintings.

'There are some papers to sign and then the formalities will be over,' Soletti concluded. 'I'm sorry there are so many but this is Italy and here we exist to serve the state – we express ourselves in triplicate.'

Half an hour later it was all over and Laura was walking to the front of the office. Five more days to go to Christmas and here she was in Rome, now a very wealthy woman but without her father. When her mother died she had kept her promise to herself and had tracked him down. Now he was dead. Maybe, she thought, work was meant to be her only purpose. It was, she knew, the one area where she could make sense of her life. Families must surely be meant for other people, not her.

She shook hands with the lawyer and turned to go. As she did so, she noticed two men standing beside the secretary's desk. Both men were short – one was overweight with small dark eyes, the other slim, balding and wore small, round-framed glasses.

'Back to New York,' she said to herself, pulling her collar up.

'Signore,' the receptionist said to the lawyer, who had accompanied Laura into the reception area, 'these men wish to see you.'

'Mr Soletti?' the short man with spectacles held out his hand.

'Yes,' Soletti answered warily.

'Good,' the little man advanced a few steps. 'I'm Mr Wessells,' he said, 'pleased to meet you.' They shook hands.

The New York accent rasped in Laura's ears as she nodded to Soletti, thanked him again and left the office.

'What can I do for you?' she heard Soletti say as the door shut behind her. Strange, a New York accent here. She shrugged and shut the elevator doors behind her.

'It's like this,' Weitz began. 'I'm looking for a great friend called Cosmo, who served with me during the war but you might know him as D'Ostia. I'm told . . . that is, I gather . . . he used to live in Positano, only I can't find him. I wanted to check out where he's gone to tell him we're all having a reunion.'

Soletti hesitated. He glanced at the door before responding, 'Why did you contact me, may I ask?'

'A lawyer in London gave me your name and said we should contact you,' Weitz smiled.

'Well,' Soletti began, 'the answer is very simple even though perhaps sad for you. I'm sorry to tell you that he passed away last week.'

The smile gone, Weitz responded sharply, 'I don't believe you!' His eyes were ablaze as he took a half pace forward – then remembering where he was, he backed down, 'That is – it's been such a long time.'

Soletti looked coldly and calmly at the man in front of him before shaking his head, 'Even so, even so – I am not in the habit of lying. I have a copy of the death certificate in my office.'

'Look,' Weitz resumed the smile, 'I'm sorry, forgive me, but it's just that it's a shock – I wonder, could I, do you think – could I see it? You see, we were planning this reunion, only now I'll have to tell all his old buddies and I just know the first thing they'll ask is whether I saw the certificate.' Weitz bowed his head and shook it again as though in shock.

Soletti hesitated again and then relented. 'Follow me and I will show you.' Weitz looked at his partner and shook his head before following the lawyer down the corridor to his office.

Pichowski sat down by the receptionist's desk and waited.

'Other people are interested in Signore D'Ostia; I heard that name before,' the receptionist said.

'What?' Pichowski darted a quick look at her – a young woman, a bit of a Sophia Loren look-alike, he thought. 'What?' he repeated. 'Who?'

'I don't remember,' she replied, coyly.

Pichowski nodded slowly before reaching into his pocket. 'OK, Signora, d'ya know what this is?' he asked as he peeled off a $100 bill.

'*Si*, I think so,' she replied.

'Now, do you think you could remember?' He placed the bill on the table.

'I think his name was Grande.'

Pichowski leaned forward. 'You sure?'

'*Si.*'

'Where's he gone?' he demanded again.

'I don't . . .' she allowed her voice to trail away. In response Pichowski peeled off another $100 bill.

'Here,' she said and slipped a piece of paper across the desk, on which she had copied the lawyer's address in New York.

At that moment Soletti's door opened.

'Quick,' Pichowski snarled, 'when did he leave?' He placed his last remaining $100 bill across the desk.

'The midday flight to New York today. That's all I have, I'm sorry.' She scooped up the money, putting it into a drawer as Soletti reappeared.

Once outside, Pichowski told Weitz what had happened and showed him the piece of paper.

'What the hell is he doing in New York seeing these people?' exclaimed Weitz.

'Who are they?' Pichowski asked.

'Only one of the most prominent law firms in New York.' He paused. 'This is Cosmo's doing. I know it, the guy's planned this.'

'But he's dead,' Pichowski exclaimed.

'Maybe, but somehow I know he planned this and Grande is part of it. We have to get to Grande before he can see these people. We've got our first break – now we must use it.'

7

America

John Grande sleep-walked his way through immigration and, after half an hour's wait at the carousel for his bag, also through customs.

Soon he was sitting on a low, patched bench seat in the back of a yellow cab bound for Manhattan – beneath him a strange concert of broken springs as the cab bumped along. In front, on the other side of the thick Perspex sheet, the driver hooted and cursed impatiently. John found himself wondering, tiredly, if the driver had understood the address he had given. What had happened to those original New York taxi-cab drivers, the ones always featured in Hollywood movies, who always knew their way around?

It was, he began to believe, as though D'Ostia had prepared it all in advance. Even though he was dead, the string still tugged. Goldstein and Davidoff. Another damn lawyer, always another lawyer. The only good thing to have happened during the past few days was that he had managed to give Wessells and his sidekick, Peach, the slip. His sudden departure must have confused them; at any rate he had seen no sign of them since leaving London.

He shook his head. 'God! What am I doing here?' His partner lay in a critical condition in hospital and here he was in New York on a bizarre paper chase. Despite the interview with Soletti, he knew no more about the diaries that the little man, Wessells, had insisted on. His only hope now was that the lawyers could sort matters out. But what if they didn't? He couldn't go on acting as a human letterbox. Stuck in the middle of this as he was, his only hope was to try to piece this together himself. Peach and his cronies were clearly dangerous and John was certain that his refusal to deal over the diaries, coming as it did after the delay with the picture and now his sudden departure, would have increased their suspicions. He knew they would see him as a threat. The moment they believed he didn't have the diaries, they would deal with him as they had dealt with his partner. He shuddered.

Once in his hotel, he threw off his jacket, kicked off his shoes and lay back on the bed. Picking up the telephone, he dialled a number.

'*Pronto*,' the sleepy voice of his uncle reminded him that it was well after 11 p.m. in Italy.

'Uncle Ralph, it's John,' he said.

'John, what a relief to hear from you.' The tone changed, the sleep disappeared.

'Just checking in. I'll have to be brief.'

'Some bad news here, I am afraid.' Ralph paused, 'I have just heard from a Detective Sergeant Mackie, he was telephoning from London.'

'What did he want?'

'He was asking about you – I didn't have much to say.'

'Good,' John replied. 'Be careful, he's the one I spoke about.' He paused. 'You won't have heard, but D'Ostia's dead. I saw the certificate in Soletti's office. I'd have called earlier but I was waiting until I got away.'

'I'm not surprised,' Ralph replied. 'He looked pretty ill last summer. Well, I suppose that's it – where are you, by the way?'

'I'm sorry. Can't say – it's for the best, that way you really don't know then you won't have to lie to the authorities.'

'Oh,' Ralph's voice was flat. 'It's not over then?'

'No, not by a long way.'

'But I thought once you'd dealt with D'Ostia's lawyer it would be finished – I hope you're not taking any risks?'

'No, no. Just being cautious.'

'You have to be – it's all terrible, simply terrible – and it's all my fault, all my fault, I got you . . .'

'No, no you didn't. You must understand this, it has nothing to do with you, that D'Ostia planned all this from the beginning and it was me he wanted to run it. You were just a useful go-between.'

'Don't humour an old man, John. I know it's bad, I want to help.'

'I know, but there's no way I want you to get involved. I have to do this alone. I'll call you – I must go.'

'Before you go, John,' Ralph interrupted, 'I've just remembered something. It might be of use to you. Remember, D'Ostia mentioned he had a daughter? Now he's dead she will probably get everything. Perhaps what you're looking for is with her.'

'Where does she live?' John asked quickly.

'I think in New York but I can't be sure.'

John's pulse quickened. 'Where?'

'No, I don't know, sorry.' He paused again. 'All I have is what he told me. It's strange, you know . . .' Ralph continued, 'he never introduced her to anyone here, even when she was staying with him. In fact, now I remember, my housekeeper said she was staying at the same time as you. Strange man, he must have been careful to make sure she was out of the way when we were there. I never met her, I've no real description – hold on, I do remember my housekeeper said she was attractive, with dark hair – something to do with television . . .'

'Tell me,' John interrupted, an idea coming to him, 'the beach at the bottom of your home, who has access?'

'Only us and two other houses. One is D'Ostia's villa and the other is that of an Italian businessman on the hill above – why?'

'I think I met her briefly,' John replied. He tried to remember the dark-haired girl's name on the beach, but couldn't. Yet if he shut his eyes he could see her clearly enough.

'I can't remember her name but I can recall her face. Can you try and find out for me?'

'I'll try the housekeeper.'

The conversation over, John climbed wearily into bed. All he could hope was that tomorrow might end this whole sorry tale.

Jet-lagged, tired and confused, he slept heavily. No dreams about recent events, no nightmares about the future or the past – just a deep sleep.

While he slept, the temperature in New York, driven by a north-east wind, dropped sharply. Heavy snow fell, covering the city. By morning, it had all but brought the traffic to a standstill.

As John walked towards his ten o'clock appointment, he watched with detached interest as drivers tried to control their large cars on the hard-packed snow. He walked steadily west along 42nd Street. Deep in thought, he crossed Broadway and then stopped. Ahead of him he could see a police car parked on the north side of 42nd Street, its red light flashing slowly. A sense of foreboding washed over him and his memory took him back to the gallery.

He walked across the road, stepping between the parked cars. The building he wanted was directly behind the police car. Outside in the biting wind a police officer stamped his feet to keep warm. Memories flooded back to John: it was the gallery all over again. He shuddered.

'OK, move along,' the sharp twang of the police officer's voice broke in on his thoughts, 'Move it, I said.' The voice was now more insistent.

'I've got an appointment at Goldstein and Davidoff – here,' John said as he approached the door.

The police officer put his arm out. 'Wait here,' he said and turned and reached for his radio – a crackle of static, then, 'Guy down here says he has an appointment with the lawyer.' He waited for the instruction, then turned to John: 'What's your name, Mac?'

'Grande, John Grande.' The policeman muttered into the microphone. At that moment, a car sounded its horn and John spun round, his nerves jangled; he didn't know whether to turn and run or go in. He felt a tap on his shoulder.

'Fourth floor, take the elevator in back.' The police officer's jerked thumb indicated the way.

Minutes later, John stepped out of the elevator and, after giving his name to another police officer, he ducked under a tape and stood in the reception area of the lawyers' office. As he went in, on the wall he noticed a brass plaque inscribed with the names Goldstein and Davidoff, Attorneys at Law. The place was a hive of activity; in the corner by one of the office doors two men were in conference, heads bowed, their voices just a murmur. Through a doorway to another room, John saw a couple of camera flashes.

One of the two men in conference turned and walked towards John. He was short with thinning hair, a large moustache and red-rimmed, tired-looking eyes. He wore an overcoat and a scarf hung around his shoulders.

'You the guy from downstairs?' The man looked up at John. John nodded. 'OK, I'm Jasinski, Lieutenant Jasinski.' The man paused to blow his nose on a grubby-looking handkerchief, which he then tucked away in his overcoat pocket. 'You got any ID?' John reached into his breast pocket, then into his side pocket, hesitated, then settled on his breast pocket to produce his British passport rather than his American one.

'What happened here?' John looked past Jasinski as he spoke.

'Mr Goldstein was found dead in his office.'

'Murder?' John asked.

The lieutenant didn't answer and handed the passport back. 'The officer downstairs said you've got an appointment?'

'Yes, at ten o'clock,' John looked absent-mindedly at his watch as he spoke, as if to punctuate his last comment.

'Who with?'

'Mr Goldstein.'

Jasinski turned and beckoned another detective behind him. 'Get Mrs Dupont out here and ask her to bring her diary again.' He turned back to John. 'Dupont was Mr Goldstein's secretary,' he explained.

John's gaze followed the detective as he walked into another room, then emerged a few seconds later with a middle-aged lady, who had a strong, handsome face, and a slim, upright stature. She carried a large black book under her right arm and, as she approached, John noticed that behind her glasses, her eyes were red and watery.

The lieutenant stepped away from John and addressed her in a much softer tone. Despite the background noise, John was able to hear all the conversation quite clearly.

'Lieutenant,' the woman answered firmly, 'you said I was free to go, but I'm still here.'

'Yes, ma'am. But . . .'

'But what?' The lady glanced over her left shoulder as she spoke towards the office from where John had earlier seen flashes of light.

'Just one last thing,' said Jasinski.

'Have they taken him . . .?' Her voice had fallen to an almost inaudible whisper.

'No, they are just about to. Now, Mrs Dupont, a few minutes ago you said that Mr Goldstein had no appointments this morning but this man says he has one. The name is . . .' Just then there was a flash as a photographer holding his camera above the policeman tried to photograph the scene inside. 'Goddam it! Get that lowlife outta here!' Jasinski yelled.

John turned to Mrs Dupont, 'My name is John Grande.' Mrs Dupont looked at John with a puzzled frown on her face. 'What time?' she asked.

'Ten.'

Mrs Dupont opened her diary and turned a couple of pages.

'Nothing here.' She looked up. 'It's blocked off, but no named appointment.'

'Are you sure?' Jasinski asked. Mrs Dupont nodded. Jasinski looked at John. 'Mrs Dupont said there was no appointment registered for you.'

'No, I didn't, Lieutenant,' Mrs Dupont interrupted, 'I said it was blocked off. Mr Goldstein regularly did that if he wanted privacy. It's just not named in my diary.'

'That's right,' John spoke quietly, 'I think you put me through and I spoke to him direct, you know, to do with Mr D'Ostia.'

'That does sound familiar but I can't confirm it. Mr Goldstein kept his own pocket diary – I used to fill it out for him, though.' She looked down at the diary. 'He rarely moved anywhere that I didn't know about – not for twenty years.'

'I spoke to him myself from Rome two days ago. He confirmed the appointment to me then. That's why I flew over here.'

Jasinski turned to the detective again. 'Go and check on his desk and in his jacket, see if you can locate this pocket diary.'

'Come to think of it, that's when he asked me to block off the 10 a.m. slot; he didn't say why.' She pointed to her diary and John could see a dark pencil mark against the time of 10 a.m.

'You said earlier on that you fixed up all his appointments.'

'Yes.'

'Did he ever ask you to do this before?'

'Yes, but normally it was only for something to do with his family.' At the word 'family', her eyes welled up with tears.

118

'Oh dear, his family, what . . . ?' her voice trailed away as the tears rolled down her cheeks.

'OK, I think you can go now, I'll get a car to take you home.' The detective arrived back as Jasinski finished speaking. 'No diary – nothing – we looked everywhere.'

Jasinski nodded at this news. 'Get Mrs Dupont a car.'

John watched Mrs Dupont as she was escorted away. Was this to do with him? Could it be that someone knew about his visit? He felt his mouth getting dry.

'So, Mr Grande, what was the appointment about?' Lieutenant Jasinski's question broke into John's thoughts.

'I think I was meant to receive some documents,' John stuttered slightly.

'Documents, what were they for?' Jasinski took a pace towards John.

'Part of – part of a . . . diary,' John stammered.

Jasinski stared at John. 'I don't suppose you can tell me what was in them?'

'No – that is, I would, only I don't know,' he replied.

'You don't know, Mr Grande, yet you flew from Rome. It's a long way to come for something you don't know anything about. No idea, I guess, why Mr Goldstein didn't arrange this through his secretary?'

'No. He just told me to be here at 10 a.m. this morning.'

'As I said, it's a long way to come. I guess the diaries must be important to you, yet you don't know what's in them,' Jasinski said. 'Wouldn't you say that's strange? You're not keeping anything from me are you, Mr Grande?'

'Yes, I admit it must seem strange but,' John paused, 'it's about a private matter.'

'I usually find that death makes private things public, sooner or later,' Jasinski replied. At that moment they were disturbed by a man in his late fifties, with slicked-back grey hair, a square pugnacious face and dressed in a three-piece suit.

'Do you want me any more, Lieutenant?' His voice was sharp and it carried authority. 'If not, I would like to go.' The lieutenant turned around, his manner changing again.

'Just a couple of questions, Mr Davidoff. I'll get to you now.' The man looked to his left to what John now knew must have been Mr Goldstein's office, nodded, then went back into his room.

Jasinski turned to face John, 'I may need to talk to you again. Leave your address with the officer at the door.' He reached into his jacket pocket and handed John a card, saying, 'Call me if you can think of anything else.'

He shouted across to the man at the door. 'Take his name and address!'

John turned to go. The policeman looked at him and was about to speak when another detective called to him.

'Wait there,' he ordered.

While he was distracted, John walked quickly out of the door and down the stairs.

He needed time to think, after all he had arrived expecting, or at least hoping, his problems would be solved. He was beginning to understand now, perhaps belatedly, that he had underestimated Peach and Wessells; they were not following him, they were ahead of him. Surely, he reasoned, this must be their work? There was no one else. It couldn't possibly be a coincidence. He wondered vaguely what the diaries might be about – if they had ever existed. He stood at the bottom of the steps and looked down the corridor towards the front entrance. Here he was, in New York, in the middle of a blizzard, unable to go back but with no idea now of how to go forward.

The snow was falling heavily and it was now quite difficult to make out the cars on the far side of the street. Those on the nearside seemed to be covered in snow, except for two police cars sitting beside the entrance with their red lights flashing. He waited until a couple of people had walked past and then stepped out of the office, walking beside them until they turned the corner of 42nd and Broadway. He stopped and searched the street for a cab. What John had failed to notice, in his haste to get away, was a large black limousine, which slowly drove along 42nd street behind him, its nearside window half open. As other cars were travelling slowly it didn't attract any attention.

John was still trying to decide if he should walk along 42nd, or wait for a cab on the corner. Distracted, he didn't see the car pull up alongside him, its engine still purring. His hands in his pocket, he fumbled with his keys, absent-mindedly pulling them out; they slipped from his hands and dropped into the snow on the sidewalk. Cursing, he bent down quickly to retrieve them and, at that moment, a plate-glass window behind him shattered. A split second later there was a dull clunk as a restraining clip on a drainpipe next to the window ripped away from its hooks.

John stood up, staring at the smashed window as a woman screamed. She pointed to the black limousine. With a muffled roar, it kicked into life and moved away quickly into the traffic, down Broadway. She'd seen a gun protruding from the car window.

'You all right?'

John turned to see a man in a dark overcoat and hat, and carrying a briefcase beside him.

'Yes, why do you ask?'

'You were in line,' the man replied.

'Look!' A short, dumpy woman beside him gestured to the side of one of the walls. As she spoke, John could see a drainpipe had been knocked to one side next to the window. At that moment two more people walked over.

'You OK?' they asked. John nodded slowly.

'I thought you were hit,' the short woman beside him continued, 'for sure.'

John looked at her puzzled, 'What do you mean, hit?'

'That guy – you know in that black limo.' She pointed over to the open spot where the car had been.

'Black limo?' John turned and looked.

'Just there. But if it wasn't meant for you, then who?'

The woman's finger was pointing to a car and then to the other side, away from the car, towards the window and drainpipe.

'You see, I told you,' the woman said, her voice insistent.

'Me?' John began to understand and broke into a sweat.

'What were you doing?' the woman asked.

'Nothing – I was just looking for – for my keys.'

The crowd grew quickly. John was aware that faces were staring at him from the smashed window behind.

'Yes, that guy there!' The same woman's voice, and all around her the growing crowd of people were focused on him as though he were an exhibit in a freak show.

'No, really, I don't think . . .' He needed a cab – fast.

'So what's it all about?' someone demanded.

'It's nothing to do with me,' John said, 'I just happened to be here.' He tried to smile, but it came out like a sickly grin.

'You from out of town?' A voice from out of the crowd.

As quickly as it had gathered, the crowd started to melt away. John looked behind him and saw the reason, a police car coming towards them, its light flashing and siren going, a cab for hire just ahead of it. John raised his arm and waved at it.

'What are you doing?' The first woman spoke again. She stepped nearer to him. 'They'll want to speak with you, they always do.' John's heart was pounding, he knew he had to get away – he cursed his luck. All those stories about hard-nosed New Yorkers stepping over dead bodies in the street and he had to meet the one exception.

John turned away from her. He needed time to sort things out and he couldn't do that with the police. Besides, they'd trace him to the incident at the lawyers' office. He walked quickly over to the cab as it pulled up – the police car was getting closer.

'No, I didn't see anything. I can't possibly . . .' he shouted over his shoulder.

'Hey, you've got to stay!' Again, her voice.

'The Algonquin, and hurry, please,' John hissed to the driver as he shut the door. He slumped back, aware of the all-pervading, flashing red light flooding his sanctuary through a misty rear window. He stared straight ahead, expecting the door to be flung open and a policeman's face to intrude. He waited. It was only as the red light faded and died that he allowed himself to look back – nothing but the snow and the strange, misty, almost dreamlike shapes of slow-moving cars.

Alone in his room in the carefully less-than-efficient and faded Algonquin Hotel, he worried about the morning's events as he hastily crammed his things into a suitcase. He was surprised to find that once the initial shock had gone, his mind was clear and he felt calm. Now, more than ever, he knew he had to put together all the pieces of the jigsaw, then stand back in order to better understand his next move. Someone out there thought he knew too much, but what did he know? Everything that D'Ostia had done had been planned down to the smallest detail, but why?

He zipped up his bag, grabbed his coat and headed for the elevator.

'Time and luck,' he muttered. 'Just one break, one simple break.'

Back in New York after only a few days away was not what Laura had planned. God, how she hated the city! The inhuman heaps of concrete, the vast inequalities of the sprawling suburbs. It always angered her when she was abroad that when people spoke of New York, they seemed only to picture parts of Manhattan. Washington Heights and the Bronx, while only a few miles away, could have been different worlds. Despite all that, she knew the city's excitement, its buzz, was the source of her adrenalin. Like a detached witness to a game of Russian Roulette, she seemed to be forever peering through a keyhole at activities that terrified, appalled, and yet at the same time fascinated and enthralled.

Laura looked to her right as the cab swung across the Triborough Bridge; she could see the buildings of the Bronx picked out by the dying gold of the late December sun. The lights of the cars on the Major Deegan expressway against the white snow looked Christmassy and hid the reality of the hopelessness, or so it seemed to her in her present bleak mood. It wasn't long before her cab was cruising past the grand apartment blocks on Fifth Avenue and then cut across Central Park, heading for her block in the West mid-seventies.

In her apartment Laura poured herself a drink, shuffling through her mail as she listened to her answering machine. There were a number of callers, some congratulating her on her new job.

'God! How did they know?' she muttered. Then Walter Harvey came on the line.

'Welcome back – sorry, you probably already saw, but in case you haven't heard, the *Daily News* got hold of your change of job and the details of the new one. Had to put out a quick statement and couldn't reach you. Please give me a call when you get back in.'

Then, 'Hi, Laura, Merry Christmas. It's Pat, Pat Danvers.' She smiled. 'I'm in Rome. Anyway, remember you asked me to find out more about this lawyer, Soletti? Well, it's no good, he's – he's dead . . .'

Laura stared at the answerphone. '. . . impossible to get any more news at the moment. I'm off on a short assignment to the Balkans, I'll call you when I get back. Meanwhile, happy days.'

She flipped the switch on the answering machine. She'd forgotten about Pat and that she had asked him to snoop around in Italy. The lawyer dead! She couldn't believe it. She stared at the machine, her mind a jumble of disconnected thoughts. Pat must have made a mistake – she'd only just seen Soletti. Laura took a drink and picked up the telephone to call Walter Harvey.

Twenty minutes later she put the phone down. Too late to worry, the news was now out, better make the best of it.

ABS was already running with it on their news bulletin. Laura smiled, she'd never had a huge amount of time for feminist extremes but nonetheless she took pleasure in beating her male colleagues. She knew it had always been tough, but she was only sure of one thing, that she was better than the rest – male or female. She was damned if she was going to let them get together some clutch of the usual politically correct clones to discuss her new job. They were bound to talk about it everywhere else but they were not going to do it on her news time. Laura smiled at the irony of her decision, now she was in charge. She laughed for the first time in days.

'Well, Dad, you might even be proud of your unwanted daughter now,' she said to herself as she looked at her watch. 'Pat Danvers, we need to speak.' She reached for the phone, hoping he would be back. But there was no answer.

Christmas Eve in a tiny, one-and-a-half-room apartment in a downbeat, prewar building just off 100th Street and Central Park West. The whole place would have fitted into John Grande's Chelsea drawing room, with room to spare. The walls were brown with a dirty white ceiling – white once, now more a urine yellow. In the corner of the main room an old two-bar heater glowed in patches but without really affecting the cold, damp atmosphere.

As he walked into the room, John stopped and looked around – now he knew he'd reached rock bottom.

He had taken the place as advertised – 'furnished rooms'. That had to be a joke. The only furniture was a fold-down bed, a wooden chair, a rickety, chipped, Formica-covered table and a battered TV in a corner. It was on a short lease, a month, and the landlord knew John needed it; only someone in need would pay what he was asking for a hole like this and no questions. Still, at least he had bought himself some time, out of sight, if not out of the minds, of those who were trying to find him.

Not that he had got anywhere with his time. For three or four days since leaving the Algonquin, he had stayed pretty much close to the apartment; he had not shaved and had only ventured out to buy some food, an old coat from a street market and a pair of glasses. He was quite pleased with his appearance now; he looked rough enough – not far short of being a bum. Yet it enabled him to get around without being recognised. He'd already spoken to the office of Goldstein and Davidoff, trying to make contact with the other lawyer, Davidoff, to see what information he had. He had waited until the police had moved on, but the office was now closed for the vacation. Not of course that he held out too much hope. Clearly, whoever killed Goldstein had been after the diaries as well.

He sat down on the hard chair and laid a brown shopping bag on the table beside him. He rubbed his eyes and gazed down at the heater.

'God, you owe me one! All I need is a break, just one break,' he said, gazing up at the ceiling and shaking his head. 'Fat chance!' He pulled the *Daily News* out of the bag and skimmed over the headlines. No point in going to the police, the first thing they would do would be to vet his name. He could imagine what the New York police would say when they found out that he was already mixed up in an assault in London, which had become a murder hunt. He shivered as he remembered how Maguire had told him about his partner's death.

Poor Richard. But he didn't have much time to feel sorry

for anyone else for he knew what the police would make of a murder in London and the murder in New York, both connected to him. Now the trail got even worse. The Italian lawyer was dead. His uncle had told him that morning when he called. That would be enough to slam him into prison faster than he could blink. No, he had to try and sort this out himself. His problem was knowing where he should start; everywhere he'd drawn a blank.

As he sat at the table, deeply depressed, he finished flicking disinterestedly through the *Daily News*. It was just as he was turning over a page that something caught his eye and he turned back: 'Top job in the news goes to high-flyer career woman'.

Underneath the headline was a picture of a slim, attractive woman in her early thirties, with large dark eyes. He looked at her carefully, something about her vaguely reminded him of someone else. He read the article beside the picture – it was about the woman's new job – 'Laura Buckley, the new head of ABS news and current affairs'. He shook his head and switched on the old TV set, sitting back with his eyes half closed.

'A disaster in Bolivia – hundreds killed – a shoot out in Washington between the police and some drug dealers', the screen flickered and he gazed with less and less interest. He got up and poured himself a whisky, and then sat down again. 'President Carson's problem gets worse – the forthcoming caucus in Iowa and the primaries in Massachusetts – Kelp catches up.' John found himself watching, only half-listening, his mind elsewhere. He was about to switch off when the same woman whose picture was in the *Daily News* flashed onto the screen. He turned up the sound.

'Youngest ever to run the news and current affairs unit . . .'

She should look happier, he thought, a new job, a great future, it was all in front of her. Had he not seen her before? But where? Perhaps it was just a familiar face – attractive, sad – no one in her position should be so sad, the world was at her feet. Pictures kept flickering through his head – a hot day, the sound of the sea, shadows. He turned off the television and swallowed the rest of his whisky.

Miles from home, he was running for his life, desperate to solve a riddle. He felt tired, empty and sorry for himself. If he didn't get something in three or four days, he'd have to go home, no point in squatting in New York. He threw his coat on the bed, and walked through to the little shower room at the back and started to get undressed. At least the water was hot. He dried himself, switched the light off and climbed into bed. Depression made bed seem like a refuge, he had never felt so tired, exhausted by his failure, worn out by the collapse of his self-esteem. Again, that woman's face, where, where . . .?

'God!' he exclaimed, sitting up and switching on the light. 'What a fool I've been!' He tossed the blanket aside and, grabbing the paper, he turned the pages quickly. He stared again at the picture of Laura Buckley.

'Is it you? Oh God, I hope so,' he exclaimed as he recalled his uncle's words, '. . .something to do with television.'

John hardly dared to believe it might be so; his uncle's other words raced through his mind, 'He never introduced her to anyone here . . . this summer . . . at the same time as you . . . dark hair, attractive.'

'You were on the beach – it was you, I know it – on the beach,' he smiled, 'now, all I ask is that you be D'Ostia's daughter.'

8

Down and Out in New York

'Munroe!' Lieutenant Jasinski's voice cut through the noise in the office. He stood in the doorway, staring into the open-plan room, full of plain-clothed police. A short overweight detective advanced towards him.

'Where's Rutgers?' Jasinski demanded as Munroe drew near.

'Following up that guy in the office across the street from the lawyers,' Monroe replied.

Jasinski nodded and walked back into his office and sat down at his desk. Munroe remained standing.

'So, what've you got?' Jasinski barked.

'Not much, so far. This guy Goldstein was quite a loner. It seems he often used to go to his office early to meet clients. Signs of a burglary but nothing taken that his secretary could see. Anyway, the safe wasn't forced. He must have disturbed the burglars. The blow to the head couldn't have killed him but forensics say he had a heart attack as well.'

'I know all that,' Jasinski shook his head as he spoke.

'But there's more. Remember that English guy at the office, the day of the shooting? Well, it may be nothing but the same morning we were in the lawyers, there was a shooting a block away on the corner of Broadway and 42nd.'

'Yeah?'

'Witnesses to the shooting said the guy they thought was being shot at was a Brit. Their description fits the man in the office perfectly.'

'So you think it may be the same man?'

Munroe nodded.

Jasinski gazed up at the ceiling, 'What was his name? I can't remember.'

Munroe shook his head very slowly.

'I don't remember either.'

'Well, check the record,' Jasinski ordered.

'I've tried . . . the thing is, I can't find any record, Lieutenant. There's nothing on the guy.'

'What?' Jasinski sat up. 'Surely the cop at the door . . .'

'No – seems he was distracted.'

'Didn't you take his name?'

'No,' Munroe hesitated, 'I didn't interview him.'

'Well, who was the last to speak to him?' Jasinski frowned.

'Well . . .' Again Munroe hesitated, 'you were.'

'For Christ's sake! You mean to tell me that no one else thought to take his name?'

Munroe stared blankly back.

'What am I running? A kindergarten?' He shook his head. 'How long you been a detective?' Before Munroe could answer, Jasinski continued, 'Well, you won't be one much longer if you screw up like that again!'

Munroe grimaced.

'What happened after the shooting?'

'The guy went off in a hurry.'

'Nobody heard where he was going, or took the licence plate?'

Munroe shook his head.

'Listen, Munroe,' Jasinski spelt out, as he sat back in his seat, 'this smart-ass fancy lawyer had friends everywhere and I mean everywhere. The mayor's on the commissioner's back and he's on the captain's back and the captain's chasing my butt all over this and we're gettin' nowhere. All we have is some English guy with no name and no address – what a screw-up! OK, you'd better get onto the cab companies to try and find out if anyone remembers taking the guy after the shooting. You'd also better get onto all the hotels, find out if they have any record of a Brit fitting that description.'

'L'tenant!' Munroe's face fell, 'that'll take for ever.'

'Don't start on me, Monroe, don't start – just do it! Take whatever men you need, but do it!'

Jasinski watched as Munroe walked into the outer office. 'There's gotta be a better way to earn a living, gotta be,' he muttered as he picked up the receiver to speak to the captain.

John walked through the smoked-glass door on the fourth floor of the tower towards the receptionist and the security guard. The guard carried a gun; it sat high on the waistband, just below his large gut, which seemed ready and willing to force its way out of the tight blue tailored shirt. He had badges all over and John wondered why every security guard in New York looked like the chief of police.

'Can I help you?' The guard looked at him impassively from under a sharp-peaked cap, his blank face broken only by the movement of his jaws as he chewed gum.

'Laura Buckley, News and Current Affairs, ABS Broadcasting.'

The receptionist stepped forward. 'Have you an appointment?' she said, looking John up and down with obvious distaste.

'Yes,' John didn't hesitate. 'Just tell me the correct floor and I'll . . .'

'Oh no, I'll have to call ahead.' The guard continued to stare at him and was right at her shoulder. 'If you'll wait,' the receptionist said, as she reached for a directory and flicked some pages over. 'Let me see . . . Buckley . . .' She tapped out some numbers on the telephone console and picked up the receiver. 'Is that Laura Buckley's office?'

John watched nervously, aware that his appointment would now be denied.

'Pardon me . . .' the receptionist said in an aggrieved tone, 'I didn't know she had moved to the twentieth floor, it doesn't say . . .'

At that moment a group of six Japanese men walked up to the desk, talking loudly to each other. John stepped back and to one side to let them through and was briefly hidden from the gaze of the guard. Walking quickly behind them, he made it to the elevator.

'Twentieth floor . . . twentieth floor,' John murmured as a set of elevator doors opened. He walked into the elevator quickly, expecting to hear a shout from the guard. But the doors closed behind him. He turned and looked at the bank of buttons, pressed the twentieth and waited for what seemed an eternity before he felt the pressure as the elevator surged upwards. He exhaled slowly and watched the liquid crystal display change as it moved towards the twentieth floor. Fifteen, sixteen, seventeen. The elevator stopped, his pulse raced, a woman got in, looked at him and pressed the twenty-second-floor button and then moved back as far away as possible from John.

At the twentieth floor, John stepped out and walked a few paces to his left. How he hoped she was in! He saw his reflection in some glass: a shambles, dirty coat, rough stubble and greasy hair. He took off the cheap glasses and looked around – three different corridors. He decided to go to one of the corners – all executives had their offices at the corner of the building, he reasoned, it was one of the great power symbols – windows on two sides.

He stopped a man walking towards the elevator and asked, 'Could you tell me where Laura Buckley's office is?'

'Down there,' the man gestured behind him. John walked

along the corridor indicated: there was a door at the far end, it was open. He knocked.

'Excuse me, I wonder . . .' he started. He faced a middle-aged woman with her hair tied behind her head and her jaw set, standing behind the desk looking straight at him aghast. 'Would it be possible to speak to Laura Buckley?'

'You don't have an appointment – and no, it's not possible,' she replied curtly. 'Now if you please . . .'

'But all I want is a few minutes,' John insisted.

'Look, if you don't go, I'll call the guard.'

At that moment the guard walked into the office. 'This man causing a problem?' he asked, his arm already on John's shoulder. 'Reception said he might be up here.'

'He doesn't have an appointment so I've asked him to go.'

'OK, mister . . .' the guard began.

'What's going on?'

John turned his head to see an attractive dark-haired woman. He immediately recognised Laura Buckley, now standing in the doorway of her office. 'What's all this about, Sal?' she asked, her puzzled face turned to her secretary.

'I don't know, just another bum who reads the *Daily News*, although this one got in, Laura.'

'Laura Buckley?' John asked quickly. 'Are you Laura Buckley?'

It all seemed rather strange to Laura as she stood watching the security guard and a rather down-at-heel man in her office. The way he was dressed, the way he looked, he should have been speaking in a New York accent and yet he spoke with a clear English voice. She was intrigued.

'Hold it, hold it a minute.' She walked around the secretary's desk and stood just in front of them. 'Who are you?'

'You won't know me,' John began, 'but I do know your father – Mike D'Ostia.' Laura started at the mention of her father's name, her eyes wide open.

'I know I don't look like much now, but there is a reason for

133

this; it's a long story.' He reached into his coat pocket for his British passport.

'Look, my passport proves my identity.' The security guard let John's arm go as he pulled out his passport. 'The picture might be a little hard to match but it's all I've got.'

Laura Buckley took the passport and flicked through the first couple of pages, stopping at the photograph. She looked up at John and back at the picture, then again at John and one more time at the picture. She closed the passport and tapped it on her hand as she spoke.

'If you can spare me just five minutes, that's all, five minutes – then if you still think I am a waste of time, I'll go without anyone having to throw me out,' John pleaded.

'OK, you've got your five minutes.' She nodded at the guard. 'It's OK, you can let him in.'

The secretary, who was standing by the door, looked appalled. 'As Miss Buckley said,' she sneered, 'you've got five minutes, not a second more.'

He walked past Laura into the office. She moved to shut the door, hesitated and, leaving it ajar, went over to the window. She pointed to a chair in front of the desk. The office was a mess, books everywhere, magazines and newspapers all in piles on the floor – at the far side, a large rosewood desk and in the corner a couple of TV sets, a bank of equipment and in some open cupboards a load of video machines. The office had the most spectacular view of downtown Manhattan, which framed her as she stood against the window. Whatever doubts he may previously have had disappeared. At that moment, he could see it was the same face that looked down on him on the beach in Positano, that strange, striking look, those dark eyes and the dark thick hair.

'The clock's ticking, Mr Grande, I don't have much time.' Her voice was flat as she tried to hide her curiosity. She looked at him closely as he sat down and began to notice something about his eyes, which made her feel she had seen him before. With each passing minute she became more certain of it, but she could not remember where.

'I'll try and be brief,' he began. 'You probably don't remember, but we met this summer – on that little beach in Positano, I'm sure it was you.'

Laura's face was expressionless and she made no movement at all.

'You were with a friend, I was sitting by a rock – you looked down . . .' He searched her face for the smallest acknowledgement; there was none. 'I think your friend was blonde,' he added.

She could remember that day on the beach clearly, she could even see him walking away from her up the hill. Odd, how little things like that stick in your mind.

'OK, Mr Grande, let's assume I remember – I guess you didn't come here to talk vacation snaps.'

'No,' he said, unsure whether she did remember or not, 'it's about your father. You see, your father asked me to sell some pictures for him – I'm a dealer in London – well, the day I met you on the beach I went to meet him at his villa . . .'

'Look,' she interrupted, 'I know nothing of any pictures, whatever my father arranged, I . . .'

'No, wait – I sold all of them, it's more than that.'

'Laura,' the secretary's voice burst in on them, 'You're meant to see Jack in fifteen minutes.' She was standing at the door tapping her watch.

'Put him back fifteen minutes, Sal.' The secretary hesitated, eyebrows raised. 'Oh, and shut the door after you, will you?' The secretary frowned at that last instruction, seemed about to say something and then, thinking better of it, she closed the door behind her.

'Look,' John continued as the door shut. 'I know your father's dead, I . . .'

'How do you know?' Laura demanded.

'I was shown his death certificate in Rome.'

'By whom?'

'A lawyer – Soletti, I think, was his name.'

As John mentioned Soletti's name, she sat up, a puzzled expression on her face.

'The only reason I was there,' he continued, 'was to receive a note from your father.' He reached into his pocket and produced the crumpled note. It was typed and there was no signature.

'A note? When was this?' she demanded again, her voice dry and thin. She looked at the note. 'This doesn't prove anything – you could have written it.'

'Yes, I could have done so, but I didn't. Just hear me out – that's the point I'm making – that's why I'm here, because of your father. The whole thing sounds strange because it is. I don't pretend to understand what's going on, that's why I've come to you. I wish I did. Your father asked me to sell a collection of paintings in London. As I said, I'm an art dealer, and so I agreed. It looked to be a good collection. Since then my partner's been murdered, the lawyer your father wanted me to see in New York is dead and I've got two people who are after me for some diaries they say your father had passed onto me to sell to them. He never mentioned a thing about any diaries, yet they're certain. The trouble is they won't take no for an answer.'

'So you expect me to believe that my father's responsible for all this?'

'I don't know. I only know I've been set up and I don't know why. I thought you might be able to help. No one else can. The lawyer in London is silent on the subject and the lawyer in Rome . . .'

'Is dead,' Laura interrupted in a soft voice.

'I know,' John muttered, his head bowed, 'My uncle told me, though he didn't know any details.'

'Not more than one day after I left him.' She watched him

while she spoke. He seemed genuinely concerned, yet he could just be a good actor, she thought.

'I shouldn't be surprised I suppose, everywhere I go someone . . .'

'. . . dies?' Laura asked quietly.

John grimaced. 'It's a familiar pattern. First my partner, then the lawyer in Rome, and now the lawyer in New York.'

'And you're trying to tell me my father is the cause of all this?' she asked slowly.

'No – yes, oh, I don't know! All I know is that I wouldn't be here but for him. Since he asked me to sell some pictures for him, everything has gone wrong.' The frustration was building up inside him. 'I'm sitting here dressed like a bum, in New York – here, I guess, because of your father – because there's no denying if I hadn't met him . . . Well, I would be in my gallery in London, not here. Now my partner has died and I'm wanted for his murder!' He looked her straight in the eye. 'That information alone passed to the police would be certain to have me back on the next plane to London. I came to see you because you are my last hope, you must know something. Everything that has happened was due to him and there is a great deal more to come, I know. I never wanted to get involved in whatever it is that I now seem to be in the middle of, but your father put me here as sure as if he had tied my hands and carried me here himself.'

His last words were soft and Laura watched as one hand gripped the other, his knuckles white.

'I'm not saying he planned this but he set up the deal and arranged for me to meet Goldstein here in New York.' He shook the note in his right hand. 'See for yourself.'

'I did,' she said quietly, 'and as I said, it doesn't prove anything at all or connect my father. I have only your word that he asked you to sell some pictures. You've produced no proof, except a cryptic note, unsigned. All because of my father, you say. Why should I believe you?'

'It *was* him.'

She shook her head. 'I've got to hand it to you, I don't know what you expect from me but I give you full marks for your lack of sensitivity. You hustle your way into this office, a few days after I get back from learning about the death of my father and you insult him. What am I supposed to do, give you a medal? My father was no saint and I am sure there are a lot of people out there who didn't like him, but I find it hard to believe that he would have set out to deliberately make your life hell. He didn't even know you. Why would he go to such lengths?'

'I don't begin to pretend I know what's going on but if you believe your father has nothing to do with this, at least help me find out who does.'

Laura stared back at him impassively.

'Look,' he continued, 'he must have set up the deal direct with the two Americans in London – Wessells and Peach. They knew all about the six Licattas, they were waiting for them . . .'

'I don't know what you're talking about.' She reached for the telephone. 'I think I've heard enough. I'm very busy and this is clearly a fairy tale from a psychotic mind. I'm going to call the police. Tell them about . . .'

'No wait. I can prove it.' An idea came to him. He closed his eyes, trying to conjure up the gallery at D'Ostia's villa. 'I can tell you which paintings he left you,' he paused, 'He did leave you some valuable paintings, didn't he?'

Laura's hand rested on the receiver. She hesitated. 'Maybe.'

'Let me see,' he said, closing his eyes. 'Nine were on one side of the gallery – religious theme . . . Caravaggio . . .' he started.

'Wait,' she ordered. 'I've got the list right here.' She reached into her desk drawer and pulled out a folder. John could just see the front cover as she opened it: Sotheby's. He swallowed hard.

'You're wrong about the number.'

'Oh.' He tried to count the pictures again – nine – he was sure, then he remembered. 'Yes, there's probably more but I'm talking about nine – oh yes, there's probably a Picasso sketch as well. I'll start with that, then an oil on canvas by Brueghel, then Madonna and Child, Caravaggio . . .'

He carried on slowly while she checked against the list.

'OK,' she acknowledged, shutting the file, 'I guess that proves you met my father.' She slid the folder back into the drawer. 'That, however, doesn't prove your allegations about him. None of it makes sense.' She glanced at her watch, 'Not one word.'

'I'm only asking you to help – perhaps he left the diaries to you, or a note explaining the whole thing?'

'No, you'll be lucky if I don't call the police. I haven't got the time . . .'

'If you don't,' he interrupted, grasping at straws, speaking first, 'you'll never know. There'll always be a nagging doubt. If I'm killed or the police get me, you'll ask yourself, could it have been different, could it have been true?' He watched as she looked away. 'I'm not asking much, I never wanted to involve you but . . . you're my last chance.'

Laura knew he was right, that she would wonder – who was her father, was he responsible, why did he shield his past when she'd asked him? He was her father and she yearned to know more – most of all, was she like him?

She reached for her diary and flicked through a few pages. 'This has got to be one of the busiest times of my whole working life,' she said, tapping her fingers on the desk. 'OK, I will give you some more time but not now, not for a few days. I'll call you – I need time to think about what you've said.'

John took a pace forward from the window. His spirits soared and it showed in his face. In response, she calmly, deliberately, pushed a piece of paper towards him and placed a pencil down on top of it.

'Before I do anything, though,' she stated, 'I'm going to run some checks. Write down details about the gallery, the lawyers you have spoken to and any telephone numbers you can remember. Before I move anywhere, I want to find out if what you say is true, and give me a contact number where I can reach you.'

John was unsure. 'How do I know you won't go to the police?' he asked.

Laura smiled again. 'You don't – as the man said, you'll just have to trust me. Oh yes, and no more stunts like that one. If you enter the building again, I'll hand you over to the police.'

Three minutes later, Laura shut the door behind him and walked back to her swivel chair. She sank down, resting her head on the back as she closed her eyes. The strange meeting flashed past her as a series of images, blurred and distant. It was all too ridiculous to be true and yet its absurdity made it all the more fascinating.

'He's gone,' her secretary said, walking into the office. 'I'm glad that's over.' She stopped on the other side of the desk. 'It *is* over, isn't it?'

'Sal, I want you to get Pat Danvers on the telephone – he should be back from the Balkans by now. There are a couple of things I want him to do for me.'

'I smell trouble here, Laura. This is something to do with that guy – he's a fake, you know.'

'I thought from the way you looked, you thought he was a bum?'

'He's no bum.'

'How do you know?'

'Bums in New York don't wear English brogues and talk in cut-crystal English accents.'

Laura raised her eyebrows. 'You're very observant, Sal.'

'You're not going to get involved in something, are you, Laura? For God's sake, surely not now of all times!'

'Now, Sal, stop mothering me and just get me Pat.'

'Are you sure?'

'You'll just have to trust me.' She patted her secretary on the arm. 'Now please get me Pat.'

'Now I know something is going on. This is New York, Laura.' She started to walk towards the door. 'Nobody . . .' she said, over her shoulder, 'in New York trusts anybody and nor should you. He's got to you, hasn't he?'

'Why do you think so?' Laura laughed.

'Because you never, ever say please, and you just did!'

An anglepoise lamp cast shadows that seemed to flicker in the light of a log fire. Much of the rest of the room was in darkness. A bookshelf on one wall was just visible through the gloom.

Jack Douglas sat in his chair, his feet up on one corner of his desk while he studied the large pile of documents. As he read, an old grandfather clock chimed the hour. He continued to read each paper carefully, marking, underlining and then occasionally writing notes on a pad beside him.

Finally, taking his glasses off, he sat still for some minutes before leaning forward and, taking his feet off the desk, he turned in his chair, pulled the pad of paper across the desk and started to write.

He was puzzled. Having trawled through a huge pile of documents over the last month and a half, he found his lines of investigation all seemed to stop with exactly the same question – where did the money come from?

What frustrated him most of all was that this question kept coming up at the end of everything he had read since the article in the *Spectator* he'd come across so recently. He knew that unless he could find the answer there was no story.

The Kelps had once been a wealthy and powerful family. Their money had been made in the nineteenth century, through shipping and property investments. It was indeed the classic American story of great wealth being built up over a generation, consolidated by another and then spent by a third. However, in the Kelps' case, it was dissipated even faster than was usual. Andrew Conrad Kelp's disastrous business and gambling debts had grown and grown, and ruined the family in the late 1930s. When Ewan Kelp had been a young boy the family had been part of the smart set of New York. Then suddenly it had all come to an end – the houses in New York and Newport had been sold, so had the cars. No more extravagant parties – the Kelps could hardly afford the low rent on their three-bedroom apartment in New York. They had, as so many before them, always persuaded themselves that their family and friends were important and that no matter what, they would always stand by each other. It was simply a matter of class. However, once they had had to leave their sumptuous homes, they found they did not matter to their friends at all. They learnt the hard lesson that families for generations before had learnt in New York: the entry ticket was money and family – no money, no standing. Worse, they became an embarrassment to society, reminding it of its obligations and they soon stopped receiving invitations.

It was with the memory of this position that Ewan Kelp had gone off to the war in 1944 as a newly commissioned officer. He'd lied about his age. Yet late in the same year he had received the Congressional Medal of Honor and a Purple Heart for leading a troop of soldiers back from an air crash through enemy lines at the time of Anzio.

At the end of the war, he set up in business with his ex-platoon sergeant, a man called Acquilan. In a remarkably short period of time, business boomed. It was this that puzzled Douglas more than anything else because he could find no reference to how the business had taken off, or what it was that they had done that had made their venture so successful, so quickly.

Douglas stopped writing and flicked through his notes. He had been a journalist long enough to know that apart from it being an interesting story, there was nothing very odd until he got to the period 1945 to 1948. Whichever way he turned, no matter where he inquired, it appeared their company was legitimate. He was sure something didn't fit, it was too much too soon. Yet there was no evidence to support his suspicions. He made a mental note to do more work on Acquilan – an interesting man from the West Side, a poor boy from a poor neighbourhood, no money, on the edge of the law – the usual story. Time, he thought, to do some more digging.

He stood up and walked over to the fire, put the fireguard in front of it and, staring into the flames, wondered whether there was perhaps nothing else. Had he become obsessed – perhaps it was time to move on? He nodded, stretched out for his pad and pencil and put a line under the last notes he had made, writing in bold, 'Time to start the Carson piece'. He put the pencil down. As he moved towards the door the clock struck 2 a.m.

Detective Sergeant Mackie walked slowly along the corridor, his pipe in one hand and a file in the other. At the far end was a grey door with a frosted glass panel. He knocked and entered, without waiting for a reply. Behind the oblong mahogany desk sat a grey-haired man in the uniform of a Chief Superintendent.

'Ah, Donald, come in, sit down.'

'Thank you – sir.'

'Cut it out, Donald, after all these years.' He gave him a wry smile.

'Well, you did summon me, sir,' Mackie said and sat down. 'You're the Chief Superintendent.'

'If you, Donald, had been a little less outspoken, a little more careful about who you insulted, you would have been here, not me.'

'I think I'm happy enough where I am, if it's all the same with you.' He put some papers on the desk in front of him. 'Anyway, we both know I never wanted to be a politician – I only ever wanted to be a policeman.'

The Chief Superintendent smiled and pretended he hadn't heard the last rejoinder. They'd known each other since training college – they were long-time friends. Each knew what the other said was correct.

'I suppose you want the latest on the gallery murder?' Mackie rummaged in his pocket for his tobacco pouch. 'Well, it's all there,' Mackie gestured to the papers in front of him.

'So, what's new?' He waited while Mackie lit his pipe.

'There's not a great deal more to say. We've got the same suspicions, the same potential suspects: the only thing that has changed is that the man in the coma is now dead and it's become a murder inquiry.'

'But you don't seem to be getting anywhere. You released the main suspect two days ago just when I thought you were going to charge him. Was he the new man?'

'Yes, Havers – the boyfriend.'

'Then why did you let him go?'

'There was not enough to connect him.'

'What about the fingerprints on that crowbar?'

'Aye, there were those, but he'd been helping to sort out the exhibition a day or two before – it could have been from then. Besides, we also have prints for Grande and we also have evidence that it had been held by somebody wearing gloves – there were some fibres.' He puffed on his pipe. 'Forensic are certain those gloves were leather.'

'Look, I've got the *Standard* and the nationals breathing down my neck. You remember the piece they wrote yesterday – 'Cabinet Minister's Son in Brutal Slaying. Police Drew a Blank'? Well, now we are under pressure because they're saying there is not enough going on.' Mackie nodded slowly but said nothing. 'From what you say, Donald, we are back where we started.'

'Well, we are still interested in Grande.'

'That's great, but you let him go weeks ago.'

'Aye, but I couldn't hold him – no real proof.'

'What about the witness you had? I seem to recall something about a man in an upstairs window.'

'Disappeared,' Mackie delivered the information without changing the expression on his face.

'Disappeared?' The Chief Superintendent stared at Mackie. 'Donald, if it was not you sitting there in front of me, I swear to God, I would have taken you off the case by now.'

'Aye, well, you may yet want to do that, but just hold on a while, there's some more here.' He puffed on his pipe for a second. 'We talked to this character and I went up to the flat where he is supposed to have seen the person he described entering the gallery. I couldn't see how he would have been able to see the man, it was too far away and at slightly the wrong angle. I don't know what his game was but his story didn't hold up at all – for some particular reason he seemed to want to point the finger at Grande. He would not have stood up in court for five minutes so he saved us a lot of trouble by disappearing.'

'OK, Donald, I've got the picture. I hope for both our sakes you come up with something fast – they're breathing down my neck. The pressure I'm under to change the team on this is huge.'

'Well, I believe it's all to do with this man Grande, not the guy we just released. He's involved in something – I don't know what – but it's quite big.'

'Drugs?'

'No, I don't think so. More likely to be something in his own line of work – art.'

'Well, let's see.' The Chief Superintendent's voice took on a sharp, sarcastic tone. 'We've got a dead art dealer, his business partner's buggered off – you've released the only suspect who seems to be connected to it; your key witness disappears and now you tell me that he had something to do with it all along! There's only one snag, Donald, we have no idea where he is. For Christ's sake, in all the years I've known you, you've never had a cock-up like this on your hands! This isn't just an ordinary murder.'

'That's your department! Only good police work will solve this and no quicker whether his uncle is a cabinet minister or a cab driver.'

The Chief Superintendent knitted his brows as he looked at his subordinate. He knew Mackie was an excellent detective, thorough and with a nose for the truth, so something, he felt, didn't quite fit.

'Come on, Donald, I think there's more – let me have it all.'

Mackie shook his head. 'The whole thing is very complicated and I am only now beginning to see the way ahead. This man, Grande – I always felt he had the look of someone who was being manipulated rather than manipulating. Seemed a detached, quiet man. He lost his wife and child in a bad car accident some years ago and his friends say it affected him very badly and, from what they say, he cut himself off from pretty well all contact outside the gallery.' He picked up his pipe, struck a match and slowly brought it to light again. 'The receptionist led us to look into the gallery's financial position; my instinct was right on that – it was in serious difficulty. Then Grande went off to Italy for three or four days to visit his uncle in Positano. The receptionist said that when he came back, she overheard him and his partner constantly talking about some big deal.'

Mackie leaned back and turned his head so he faced the chief inspector. 'It seems the deal didn't come off. The receptionist said they started to argue. It ended with a shouting match with Grande threatening his partner.' He picked up the file and opened it. 'Then there was this man called Peach, an American; again, the receptionist seems to think he was something to do with this big picture deal. She couldn't tell us anything else but Peach was in and out of there quite a lot. Then there was another man – no name – who seemed to be linked with Peach.'

'Anything more about this man, Peach?'

'Nothing – bought some pictures, paid for them all by cheque, money was cleared through a NatWest bank account but it originally came from a numbered Swiss account. Most other dealers think the price was much more than those pictures should fetch in the open market.'

'That's a lot of loose ends, Donald.'

'Aye.'

'You've no idea where Grande is now?'

'Well, I know he went to visit his uncle in Positano. I've spoken to the uncle but he wasn't giving anything away.'

The Chief Superintendent perched on the corner of his desk. 'Sounds to me as if everything points to Grande, that he did it.'

'He may well have done – that's always a possibility but I'm not at all convinced . . .' Mackie shut the file and tapped out his pipe in the ashtray. 'Things are happening around him, he'll show up and we'll be hearing about him pretty damn soon.'

'More than probably dead by the sounds of things.'

'Maybe he's got something too many people want. I don't know when but once we find him, we'll sew this case up.'

'OK, it's yours for a bit longer. You had better deliver – both our reputations are riding on this one.'

'Aye, well, as I said, only good solid, boring police work will sort it,' Mackie nodded as though agreeing with himself.

9

Sins and Opportunity

In a corner of a large hotel dining room in Washington, six men sat at a circular table. Around them, waiters were clearing the debris of a campaign-fundraiser dinner at which Senator Ewan Kelp had just spoken. They were deep in animated discussion; an argument had broken out between two of them.

'Bullshit, Jim!' A thick-set man in his mid-forties was shaking his head. 'Ewan's right about the *Post*, Douglas is on a vendetta and we all know why.'

The thinner man at the side of the table, who was the focus of his attention, shook his head.

'You'll eat your words when you see the effect his column has on Carson.' He threw the following day's *Post* across the table. 'He's lifted the lid – the packing of the meetings – it's a great piece.' He paused as Mason read it. 'Look, I never said he liked Ewan – hell, I know he doesn't – but he's too good a journalist to be as openly biased as you say he is.'

At that moment they were joined by two more people, Ewan Kelp himself and Victor Acquilan. Kelp placed his hands on Jim Donald's shoulders.

'So, Sam, how did we do?' Senator Kelp was first to speak as he looked across the table.

'Good, good – hard to say exactly but we raised at least $200,000 give or take,' Sam Eadie spoke while glancing at a piece of paper.

'Got some good reactions for tomorrow,' Donald, his press secretary, cut in quickly.

'Not from the *Post* though,' Dick Mason's voice was sharp.

'How are the networks?' Kelp asked, exchanging glances with Acquilan, who stood beside him.

'OK – they will be in Iowa for your whistle stop next week and then in New Hampshire.' Jim Donald looked apprehensively at Mason. 'I know you can't stand Douglas, Ewan,' Donald continued, 'and you think he is out to get you, but he's written a piece that won't make life easy for President Carson – he's laid bare what they have been doing in all those meetings in Iowa.' Donald pointed to the newspaper in front of Mason. 'The networks will follow, they always do.'

'God help us the day we thank Douglas!' Mason spat the words out, passing the paper to Kelp.

'Look, Jim, you'd better make sure that Douglas and the others aren't about to do a job on me next,' Kelp spoke slowly. 'I know them, particularly Douglas, and far too many in the media take their lead from him.'

'Douglas has always been a law unto himself,' Donald replied, 'I can't stop . . .'

'Goddammit, what's the use of a press secretary who can't?' Mason responded aggressively.

'OK, OK,' Kelp cut in, 'lay off him, Dick! Jim's right, we should be thankful that Douglas has laid Carson wide open.' He turned reassuringly to Donald. 'We don't have to trust him, though. Next month California, then New York. We'll go straight for them through the networks – right, Jim?'

'That's how we planned it,' Donald glared defiantly at Mason. 'If Dick lets us . . .'

Acquilan watched and listened without saying anything but

he exchanged glances with the man on the far side of the table from him, Bernie Weitz.

As the meeting broke up, Kelp took Acquilan's arm and guided him away from the others.

'What's happening about Cosmo?' Kelp asked.

'All under control, Ewan.'

'That's what you said before,' Kelp countered.

'Calm yourself, it's good news, we've got the paintings.'

'All of them? They're all here?'

'Not exactly, but they're in New York, safe and sound,' Acquilan answered. 'They'll be taken care of.'

'Good, the sooner they're destroyed, the better we'll all be. We can't take any chances, they're like a dagger at my heart.'

'Trust me, it's all settled,' Acquilan replied.

'What about Cosmo and the diaries?' Kelp continued.

'Good news there too, Bernie saw his death certificate – he's dead, even been cremated.'

'Dead?' Kelp stopped walking and turned to face Acquilan. 'How? Where?'

'Switzerland – cancer.' Acquilan turned to Weitz, who had joined them. 'That's right, isn't it, Bernie?'

'Sure, cancer,' Weitz shrugged.

'Are you sure? It's real, no games from him?' Kelp stared at Weitz.

'I saw the certificate, Ewan. What more can I say?'

'After all these years he's gone,' Kelp began. 'The one man who could destroy us all – the moment he starts his move, he dies.'

'Well, I guess we left it too late for him, for once his planning wasn't so good,' Acquilan muttered.

'Yeah, maybe,' Kelp spoke slowly. 'It all seems too easy though. I don't trust him. What about the diaries, Bernie?'

'Well,' Weitz began, 'We don't think he ever had them, it was all bluff. Either way, there's nothing he can do now.'

'You think they really were destroyed in the warehouse fire after all?' Kelp looked quizzically at Weitz.

'I guess so,' Weitz replied.

'Don't worry,' Acquilan cut in, 'we're still working on that, we've got that covered.'

'I hope you're right, Victor, but you know, I've still got a funny feeling about this – it looks too easy.' Kelp shook his head. 'Well, I guess I'll just have to leave that to you. There's enough of a problem on the campaign.' Kelp smiled briefly at them both and walked to his car, where Mason was waiting for him. Before he entered the car, he looked back towards Acquilan, 'I don't know – I've just got a bad feeling about Cosmo – it's too good to be true.'

Acquilan and Weitz walked to another car. 'He's calm enough now, Bernie,' Acquilan said, as the car pulled away, 'but he's right, it all looks too perfect.'

'Well, we've still got to find the English guy, he's just disappeared, Victor,' Weitz said slowly, his mouth tight. 'To top it all, the Italian lawyer's dead.'

Acquilan turned to Weitz in surprise, 'One of our . . .?'

'No! Nothing to do with us. It's like that English guy's partner, I have no idea who did it, or why.'

'Get this, Bernie,' Acquilan's voice had fallen to almost a whisper so that Weitz had to bend forward to hear. 'One of those pictures, the one you said was late, well, it's been patched up. I noticed when I was cleaning it up.'

'Must have been Cosmo.'

'Perhaps, but I don't think so – he'd never have touched those pictures, they were his bait,' Acquilan answered.

'Grande?'

'Could be. If it was, he knows more than we thought.'

'That's something I never understood, Victor. Why didn't Cosmo just wipe them clean and sell them? All that money, all those years.'

'You've got to understand, Bernie, Cosmo and me we

were both out of the same bottom drawer. Same neighbourhood – we both wanted the same things. Never seen real painted pictures as kids, just concrete and iron. We both wanted out – but we wanted out with class.' He looked at Weitz. 'You, you're different – New Jersey, Jewish, at least you got some education. You had some expectations, not us. With Cosmo and me it had to be the hard way.' He paused again and gazed out of the window, 'You know the difference between the really rich and those who are just comfortable, Bernie? I'll tell you, the really rich collect – they collect pictures, statues, Chinese vases, stamps, houses, even women – everything has a price, it's all about possessing that beauty.'

'I don't understand. Surely Cosmo would have cleaned them up on that basis? It would have added to his collection . . .'

'No,' Acquilan shook his head. 'What you've got to understand is that there was one thing Cosmo wanted to collect more than anything else in the world – it was me and Kelp. Not even you – after what happened, he only ever wanted to get back at us and he knew that those six pictures were the key. Of all the things we found, he knew I wanted them, they were mine. He hated me enough to keep them, to constantly remind himself and me, that one day . . .' He sighed. 'He knew I would have no peace of mind until I got them back. That's why I know, dead or not, he planned all of this – he wants us.'

'The diaries?'

'God knows. We don't even know if they exist. But if they do and they're what Ewan remembers writing, then they'll connect us to the pictures, and it'll all be over.' The car pulled up at the hotel and Acquilan leaned forward to get out. 'Dead or alive . . .' he hissed, 'Cosmo's hand is in this. For some reason, the whole thing hangs on this English guy. Get him and get him soon. And put Pichowski with Ewan, I don't like that idiot Donald – I don't trust him. Tell Pichowski to watch him for a couple of weeks.'

Weitz nodded as Acquilan left the car.

Laura walked into her office as the telephone buzzed. She was pleased with herself because she'd just won her first battle over the schedules, holding onto her extra news coverage despite the sports department's drive to get an extra half-hour for basketball.

'Yes.'

'It's Pat Danvers,' her secretary said, 'calling from Rome.'

'Put him through.' There was a click.

'Laura, you there?'

'Sure, Pat, how's things?'

'Fine, sorry to take so long, this guy Grande's been a busy boy.' Laura reached for a pencil. 'It's been quite difficult to extract information from the British police. They wouldn't confirm anything about him. I got a bit more from the gallery though – you were right, it is his, at least he owns half. Well, I guess that it's all of his now, his partner is the one that was murdered. The receptionist hasn't seen Grande for quite some while and the place is being run by an Irish guy. Weird guy, when I asked where Grande was, he told me to piss off – I'm sure they sell a lot of pictures real fast there now!'

'Nothing at all from the police?'

'Zip! No one has ever been charged although the local press are taking a real interest.'

'Anything else?'

'Yes, I discovered he has an uncle in Italy, Positano to be precise. I called him, nice old guy – didn't say much, sounds as though he is protecting him. You might find it of interest that, when I called and asked to speak to the uncle, I think it must have been the maid who answered. She said that Grande had not been there for over a month. I didn't get any more out of her, though.'

153

'Thanks, it might be useful.'

'Laura, you still there?'

'Yes, sorry, I was thinking.'

'That's about it. I'll keep digging if you want.'

'Thanks, you've done a lot already.'

'Look, Laura,' Pat Danvers suddenly sounded hesitant, 'take it easy. Sal told me about the strange guy in the old coat.'

'Don't worry, I'll be OK.'

'You know what I mean, Laura, whatever this is about it's no picnic. You're not getting me to do this because there's a story in it, it's something else.'

'No, there is nothing to worry about,' she said firmly. They said their farewells.

Laura sat back. Pat Danvers had always been reliable. He never fussed, just spoke plainly. Perhaps he was right, she thought, Grande might be dangerous. Then she remembered the man sitting in her office, the man who looked so lost, harassed, bewildered – she had felt he was not a dangerous man. She began to waver but recognised that Pat had a point.

'Laura, Walter Harvey wants you in his office – he seems pretty steamed up.' Sally's voice broke in on her thoughts.

It was 7 p.m. before Laura returned. For the last few hours she had been engaged in a furious debate about schedules as a result of her dismissal of the proposals put forward by Jack Krammer, the Head of Sport, at the previous meeting. She eventually won her point but not before clearly exasperating Krammer, who did not like being crossed.

She told her secretary to go home, kicked off her shoes and put her feet on her desk. From where she sat, she could see the tops of the Manhattan skyscrapers casting their usual patchwork quilt of cold bright light. Up in these air-conditioned towers, away from the noise on the streets, it looked almost romantic.

All her life she had worked hard to stay of it but not in it, to remain aloof from the affairs of the rollercoaster city. Cautious, cool and determined, she had kept everything at arms' length and, if not always in control, she made sure she was the observer rather than the engaged. Then Grande appeared in his coat with his unshaven face. The way he arrived was pure New York hustle and yet it contrasted so much with his lack of self-assurance. Most of the men that Laura came across either during her work or social life seemed so certain of themselves, so confident. She unclipped her hair and shook it loose and began to think that Pat Danvers might be right – perhaps John Grande was dangerous. As Pat said, things happened around him. But why did he approach her the way he did? It made no sense to involve her – what did he want?

She walked slowly over to the window and leaned her forehead against the glass – it was cool to the touch. Below her, the city grew more and more opaque as her breath misted up the glass. Down there, she thought, was Grande. Perhaps there was nothing for it but to stop it all here, to take no further part in this. Laura stepped back. Her breath had formed a rough pattern on the glass and absent-mindedly, she slowly traced a large V through the pattern with her finger. Then she turned back to her desk and reached in the drawer for her car keys. As she pulled them out, a piece of paper fluttered to the ground. She bent down to pick it up and was about to throw it away when she saw a telephone number scrawled on it, and an address – it was John Grande's details. She hesitated, then sitting down at her desk, she pulled the telephone towards her and dialled the number.

'Yes!' The echoing voice that answered was flat and aggressive.

Laura hesitated again, the name on the scrap of paper said Johnson; she remembered that he had told her he was using that name. 'Is Mr Johnson still there?'

'Maybe – who wants him?' the man snarled.

'Well, if he is, I would like to speak to him.' There was no answer and then she heard a man's voice shout, 'Johnson!' There was a few seconds' gap before, 'Johnson!' rang out again. Another longer pause and then slow breathing on the end of the line.

'No answer, lady.'

'Well, if he is out, I'd like to leave a message.'

'I don't take messages – like I said, no answer.'

'So is he in or out?'

'Look, I ain't no message boy!' The line went dead.

Half an hour later a cab pulled up outside a grey building with a large flight of steps leading up to a heavy door.

'You sure you want this address?' The cab driver looked back over his shoulder.

'Thanks,' Laura pushed the money through the grill behind the driver's head. 'Will you wait?' She followed the first payment with a $50 bill.

'How long?'

'Ten, maybe fifteen minutes.'

The driver nodded. 'I'll drive around.'

Looking carefully left and right, Laura walked up the steps. At the top was a large double door and to the right an entry-phone system. She looked down the buttons until she counted to number three and pressed it. While she waited she checked the street nervously. Apart from a few cars passing by, the street was quiet; half the lamps were broken and the few that were left cast weak light around them: everywhere else was dark. As she became aware of the sound of feet coming along the sidewalk towards her, she pressed the button again. Still no response. Trying to control her sense of unease, she pressed the bottom button marked 'super'.

'Who is it?' The speaker entryphone crackled into life.

'I'm here to see Mr Johnson.'

'So press *his* button!' he replied.

'Wait! There's no answer – I spoke to you earlier. Please let me in – I want to leave a message for him.' There was a pause and then the door buzzed and clicked open.

Laura stepped inside and quickly shut the door behind her. She leant back against it, breathing hard. There was one light bulb burning behind a set of stairs in front of her; the bleak shadows hid most of the dirt but there was a stale, airless smell. Almost immediately, the door on her left opened and a large bar of light fanned out into the open hallway. A tall heavy-set man stepped out. The light was behind him and his face was lost in the gloom. As he came forward, she could smell the rancid mix of old sweat and alcohol.

'It's the last one on the right, down the corridor.' She pulled her coat tighter – she suddenly felt very cold.

Before she knew it she was at his door. She knocked sharply, waited and then knocked again. Still no answer. She listened – nothing. She half turned to go but as she did so, she laid her hand on the door handle and pressed lightly; to her surprise it opened. She pushed the door open and walked a couple of paces into the room. There was a very strong smell of whisky. She screwed up her face. How low can you sink? she thought – he's a drunk.

'Mr Grande?' She reached to her right and fumbled for a light switch. At a touch of the switch, the single bulb hanging in the centre of the room cast a harsh light that dazzled her.

In the centre of the room was a chipped Formica table with a couple of chairs, to the right a television set. She noticed over to her left, in the corner, a bed and as her eyes became more accustomed to the light, she could see that what she had first thought was a pile of blankets was a man in an overcoat – Grande. She screwed up her face in disgust. 'God, he really is a bum!'

She walked over to the bed where the whisky smell was strongest. John stirred slightly and turned his head. As he did so, she noticed a bloodstain spreading out from behind one side of his head on the pillow. Frightened by the blood, she stepped back and her heel crunched down on some broken glass. Under the table glass from a broken whisky bottle was scattered across the floor; she kicked at it and then looked back at John, bending down to inspect the matted hair and the swelling the size of an egg on the left side of his face.

His eyes opened slightly.

'Who did this?' she exclaimed.

He shook his head awkwardly, clearly in great pain. 'I don't know . . .', his voice faded away.

'I've got to get you to a hospital,' she whispered.

'No police,' he managed, 'please.' His breathing was heavy and he closed his eyes.

Laura knew she should call an ambulance but that would involve the police. She hesitated – an inner voice screamed call the ambulance and be done with it but something held her back. Then she realised he'd not been drinking, that he'd been attacked.

'Don't worry,' she found herself reassuring him, 'no police, I promise you.' She reached into her pocket and pulled out her mobile phone. It had occurred to her that there was another way.

President Carson pressed the button on the remote control and switched the TV set off. He puffed slowly on a Havana cigar. Inside the room with him were Dan Petrone, his campaign manager, and the resident pollster, Seth Gold.

They were sitting in the presidential suite of the Sheraton in Des Moines, Iowa. In the room outside, secret service agents mingled with campaign and White House staff.

They were three days into a four-day tour of the Midwest culminating in a stopover in Des Moines, with a speech to come in the evening and another day 'pressing the flesh' around Iowa. The President should have looked tired but instead he glowed, enjoying every minute. He was, as his staff had come to know, a campaign animal. He thrived on an endless round of speeches, meetings and media interviews. In a sense, he had never stopped campaigning throughout his first term. He liked nothing better than to be out in the crowds, grinning broadly and getting close to them. He knew the cameras picked up his enthusiasm and the American public saw it each night on the news, coast to coast.

The unexpected challenge of Senator Kelp had, however, disturbed his usual confidence. The Carson team had been galvanised into action by the President. At first, they'd tried to dismiss the Kelp campaign as cheap opportunism but that had failed to stop his advance. Then they tried to manipulate the caucus in Iowa to get a false poll reading ahead of the vote and mislead the pollsters. That hadn't worked – the media had been expecting it. Finally, President Carson took a hand and started campaigning earlier than planned.

Petrone and the campaign team were excited – it appeared the President had done it again. Kelp's rise had slowed and he was now four points behind. They hoped the worst was over and Kelp's challenge would fade. His gamble to get ahead and use Iowa as a springboard to the more important Massachusetts primary seemed to have failed.

Carson had caught this enthusiasm and, as he sat back in his chair reading through his speech, he felt comfortable. He glanced at the screen: the main evening news was about to begin.

'Dan, what's keeping Frank?' Carson muttered as Johnson left the room.

'Should be here any time now.'

The door opened and Frank Parry walked in. 'Mr President, have you got a minute?'

'Say, Dan, give me a few minutes,' Carson began as he levered himself out of his seat. 'And Dan, this looks fine for tonight,' he said, passing the draft of his speech across to

Petrone. 'I've made corrections so let's run through it again before I speak.' He put an arm around Petrone's shoulder and guided him to the door. 'You're doing great, Dan. Great.'

'The news isn't good,' Parry began as Carson shut the door. 'The land deal?'

'Yeah. Haskins' partner – I hear he's said he'd swear under oath that you tipped her off about the sale of the land and they were able to get an early offer in as a result.'

'So? He's been saying that for a while . . .' Carson flopped down and puffed slowly at his cigar. In the background, the television news began.

'No, this is different!' Parry sat down opposite him, 'This could mean real trouble.'

'What do you mean?' Carson sat bolt upright, 'You said we were OK.'

'I know, but it's changed. The guy's got a note. He says it shows Haskins knew about the sale before the official announcement by your office.'

'So?'

'Well, that plus the sister's statement that you were having an affair.'

'But she's been saying that for weeks!' Carson snorted.

'Put them together and you have a problem. They can't prove anything but some of our side have wobbled, even said they'll abstain.'

'What!' Carson stubbed his cigar out, 'What a weak bunch of fools!'

'Sure, sure, but that'll be enough to reopen the enquiry.'

Carson walked to the window and stared out. In the background he could hear the TV news. With perfect timing it moved to Kelp's tour of Massachusetts: 'Keep it clean with Kelp!' His supporters cheered. Carson shook his head slowly.

As if reading the President's mind, Parry glanced from the screen to the President.

'This'll really help that son-of-a-bitch,' Parry muttered.

'So what can we do, Frank?' Carson asked, lighting up another cigar.

'Try and make the enquiry look like a witch hunt and make sure it doesn't come up with anything,' Parry continued quickly, 'The note doesn't prove anything and the sister has no proof – it's their word against yours. I can't find any financial links back to you but we've still drawn a blank on the girl.' Parry watched as Carson slumped into the chair in front of him.

'It's not enough, is it?'

'No, unless Kelp can be got at. He'll use this and it'll hurt you.'

'Has Dan got anyone good on Kelp? Has he come up with anything?'

'Not yet, but he's working on it. So far the guy seems clean – war hero, good on charities, successful businessman . . .' replied Parry.

'I know, I know,' Carson sighed. 'We've gotta rip the guts outta this guy – go deeper, get something, *anything.*'

Parry knew exactly what the President meant. If they couldn't stop the enquiry, they had to stop Kelp. If Carson was unchallenged then the Democrats would hold together, but if Kelp was still there by the Convention, they'd break apart. He knew that while the polls still gave Carson good approval ratings for the economy, they were already showing that the stories about the land deal were eating away at the trust factor.

'What's the worst that could happen?' Carson's question broke in on his thoughts.

'That Kelp runs you all the way to the Convention.'

'Could I survive that, Frank?' Carson asked, stubbing out his cigar.

'Hard to say. If it was just you, my money would be on your survival against the Republicans.'

'Against Kelp?' Carson asked.

'Depends on the timing. If it runs on and he's doing well – well, you never know . . .' Parry said, his voice trailing away. 'This is high stakes . . .'

'Sure it is. Our survival. Nothing higher than that. Hell! We've done it before, Frank. You know what it takes.'

Parry knew exactly what he meant. 'I guess we'd better access a few files,' he muttered. 'We'll need the NSA.'

'Good, now we're on the same wavelength.' Carson rubbed his eyes, 'Get Pete onto it.'

Pete was Pete Neal, his national security adviser, who would have access to some of the most sensitive information. They both knew that asking him to do that was against the rules and a large escalation.

'I'll call him tonight,' Parry said firmly.

'Just the four of us should know – no one else,' Carson said slowly, carefully.

Parry nodded.

'Sure, just the four of us.'

10

Discovery

Ewan Kelp stood on the platform of the conference hall in Manchester, New Hampshire, slowly acknowledging the cheers and applause from the crowd of supporters. While his wife walked to the platform, he waved to them. Slipping his arm around her waist, he smiled at her, kissed her and they both waved – then a chant began to sweep the hall.

'America, America, you need help – bye, bye, Carson – send for Kelp! Carson, Carson, time you went – we want Kelp for President!'

The cameras panned around the crowd as the chant faded away. It was followed by a great cheer. Kelp gave a final wave, grinning at his wife, and then walked off to the back of the stage with her.

'Great, well done!' Kelp shouted in Dick Mason's ear as they walked off the platform. Then he turned and glanced back at the curtain separating him from the hall. 'Listen to that!' He patted Mason on the shoulder and followed him down the steps to the back of the hall. Mason stopped before the exit.

'I'll see you back in Washington next Saturday,' he said to his wife; there was a perfunctory kiss from her and she was gone.

163

'Remember, Ewan,' Mason whispered in his ear, 'straight down to the car and then away.' Mason's voice was insistent. Kelp nodded, still smiling. 'Say nothing, keep it for *Meet the Press*.'

He emerged, stopping briefly to wave to the small crowd gathered outside, a smile for the cameras and then they were in the car and away.

'It gets better all the time, Ewan,' Mason was smiling as he sat back in his seat.

Kelp nodded, 'What time is the programme?'

'Nine-thirty, two and a half hours from now.'

'What else?'

'Jim wants to see you before, let's say 8.30. He wants to go over the list of those who will be in the audience.'

Kelp nodded, 'They're all local reporters and editors tonight, aren't they?'

'Well, yes and no,' Mason glanced nervously at Kelp. 'That's how it started out,' he continued, 'however, some of the big boys asked to be there and ABS wanted to clip it to their *Marriott* programme tonight.'

Kelp's brow furrowed, 'It was meant to be the local papers not the nationals or TV! Why the change?'

'Jim felt it wouldn't hurt to have some nationals there too.'

'Why didn't Jim ask me? I *am* the candidate!' Kelp calmed down slightly. 'I just wish he'd told me. Not Douglas or the *Post*?'

'Well, Douglas is . . .'

'No, dammit! He'd better not be there – no way!'

'Come on, Ewan! Jim Donald's trying to keep the Press on our side, and Douglas and the other columnists – well, they have a lot of pull. Besides Douglas wrote that piece on Carson. Look, Jim's your head of communications . . .'

'Donald! Whose side is he on? And you, no wonder you didn't tell me before. Douglas and his paper are poison! Since

I declared, they've hardly had a good word to say about me – it's nearly always pro-Carson.'

'We're running only three points behind in Iowa, the same in New Hampshire – and closing – and it's looking good elsewhere.' He paused to emphasise the point. 'We all agreed you wanted a good show in Iowa, and that's what you're going to get, Douglas or no Douglas. If we block him, it'll be bad news for us – everything's working, Ewan.'

Kelp fell silent, deep in thought. Though he'd always wanted to be President, up till now he'd been reluctant to run, endlessly resisting the urgings of Acquilan. Fearful and cautious, Kelp felt his past was like a gun pressed to his temple. Even fifty years later, it was still there, nudging him daily. Cosmo, he was constantly reminded, seemed to be able to reach into his innermost thoughts at unguarded moments or shadow him in his dreams. But now, after all these years, for the first time Kelp knew he should feel a lifting of the burden, an end to his worries. After all, he kept reminding himself, Acquilan had told him Cosmo was dead. As so often before, Acquilan, the great gambler, appeared to have got it right. His plan to draw Cosmo into the open had worked and now Kelp knew he should have peace of mind. If Acquilan was right, Kelp thought, then destiny had played a hand – the sordid past would be banished for ever to be replaced by a future that hinged on the present alone. Perhaps, he mused, Acquilan was right: this time no false starts. The time for caution was over – all he had to do was reach out and fulfil his ambition.

Mason watched Kelp nervously. Then Kelp turned and surprised him by smiling.

'OK, maybe you're right, maybe you're right after all, Dick.'

Across New York, Bernie Weitz sat in his office halfway up the Empire State Building, the telephone clamped to his right ear. Smiling faintly, he put the receiver down, picked up a pen and wrote quickly in the margins of a sheet of paper in front of him.

Then he sat back in his seat; again, a thin-lipped half-smile. With one gesture, he swept up some papers, pushed them into a folder, tucked it under his arm and walked out of his office to the elevator.

'Go right in, he's expecting you.' Acquilan's secretary hardly looked at Weitz as he approached.

Weitz tapped on the door, walked in and shut it behind him. Sol Levinson was sitting at the long conference table to his left, papers spread across the table, and in front of him was Acquilan. Levinson was looking down at the printouts, his finger running up and down the columns, jabbing at them as he spoke.

Acquilan looked up, 'Bernie, come over here.' He pointed to the seat beside him. 'So what you're saying, Sol, is that you've now got it back on target?'

'No, Victor, for the moment it's looking positive, but . . .'

'No, Sol, you're doing yourself no favours. Compared to this time last week, it's much better.'

'Not good though, Victor,' Levinson said leaning back. 'I'm still putting the figures together but although we've stabilised it for the moment at this rate we could still lose the investment.'

'And we can't get out of it?'

'No. We're locked in for another year. All those rumours about our liquidity were what started it. They all rushed to take their money out. I'd love to know who was behind it.'

'Sure,' replied Acquilan, 'you and me both.'

'I'll have those figures complete by tomorrow,' Levinson said as he gathered the papers together. 'If you'll excuse me, Victor . . .' he said as he stood up, 'I'm expecting a call.' And with that he left the office.

'Bernie,' Acquilan sighed as he turned to Weitz, 'we've got big problems with the Seattle investment.'

'How big, Victor?' Weitz asked. He knew Acquilan had put $50 million into the development. There had been difficulties over planning with City Hall but nothing unusual. The potential profits were enormous. He also knew that Acquilan had expected cash-flow problems early on in the project and had had to take in another major investor, a finance company based in Liechtenstein, which held a 20 per cent stake.

'Remember that operation in Liechtenstein?' Acquilan continued.

'Sure.'

'They pulled out two days ago and are talking about legal action.'

'Why?'

'Said the thing was a disaster – badly run and lacking the correct finance. What's worse, they threatened to make public some payment to City Hall, which they know was way above the share price, unless we bought them out.'

'So you did?'

'I had to. No time – if we got into a fight with City Hall, the project would collapse and so I paid up. Now everything is on the line.' Acquilan lit his cigar. 'Thing is, the project's OK. But it couldn't have happened at a worse time. It was the money I was putting aside for Ewan's campaign – *his* money. Now we've got no more money for the campaign.'

'We'd better keep this from Ewan.'

'That's for sure.' Acquilan stared at his cigar. 'You know, there's worse than that, Bernie. The worst is, we've been set up.'

'How?'

'That Liechtenstein company.'

'It's just an investment vehicle.'

'No, it's Cosmo.'

'I don't understand. You said to Sol you didn't know who it was.'

'That was to Sol,' Acquilan cut in. 'No, Cosmo has watched every move we've taken since the war. Waited for his opportunity. This deal offered him the perfect moment to increase the pressure. Everyone knew we were planning to fund most of the campaign from our own money, so the opportunity arose to put the squeeze on and he moved in.'

'How do you know it was him? Aren't you getting . . .'

'Paranoid?' Acquilan smiled. 'No, too much points to him. There was no reason to pull out of the deal, it was looking good.' Acquilan snorted. 'He even rubbed it in.'

'How?'

'Look at this,' Acquilan held out a piece of paper and pointed to two typed words – 'Consolidated Monopolies'.

'That's the company name,' Weitz said calmly. 'So?'

'Look again at the name – I've only just realised.'

Weitz shook his head and frowned.

'C-O-S-M-O,' Acquilan spelt out. 'You see, he's been ahead of us all the way.'

Weitz leaned forward. 'I don't know, Victor . . . It would be pretty incredible planning. . . I don't know.'

'That, Bernie, is what we're up against. Just don't tell Ewan – he might panic.'

'You're right, seems we've really underestimated Cosmo.' He shook his head, 'What's clear now is that the whole thing, *everything*, has been planned.'

'Even Grande?'

'I mean *everything*, Bernie,' Acquilan took a deep breath and let it out slowly before continuing, 'Is Pichowski still with Ewan?'

'He's been with him for two weeks but there's not much to report. He says Donald is too sweet on most of the Press, but nothing else.'

Acquilan wasn't really listening. The near disaster in Seattle had brought it home to him that they were back in a 50-year-old fight. While he couldn't be sure that Cosmo was dead, he felt certain that he was behind it. What he couldn't understand was why he hadn't used the information he had. The diaries . . . the diaries – what about the diaries?

'Victor?' Weitz spoke softly, 'Victor, about the campaign . . .'

'Campaign?' Acquilan nodded. 'Sure . . . look, Bernie, if Cosmo had the diaries, he would have used them before now, right?'

'I guess so, or why keep them?'

'Precisely. But he hasn't.'

'Anyway,' Weitz said, 'I always figured it would be his word against ours – and we'd say they were forgeries and blame the death of Morrow in the fire on him.'

'But how does this guy Grande fit in?'

'I don't know but it must be Cosmo who set him up – we have to find him first!'

'Sure, if we . . .'

'No ifs, Bernie,' Acquilan stopped pacing. 'Without him we're in the dark.'

'What worries me, Victor, is that I still haven't a clue how much Grande really knows.'

'There was the picture that was tampered with, remember?'

'Sure, but Grande probably thought it was just an art fraud.'

'Maybe, but why would he patch it up again? No, I got a bad feeling about him.' Acquilan looked down at his hands. 'Makes you wonder what else Cosmo planned.'

'Grande's going to have to surface soon,' Weitz said. 'I've got people out everywhere. If he's in New York, Victor, it's only a matter of time.'

'But that's what we don't have, Bernie. We don't have time!' Acquilan replied tersely.

'Hold it, Victor – just think, what if this has been a bluff from start to finish and Cosmo never had any diaries? What if they went up in the fire, as we first thought? What if there's not enough in them? How dangerous is this British guy, Victor?'

'Go on.'

'Well,' Weitz continued, choosing his words carefully, 'if there are no diaries, Victor, surely then there is nothing on any of us and you're right about him needing more time. Because as long as we believe the diaries exist and are held by Cosmo, we chase around after them and we start to make mistakes.'

'Even if you are right, we've got to find Grande.' Acquilan turned his cigar around in his hand.

'Don't you see, Victor? Chasing after Grande means we're setting a trail, which also leads back to us. That's what worries me.'

'We don't have a choice,' Acquilan replied sharply.

'But Cosmo's dead, Victor.'

'Maybe, who knows?'

'But I saw the certificate in Rome . . .'

'Sure, but did you ever see the body?'

'No, but . . .'

Acquilan waved his hand dismissively at Weitz. 'You have a point about the trail we're leaving – sure, perhaps we're being strung along.'

'It could be that all of this was set in motion before Cosmo died,' Weitz replied. 'That it's over now.'

'Maybe, maybe – who knows? I've reached the stage where I don't believe anything any more. We're going to have to keep this tightly under control, Bernie, but I'm also concerned about Ewan. He's got to keep his act together. We didn't spend all this damn money just to see our hopes collapse.' Acquilan turned and looked at Weitz. 'That's why Ewan mustn't know any more, Bernie. No more talk of the diaries or Cosmo.'

'But what if . . .?'

'No ifs, we'll figure it out.'

'And Grande?'

'As far as Ewan's concerned, he's gone, never knew anything anyway, there was no problem.' He leaned forward, his hands on the table. 'We've got to build his confidence right up, Bernie. This is my – I mean, our – last shot.'

Later, alone in his office, Acquilan thought back over the last few months. He had always feared that Kelp's run for the Presidency was what Cosmo had been waiting for. It was the big gamble, a game of poker. Despite his hatred of Cosmo, Acquilan couldn't help but admire the way he'd waited, certain that Kelp would eventually run. Nothing was left to chance, from London to Seattle, everything planned in detail. Acquilan knew that Cosmo's death – if it were real – wouldn't stop him. He knew Cosmo wanted everything or nothing, either Kelp was going to claim the prize or go down, destroying everything they had built up.

Despite the high stakes, Acquilan was calm; he felt no fear, just that extra edge, the heightened sense of anticipation. They could only carry on and wait for Cosmo's next move. Acquilan knew that this was always the real ambition – all the business, the money, was for one reason: to put Kelp in the White House. And Cosmo had known it too.

'I nearly forgot,' Gene Meyer said, as he pushed some notes over to Jack Douglas. 'Jack, we've drawn a blank on Acquilan and Kelp 1947 to 1948.' Meyer shrugged. 'In short, they're clean.'

Meyer watched Douglas as he read the notes. 'What is it, Jack? What are you looking for? 'Cos it sure as hell ain't there.'

'I was hoping for more, perhaps too much.'

'They followed every lead you gave them – nothing,' Meyer continued. 'I could've guessed as much . . .'

'What about those stories about the Mafia and other organised crime?'

'Just rumour, Jack. You know I can't print that – it's not substantiated.'

'The trouble is, there is nothing here about the war record – 1944 to 1946.'

'Hold on, Jack! Kelp's got an exemplary record – Purple Heart, Congressional Medal of Honor . . . You know well enough he's bomb-proof there – there's no point. He even volunteered when he was fifteen, saw action when he was sixteen – Acquilan almost the same.'

Douglas nodded. 'Can I keep this?' he asked.

'Sure, sure, go ahead – take it,' Meyer said. 'It's only going into the bin if you don't.'

'Something's not right, I can't put my finger on it but . . .'

Meyer watched his mentor as he walked towards the door. He looked tired.

Jack, I hope old Schwartz isn't winding you up. You know I put some good guys on this and they drew zip. Don't you think it's time to let it drop? There doesn't seem to be much there.'

Jack smiled faintly as he shook his head. 'Don't worry, I'm on the Republicans next week, just before the primary, and President Carson after that. Perhaps I'll put this down to experience. Thanks.' He half-waved and left the office.

Outside he stopped, scrutinised the notes in his hand again and then, with one movement, folded them and ramming them into his side pocket, walked towards the elevator. Minutes later, Jack was sitting in the basement surrounded by books and papers, a plastic cup of lukewarm coffee in one hand. Across the table was an animated Joe Schwartz.

'I could have told Mr Meyer all that, Mr Douglas. High-price, fancy effort, but not worth a darn thing! They didn't check his war record.'

'I know, I said as much.'

'Yes, but I did.' Schwartz reached into his top drawer and produced a large box file. He smiled broadly as he opened it up. 'Look at this.' He handed two sheets of paper to Douglas.

They were two photocopied pages from an article just after the war. 'GIs GO BACK,' was the headline. Jack started to read the first paragraph:

'Less than one year after the war is over, a group of veterans are returning to the scenes of their battles.'

'What's this got to do with it, Joe?' Jack was puzzled.

'Turn to the other page, Mr Douglas, read the names.'

Jack turned the page over; there were a list of names, some fifteen or so. His eyes stopped near the top – ex-sergeant Victor Acquilan. He read on. At first he couldn't see it, then after a second glance, he saw what he was looking for – Lieutenant E J Kelp. He looked at Joe and smiled. 'Very interesting, Joe, but I'm not sure what you're getting at with this battlefield tour list.'

'The question I want to know is, why the hurry, why go back so soon?' Schwartz asked. 'Most of us couldn't wait to get the hell out of it. Look at the date – under a year after the end of the war. It just don't feel right.'

'Joe, we need more to go on than this, hunches and gut feelings. I can't run with this.'

'I know, I know. It is only a start, Mr Douglas, but you've got to agree that it's something.' He put the papers away reluctantly.

'Certainly, Joe,' Jack said, patting him on the arm. 'It's a start all right but we two old-timers had better come up with more than this, if we're going to get anywhere.'

John Grande gazed at the flat, featureless ceiling while a nurse fussed around him, finishing off the new dressing on the side of his head.

He tried to remember what had happened, without success. How his head ached, and the stitches behind his ear throbbed, every time he moved. The doctor had mentioned something about Laura Buckley, but he couldn't remember that part very well. He touched his brow . . . if only he could remember. His arm dropped back onto the bed. What puzzled him most of all was why Laura Buckley should have been involved. He remembered that he had already given up on her. Yet that doctor kept mentioning her name.

He closed his eyes and, as he did so, he could see himself, standing at the battered doorway in the cheap tenement, keys in hand. His door was open, he remembered. He'd pushed it and gone in. It was dark inside. Then he remembered feeling a sharp pain on the side of his head . . . a struggle, then another blow. He remembered pitching forward, with someone's hands on his shoulders. Somehow, in the confusion, he kept hearing the sound of breaking glass. There was the tang of whisky.

'Hello, may I come in?'

His reverie was broken by the sound of a woman's voice.

John opened his eyes and found himself facing Laura Buckley, framed in the doorway. She had a quizzical expression on her face.

'The beard,' she said, as he ran his hand across his chin, 'I didn't recognise you without the beard.'

It seemed to Laura that without the beard, John Grande's rather large and sad-looking eyes were even more dominant.

'How are you feeling?' she asked.

'As though I'd been out drinking for a week and fallen down a hundred stairs.' He smiled. 'I gather,' he said, hesitating, 'I have you to thank . . .'

She shook her head and waved her hand dismissively. 'It was nothing – anyone would have.'

'Not at the doss house where I was staying,' he said quickly. 'Anyway, thank you. And can I ask you a question?'

'Sure.'

'What were you doing there?'

'Trying to speak to you.'

'I don't understand . . . when I didn't hear from you, I assumed you'd decided not to take it any further. To be honest, I always knew it was a fairly long shot. My story must have sounded completely absurd, probably still does. No reason why you should want to get involved but I was desperate.'

'I only intended to tell you that there was nothing much I could do for you. Instead, you ended up here.'

'Seems a pretty good place to be,' he replied, 'in the circumstances. Oh yes, the doctor came in very early this morning to tell me that the injury was a result of a domestic accident. My memory is clearing and although I'm a little hazy, I know this is not . . .'

'No,' she interrupted. 'No, not a domestic accident.' She sat down on the chair next to his bed. 'I found you in your room, there had been a struggle – you were badly hurt.' Laura took in the clean room with its crisp furnishings. 'I called a friend of mine – the doctor you referred to – and he put you in here for the night.'

'You rang for an ambulance?'

'No, I didn't think it would be a good thing.'

'Why not?'

'You told me not to. And you were right, the police would have been informed. And so you're here in one of New York's most exclusive clinics, only 150 beds you know!' she laughed.

'But why didn't you call the police or an ambulance? Surely you didn't . . .'

'. . . trust you?' Laura cut in. 'I don't know myself – it's the most illogical thing I've ever done but I guess I decided to give you a chance.' Her eyes caught his while she spoke and he started to smile. 'I wouldn't smile too soon, we both may live to regret this decision. Now listen,' she said, her face hardening, 'I've arranged for you to stay at a friend's apartment for the next few days.'

'No,' he said, sitting up, 'I've involved you in this too much. Once I leave here perhaps I'd better sort myself out. You shouldn't become directly involved. All I need to know is whether the diaries exist.'

175

'You still don't understand,' she said shaking her head. 'Who do you think was responsible for all this?'

John shrugged.

'It was the super, he got your real name.' She walked towards the end of his bed.

'*My* name? Why would I be of interest?'

'Look, people like that guy feed off the strays like you. All he's interested in is what you're running from. God,' she said, smiling, 'you're not very streetwise, are you? You see, for you to take a place in his building, it's a fairly safe bet that you're hiding from something or someone. To a man like that guy, it means money. You must have come back before he'd finished going over your room.'

'I see. He couldn't have found out anything about me.'

'What makes you so sure?'

'I keep my passport and other papers on me.'

'There are other ways,' she said as she laid a hand on his suitcase. 'This was in the corner of your room, on top of a pile of clothes.'

'But it was empty . . .'

'OK, but what's this then?' She bent down and held up the name tag, which was hanging from one of the handles of the suitcase. He looked at it blankly. 'Perhaps now,' she said as she stood up, 'you'll understand why I had to move you . . .'

John was struck by how calm her voice was. She was right, he was lost in New York in every way. He sighed, then it dawned on him that he was lucky he wasn't dead already.

'After all,' she continued, 'you don't spend time as a journalist in this godforsaken city without learning a few things.'

As she finished, a tall, handsome man in his late thirties walked into the room.

'I'm not disturbing anything, am I, Laura?' He asked smoothly as he stopped by the end of the bed.

'No, certainly not,' she said as she smiled. 'John . . . Johnson meet Dr Ben Bergen, clinician and friend,' she said with a flourish.

'We have already met,' Dr Bergen said. 'I am pleased to tell you that you have a clean bill of health. Amazingly, no fracture – you must have a head made of rock. Just severe bruising, and the cuts, while ugly, should heal quickly, so I'm discharging you this afternoon.'

'Are you sure?' Laura asked.

'Quite. Well, perhaps I would normally keep him in for another day, but given his particular needs, I think you and he probably want to go as soon as possible. Laura, I wonder if I might have a word in private.'

'Johnson?' John mouthed at her.

She nodded gently before following the doctor out of the room and into an empty one nearby.

'Are you sure he's all right?' Laura began.

'Sure, he'll be fine. All he needs is a week's rest and he'll be OK.' He perched on the end of a bed. 'That's not the real problem, Laura, is it? What have you gotten yourself into? Why didn't you call an ambulance?'

'Because,' Laura looked away from him, 'the man is in trouble.'

'So call the police!'

'No, that would only make matters worse, at least right now.'

'Why? Do you know him well?'

'Yes and no . . .'

'Oh, come on, Laura! I've known you since we were kids! I've never seen this guy before – it's you I care about. When he came in yesterday he looked like a bum! I wasn't aware that you were involved with a low-life.'

'He's undercover . . .'

'Pah!' he exclaimed, 'we've known each other too long, Laura. I've stuck my neck out for you. You know this clinic doesn't take accident cases and I've registered him under a false name – if I'm discovered . . .' His voice trailed away.

'Look, Ben,' Laura began, squeezing his hand, 'I know what you've done for me is magnificent. I couldn't have managed without you. But I don't even know the full details myself and anyway, it is probably better if you don't know. It'll only make it more difficult for you in the end.'

'He must be pretty special,' Ben retorted bitterly.

'No,' she said shaking her head. 'No, I just feel kind of responsible. It's got something to do with my father.'

Dr Bergen shrugged his shoulders. 'Well,' he said as he walked to the door, 'he'll have to go in the next hour – we need the bed.' He kissed her on both cheeks, 'I hope you know what you're doing, Laura, I really do. I've got a bad feeling about this.' He put both hands on her shoulders. 'I hope it works out for you, Laura. God knows, you deserve it!'

'Don't say anything to the police, will you?'

He stared at her before nodding slowly in agreement.

11

The Puzzler

Jack Douglas fed the last page of his column into the fax. Then, pulling the pages together, he fastened them with a clip.

Tossing the papers onto his desk, he glanced up at the clock in the corner. It was just coming up to 6 p.m. He was about to leave his study when the telephone rang.

'Mr Douglas, it's Joe, Joe Schwartz.'

'Joe, how are you?'

'Fine,' Schwartz answered, breathlessly, 'I need to speak to you, though.'

'OK. How about tomorrow morning?'

'I guess, if you say so, Mr Douglas.' There was a pause, 'But if it was left to me, we'd meet right now.'

'Where are you, Joe?'

'At the *Post*, Mr Douglas.'

'Can't it wait until tomorrow?'

'Sure, sure it can but I was hoping . . .'

Douglas paused. It was unlike Joe to get excited or to ring him at home.

'I'm about to go out to dinner with my wife and some friends,' he hesitated. 'OK, look, I'll drop by on my way there. I can only spare a few minutes, though.'

'That's all you'll need,' Schwartz replied.

As usual, Douglas had little trouble explaining to his wife that he'd have to follow on after he had this meeting and join them later. She had been married too long to a newspaper man to complain. She just sighed heavily and fixed him with her sad blue eyes.

'Jack,' she said, 'all these years you've been doing this to me. Each time you behave as though it was the first time. Don't you think it's time you called it a day and retired properly like everybody else? I mean, Jack, you're not getting any younger. Surely, enough is enough?' She gave him one of those old-fashioned looks, the sort of look that she reserved for her grandchildren when they'd done something they shouldn't have.

An hour later Jack was sitting at Joe Schwartz's desk in the basement.

'It's all here,' Joe said, as he laid a paper out in front of him. 'Remember the last article I showed you – you know, the one with Kelp's name on it?'

Jack nodded.

'Well, look at this.' He pointed at the sheet under Jack's nose. Jack skimmed the headlines of the *Daily News*: VETERANS' TOUR ENDS IN TEARS.

He read on. The short article covered a disaster in Naples; the year was 1946. Two members on the tour that he'd read about previously seemed to have been killed in a fire in a warehouse. The rest had come back to New York, ending the tour early.

'Look down there, Mr Douglas.' Joe pointed to the bottom of the column. The two dead were named as ex-Corporals Morrow and Cosmo. Then there was a list of another ten people, all of whom arrived back in New York at the same time. Jack rubbed his forehead as he read the column and frowned.

'I don't get it, Joe. Sure, there was a disaster but so what?'

'Look again, Mr Douglas, only this time look at the unit that they came from, it's listed next to them.' Jack went over the list again. As he did so, he could see the two who died belonged to a different unit from those who had returned.

'Don't tell me the two who died were in the same unit as Acquilan and our friend Kelp?'

Joe nodded quickly. 'Look again, Mr Douglas, what else do you notice?' He smiled and Jack again read the list and still couldn't see anything new.

'It's in front of you, Mr Douglas – it's not what you see, it's what you don't see.'

'Ah!' Jack smiled. 'Of course, Kelp and Acquilan are not on the list of those returning.'

'Correct,' Joe paused, 'And there's one more thing . . .' He pulled the original article out of his box file and pointed to one of the names listed there. 'Look, Weitz, D B Weitz.' Joe reached into his box file for another sheaf of papers. They were rather grey photostats of old New York Port Authority documents, and he was running through them too quickly for Jack to take proper account of what was there.

'These documents, Mr Douglas, they also tell us something else.' Joe stopped flicking through them and sat back. 'They confirm there were two bodies brought back, and the names.'

There, at the top, was a note that the bodies were those of Morrow and Cosmo. Jack remained puzzled.

'There's more too.' Joe pulled another sheet of paper out. 'Remember the *Daily News* story about the Congressional Medal of Honor and Purple Heart awarded to Kelp? You remember last time I said something about there being another story with a picture? Well, here it is.' He handed it over.

It was a short piece, but the most significant thing was the picture at the top. There were five of them standing against a backdrop which must have been Naples harbour. In the centre was a very young-looking Kelp, on his left, Private

First Class Weitz, on his right Sergeant Acquilan, and to the Sergeant's right, the two corporals, Morrow and Cosmo. The article was headed, THE BOYS WHO CAME BACK ALIVE.

'This story just confirms what we knew before, Mr Douglas. Kelp and the others got medals for getting back into Allied lines after they'd crashed in a Dakota behind German lines in Italy, north of Anzio, leaving them a long way from US lines. They arrived back in captured German trucks. Now look at the original article again. You see, all the same names. They all went back out together, after the war, and the only ones who came back were Morrow and Cosmo – in boxes.'

'Joe, you've got me,' Jack had a puzzled expression on his face. 'I don't know what this all adds up to. Slow down, I need more time.'

'You see, Mr Douglas, I knew there was something.'

'Now, let's see,' Jack continued, 'as you said, a battlefield tour much earlier than all the others. All five survivors in Kelp's platoon are there, somehow they get caught up in some warehouse fire and only three survive: none of them returned with the rest in the tour party to New York. Where did they go? That's the big question and when did they come back? We'll need to find that answer first.' He glanced down at his watch and then sat up with a jerk. 'Oh my God! This means trouble.'

'What is it, Mr Douglas?'

'I was due at dinner at eight,' Jack said ruefully, 'and I promised I'd be there, at the latest by nine, it's now nine-thirty.' He shook his head and his face crinkled into a smile, 'My poor wife! God, what she's had to put up with, Joe. Perhaps we should give this up – what do you say? After all, everyone will think it's just the wild imaginings of a couple of old men.'

'No, sir, not you. These people who call themselves journalists, they've got no real nose for the job. A good story has a real smell to it. That's what this is all about, Mr Douglas – a bit here, a bit there, hard work and a good nose.'

Jack stood up, handed the papers back to Schwartz and laughed. 'Perhaps, or perhaps it is just the last throw for two old-timers,' he said as he walked towards the door.

At nine o'clock the following morning, Jack Douglas walked into the editor of the *Post*'s office. There were three people in the room.

'Jack, look I'm busy for another ten . . .'

'I'm sorry, Gene, I need to see you right now. It's really important.'

'OK. Leave us, will you boys, I'll call you back.' He waited for them to leave before turning to Jack, 'This is unlike you, Jack, what have you got?'

Douglas told Meyer about his conversation with Joe Schwartz the night before. He showed him some photocopies and started to explain.

'There,' he began, 'you see, there is something to this.'

'Wait a minute, Jack, this is interesting but it won't prove anything.' He looked at the copies of the articles in his hand and tossed them down onto the desk. 'Sure, I agree, it's got a feel to it, but you know better than I do that it isn't enough – you must have something more, much more.'

'I know, no need to tell me.'

'Then what?'

'Well, there's a strange story here, Gene. It can't all be coincidence. My instinct tells me that if we dig a bit more we should come up with something else.'

Meyer watched Douglas carefully as he spoke. 'I hear you, Jack, but you didn't come here to tell me that. You'd have thrown me out of this office if I'd come to you with this and kicked my butt out of the building.' He smiled slowly, 'So tell me, Jack, what do you have in mind?'

'I need someone else working on it.'

'What for?'

'It needs much more work and I haven't got the time.' Douglas tapped the side of his nose gently. 'Gene, there's something here, I sense it.'

'Your instinct could be wrong, Jack.'

'Maybe, maybe.'

Meyer flopped back into his seat. Only a week before he remembered urging his mentor to drop the whole thing and concentrate on the other candidates. Typically, Douglas had then slammed in three brilliant pieces in almost as many days on everyone but Kelp. The fourth piece, which had arrived on his desk today, had been equally good, even if deeply cynical, pouring scorn on the whole lot.

'Hell, Jack! I didn't even know Schwartz was back on the payroll until you told me.' He shrugged, 'Go on. You'd better take him, saves me getting rid of him again.' He laughed softly, 'I don't believe this, an ex-editor and columnist, one of the most respected men in the business, teams up with a geriatric librarian – this place has gone mad. They'll be making a movie of this one day – I can see it now,' he snorted, 'Woodward and Bernstein on Golden Pond! It had better be good, Jack – it had better be good.' He shook his head as Douglas left his office.

Victor Acquilan pushed his breakfast plate away. He sipped the last of his coffee as he listened to his wife. She was talking about the fundraising dinner they'd given the night before in New Hampshire. Her slow Southern voice contrasted with her biting sarcasm and stiletto-sharp comments about all who attended the event – and one of the women at their table in particular. He watched her, his head resting gently on the back of his chair, his hands folded around the sides of his cup. Her sensuous beauty always held him. Her Madonna eyelids made her look as though she'd just woken up, particularly as they were framed by thick black hair falling across her shoulders; she was as captivating to him in the morning as last thing at night. Thirty years younger than him, she was for Acquilan, at one and the same time, a fine work of art and an exacting companion who stimulated all his senses. He laughed gently and she smiled.

'You're right, Victor – you've got to laugh at her and her absurd dress sense,' she continued. 'It's the only thing to do.' She looked down at her watch. 'Now, when are we going to New York?'

'Ten-thirty. We'll take the helicopter to the heliport and a car will be waiting for us there.'

'I'd better pack,' she said, standing up. She moved like a panther, never hurried, languid. His eyes were glued to her every move. She walked over and kissed him, her lips clinging to his as her perfume filled his senses – and he closed his eyes. 'I guess we don't want to be late,' she said, slowly stepping back, 'that is unless you've got other ideas . . .' She smiled to herself and before he could answer, she ruffled his hair and walked away, aware of the effect each movement was having on him.

Acquilan stared after her, mesmerised, considering her last words. Then as she disappeared out of the room, he stood up and forced himself to head off in the opposite direction.

As he walked down the corridor, leading away from the dining room, he smiled. Here in his mock-Georgian mansion set in 200 acres of parkland in Easthampton, he was able to dedicate himself to his great passion: art.

Acquilan walked to the rear of the house, through a door covered in green baize and down a dark set of stairs to an almost identical corridor below. He took the first set of doors to his right and, switching on a light, walked into a square room full of crates and boxes. Beside the bookcase, at the rear of the room, he stopped to stroke the protruding marble arm of a statue, half unpacked. This elegant, disembodied arm was smooth to the touch and, as he stroked it, he was soothed by the cool, unyielding feel of the polished marble. He looked around the room slowly before turning to a bookcase, full of what appeared to be leather-bound books. He pulled the back of a volume of collected poems by Longfellow and the whole row came down with it on a hinge. Instead of holding books, the shelf contained a section of false backs, which opened up to reveal a keypad in the centre. Acquilan tapped in a set of numbers and waited; a red light came on and he tapped in another set of numbers. Almost immediately the light turned to green. There was a little hum followed by a click and the door sprang open a few inches. Acquilan pushed the door and, as he did so, a number of spotlights came on in the room beyond the door.

The room was very different; the floor was bare, just a large expanse of highly polished oak. The walls were painted white and the ring of spotlights in the centre of the ceiling picked out a number of pictures hanging on the walls. Acquilan shut the door gently and looked slowly round the room. His eyes rested briefly on each picture before drifting over to the far wall where six paintings hung in the row he'd placed them in the night before. He shuffled towards the first picture on the left and stared at it. The only sound was the gentle creak of the floorboards and the soft hum of an air conditioner. He exhaled slowly and through pursed lips laughed softly, 'At last, at last.' He stroked the first one gently. 'You've come home.'

High up in the ABS office in New York, John Grande was sitting facing a TV screen with Laura Buckley.

'Nothing so far, are you sure?' Laura asked, her eyes fixed on the screen in front of her. 'Try this one,' she handed John another cassette and he changed them over. The screen flickered back into life and they found themselves looking at the same scene, the Kelp press conference.

This time the camera angle was perfect and, not only were Kelp and his wife in view as they walked towards the podium, but at the back, another man could be seen behind him and to the right.

'Yes, there he is. Let's freeze it,' John said quickly.

Laura prodded a button on the machine and the image froze. She then slowly tracked back until the picture was clearer.

'Yes, he looks very familiar,' he murmured as he stared at the screen.

'Well, surely you can make your mind up. Is this the man Peach, or isn't it?'

'Yes, I'm sure but . . .' He peered hard, 'something is missing. Have you got a felt pen?'

She reached into her handbag and produced one and handed it over to him. Before she could stop him he'd reached across and marked the screen in front of him.

'What the hell are you doing?' she exclaimed. 'Are you out of your mind?'

'No.' John sat back again and this time he was smiling broadly. 'It is him, now I'm certain.'

'Why all of a sudden?'

'Moustache – Peach had a moustache. That's what's been missing, so there, look.' He was pointing back at the screen. Laura followed his finger. She could now see what he'd done.

'You sure?'

'Pretty nearly certain, I can't be one hundred per cent until I see him in the flesh but it's as near as damn it.' Again he smiled and he looked at her. She couldn't help thinking John looked just like a small boy.

'Well, you've got to find him first.'

John's smile dropped away.

'So was he the one, you know, the one you think tried to kill you?'

'God knows! I only know that he and his partner Wessells could solve this for us.'

'Is he in the picture?' Laura glanced at the screen as she spoke.

'No, I can't see him.'

'He's the one who bought the pictures – right?'

'Precisely, your father never told me a thing – except about the pictures. The first I knew about these diaries was when Wessells told me he expected them and from me. I don't even know if the damn things exist.'

'Well, at least you made a positive ID.' She flicked the screen off and took the tape out of the machine.

John smiled to himself. Less than two weeks out of hospital and they had a lead. He'd been watching the news a couple of days before when, very briefly in the corner of the screen at a press conference for Ewan Kelp, he thought he'd seen the man he knew as Peach. Laura got the original film and they'd played it back again and again until he was quite certain.

John was staring out of the window, lost in thought. Laura noticed how the pale unhealthy look had vanished. With the bandage gone and the swelling and bruising down, the look she remembered from the beach was returning. He smiled, almost absent-mindedly, and without knowing why, she returned his smile.

'I guess you have a right to be pleased, something at last,' she said softly.

'This guy Peach, or whatever his name is, that must be a start. Could he be one of the officials in Kelp's campaign team? He's got to have some reason to be there.'

'Well, whatever,' Laura shrugged, 'if it's him, we'll soon know.' She frowned. 'It puzzles and I guess worries me. Was this my father's way of getting even, of getting something out into the open using a proxy? Maybe these diaries have the full story. You must have been meant to disclose them.'

'That's a lot of surmising. Whoever has them now knows I've got nothing to go on, but they won't be able to ignore me.'

'But who?'

'That guy Peach for one.'

'Yes, but was he and the other guy, I forget his name, were they on their own or . . .?'

'. . . with Kelp? All sounds a bit far-fetched, doesn't it really? I mean, a presidential candidate.'

'Yes,' Laura replied, 'not much but it's a start – we need to find this guy and ask him a few questions.'

'What do you mean?' John stared at her. 'You can't just go asking a man like him questions.'

'Let's find out about him first, then we'll see. As I said before, I'm in it now for better or worse and we've got to go with what we've got. And so far this is it.' She tossed the tape into her bag as the door to her office burst open. Jake Laarson, one of the senior researchers on the *Marriott* programme, walked in, holding a sheet of paper.

'Not now, Jake,' Laura snapped. 'I'm busy.'

'I'm sorry, Laura, but this is something I thought you'd want to know.'

'OK, it'd better be good, though.'

'It is. Look, I hear that they're going to push for a vote tonight. They want to reopen the enquiry into the land deal.'

'But they'll need Democrats to vote with them.'

'I hear they've got some to abstain.'

'That means a prosecution – that'll really hurt Carson. They must be Kelp supporters.'

'Yeah, they are.'

'But they still don't have much to go on. It's Julia Haskins, the one who died, it's her sister's and her partner's word against Carson's – and anyway, Haskins' testimony originally cleared Carson.'

'Julia Haskins testified?'

'Sure, under oath.'

'And now the sister says she was having an affair. It's bad for Carson. If they prove Haskins was having an affair, then her testimony looks very weak.'

'OK, better go with this tonight. Dig up some pictures of Carson as Governor, and any you can find of this Haskins woman.'

Jake nodded.

'Oh, and see if you can get something from Kelp,' Laura said as he left her office.

'Impressive,' John said as the door shut.

'What?' Laura turned, her face flushed and eyes sparkling. 'Oh, *that*!' she said, 'I'm sorry, I thought it best to take his mind off you – I'll also get someone to follow this up. You'd better go back to the apartment.'

John nodded, his eyes never leaving hers. He had never met anyone like her before and he was transfixed. She seemed to glow as though charged by some extra power source.

'Well?' she asked gently, enjoying his gaze.

'Oh,' he said, turning away, 'I'd better go.'

'You're right,' she said.

12

The Collector

Lieutenant Jasinski walked out of the men's room, still doing up his zipper.

'Hey, L'tenant!'

Jasinski looked up and saw Munroe bearing down on him. 'L'tenant!'

'I heard ya!' Jasinski barked over his shoulder as he went towards his office. 'What is this, a man can't go to the can without some guy screaming at him!' He walked past Munroe and then beckoned him to follow. 'So?'

'I think we've got something,' Munroe said excitedly.

'That'd be new,' Jasinski replied, as he sat down behind his desk.

'It's like this, it's our first real breakthrough . . .'

'I haven't got all day, Munroe!' Jasinski interrupted him impatiently, tapping on his desk with his pencil.

Munroe continued, 'the word is, there's someone in Tribeca got information about a British guy – could be something.'

'Is that all? What about the hotels? What about the British police?'

'Nothing, L'tenant. Do you know how many Brits have been through New York in the last few months?' Munroe felt uncomfortable as Jasinski's eyes bored into him. '. . . thousands and . . .'

'Your source good on this guy?' Jasinski demanded, his voice calm, flat.

'The best. The only problem is, Rutgers went down there this morning and the guy'd gone. The super ain't playing ball either.'

'Well, perhaps it's time we paid the super a call – get your coat.'

Ten minutes later, they pulled up outside a run-down three-storey apartment block.

'What a dump!' Jasinski looked at the building through the car window. 'This guy Grande must be one scared *hombre*. But he's smart.'

Munroe looked puzzled as he stood on the other side of the car. 'What's so smart about being in this dump?' he asked.

'Well, can you think of a better place to lose yourself than here?' They walked up the steps to the front door. Just as they got to it, an old lady came out. Munroe grabbed the door quickly before it shut and Jasinski walked through.

Inside, the hall was dingy, the only light coming from a dirty broken window above the stairs in front of them. Their noses were instantly assailed by the harsh smell of urine and disinfectant. In the background there was the constant noise of televisions and children, of pop music and soap theme tunes, laced with shrieks of laughter and the sound of raised voices as adults shouted and doors slammed.

'New York, New York,' Jasinski spoke quietly to himself.

'What's up, L'tenant?'

'Nothin' – it reminds me of a place I used to know, as a kid, a long time ago – that was a dump too.'

The door on the right opened and a boy of about six poked his head out.

'Hey, kid!' Jasinski barked, 'where's the super?' The boy stared at him for a couple of seconds and then shut the door quickly. Jasinski smiled and looked to his left as Munroe pointed to a door set back from the stairs.

Before they could move, the door opened slowly and a large man stepped out, wearing a torn pair of tracksuit trousers, trainers and a dirty singlet. His eyes were set back into the mounds of unshaven smoke-stained flesh, a cigarette clamped between his teeth.

'What do you want here?' he challenged, walking slowly towards them, then he stopped and squinted. 'You're cops!'

'Well, ain't you the bright one,' Munroe retorted as he walked forward. 'You the super?' he demanded sharply as he stopped a few inches in front of the man.

'Maybe.'

'Good.' Jasinski flicked up his badge.

'I'm Lieutenant Jasinski and this is Detective Munroe. We've got a few questions.'

'Big deal! I got nothin' to say to you.' He stepped back towards the open door. Munroe moved rapidly to get behind him and held the door open.

'Listen, you low life. We're here to ask some questions.'

The super looked first at Munroe and then back to Jasinski. 'I mind my own business. I keep myself to myself.' He glanced nervously towards the top of the stairs and back down the corridor to their left. A few people had gathered. He raised his voice, 'I told you, I've got nothing to say.'

'I'll be the judge of that.' Jasinski spoke sharply and took half a pace forward. The super walked back into his doorway, his eyes darting from one to the other.

'You got no right,' he hissed. 'Cops in here! You'll give me a bad name.' Munroe was about to grab him when he caught sight of Jasinski, who was shaking his head. He let him go and the door slammed shut.

'I'll go in and lean on him, L'tenant, it's obvious he's hiding something.'

'Wait, you won't get much from him here. He's too scared. We'd better take him in.' Jasinski looked around as, one by one, the few people standing at the top of the stairs and by the end of the corridor drifted away. 'If he talks, it won't be here. Someone's got to him before us. I'll stay and talk to a few more people, see what they come up with.' Jasinski looked back at the door, where the child's face had appeared. 'I'll start there.'

The door opened, but stopped on the chain; behind it Jasinski could just see the face of a woman, dark, with tired-looking eyes.

'Yes, who is it?' The woman's voice had a strong Mexican accent.

'Police,' Jasinski said as he showed her his badge, 'can I come in?' There was a pause and the door quietly shut. A few seconds passed as the chain was taken off on the far side of the door before it reopened. Jasinski stepped inside and looked around as the woman shut the door behind him. There was only one room with a small kitchen area off to the right; there were two armchairs, a battered old table and two beds. In the corner was a shower cubicle and a small toilet in a tiny cupboard just in front of that. On the floor by one of the armchairs the same small child was playing.

'I don't want no trouble, mister.' The woman's voice trembled slightly. Tall and slim, he thought, she must be in her mid-thirties although, with the remains of make-up from the night before left on her face, she seemed older.

'I'm making inquiries about someone I believe stayed in this apartment block. You know, a British guy.' He reached into his pocket and pulled out a photograph and handed it to her. He tapped it once as he spoke. As she looked at it, Jasinski walked slowly towards the big bay window at the far side of the room; there was silence as he parted the curtains and looked out. The front of the block was in view, including the steps down to the street.

'As I said before, mister, I can't help you.' The woman spoke quietly but forcefully. Jasinski let the curtains fall back again.

'Oh, I think you might if you try – he used to live here.' Again the woman shook her head and Jasinski watched as the little boy peeped out from between her legs. 'Look again, please.' Jasinski bent down and offered the little boy some chewing gum. A tentative hand reached out and took it. 'I don't want much – I just need to know if he was here . . .' Jasinski said, smiling at the boy again as he slipped behind his mother. 'Was he unshaven? Did he have a beard, glasses?'

The woman looked at the picture again, 'There was a man.' She spoke very slowly and softly. 'But he kept to himself – like everyone. Didn't shave – glasses.' She handed the picture back. 'I don't know.'

Jasinski took his pen out and drew some lines across the picture to form a rough beard. He handed it back to her. 'Like this?'

'Maybe.'

'Do you remember what happened to him?' Jasinski took the picture and put it in his pocket.

'He went.'

'When?'

'A week, maybe more. There was a problem.' She was nervous. 'You must go now.'

Jasinski reached into his breast pocket and pulled out his money clip. 'What sort of problem?'

The woman's eyes dropped down to the bills in Jasinski's hand. The child still clung to her leg. 'You must go now – I don't want trouble.'

'Was it the super?' Jasinski walked slowly towards her, tapping the wad of dollar bills on the flat of his hand.

She looked down and shook her head; her hand dropped to her child's head. 'Please, you mus' go.'

'One last question,' Jasinski stopped beside the door, 'how did he go?'

The woman stared back at him for what seemed an age before answering quietly and very slowly. 'A smart woman, she come and take him. He was hurt bad – they went by cab.' She started to open the door and spoke quickly as she did so. 'Go now, please.'

Jasinski nodded and put his hand out to stop the door from opening any further. He looked down at the child and as he did so he peeled off a $50 bill, rolled it up and held it out to the woman. She took it and stuck it in her kimono pocket. He then reached into his top pocket and held out a card and handed it to her. 'If you think of anything else . . .' His voice trailed away. He heard the door shut behind him and the chain fasten across.

As he stepped out, he saw Rutgers standing in the main hall. 'Where's Munroe?' Jasinski asked. Rutgers inclined his head in the direction of the super's room.

'Well, what are you waiting for? Get in there, get him out and let's get going.' Jasinski strode towards the front door and outside. It was only when he got in the fresh air that he stood still, the sensation of being stifled falling away as he breathed in deeply.

'Well, Victor,' Weitz spoke quickly but carefully, 'it's as you said last time. We still don't know how much Grande knows but we have to assume he's dangerous. No sign of the diaries yet either.' Weitz leant forward as he spoke, his voice lowered, almost conspiratorial.

'So what about this place in New York you were telling me about?' Acquilan's face was impassive as he spoke.

'It's pretty clear Grande stayed there. Trouble is, the cops are also looking for him and they picked the super up and took him in for questioning.'

'It's too late for us to do anything, anyway,' Pichowski interrupted, 'I tried – but when I got there I was too late. The police had already found him dead in his apartment – hanged. They're all over the building.'

'*What*!' Weitz exclaimed.

'It had been made to look like suicide but it's too suspicious,' Pichowski replied.

'Anywhere Grande goes, someone dies, just about the time we arrive on the scene,' Weitz muttered. 'Anyway,' he continued, 'we asked around and it seems Grande was pretty badly hurt. Some smart-looking woman took him away in a cab.'

'It doesn't fit together,' Acquilan spoke quietly, so quietly that he was almost talking to himself. 'The only thing we've got is this guy Grande.'

'What I don't understand, Victor,' Weitz began carefully, 'is if the diaries exist, why haven't they been used by now? After all, they're what counts. Why doesn't Grande use them? If he doesn't have them, then Cosmo – or whoever – why don't they publish?'

'I'm not sure, Bernie,' Acquilan said slowly, 'We both know Grande is unlikely to have them so the only question is, does Cosmo? Did he ever have them? Even if he does, then maybe he needs something else.'

'I don't get you.'

'Timing, Bernie, timing – that's the key.' Acquilan levered out of his seat slowly and stood up. 'What is Grande doing? I mean, it's unlikely he knows much, though one thing's for sure, he knows the paintings he saw were frauds.'

'You mean the delay in London?'

'Precisely – accident or deliberate, it doesn't matter, we're being set up.' Puffing at his cigar, he continued, 'Look,

Cosmo's done everything according to a tight plan. Yet one thing puzzles me, why in hell's name did he choose to put the pictures through Grande and why get him involved? He didn't need to. At first I thought it was to get me into the open but then I realised there's something more significant, something much more powerful than just that. Grande's not just an accident, he's got to be part of all this – but why?' He puffed at his cigar again. 'We've been running to Cosmo's tune for far too long and it's time we broke free.'

Acquilan turned to Pichowski. 'I want you to get back to London and find out everything you can about this guy Grande. Not just about him but who his parents were, what they looked like, where his money comes from, everything. I've never even seen a picture of the guy. Get me one!' He let out a small but audible laugh, 'Here I am worrying about him and he could walk right up to me now and I wouldn't know who he was.'

'No problem, Mr Acquilan,' Pichowski answered, 'no problem.'

'We've got to get inside Cosmo's head, Bernie. I got to find out why he's using this guy. There's more to him than simply a dead letter.'

A meeting was breaking up in Laura Buckley's office as Walter Harvey walked in. 'Well, you got lucky. The board's just approved all your new schedules.'

Laura stared at him before breaking into a broad smile.

'Now,' he continued, 'it's up to you to make them work. Look these papers over – only a minor change or two.'

Laura looked up at him. 'I thought you said . . .'

'I did. You'll find the changes are only suggestions,' he smiled, raising his hand defensively, 'you don't have to accept them. It's all yours anyway, what's important to you is that sport lost that half-hour.' He laughed.

'Good,' Laura smiled again.

'A small word of advice, Laura, you'd better get something in fast, you don't have a lot of time.'

Laura nodded. Harvey turned to go and then hesitating, he turned back. 'You know, Laura, I haven't seen you so motivated for months, the move seems to have suited you, you're back to your old self.' He smiled. 'The board thinks so too!' he said over his shoulder as he left.

She flushed slightly. He was right about the motivation but wrong about the reason; her future was locked to a total stranger. Furthermore, she already knew it was a voyage of discovery and while common sense told her that her dead father and an unknown past shouldn't be disturbed – she'd decided to plunge on. To go through life not knowing, always wondering, tortured by all the unanswered questions about who she was – she'd made her mind up that she wanted something different and the odd Englishman held the key to it all.

She was about to risk all that she'd worked for so hard and so steadily against massive odds, fully aware that others would say her behaviour was irrational, yet she felt certain her only course was to see it through. As she looked out of the window, she found the face and form of John Grande in her thoughts. What she hadn't fully understood but was just beginning to, was that this soft-spoken, almost shy man was changing everything. Her steady, controlled life had been crossed by someone hell-bent on an erratic course. Instead of rejecting such madness, she had changed her own course to be swept along with him. He was so unlike the men she normally saw. She began to wonder about the way his presence seemed to influence her thinking and dominate her thoughts. She smiled and shook her head.

'Sal,' she said, walking to the door, 'that new researcher, you know, the one who started with May yesterday. Tell her to come here now, will you?'

Laura walked back into her office and put a video cassette

in the machine on the table beside her desk. The picture flickered as she repositioned the image. She'd just finished as the new researcher arrived.

'Come over here,' she waited as the girl walked in front of the video. 'Sorry, I've forgotten your name . . .'

'Karen,' the young girl's voice was hesitant, nervous.

'Relax, take a seat, Karen. Look, you see that man,' Laura pointed to the screen and the girl nodded. 'I want you to get a print of this so that you can make out his face clearly. Then, when you've done that, go get a press badge and get over to the Kelp Election Headquarters and find out who he is. You may have to ask around but don't leave without an answer. Get anything else you can on him as well. Oh yes, and if anyone asks, say you're bringing all the records up to date – got it?' The girl nodded.

'Good, then here you are,' the video popped out of the machine and Laura handed it to her. 'Off you go.'

As the girl left Laura poked her head round the corner of the door. 'Sal, can you check with the news desk what the police are up to on that New York lawyer's case, you know the Goldstein one – big society lawyer, murder or something like that.'

'Why?' Sally looked up at her, puzzled.

'Simply because I want to know. Is that all right?' Laura frowned, 'Actually, even better, ask whoever's been dealing with it to give me a briefing, will you?'

Laura's secretary gave her a long quizzical look.

John Grande was assessing his reflection in the mirror. He noted with some satisfaction that the bruising had gone down and with it his face had slimmed to its natural state. Yet, at Laura's insistence, he had started to grow a moustache which, after four days, had begun to change the appearance of his face again. He had been thoroughly relieved to get rid of his beard. As he stared into the mirror, he smiled. Then, placing the glasses on his nose, he grimaced – the transformation was complete.

For the first time since the attack, he felt he was ready to carry on: free of the headaches and with a new sense of purpose after sighting Peach at the TV press conference. While they discussed the best way forward and agreed that Laura would try to find out more about the man, John felt he needed to get moving much more quickly. Without telling Laura, he'd decided to find out about Senator Kelp. He needed more than the biographical details Laura had given him. He didn't know what he was looking for but doing something, he reasoned, was better than nothing. His first step was to go to the library, where he would find out what business relationships, if any, he still had. Then he'd use the computer to lock into the business records lodged at Albany and hope to find something.

He left the apartment relieved that at best he had a sense of direction.

Tired and hot, Ewan Kelp slumped back into his armchair.

It was five o'clock in the morning and outside his quiet refuge the noise of the party carried on unabated. He closed his eyes, awash with memories of his triumph. To have come from behind to win Massachusetts was breathtaking. Around his feet, the early editions of the newspapers lay scattered.

BODY BLOW TO CARSON.

RACE WIDE OPEN.

CARSON COUNTS THE COST.

The *New York Daily News* was the clearest: PROSECUTOR DAMAGES CARSON'S RE-ELECTION.

He chuckled to himself. After Iowa, where he had come second, having lost momentum, he knew his chances had faded, despite the bright start. Massachusetts was a critical state to win, not because of the number of delegates, which was small, but because it was seen as a 'must win' for the eventual winner. Indeed, it was often an early indication swing state.

The door opened and a flood of sound filled the room, then the noise was smothered as the door was shut.

'Ewan,' Mason began, 'time you got to bed.'

Kelp opened his eyes, smiled and nodded. 'We did it, Dick!'

'I knew we would, Ewan. You played it just right when the land deal stuff broke, refusing to comment, statesmanlike, you buried him in unspoken contempt.'

'It's all he's worth, Dick.'

'Sure, we needed a stroke of luck. The reopening of the land deal enquiry really hurt him. For once he can't talk his way out of this.'

'Yes,' Kelp replied, 'it was touch and go.'

With Carson hurt and Cosmo dead, Kelp felt that he could go all the way – after all these years, he thought, years watching from the sidelines as others picked up the challenge which he coveted but couldn't touch. He'd had to watch as others took up the challenge as he remained the kingmaker, never the king. Now it was his turn – long overdue – and he meant to seize his chance.

'We need to look to New York as our next big prize.'

'Of course, but I have it that Senator Wall will now declare for me.'

'Did the Senator say as much, Ewan? I mean, he was all over Carson last week.'

'Well,' Kelp answered shrugging, 'that was last week and a lifetime ago. He's up for election in two years and as my partner in the Senate, he owes me.'

'Maybe, but I hear he's having trouble putting money together for his campaign. Although you might be friends, his bank balance is what drives him even more.'

'Don't worry, Victor is seeing to that,' Kelp yawned, 'Now, I think I'm going to sleep this victory off,' he stretched and turned towards his bedroom. 'You were right and everyone else was wrong, Dick – I owe you – we came good at the right moment.'

'You might consider that you owe President Carson even more than me,' Mason muttered, and continuing in a low voice, 'now maybe, Senator, we can try to win this goddamm contest.'

As Laura sat in the cab, she felt depressed. Her hopes had come to nothing, even the men on the tape didn't seem to make any sense to her. She felt herself getting drawn closer to John even though she wanted to keep him and his problems at arms' length. She told herself that she would set him on the right track and then walk away. Yet she was beginning to realise that walking away seemed to be getting more and more difficult. The nightmare problem he was trying to solve was their only attachment but she knew a deeper emotion was stirring. His distance, almost shyness, should have made it easy for her to stay detached, yet she found herself becoming more deeply involved with each passing day. A warning voice told her that he had the power to take her to her limits and she needed to get back in control. As each piece was slowly placed in the jigsaw, she saw a dark picture developing. It was getting to be that she feared the next piece, but couldn't halt the process.

Laura unlocked the door to her friend's apartment and walked into the small study on the right. John was sitting at the desk, writing on a yellow pad in front of him.

'I've got something here you'd better look at,' Laura said gently and handed some papers to him. 'The pictures weren't very good,' she continued, 'but at least they came up with a name.' She looked at the face in the picture, 'Pichowski, if I got the spelling right.' John showed no sign of recognition. 'Well, anyway, it seems he only worked there for a short period – he's gone now.' She flung her coat on the back of an armchair and sat down.

'The face could be his, but the name doesn't ring any bells,' he said slowly. 'What do you mean, he's gone?'

'That's what they say,' Laura sat back. 'From what we can gather he was part of security.'

'Are you sure?'

'Well, they all said he was packing a gun,' Laura answered.

'A gun?' John frowned.

'There are a lot of strange people about – a candidate makes a good target and needs protection. Anyway, he's gone – and no one knows anything about him.'

'Pichowski, you're sure?'

'Yes.'

'Well, it looks like him,' he murmured, 'but the name . . .'

'I'll see if I can run a check on it back at the office.'

'Before you continue,' he held up a sheaf of papers, 'I went to the library and did a bit of research on Senator Kelp. I used the internet to look into the company records held in Albany.' John smiled in a self-satisfied way. 'I checked all his entries; they make interesting reading.' He opened the pile of papers on his lap. 'It's strange, you know, Italy seems to crop up a lot throughout all of this. Anyway, after cross-checking, it appears he's a large stockholder in a private company. All I had to go on were media reports. But I did get something that kept repeating itself. There's a man called Acquilan, who seems to head the private company and another board director called Weitz – their names reappear in different companies; there are others, but with Kelp those three seem to be the main stockholders. Can we get anything on Weitz or Acquilan?'

'Sure,' she said glancing at the sheet, 'I know something about Acquilan already – wealthy businessman, close friend of Kelp's – he's also one of the major financial backers for Kelp's campaign but I don't think I've ever heard of Weitz before.'

'Might be worth finding out whether Pichowski's got anything to do with them.'

'I'll get somebody on to it tomorrow. The way to get at this is through his returns – to try and find out what line of work he's in – oh yes,' she said, looking up, 'there's more: a little bird tells me that the police are still looking for you. I don't think they know your name but I hear they've got a picture of you.' John nodded. 'If the police have the photograph,' Laura continued, 'it won't be long before they get someone to identify you.' Her face flushed and a tremor of excitement shot through her.

John frowned. In the dying light from the window behind her, her face was in shadow and he couldn't make out her eyes. She was breathing slightly faster than normal and her lips were open. As he walked towards her, she turned. Her eyes caught his and they held him.

'What . . . next?' she said slowly and carefully.

With an effort, he turned away from her and stared out of the window into the growing gloom of the early evening. 'It all hinges on this man Pichowski. If we can find out who he is . . . then maybe we can find the man who bought the paintings.'

'If they still exist.'

'Oh, I'm sure . . .'

'Why?' Laura asked. 'Surely he'd have disposed of them by now?'

'They still exist,' John said firmly.

'They know it would be mad to keep them,' she said, exasperated at his certainty.

'Whoever got them,' he continued, 'wanted them for keeps. Those paintings are an Achilles' heel and your father knew it. This is about desire, a desire of the collector for that ultimate piece, the jewel in the crown.'

'But whoever has them must surely know that they could all lead straight back to him. It would be madness to risk everything for some paintings.' She frowned, her head at an angle, questioning.

'Oh yes,' John replied, 'seen from our perspective but it's all part of the game.' He smiled at her. 'It's the ultimate excitement, to own the very thing that could ruin you. Have you ever asked yourself why all those people in positions of power – the people you interview – go so close to the wire, putting themselves in the most dangerous situations when they know the risk of being found out? It's because the extra risk of being found with such vast consequences heightens that pleasure, to gamble all and win. This collector is no different, he wants the pictures for himself, nothing else will do.'

He was aware that Laura had moved closer to him as he was speaking. 'That's it, that's what it's all about.' He was possessed by the character of the man he sought, his anger boiling up again inside. 'Find that man and the whole story unravels.'

Laura nodded as he finished. She was intrigued by what he had said but also by his reaction to his own comments. He had stiffened and seemed to look right through her. It was as though there was an invisible boundary around him which she had almost breached. He was a strange, wounded man. Listening to him, she understood for the first time what he meant, how that aura of danger stimulated – she felt it now. For a moment, her hand touched his and stalled. He smiled faintly and withdrew his hand. He had remembered Julia and he felt ashamed.

Across town, Acquilan leaned on his desk. He didn't move, his concentration kept him fixed, his eyes focusing on the photograph. The anglepoise lamp was bent low, throwing a circle of light over it. The study was quiet save for the occasional nervous shuffling of another man in an armchair in front of the desk. The old leather seat creaked every time the man moved. The longer the silence, the more nervous Acquilan's guest became.

'So tell me, Pichowski – what about Grande?' Acquilan

tapped the picture, opened a box and took out a cigar, rolling it between his fingers before putting it in his mouth and leaning forward, his elbows on the desk. Pichowski stood up, reached for his lighter and lit the cigar.

'Not much, Mr Acquilan. The guy's father served in the war in the British Army. Seems he was some kind of art expert before the war but after it, from what I gather, he moved into the family business. Spent the last few years in a mental institution before committing suicide. The family business was sold and split 50–50 between Grande and his uncle, who lives in Italy – not much left after paying all the bills – mother died of cancer when Grande was young.'

While Pichowski was talking Acquilan walked towards the window. The view was out across undulating parkland and down to the sea. The sun had just gone down and the night was laying its dark cloak across the ground. Pichowski was still talking when Acquilan turned to face him.

'So, Mr Acquilan,' Pichowski continued, 'Grande spent most of his money on the gallery business; whatever little's left got tied up in a few shares.' He placed another photo on Acquilan's desk. 'Oh yes, there was his wife.' Acquilan bent the anglepoise lamp until it shone more clearly on the photograph.

'She looks gentle,' Acquilan said, 'sort of homey . . .'

'She got killed. Hit and run.'

'How long ago was that?'

'From what I hear, about a year before Cosmo got in touch with us.'

Acquilan nodded slowly and turned, again looking at the two photographs on his desk. He shook his head gently and then stood back. 'Where did you get the pictures from?'

Pichowski puffed his chest out, 'You'd be surprised how easy it is to impersonate a British cop. I got this private detective to dig around, people always want to help. Oh, there's more,' he continued, 'they had a small boy, about five, he was killed too – same time.'

At that moment a knock on the door announced Bernie Weitz.

'OK, Pichowski, thanks – you've done a good job.' Acquilan took the file from Pichowski and ushered him towards the door. 'Go and get a drink while Bernie and I discuss a few things.'

'I came as quickly as I could, Victor,' Weitz said, as soon as the door was shut.

'Good. We've got some problems, Bernie.'

'I don't understand – Ewan's doing well in Georgia and most of the southern states, we've now got a lead over Carson . . .'

'No, no,' Acquilan held up his hand, 'it's Cosmo.' He took another puff on his rapidly shrinking cigar and then stubbed it out, half-finished. 'We've been fools, Bernie, damn fools! When I think of what's been going on . . .' his voice trailed off. 'With what he's got, it should've exploded on us already.'

'What do you mean?' Weitz sat forward in his seat.

'Look, Cosmo made contact with us last year. He made it clear we could buy back the pictures and he agreed to give us the diaries as well. He was the one who chose the go-between in London – this guy Grande – as I said before, why him? Anyway, it turns out there's a delay, during which time the guy's partner gets murdered. He sells the pictures and before the police can arrest him he disappears. You then follow, he visits Rome and that lawyer, so do you. The lawyer dies, murdered – Grande comes to New York, goes to see Goldstein, but the lawyer is also killed. Then there's an attempt on Grande's life, then the attack in Tribeca.'

Weitz sat silently, nodding occasionally.

'Don't you see, Cosmo's been carefully linking us to a series of murders from London through Italy to here,' Acquilan continued. 'It's a line that will run from Grande to Ewan, it's a trap that was baited with the pictures and we've taken the bait.'

'But what about the diaries?' Weitz asked, puzzled.

'Perhaps the diaries weren't enough, maybe he thought we could pass them off as false, perhaps he wanted to twist the knife before sticking it in – who knows?' Acquilan sat back in his chair and looked at Weitz. 'There's still that one thing that doesn't fit; why hasn't he exposed us by now? Why hasn't he used those diaries? What's stopping him?'

They sat in silence; then a small smile broke the normally impassive face of Bernie Weitz.

'It's staring us in the face, Victor, he needs Grande. He's the link and he must have lost him! While Grande's still loose,' he said, 'the police think he remains the main suspect. There'll be no link to us. But if they catch him, or if Grande were to be found dead, with the diaries and all the other evidence – well, it would all point to us. Cosmo must have planned it all. But now this guy Grande is gone, he's skipped.' He frowned, 'It must have been us who broke the chain when we visited Goldstein's office – it was just after that Grande disappeared.'

Acquilan quietly puffed on his cigar, his eyes fixed on a picture on the wall behind Weitz while he listened.

'So, Victor,' Weitz continued, 'there's a window of opportunity. You're right – Cosmo, or whoever is following through his master plan – must be looking for him too.'

'After all we've gone through, we're not going to throw it all away. We've got to find Grande first and make sure he disappears for good.' As Acquilan finished speaking, he flicked the picture of Grande with his fingers, 'You'd better take Pichowski. Do whatever it takes, Bernie – just find him and get rid of him, otherwise we're all finished.'

Weitz now studied the picture of Grande, turning it round so that it was facing him. He nodded in response.

'Strange, Victor,' Weitz murmured, 'but I always thought Grande's face looked familiar, real familiar – I don't know why.' He looked up and he could see that Acquilan was staring down at the picture as well.

'Yes, I thought so myself,' Acquilan agreed. 'I can't get it out of my mind – there's somebody that he reminds me of.' He shrugged. 'Just get him out of our lives.'

As Weitz left, Acquilan sat down, in his hand the photograph of John Grande. He gazed at it, his brow furrowed, then he nodded, 'Yes, Bernie, familiar,' he muttered, 'real familiar.'

Carson leaned back in his chair as his national security adviser and then his chief of staff walked into the Oval Office. Their faces were grim, matching Carson's mood.

He'd lost Massachusetts and with it the chance to finish Kelp once and for all. Now the Prosecutor was beginning to get to him, and his reputation was clearly suffering from the constant speculation about his future. His campaign was still holding up but Kelp had drawn ahead of him.

'So, Frank, Pete, what've we got?' Carson began.

'You may have to give evidence, Mr President,' Frank Parry began, 'It's some way off, but that's what they'll go for.'

'I'm not going to do it – you can forget that.'

'There's no way . . .'

'Bullshit,' Carson hissed. 'It'll demean the Presidency.'

Parry raised his eyebrows and glanced at Pete Neal.

'Forget it,' continued Carson, 'I'm not going to testify . . .'

'Well, there may be a way out,' Parry said, his voice soft. 'They might be persuaded to do it remote – you don't have to leave the White House.'

'You haven't been talking to them, have you?'

'No,' Parry continued, 'my plan is that we delay the Prosecutor as long as possible but if we have to, that is, if you're happy . . .'

'Happy?' snorted Carson, 'This should never have got this far.' He swivelled his chair around and watched as a weak sun filtered through the clouds. Politics had been his life since leaving college, it was all he'd wanted to do, but just now, for the first time in his life, he wondered what it would be like to be one of the ordinary people scurrying past the White House railings. He'd always been a politician, even when he was a lawyer, it was politics first, last and always.

'Mr President . . .'

Carson turned slowly, aware of Parry's voice.

'Shall I deal?'

'Delay as long as you can first,' Carson replied. 'Are you sure there's nothing on the child?'

'We've drawn a blank. The trust was in Julia Haskins' name, no link to you, and then it was closed. So far nothing,' Parry shrugged, 'Unless they do better than us, they'll have nothing, then we can accuse him of muck-raking.'

'I won't need to give evidence?'

'Best to offer at the last moment before going on the attack.'

'So, Pete,' Carson said, turning to Neal, 'Give me some good news. Kelp will trample all over me with this. How do we get to him?'

'Well,' Neal began, slowly, 'it's not going to be easy, but there is something.' He opened his briefcase and took out some handwritten notes. 'His business record is clear, taxes paid on time, etc. And as you know his war record is clear too. But we've looked again at his finances and there seems to be something. More of a question really and I don't yet have any answers. Where did he get the finances for his company in 1946? There's a second question mark too, his first election success in New York – some concern about the result – we're looking into it.'

'Not much.'

'No,' he shrugged, 'so I've started looking at his partner, Acquilan.'

'OK,' Carson sighed. 'We need something on Kelp – fast. I've got to stop him taking advantage of this creep.'

'You know, Pete,' Parry said turning to his colleague, 'that columnist Douglas on the *Post* seems to have started delving into Kelp, might do to keep an eye on him too.'

'Sure, we will,' Neal said as he put his notes away, 'but this time, I can't put just anyone on it. I've got to be careful – accessing FBI files isn't easy.'

'Leave that to me, I'll speak to the Secretary for Defense,' Carson replied.

'OK, Mr President,' Neal said firmly, trying to sound reassuring, as he stood up. 'Unless the guy is God almighty, we'll find *something.*'

'It's a race now,' said Parry, 'we'll have to play for time – I'll string out the negotiation on the interview with the Prosecutor. Pete's right – I'm sure we'll come up with something.'

'Oh, I know that,' Carson replied, 'that's not the problem. The question is what and when?'

13

Detective Health Care

Jasinski had just hung his coat up when he heard a tap on his open door. Framed in the doorway was Detective Rutgers and behind him stood Munroe. Their smiling faces angered him.

'You two don't have any reason to smile!' Jasinski snapped.

'We got some good news, L'tenant,' Munroe spoke quickly as they walked in. He pointed through the glass window to their desks. Sitting beside Rutger's desk was a heavy-set, balding man in his fifties, fidgeting nervously. 'That guy,' Munroe continued, 'remembers picking up someone who was badly hurt from the tenement building.' Jasinski nodded, 'Sounds like Grande.'

'OK, bring him in. You showed him the picture?'

'Yes, he thinks it could be him but says the guy had a beard and a moustache. Looked pretty rough, beat up too.' Seconds later the cab driver walked in, followed by Munroe. The man wore an open-necked shirt, jeans, a thick sweater and an old jacket. He had a broad face with a scar down the left cheek and a badly broken nose.

'This is Mr Maloney, L'tenant,' Munroe said. 'Sit down,' he muttered to the man.

'So, Mr Maloney,' Jasinski began, 'the detective here tells me you've got some information.'

'Well, L'tenant, I saw your notice on the board at work – I thought maybe, maybe it was the dame I picked up. Jeez! I hope nothing happened to her . . .' His bloodshot eyes were half-closed.

'Why don't you take it from the top?' Jasinski leant back in his seat and waited.

'Like I said to the detective, you know, she was a classy dame, picked her up, must have been her office at around 7.20 p.m., and took her down to this shithole in Tribeca. At first I thought, she must've got the wrong address, couldn't figure what a dame like her was doin' going to a place like this. When we gets there, she wants me to wait but in that neighbourhood you don't know what might happen, so I says no, but then she handed me 50 bucks. So, I look at the money and I cruised.' He twitched his mouth, as though seeking approval and recognition. 'Well, like I said, she goes into the place – she got balls, that dame! Then she came out ten minutes later and I pulls up. That's when she asked me to go back in with her! Can you imagine, in this city? So I says no way! But that's when she pulls out another 50 bucks. Well, like I said, she was OK and it seemed pretty quiet so I says, yeah, why not? Then the next thing I know, I'm helping this guy, who's got some whack on the head, out to the cab – should'a had an ambulance, looked pretty bad. Anyway, she screams out an address and we goes up to St Teresa's, where I dropped them off.'

'What was his name?' Jasinski leant forward, staring at him.

'I didn't ask.' The man looked away as he answered.

'And hers?'

'I didn't ask that either.' Again the man looked away.

Jasinski sat back and smiled. 'OK, Mr Maloney, so you didn't ask – I didn't ask you if you asked – I asked what's his name?'

The man gazed down and then looked back at Jasinski. 'I don't remember.'

'Look, I know you know, do you want me to book you for obstruction?'

'OK, OK. So, I saw the label on his suitcase, the name was Grande – G-R-A-N-D-E.'

'Grande, you say, and hers?'

'I don't know, that's the God's truth!' He looked up at Jasinski and stared him straight in the eyes. 'That's all I got, honest.'

'Rutgers, take him out.' He looked up at the cab driver as he stood up. 'Thank you – we may need to talk with you again. Make sure you leave your name and all your details with the detective before you go.'

Munroe edged his seat forward and leaned on the desk after he had gone, 'That gives us something to go on, L'tenant, I'll pass that around the hotels and we'll see if we can get onto Interpol and the British police.'

'Sounds like him – anyway, we'll go with it,' Jasinski said, standing up, 'Now it's time we did some hospital visiting.'

Half an hour later, Jasinski and Munroe entered St Teresa's. The reception reeked of efficiency, cleanliness and calm. To Jasinski, this very modern private hospital smelt of more than that – it reeked of money. It looked just like the sort of place that operated on your wallet first before it did anything else. Quality is a great thing, he thought, as long as you can afford it.

In the manager's office he was greeted by a short, heavy-set woman wearing thick red glasses with her auburn hair plaited back from her face. She had an unsmiling, no-nonsense look as she turned towards Jasinski.

'I'm sorry, Lieutenant,' she said in answer to his first question, 'that would be privileged information. Anyway, I have to tell you this is not a general hospital, this is a specialised hospital and we only take referrals.'

'Are you sure?' Jasinski glanced at the computer behind her, 'I mean, have you checked your records?' The woman looked surprised at his question and hesitated. 'You see, ma'am, I just want to know if you did take anybody in with head wounds on that night and who it was. Then I'll be out of your hair.'

Again the manager hesitated.

'OK, I'll have a look but I'm warning you, you're wasting your time and mine. We don't do things that way.' She indicated two seats in front of the desk and swung her own round under the computer. For the next few minutes there was silence as she stared at the screen, typing occasionally.

'No, nothing,' she said with renewed assurance, 'No Mr Grande was admitted that night or, for that matter, on any night, so if . . .' she turned back to him.

'Hold it, ma'am,' Jasinski looked puzzled, 'did you check for head injuries?'

'Sergeant . . .' she began, standing up.

'L'tenant, ma'am,' Jasinski said, remaining seated.

'Lieutenant, this hospital doesn't take emergency work unless it has been referred by one of the consultants. They go elsewhere.'

'But you wouldn't refuse one – in an emergency, a real one, would you?' He looked at her; she was becoming a little flustered.

'Well, of course not – that is, it depends on the doctor's opinion, whoever is on duty or on call.'

'So, someone could have been admitted by one of your doctors?'

'Yes, in exceptional circumstances. Now if you'll excuse me, I . . .'

'One moment, ma'am, I repeat, could you please check and see if there were any head injuries around nine o'clock that night – real emergency work as you said, not pre-booked.' He noticed as he spoke that her eyes narrowed and her mouth began to set. 'It really would be a help, ma'am.'

'OK,' she sighed with clear exasperation and sat down again, 'But this has to be the last request.' Again she swung round on her seat and faced the computer. This time her actions were different; she started writing on a pad of paper as she looked at various files of information. After a few minutes, she swung round to face Jasinski.

'Have you got anything?' Jasinski leant forward, seeing that her face was flushed.

'Maybe.' She studied the pad of paper in front of her. 'There were half a dozen general cases that evening, but only two around that time.'

'Were they emergency?'

'Only one.'

She looked up at Jasinski, reluctant to pass any further information over.

'Can I ask you for the name, ma'am?'

'A Mr Johnson,' again she glanced down at the note as she read out his name. 'Now,' she stood up slowly, 'if that's all . . .'

'And the ward?'

'The Eleanor Roosevelt floor – a series of private rooms, we don't have wards. I must now ask you to leave. I am very busy, Lieutenant.' She walked to the door and grasped the handle.

Jasinski stood up slowly. 'I wonder, could I just speak with the doctor, the one that was in charge?' Jasinski smiled again; he was almost excessively polite, yet his voice carried not so much a question, more an insistence. It was clear to her that he wasn't going to go until he spoke to the doctor.

'Really, Lieutenant, you promised,' she spluttered, 'I have a hospital to run.'

'I know, ma'am, I'm really sorry – just a couple of minutes and I'll be out of your hair.' He smiled again at the repetition.

'Well,' she paused and opened the door, 'you'll have to wait outside while I try and find him.'

Outside Jasinski moved back into the reception area and sat down. Munroe sat down next to him.

'Johnson, Johnson.' He looked at Munroe, 'get into the Roosevelt floor,' he whispered, 'talk to a few of the nurses – find out about that night. While you're there, get some descriptions of whoever came in with him.' Munroe nodded.

Doctor Ben Bergen walked into the manager's office some five minutes later.

'Ben,' the manager paused as he sat down in front of her, 'we've got some visitors – the police.' Bergen looked surprised.

'Why?'

'About someone who was admitted on a night when you were on duty.' She hit a couple of buttons on the computer screen with her left hand and then pointed to the file. Bergen walked round behind the desk and, watching over her left shoulder, he frowned. 'There,' she said, the exasperation clear in her voice, 'why did you admit him?'

'I don't fully remember – I suppose he needed attention,' he walked back and sat down.

'But he wasn't a referral,' she frowned, 'you must have known that.'

'I know, but he had concussion and a bad head wound. I thought it best . . .'

'That much is clear,' she leaned forward, 'that's why you over-rode all the rules.' She paused, glancing back at the screen. 'However, I see from this that he paid cash, both the deposit and the final bill, not even an insurance reference.' She looked at Bergen and he nodded. 'You know, Ben, that's against all the hospital rules.' She shook her head, 'Cash in a place like this!'

'I know,' Bergen's heart was pounding, 'but it was only the

once.' He attempted to force a smile – he knew his charm normally worked on her.

'Did you know the man?' The manager ignored his smile, growing angrier as she spoke.

Bergen shook his head in answer. His face looked calm but deep down inside his emotions were racing. Inwardly he cursed Laura for what she had done, as his mind sought to find a way of keeping the whole thing from exploding in his face.

'Look,' Bergen spoke slowly, 'I don't think there's any need to get the hospital involved in anything to do with this – we should simply tell the police that he was admitted, was treated, paid in cash and was discharged. I don't see what all the fuss is about – oh yes, I know, I broke the goddamn rules! But that's got nothing to do with the police. At the very least we acted in a humane way.'

'What's done is done, Ben – I accept that. As you know, my job here is to make certain that the good name of this institution is not dragged through the mud. I don't know what this is all about but I intend to bring it before the board and I'll leave it with them. They'll be aware that this is a major transgression.' Bergen nodded as she buzzed his secretary on the intercom, 'Get the policeman back in here, please.'

'Thank you, Doctor,' Jasinski said as he sat down. 'I'm aware you must be very busy. The manager tells me that you were the doctor responsible for this Mr Johnson's admittance?'

'Yes, although I wasn't the only one to see him in the 48 hours he was here – there are a lot of other doctors here too, you know, Lieutenant,' Bergen smiled patronisingly.

Jasinski watched as he answered the question, aware of the superior tone, but he'd been expecting it. It simply confirmed his initial impression of this tall, handsome man. He was everything Jasinski found irksome, a Cary Grant lookalike, who thought the right connections, his money, his charm and a cultivated accent put the world at his feet – everything without really trying.

'Of course,' Jasinski said slowly, 'Of course, but you did OK his admittance.'

'Yes, I did.'

Jasinski reached inside his breast pocket and took out a photograph of Grande and handed it across to Bergen. 'Is that him, Doctor?'

Bergen stared at the picture. Whatever doubts he had that Laura was involved in something serious were dispelled. The man called Johnson was staring back at him. He frowned as though not quite recognising the face and then looked at Jasinski. 'Could be. I can't remember exactly – I treat a number of patients. Anyway, I seem to remember he had a beard when he came in.' He handed the photo back to Jasinski.

Jasinski had noticed the hesitation, the initial surprised look in Bergen's eye when he saw the picture. He pocketed it.

'Why did you admit him?'

'He needed treatment.'

'But your manager here tells me that you don't admit people into a place like this for emergency work, unless there's a referral.'

'Normally, yes. We – we are able to take accidents sometimes, if we can.'

'Whose decision is that?' Jasinski looked across at the manager.

'Normally mine, but doctors have the final say on clinical matters.'

'So anyone could come in, in theory.' A puzzled expression crossed Jasinski's face.

'With certain provisos.' The manager shifted uneasily in her seat.

'You mean, they or someone has to be able to pay?'

'In short, yes. That's correct. This is not a general hospital.'

'So let me get this right, your policy is not to admit when

it's pretty serious, without a referral, but you make exceptions in the case of a clinical emergency, depending on whether they can pay, or have insurance, I presume. But you said, Doctor, he was discharged some 24 hours later – couldn't have been that serious.'

Bergen nodded, walked around the desk to the computer, reached past the manager and tapped some keys, waiting as the screen changed. 'I'm just bringing up his record, if you'll bear with me. Not serious in the end but he had received a severe blow to the head, causing concussion, bruising and a rather nasty cut. There were also some glass splinters in the cut – yes, it turned out not to be too serious but it could have been otherwise.' He turned away and walked towards Jasinski, 'Look, Lieutenant, if you've really finished I've some patients to see.'

'Certainly, Doctor. Just a couple more questions.' Jasinski glanced at the manager, who was watching Dr Bergen with a face like thunder. 'Was anyone with him?'

'No, I don't think I remember anyone,' Bergen shook his head. 'Perhaps the nurse on night duty . . .'

'You don't remember a dark-haired woman in her late twenties, early thirties?'

Bergen froze as Jasinski spoke. He knew that Jasinski wasn't asking him a question, simply letting him know that he was aware of Laura's presence that night.

'Now you mention it, there was someone rather as you describe – although I don't remember her too clearly or her name.'

Jasinski nodded. 'Thank you,' he said as he stood up to shake hands with the doctor and the manager.

'What, Lieutenant,' the manager looked surprised. 'No more questions?'

'No, ma'am.' He smiled at her. 'Anyway, not just now.' He walked towards the door, 'Oh yes, I nearly forgot, can you tell me how he paid. Insurance?'

But the manager was wary, saying, 'I believe the bill was paid in cash.'

'Cash?' The lieutenant looked puzzled again, 'I didn't think a place like this took cash. I've never been treated in such a hospital, but I would've thought you don't take cash.'

'That's true,' again she looked hesitant and flushed slightly, 'but he paid,' she paused, 'at the end.'

'Oh, and how much would that be?'

'Two thousand five hundred dollars.' The manager checked the computer screen as she spoke.

'That's a load of cash,' he smiled, 'a load.' He looked back at Bergen. He could see tiny beads of sweat forming on his brow. Turning, he left the office.

Back at the precinct, Jasinski called Munroe into his office with Rutgers.

'It was Grande all right.' Munroe spoke first. 'The nurse on duty remembered.'

'Did he have a beard?'

'No, well, at first yes, but they shaved it off.'

'So that doctor was lying – he said he couldn't recognise him because he had a beard,' Jasinski said firmly. 'Go on.'

'Not much else except she said some dame visited him once. Good-looking, thinks she's seen her face before. In a magazine or on the television – couldn't remember.'

'Well, that confirms it. The doctor got them into the hospital. He must have known the woman. Munroe, get back to the hospital this afternoon, see if you can identify the woman.' He turned to Rutgers, 'How d'you get on?'

'Great. We got a return from Interpol – seems this Grande is wanted in connection with a homicide in London.'

'The woman at the tenement?'

'Gone, L'tenant,' Rutgers paused, 'seems she left about the same time the super was found hanging. I had a talk with a few others at the same place, seems he was screwing her big-time. She's an illegal. I suppose it kept him quiet and it paid the rent.'

'Yes,' Jasinski's voice was soft as he thought back to his interview with her, 'that figures. Well, better get on, put out an APB.' He looked up at Munroe, 'Oh, and find out which companies operate from the buildings around where that cab driver picked up the dame.'

'But, L'tenant, that's a busy place.'

'Sure, but think about it, you're looking for someone who this nurse seems to think she's seen on TV or in the papers in the last month or so. So use your nose, go through the list – it may give us something.'

As Laura put down the receiver, her heart was racing. For the first time in her life, she felt really scared. Being out of control was a completely new experience for her. The call from Ben Bergen had changed everything. He'd told her all about his interview with the police and even worse he let her know that other people had been poking around asking questions over the last two or three days. She felt bad because she couldn't tell him anything, but she was deeply grateful; he'd bought her a bit of time and she meant to use it. He told her he couldn't delay much longer, he'd have to remember her name before the police came back.

As she hung up, she remembered receiving some important information just before Bergen's call. She picked up the receiver again and dialled John's number. She decided to tell him the positive news first, the news about Pichowski: that he was a private investigator, was registered in the state of New York and licensed to carry a handgun. The strangest part, however, was that he had no office, just a PO box. Further inquiry revealed that those who knew about him said he only had one client – Atlantic Import Export.

Before she could say much more, however, John had made the connection and he let out a whoop of joy.

'That's it!' he cried, 'there's the connection! Atlantic Import Export, it's Acquilan and Kelp's company. Now, if I'm right and that is Peach, then we know where the pictures are.' He wanted her to say something, anything; he assumed that she would be as excited as he was. Yet even down the telephone he could sense the tension. 'There's something else, isn't there?'

'I suppose nothing we hadn't expected,' her voice was almost inaudible.

'The police?'

'Yes, they're already asking questions at the hospital.'

'Your name,' he asked urgently, 'have they got your name, Laura?'

'I don't think so, at least Ben doesn't think that they've found that out, but it's only a matter of time. There's more – it seems there are others asking questions. It's not the police I'm so worried about,' she continued. 'But these others . . .' her voice trailed away. 'The super's been killed – murdered – found hanged – others have been asking around and now at the hospital.'

'I knew it!' John declared. 'We've got to move – it won't be long before they get on to you. I knew I shouldn't have involved you.'

'You didn't have the choice – I decided,' she snapped, 'but I didn't think . . .'

'I know, but you've got to get out with me.'

'Where?'

'We're getting close, we need to buy some time – throw them off the trail, we'll have to go somewhere else.'

Laura stared at the wall before nodding, as though John was sitting in the room.

'OK,' she put the receiver down and surveyed her office – everything she had worked for and she was about to throw it all away. As her pulse raced, she shook her head and sighed. Now, she knew, was the time to walk, to get out of this mess, *his* mess. Reaching for the telephone, her hand on the receiver, she hesitated. She saw John's face and she let the receiver go. She had been swept into the vortex, she was part of it – walking away was no longer an option. It wasn't his problem, it was just as much hers. She glanced down; in her left hand she still had the folded page of the *Post* containing Jack Douglas's column. She had scribbled some questions beside it in the margin. She'd already tried twice to call Douglas and leave a message but without success – his tape had cut out. There were questions about Kelp's past – where the money had come from, what her father's connection with all these people was . . . She sighed, her head was spinning.

She took a deep breath – there was no other way and she knew it. She reached across her desk and grabbed a sheet of notepaper. A few quick lines and her request for unpaid leave was complete. Folding the notepaper, she placed it in an envelope, sealed it and wrote Walter Harvey's name carefully on the front. She picked up her bag and coat.

'All this,' she whispered, 'career, my whole life . . .' She shrugged and stepped into the outer office. 'Sal, give this to Walter Harvey, will you.'

'Where are you going? You've got a two o'clock.'

'Cancel it.'

'What do you mean?' Her secretary stared at her. 'When will you be back?'

'I don't know,' Laura smiled faintly, 'I just don't know.'

'You're not coming back, are you?' Sal said, standing up, her face white.

'No, I'll be . . .' Laura muttered, without commitment, 'I'll be back.'

'I know you won't be,' her secretary interrupted, 'it's that Englishman!' She shook her head. 'All this, Laura . . . all this . . . is he worth it?'

'You're wrong. I'll be back – I just don't know when. I'll call you to let you know what's going on.'

'I hope so,' her secretary replied. 'Look,' she said, writing a number down on the piece of paper and thrusting it into Laura's hand, 'use this number.' She held onto Laura's hand for a few seconds. 'I knew he was trouble, I just *knew* it!'

Laura was about to protest. Instead, she looked hard at her secretary, nodded in acknowledgement, then left the office.

14

Independent
Columnist

As Jack Douglas locked his car door in the half-full basement garage and walked towards the elevator, his thoughts were on the last seven days. His column on Kelp had produced a storm of angry comment. There were official complaints about it from the Kelp team to the editor and the board. A succession of Kelp supporters appeared in the media, condemning his malice and calling for him to withdraw what they claimed were his unsubstantiated allegations. There had even been Kelp supporters in the audience on ABS's *Opinion to Opinion* programme, accusing him of bias. Then, just as all of it was dying down, came the counterattack. The day before yesterday, the *Los Angeles Times* produced an article alleging he was running a personal vendetta against Senator Kelp, their evidence being two incidents in the past in which Kelp had crossed Douglas.

The article dredged up his time as editor of *The Courier* in 1955, a small independent newspaper aimed at New York commuters. He had at the time opposed Kelp's candidature for the state legislature and had backed his opponent. Kelp, however, had gone on to win and had held up Douglas's editorial, prophesying that Kelp would lose, to the cameras, just as President Truman had done when he won the

Presidency. The article also referred to the time when he had just taken over as editor of the *Post*. There had been a diary piece insinuating that Kelp was seeing other women. Kelp sued, the *Post* settled immediately and apologised. The *Los Angeles Times* used these two incidents as a sign of lifelong bias by Douglas against Kelp.

Douglas poured himself a cup of coffee from the stand and walked towards the editor's office.

He hadn't been surprised when Gene Meyer called him in. He felt sorry that Meyer should feel so embarrassed about making the call. Douglas knew Meyer understood how this had been engineered by the Kelp campaign team and the sprinkling of coverage that had been achieved was more because of a journalistic laziness than any genuine belief in the allegations of bias. It was also good knocking copy for rival papers. Of course, in the wake of the allegations, there had been the inevitable calls for his contract to be withdrawn, but these had been from predictable quarters and had died down almost as soon as they'd begun. It was all too absurd, he knew, but sometimes the most absurd things had a habit of being remembered.

Perhaps Gene Meyer had been right, Douglas thought – he should have taken it all a little more seriously when it first started. Whatever the charges, Douglas had felt there was nothing to be gained by legitimising them through any counter comment on his own part.

He peered round the editor's door. Gene Meyer was sitting with the receiver cradled between his shoulder and his ear. As soon as Meyer saw Douglas, he beckoned him in with his left hand.

'No,' Meyer was saying, waving at Douglas and pointing to the chair in front of his desk. 'I don't believe it for a moment . . . Well, they're just plain wrong . . . As I said, this paper certainly isn't conducting any vendetta . . . No! That's not how Jack Douglas works and you . . . Well, is that so? Then I must be blind and anyway I don't see any letters from those smart-ass lawyers – no writs . . . No, ma'am! No defamation and they damn well know it . . . Frankly . . . You know, I know, and every other lazy journalist in this game knows, that they were all legitimate questions about Kelp's tactics in Massachusetts and . . . I don't know if Jack wants to continue with the line.' Meyer became very animated, jabbing his finger into the air. 'Sure, I appreciate that . . . I know, we always have been and always will be about the facts – this paper doesn't kiss anyone's butt, I don't . . . sure, I'm a hundred per cent behind Jack and I think that should be enough . . . No, not obsessed . . . OK, I'll say so – thanks for your help.' With that he slammed the receiver down and sat back in his seat, flushed and shaking his head.

'Let me guess, Gene,' Jack began, 'the proprietor calling to express thoughts on your supposedly biased, vendetta-ridden columnist's view of Kelp's life. An old man who should have been pensioned off and his column handed over to a younger journalist,' he chuckled.

'You forgot obsessed,' Gene's voice was dry, with just the hint of a smile creeping across his face. 'Well, the shit's in the air, Jack. Everyone's edgy, the Kelp team have really gone to town on this and worked us over. Boy, did you strike a raw nerve! It's bullshit, I know, Jack – but I just wish you'd remembered those previous encounters you'd had with Kelp. But what the hell, it's ancient history.'

'But Gene, what the *Los Angeles Times* didn't say,' began Douglas slowly, 'was that *The Courier* was bought by a front company for Atlantic Import Export – you know, Kelp's company. When they said I lost my job after the article, I actually got my marching orders from them. And the diary piece – I wasn't even editing the paper. I was away on holiday. As soon as I came back the next day, I made the decision to settle and apologise – even though what appeared was probably correct.'

'We can throw some muck back at them, enough to kill the issue,' Meyer replied, 'but we'll have to think carefully about what we do now.'

'We go on,' Douglas said, sitting up. 'I've hit a raw nerve with Kelp. I'll need to look a bit harder.'

'It's gotta be really something, Jack!'

'I think there is, Gene. Joe's got information that seems to be leading somewhere. I admit, we're still at the stage where we have more questions than answers but this baby has a real smell about it, Gene – a real smell.'

'Maybe. However, our problem, Jack, is that we just don't have enough . . .'

'Look, Gene, we're really on to something . . .'

'Hold it!' Meyer ordered, 'Let me finish. I'm giving you another pair of eyes, a new guy who started this week. I've sent him on down to join Schwartz.'

'What about the call you've just taken?' Douglas asked smiling, 'the powers that be . . .?'

'Sure, well, as I always say, it's difficult to control an independent columnist,' Meyer said drily, 'as I promised her,' inclining his head towards the telephone, 'I'd speak to you – so I'm speaking to you.' Meyer scratched his forehead. 'Well, go quiet for a bit until you come up with some hard facts and then . . . Well, I guess you taught me not to get pushed around, Jack, and you taught me too well.'

'Don't worry, Gene, if this doesn't fly, I'll retire and die gracefully.'

'Oh yeah, and then we'll get faxes from your coffin,' Meyer watched Jack leave the office and he slowly shook his head. Maybe she was right, he thought, maybe Jack was obsessed. 'No,' he muttered, 'Jack backed me too often against their better judgement. God damn them!' He picked up a bent paperclip from his desk and threw it at the corner of the room. 'It just better work out, that's all.'

Twenty minutes later, Douglas walked into the VIP guest room at the Washington office of ABS Broadcasting to do the *Opinion to Opinion* programme. There were already five people in there. Four of them were political commentators like himself, the fifth was Jack Marriott, the show's host – Marriott the talking head, he thought. He smiled at him but, try as he might, he just couldn't bring himself to like the man. It was his grating pomposity and lack of sincerity that nagged at Jack whenever he was near him. To listen to him talk, Jack thought, you'd be forgiven for assuming the man had invented political journalism.

As the others greeted him, a serious young woman walked in and without ceremony took him by the arm and ushered him through the door and into make-up.

'God, I hate this!' he complained. 'Look, Mary, I'll do a deal, no make-up and I'll turn up on time in future.'

'No dice, Jack,' Mary Ward laughed, 'you'll shine like a seal's butt, if you don't.' Her deep voice made him smile again as he slid into the chair.

'Mary?' Another girl poked her head in through the swing door.

'Yeah?'

'Jimmy Randle wants you.' The make-up girl held the door open as Mary Ward turned and left the room.

'Just a light dust, please,' Douglas said as the girl covered his body in a white nylon gown.

'Uh huh,' she intoned, without even catching his eye. She worked without talking for two minutes and then, pulling off the gown, she turned and, grabbing her mobile and make-up box, left the room. Jack was just about to follow her when the door opened again. He half-expected to see the make-up girl, but instead he was pleasantly surprised to see Walter Harvey of ABS Broadcasting.

'Walter, what on earth . . .?' he began.

'Jack, I know, it's been a long time.'

231

'Too long.'

They shook hands.

Jack Douglas and Walter Harvey had known each other since the Korean War. Douglas had been a war correspondent and Harvey, having been wounded up at China Lake with the Marines, was looking after the press for a time at head-quarters. They'd got to know each other well and after the war, when Jack had become a young editor of the *Courier* in upper New York State, he'd given Walter his first job in journalism. Their paths had gradually drifted apart. Harvey went into television and Douglas stayed with newspapers.

'What are you doing here? Aren't you based in New York?' Douglas asked.

'Yes,' Harvey answered and then shrugged, 'but there's a little local difficulty.'

'Must be a hell of a lot of difficulty to bring a big white chief like you here.'

'I'm looking after the news and current affairs section.'

'But that's the new woman's job, isn't it? You handed it over to her, didn't you? She seems good, she knows what she's doing,' Jack glanced towards the door, 'though how she deals with that pompous stuffed shirt Marriott beats me.'

'Oh yes,' Walter Harvey smiled, glancing at his watch. 'You're due on now, so I thought I'd walk with you to the studio.'

'Sure,' Jack watched him as he turned, 'Something on your mind?'

'It's that noticeable?' Harvey followed Douglas down the corridor and through the next door before continuing. 'Look, I'll be honest with you, it's about that same woman, Laura Buckley.'

'What about her?'

'Well, it's hard to believe,' Harvey continued. 'but she's just upped and gone – taken unpaid leave and get this, it was all at one hour's notice. It's completely out of character.'

They walked up a flight of steps as Harvey continued, 'I mean, this is one of the most responsible people I've ever come across in the business. A tremendous brain, great organising skills, imagination and real determination – she was going places and then this.' He shook his head.

'Sounds very strange,' Jack interjected, 'but I don't see how I can help.'

'I'm sorry, Jack, I should have started with this,' he reached into his pocket, pulled out an envelope and took out a slightly crumpled newspaper cutting. 'I found this on her desk, the same day she wrote her goodbye note to me.'

'Oh yes, my American dream piece,' he smiled. 'The one that's caused Kelp to go mad, but what . . .?'

'There were some comments she had scribbled in the margins, see?' he pointed to one scrawl, 'Call Jack about the money,' he read. Walter passed it to Douglas. 'The strange thing is, Laura never kept any of the newspaper cuttings, she usually just marked them and gave them to her secretary.'

'I see, and you think that maybe if I had spoken to her, I might shed some light on all this?'

'I was hoping.'

'But I'm sorry, Walter, I hardly know her and certainly haven't spoken to her since she asked me to be on the programme.'

'The thing is, Jack, normally I wouldn't be so bothered,' Harvey continued. 'I mean, it was bad enough her taking off like that, I might just manage to swing that with the board – after all, the schedules are all in place and the new organisation is working pretty smoothly – but the thing is, yesterday the police came round asking about her.'

They stopped outside the studio door and Douglas looked at Harvey, puzzled. Harvey looked away. 'It's not just that she's taken off. No one knows where she's gone. She's left her apartment and the police have searched it.' He turned and looked at Douglas, frowning. 'I think she's mixed up in something, Jack, something pretty strange. I can't find anyone else she's talked to about this before she left the office.' Harvey seemed unsure of what to say next. 'There's something else, too, there was some strange guy dressed like a bum whom she spoke to in her office. Her secretary says he was English – it all seems connected.' He took the article back from Douglas. 'Anyway, the point is, she might still call you. If she does, would you let me know?'

'Of course I will, but I doubt she'd call me, I can't see how I'm connected. It's probably just a coincidence, Harvey, just a coincidence.' He squeezed Harvey's arm, 'She's a smart girl, don't let it worry you too much.' Through the glass panel of the studio door he saw Mary Ward waving at him.

'Look,' Harvey handed the article back to Douglas as he turned to leave, 'You keep it – you might think of something. If so, give me a call.'

All over the floor there were cable runs and cameras on large metal frames, gliding around.

'Jack, quick, we're nearly on!' Mary Ward whispered, standing by his chair with a clipboard in her hand and a headset on.

'We'll talk about it later, Jack,' Harvey said, waving to him.

As Douglas took his seat, his mind drifted back over their conversation. At first it had meant nothing to him, but then he remembered a strange message on his answering machine some days before. No name and it cut off because the tape ran out. It must have been about the same time, he mused. Perhaps, he thought, there was a problem after all.

'Jack, did you hear me? Can you please give us some level? What did you eat for breakfast?' Mary Ward's voice broke into his thoughts.

'Must have been a coincidence, just a coincidence, that's all,' he voiced his thoughts aloud.

'Great! OK – we're all set!' Mary Ward cut in. 'Ten and counting,' she shouted as she stepped back and pointed towards Marriott, '. . . Nine – eight – seven – six – five – four – three – two – one.' She pointed at Marriott again and the music rolled.

The police car pulled up outside the precinct building. Minutes later Detective Munroe was knocking on the door of Lieutenant Jasinski's office.

'Lieutenant, this is Detective Sergeant Mackie – you know, British police.'

Jasinski watched as a short grey-haired man, wearing a tweed jacket, grey flannel trousers and brown shoes, stepped forward. With his thinning grey hair, strong jaw and deep brown, intelligent eyes, Mackie looked more like a teacher than a policeman.

'Detective Sergeant Mackie – good to meet you,' he said as they shook hands.

A jet-lagged Detective Sergeant Mackie lowered himself into the hard seat opposite the lieutenant's desk. Through the glass panels to his left he observed the men and women as they shouted, telephoned, typed, questioned and ate. His mind was overwhelmed by the sights and sounds of New York – the huge contrasts with home. He glanced at Munroe and Rutgers, who had attempted to tell him their side of the Grande case in the car – but he hadn't understood much.

'My men fill you in?' Jasinski asked as he sat down.

Mackie nodded, 'Aye, thank you, Lieutenant. A pretty good summary.'

'Good, good.' Jasinski studied Mackie's face carefully as he answered and then he reached into his top drawer and pulled out a brown file. 'Here,' he pushed it across to Mackie. 'It's all in there, something to read tonight. Just in case my detectives left somethin' out.' Rutger's face fell and he stopped chewing his gum. Jasinski saw Mackie smile.

'Aye,' Mackie said, 'that's him.' He was looking down at the photograph pinned to the inside front cover of the file. He flicked through the file for the next few minutes, stopping to read the interim report.

'Well, how about a coffee?' Jasinski glanced up at Munroe as Mackie began tentatively, 'Thanks, but I don't suppose you have tea, do you?'

'Sure,' Jasinski glanced across to Mackie and then again back at Rutgers. 'Get the detective sergeant here a cup of tea, will you.'

'But, L'tenant, we ain't . . .' Rutgers began. Jasinski cut him short with a wave of his hand and he shuffled off.

'L'tenant,' Munroe spoke quickly. 'I'm going over to see that friend of Buckley's – you know, the one the secretary put me on to – that van Buren woman.'

'Get some background on Buckley – you know, guys, vacations, anything,' Jasinski spoke as Munroe started to walk towards the door. 'Six-thirty, look, why don't we get you to your hotel?'

Mackie nodded, 'I'd appreciate that.' Jasinski slipped a revolver into a holster clipped to the back of his belt as Rutgers returned with a plastic cup in his hand.

'Christ! What's that?' Jasinski looked at the teabag hanging limply in the cup on some string. The water inside the cup was barely warm and the teabag had hardly stained the water. 'Roach piss!' Jasinski pushed it back towards Rutgers.

'There ain't no boiling water here, L'tenant,' Rutgers complained.

Jasinski snorted as he slipped on his coat. 'Never mind that. First thing in the morning, get down to ABS Broadcasting and see if you can look around Buckley's office. Go through her notes, see if there's anything there she wrote before she went. Ask around, you know. There was nothing in the apartment, you'd better find something.' Rutgers nodded as Jasinski spoke. 'I'm going to take the detective sergeant here to his hotel.'

As they left, Mackie's mind drifted back over the last three days. Summoned by the chief inspector, he'd been informed that Grande had turned up in New York. The New York Police Department had been told that London thought it was a straight murder inquiry and Grande was a prime suspect. In return, the superintendent had then been asked by the NYPD if someone who knew about Grande and the case could go over and help them. The chief inspector told him to pack his bags as he handed him his ticket.

'Strange,' he said as they parted, 'it seems the Cabinet office have specifically asked for us to help the New York Police Department. The Home Office too, by request of someone in the White House, I'm told.'

It was the chief inspector's way of letting him know that the politicians were watching him; that only angered him. Mackie hated politicians.

The past few months had tested Mackie's patience and certainly that of the superintendent. His plan to wait until Grande surfaced had become thoroughly discredited, yet it seemed that, at the eleventh hour, it had been saved. He'd known in his bones that Grande had been set up; all the evidence he'd seen pointed to that conclusion. However, the chief superintendent demanded Grande be put on the Wanted List and, while Mackie disagreed that Grande was guilty, he knew that running it through Interpol might turn up a connection – it had.

Two hours later Lieutenant Jasinski and Detective Sergeant Mackie were sitting in the hotel restaurant, the remnants of a meal scattered around them and in front of them two cups of black filter coffee. They had spent the last two hours exchanging information about the case. When the coffee arrived, Mackie rejected his in favour of tea, and while they waited for it, there was silence, each pondering the other's words. Mackie pulled out his pipe and puffed away while gazing at the ceiling.

Watching him, Jasinski was reminded of his father. An immigrant Pole, he'd worked the docks all his life, never borrowed anything or had a day off sick until the day when a crane dropped a packing case on him. It broke his back and he spent the rest of his life – twenty years – in a wheelchair, paralysed from the neck down. Jasinski remembered how he'd fill the pipe for his father after meals and then hold it so he could smoke it. Three of them had shared a one-bedroom apartment in a rundown tenement in the lower East Side. It was curious, he thought, how often his mind travelled back to the old days now. So much of this city had changed and yet far too much had remained the same.

'If you catch him, you know my lot will be applying for extradition,' Mackie said, still puffing away.

'So you got a case against him?' Jasinski spoke quickly and, finishing his coffee in one gulp, he wiped his mouth.

'They'd need to break him,' Mackie looked down as he spoke, 'during questioning. They just want someone, it appears anyone, and Grande is their best target. It's the pressure from outside.' Mackie explained, 'His dead partner was gay and the son of a politician, you see – what we call a Cabinet Minister – the Establishment. They've already attempted to portray Grande as a homophobe, which is crazy! I suppose I shouldn't be surprised,' he sighed, 'Justice is always the first casualty when people want a hanging.' He put his pipe back in his mouth and puffed away slowly.

'So tell me about it!' Jasinski muttered, 'This guy Goldstein was very big here. Leader of the Jewish community, big philanthropist, personal friend of the Mayor. He was even on the previous mayor's crime commission.' With that he gave a snort of derision, 'In those days it was the usual crap, if you come from a poor home – you know, you're entitled to commit crime. What you need is more money.' Again he snorted. 'Anyway, my balls are nailed to the wall on this. I've got limited resources and a crime list as long as your arm – so I have to do this myself with those two boys you saw earlier. It don't matter that I got years of good policing behind me.' Mackie nodded as he listened.

'You see,' Jasinski continued, 'it just don't fit. The guy turns up after the murder – I don't buy this crap that Grande committed murder then came back the same day: it makes no sense. All these years in police work, I've never seen that before. No, this looks like some sort of set-up, but,' here Jasinski paused, 'I've still got to get him in.'

'Aye, it seems there's a pattern developing – Grande tied in to the murder in the gallery, runs away, then there's a murder of a lawyer in Rome – Soletti, Grande was seen with him. Then the murder of Goldstein – Grande shows up after it – and then the shooting up the road. He runs again, ends up in a rundown part of town, gets hit on the head, rescued, taken to hospital and the super of his building gets murdered. And now you say some woman at the television studios has disappeared. What d'you think, was she the one who took Grande to the hospital?'

'Looks that way, but she's not just some woman, she's head of news and current affairs at ABS. I can't figure it out.' He looked at Mackie, 'If the son-of-a-bitch knows someone's after him, I don't understand why he doesn't hand himself in – unless he's guilty.'

'Probably our fault,' Mackie lowered his pipe and placed it on the table.

'Eh?'

'My chief superintendent, remember, he's the one who insisted on making it clear he was our prime suspect. And anyway, it was the only way to be certain that we'd find him, if he turned up somewhere else. Grande's obviously in touch with someone in London. My money's on the man who's looking after the gallery for him – he must have been keeping him informed.'

'What about this guy in Italy, his uncle?' Jasinski leaned forward as he spoke.

'The Italian police had his wires tapped until last week. Nothing. Poor bastard! I don't think he knows anything. You remember the paintings I spoke about?'

'Sure.'

'Whoever wanted them, must have got them now – it's my guess they're somewhere here. Grande was used specifically for this handover. At first I thought it was drugs, but going through the inventory at the gallery, there was a hell of a lot of money passed across their books for six pictures, which would never normally fetch prices like that.'

'What about this guy D'Ostia, have you got anything on him?' As Jasinski spoke a puzzled look crossed his face.

'Not much. Covered his tracks pretty well. A naturalised Italian, originally on a Swiss passport before that, a one-time resident in Monte Carlo. Oh yes, all bank accounts were Swiss. Soletti was his lawyer. I've got someone almost full time on it. The Swiss have just given us permission to check the passport records.'

Jasinski felt strangely comfortable with this quiet Scotsman. About the same age as himself, with a lifetime's service in policing, they were already beginning to strike up a rapport. He liked the calm deliberate way Mackie approached his work. The conversation had built up a picture for Jasinski, it helped him to understand his quarry. Grande himself probably didn't know much but for someone else he must hold the key.

'How sure are you of the identity of the woman?' Mackie tapped his pipe out in the ashtray.

'Pretty sure. Didn't show up on Monday, the company says it's unpaid leave. Anyway, it all fits because the cab driver,' Jasinski waved his hands in the direction of Mackie's brief-case, 'he remembered picking her up; it turns out that the ABS offices are right there.'

Out of the window, Mackie could see Central Park. It was

raining, people hurried by with umbrellas up and raincoats buttoned around their necks. Why did everyone always hunch their shoulders when it rained? Mackie mused, it didn't change how wet they got. They knew it, yet they still did it. He smiled as they scurried past – and why did everyone want to know the answer before they knew the question?

'Could she have known about your visit to the hospital?' Mackie asked.

'Maybe that doctor coulda tipped her off.' He caught the waiter's eye – good coffee, why couldn't he make it like this at home? 'More coffee,' he called.

'Buckley's secretary,' Jasinski continued, 'wasn't saying much. It was all I could do to get the name of Buckley's friend – that's why I thought Rutgers should pay her a visit.'

'Something must have happened to make Buckley suddenly up and go,' Mackie watched as the waiter poured more coffee for Jasinski.

'Yeah,' Jasinski answered, 'she shouldn't be scared of us, she ain't done nothing. But then again, maybe someone's leaning on her. The truth is, we just don't know.' Jasinski blew across the top of his coffee, then draining the cup, he continued, 'Let's see what Munroe and Rutgers come up with.'

Mackie stifled a yawn. 'It's a quarter of ten,' Jasinski said, 'time to go – you must be tired.' He stood up and they shook hands. 'The car will be here at eight tomorrow morning – OK?'

15

Laura

Laura sank back into an old worn armchair and rested her head. Outside the rain was sliding down the window. She was tired, bewildered and also scared. The last few days had flown by with hardly any time to think. Absurdity piled upon absurdity. Some weeks ago, she had met a strange unshaven Englishman who suffered, she'd thought, from paranoia. Yet now she was sharing a small one-bedroom apartment in Chelsea with the same man. She smiled at the thought of how, despite the one bedroom, it had all been so intensely proper. He slept on the couch and she had the bedroom – such propriety, she mused, in dire circumstances. He was, she had to remind herself, a man who was wanted for one murder and connected to at least two others. Yet despite his undeniable aura of danger, she could also see he had built a wall around himself behind which dwelt a lonely, reserved and shy man.

She knew nothing about his past and found herself intrigued by the way he blocked all her inquiries. Superficially, he seemed clear-headed and determined, all action, but there was more. She knew well enough that New York was stuffed full of men competing with each other to be dollar lords and for whom every polished surface was simply a potential mirror. What little interest she had in them had long gone. She had become weary of the mating merry-go-round. Tired as she was of the men in the city, she was fascinated by her women friends, all career, fashion and fun on the outside, yet seething with insecurity inside. The game they played still had strict rules; they must show the men they had no interest in commitment, only in their careers. Sex without demands. She watched as the years created an outer hardness. But underneath hope coursed for an offer of the thing they said they wanted least, that island of mutual well-being and stability.

She had insisted that her way was not theirs. Their hypocrisy was all she saw, their fears were alien to her and their hopes were too much a part of their fears to interest her. Now, against the whole grain of her life, she found herself close to a man, albeit a very different sort of man, in a way that she would have laughed at a month before. John's detachment and distance enhanced her feelings. She laughed now when she thought of how Alice van Buren would ridicule her for being so interested in an unsuccessful man, a nobody, someone about whom Laura knew so little. Yet she realised she no longer cared and this thought surprised her. She'd always valued her friend's opinion before, why not now?

From her bedroom she heard him moan nightly – trapped in some vicious nightmare, often repeating a woman's name – Julia. What would Alice think of that? On a couple of occasions, she'd crept into the room and seen him tossing about relentlessly. Not a night went by but as dawn broke, the same nightmare seemed to return. Yet he would say nothing of his thoughts or dreams to her. Once she'd seen him gripping onto the bed with his eyes closed, hanging on as though his life depended on it. She wanted to help, to reach out, but she didn't dare to try to break through.

What most surprised her was that she had hardly thought about the job she had left behind. The only real success of her life. She had walked away from it with too much ease – not a backward glance, not even a regret. She had loved it – the excitement, the power and the sense of purpose she found in her work each day. Yet all that was being replaced by a strange man's helter-skelter existence and the impenetrable cloak of danger that hung around him. Her one and only real regret was that she had left poor Walter Harvey in the lurch, a man who always played straight with her and who, in a way, had become a mentor, more than just her boss. She knew that he would be hurt and worried by the turn of events and that gave her cause for thought. Yet her decision had been made and, despite her present fears and concerns, she knew it was the only course.

Laura checked her watch. She had fallen asleep and during this time John had left the apartment – for food, the note had said, but that was an hour ago. She felt strangely alone and worried. He shouldn't take chances, he might be seen, recognised. She switched the television on and absent-mindedly started flicking across the channels. She stopped and smiled. The programme she had recently launched, *Opinion to Opinion*, was on. She turned the volume up. It seemed like light years ago.

At that moment there was a knock on the door. 'It's me, John.'

Just as she got up to answer the door, Jack Douglas appeared on the screen. Douglas – strange – what was it? She paused halfway to the door, a half-lost thought nagging at her in the recesses of her memory.

'Laura? Are you there?' John shouted again.

'Coming, John,' she called out, but she couldn't move. What was it? She should remember – she couldn't.

'Of course,' she realised, 'The article! Jack Douglas's piece on Kelp!'

'Laura!' John shouted again. 'Open up!'

Shaking her head, she opened the door. 'I've just remembered something. I'm an idiot!' she shouted. 'Jack Douglas
wrote something on Kelp in the *Post* the day I called you
about the police. Something about Kelp's money – where it
came from. It looked like he had an angle, so I tried to call
him, without success – I meant to call him later, but you
know what happened next.' She emerged from the bedroom
in her coat and walked towards him. 'I got a little distracted,'
she smiled, 'I should have remembered though.' She smiled
again at him.

'Where are you going?'

'Off to call Douglas.'

'But – he's on TV,' he said pointing at the screen, 'you just
said so. Surely you'll have to wait until . . .'

'No, no. That was recorded this afternoon. He'll be back at
home in Washington, that is, at his home in Alexandria by
now.' She paused only inches from him. He seemed edgy,
reserved. 'Look,' she said, 'it's a long shot but maybe Jack has
found something.' She laid her hand on his shoulder, leaned
forward and kissed him gently on his cheek, the way a mother
might a child before he went to bed. 'I won't be long.' With
that she slipped out of the apartment.

John knew that she was going across the road to the bar
on the corner. All the other apartments had their own
telephones; however, this one had been cut off before
they arrived and they thought it wiser to leave it at that.
He remembered when he had mentioned mobile telephones, Laura had said in an exasperated tone that
suggested he should have known better, 'Cell phones are too
easy to trace!'

He walked over to the armchair and flopped down. For the
first time since the death of Julia and his son, he'd begun to
feel like a human being again. Someone cared whether he
lived or died and that had begun to make him care too.

Someone whose kindness and laughter was beginning to break through. Part of him felt exhilarated by her vitality, the other part guilty and confused. Although he had been desperate and had gone to see her for help, he was now worried about her.

The grandfather clock in the corner of Jack Douglas's study struck half past ten as he typed the final words on his computer. He finished, checked them through, then printed them off. He still wasn't used to the computer, having only started using it the year before. Even now, every time he shut the machine down, there was that moment of panic when he wondered whether, when he turned it on again, there would be anything that he'd typed left on it. He shook his head, looking at the heavy old manual typewriter on the table by the door. He recalled how it folded away into its case ready to carry. It had gone everywhere with him. He turned back to his work, back to Kelp – where did that money come from? The same question he asked himself over and over again.

He folded his glasses and reached into his pocket, searching for the case; instead his hand caught a piece of paper. Unfolding it, he saw it was the cutting Walter Harvey had given him. He started reading it again.

'Why did Laura Buckley call?' he wondered. 'What was it that created the interest?' He placed it down on the desk. He remembered how Walter had told him about the strange visitor, the rough-looking Englishman. Walter had confided in Jack that he thought something serious was going on, perhaps even dangerous, and that she, Laura, was mixed up in it. But why tell him?

He stood up slowly and stretched, then leaning across the desk he switched off the light, just as the telephone rang. He paused, irritated by the nagging shrill tone. For a moment he wondered whether he should answer it or not. Again and again it rang, rasping through his head like a serrated knife, intruding, demanding. He sat down again, sighed, switched on the light and reached for the receiver.

'Come on, come on!' Laura Buckley muttered as the telephone rang. Nervously, she glanced around the bar behind her; it was noisy and full. She needed one hand on her other ear, to enable her to listen through all the noise. The payphone she was using was situated in a corner just by the lavatories and she felt distinctly uneasy using it. Every time the door to the men's room opened, she could feel the stares.

'Hello, Douglas speaking.'

Laura pressed her ear to the receiver, her heart pounding. 'Jack!' she shouted. 'Jack, it's Laura Buckley.'

'Laura? Laura Buckley?'

'You know – ABS Broadcasting. Look, I need to see you.'

Douglas found it hard to hear what she was saying. The noise of rock music in the background, laced with laughter and shrieks, cut across her words.

'See me. Certainly, but . . .'

'Tomorrow morning,' she cut in.

'OK, where are you, can you come here . . .?' It was just as he spoke that he realised that he was assuming she was in Washington. 'That is, I'm not free till ten-thirty.'

'In Washington then. Where?'

'Vietnam Memorial, at the statue.' He found himself shouting at her as she had been shouting at him.

'OK, we'll be there.'

'We'll? Who . . .?' But the line went dead and he was left looking at the newspaper clipping. He put the telephone down and stared again at the cutting.

Laura's face broke into a smile. She stepped out from the corner and into the bar. As she tried to walk towards the door, she found her way was blocked by three women, two black, one white, standing sideways to her. They wore tight skirts and tight tops, their heavily made-up faces looked tired and each of them chewed gum mechanically, jaws going round and round. As she tried to edge past them, her eyes followed their stares. Six feet to her right, leaning against the wall, stood another woman, dressed in similar fashion to the others, her face also made up, but she still looked young, even pretty. Laura was struck by the contrast. An unshaven pot-bellied man was leaning up against her, his left hand held a can of beer, his right was attempting to get between her legs. The woman kept pushing him away, but he persisted, encouraged by a group of men sitting on a table a couple of feet away.

'Come on, baby, don't be so shy!' His voice was rough and his pale fat face glistened with sweat. The woman tried to move away but he held her by the simple device of leaning against her.

'Hey!' one of the women in front of Laura shouted, 'let her go!' The man turned his head towards them.

'Don't be in such a hurry, there's enough of this,' he glanced down, 'to go round.' His voice trailed away as he looked at Laura. He turned away from the woman against the wall and swayed before moving forward.

The first man shouted to his friend and walked towards her, 'Man, this is some classy piece of ass!' They all roared with laughter.

Laura stared in horror at this mountain of wobbling flesh coming towards her. She took a deep breath while her heart pounded away and she wished the time she'd spent in those self-defence classes had been yesterday rather than two years ago. Now what was it? Smile – put him at ease – not too close – now! As he grabbed at her, Laura swung her knee sharply up into his groin. For a split second, which seemed to her an age, nothing happened. Then, as he exhaled, she was hit by his foul breath, his eyes rolling as he started to lean forward. Moving her right hand across her body and straightening it out, she brought it up into his face as hard as she could, aiming for his nose. She felt the nose give slightly and his face jerk back to one side as he straightened up. Now she was staring into his face; his breath was short and laboured, some blood trickled down his left nostril and his small bloodshot eyes were watering. His drunken, uncoordinated hands grabbed at her again, but she ducked and pushed both his shoulders as hard as she could.

He stepped back and hit a chair behind him. Off balance, he sat down heavily, his momentum carrying both him and the chair onto the rear two legs. At that moment, the first girl by the wall took a pace forward and kicked the right leg as hard as she could. The leg gave way and the fat man crashed to the floor, amid roars of laughter all around the bar.

Laura stood, frozen to the spot, her heart racing, amazed at what had happened. She grimaced at her hand as she wiped it on her raincoat. The woman by the wall smiled.

'Let's go!' The women screamed and, grabbing Laura by the arm, they pulled her towards the door.

'You're all right, you know that!' The younger woman exclaimed as they left the bar. She smiled and turned to the other two, 'Ain't she?'

'Sure is! Uh huh!' they intoned together.

'Look, lady, if ever you need help jus' ask in there for Ari,' she said as they walked quickly down the road.

'Ari?' Laura's face looked puzzled. They stopped on the corner.

'Yeah, Ari – Ariadne,' the woman laughed, 'some name huh? You see, my mom watched some Greek film, said it was romantic . . .' Again they all laughed. 'Just ask in there, anyway.'

'But I thought . . .' Laura began.

'Hey, what's your name?'

'Laura,' she said, quietly.

'Well, Laura, don't mind them, they'll forget all this tomorrow.'

'Where you from?' the woman called Ari asked. Laura pointed to the block across the street. 'Well, sister, I owe you one and I always pay my dues.'

With that, the three of them glided up the sidewalk. Laura watched them, her heart pounding. A burst of music from inside the bar served as a reminder of where she was. She ran across the street and into the apartment.

Inside, it was dark, save for the television, which flickered in the corner, the volume turned down. Laura pressed herself back against the door as she shut it, breathing hard. As her eyes got used to the light, she saw John sprawled out on the armchair, sound asleep. She walked closer to him. She bent down and smiled, her face just above him. His eyes opened, then she felt a hand reach up into her hair and pull her gently forward. With adrenalin still pumping from the incident in the bar, she lowered herself onto him. His kiss was passionate and hard.

Across town, a cab pulled up outside a hotel near the Park and after a few minutes an old man got out. He walked slowly into the lobby and gazed around him, unsure but unhurried. It had been a long journey from Positano and he felt every bit his age.

The room was filled with the post-theatre crowd, groups of friends, animated yet comfortable in this womb of security. As the old man finished signing in, he leaned back heavily on his walking stick. His attention was then caught by two men standing behind him. One was tall, young and heavily built, the other middle-aged. There were no handshakes or smiles – the greetings were cold and formal. They walked across the lobby, talking. Then they parted company – the old man moving towards the elevator, they out onto the street and into the night.

'Mr Grande?'

The old man turned and looked at the young girl in front of him.

'Your key – you forgot it.' She smiled.

President Carson stared through the window at the press corps assembled outside on the White House lawn waiting for his departure from the South Lawn by helicopter. As ever, his smile was light, the same winning smile – in good times and bad, it never changed.

'Kelp's broken through and my campaign is virtually dead,' Carson shook his head slowly as he spoke. 'Another one-term President, is that what I am to become?'

'Well, that depends . . .' Pete Neal, the national security adviser began.

'On what?' Carson growled, turning around.

'Kelp – there may be something.'

'What do you mean?' Carson demanded, staring at Neal.

'We've been doing some checking. There's been a lot of activity in his office.'

'What's that got to do with it?'

'Not sure. But his number two, Bernie Weitz, travelled to London – twice.'

'So?' Parry muttered.

'Well, it's strange. I understand he used a different name while he was there. Went with this private investigator, Pichowski. We checked on him too. He only works for Acquilan, no one else.' He glanced at Carson, who was leaning against the edge of his desk, hanging on to his every word.

'Anyway, seems Pichowski's also made several trips to Italy.'

'London, Italy – I don't get it,' Carson said, walking over to a sofa by the fireplace. 'What'd they do . . .'

'They bought some pictures . . .'

'Goddamn it, Pete, give it to me straight,' Carson snorted.

'There's a little more . . .' Neal continued, 'the guy they bought the paintings from in London is wanted for murder and,' he paused for dramatic effect, 'he's turned up in New York.'

'How do you know?' Parry asked.

'New York Police Department made a request through Interpol and turned the guy's name up.'

'What's the connection?' Carson asked, sitting back.

'I'm not sure . . .'

'What do you mean – not sure?'

'It's too early to say but it's pretty suspicious,' Neal replied.

'I don't know,' Parry began. 'We shouldn't jump to conclusions.'

'Come on, I mean, why use a false name unless something's going on?' said Neal quickly. 'And a man wanted for murder ends up in New York near the man he sells his pictures to.' He let out a short laugh. 'Now he's wanted in connection with a homicide here as well – I reckon there's much more but it's our first breakthrough.'

'You're right, Pete,' Carson said, smiling at him. 'Thanks. I guess he may have something after all, Frank. But what about the police, do they need any help? They have to catch this guy.'

'Don't worry,' Neal assured Carson, 'We've seen to that. An officer from Scotland Yard, who knows about the case, is on loan to NYPD. I didn't tell you but I made sure everyone over there knew how important it was that the cop was sent over. If they get the guy, it could turn out to be big for us.'

Parry smiled faintly, 'Well, maybe there is something Senator Kelp would rather we didn't know about. You'll just have to keep going, Pete. You're all we've got.'

16

Unprovable Truth

In a hollow to the right of the Lincoln Monument, a black V-shaped structure cut through the grass like a shadow, its highly polished granite shimmering in the sun.

It was the first time John had seen the Vietnam Memorial and he was struck by the way it seemed to absorb the people in front of it. It was sombre yet, as he watched a small group of young children cascade along its front, it seemed to embrace them, picking up their noise even before their parents chastised them. The names carved into it seemed like smudges on its polished face.

Laura tugged at his arm. 'That's him,' she whispered, pointing at a grey-haired man walking very slowly along the wall, 'that's Jack Douglas.'

John started forward but he felt her hand tighten on his arm as he did so.

'No, wait,' she whispered. 'Wait here – he's busy – we'll give him some more time.'

John looked from her to Douglas, bewildered. Douglas had stopped at the apex of the V and, half bending, he touched the wall with his finger, gently, slowly. As John watched, he could see he was tracing a name – a woman was doing the same at another part of the wall – and he understood.

Douglas bowed his head before stepping back. He turned and walked up the path. As he reached the top, he caught sight of Laura.

'I'm sorry,' he said as he walked up, 'I didn't see you there – you're early.'

'Yes. We got here quicker than expected – we caught an early flight out of New York.' She looked back at the monument. 'I'm sorry, Jack, I didn't know . . .'

'Oh,' Douglas said, 'no reason why you should. Funny though, it would have been my son's forty-eighth birthday today.' He shrugged, 'Strange, he never celebrated his birthday when he was alive. He hated all of that – I guess he wouldn't have wanted this either.' He smiled as he looked at her, 'Now, is this . . .?' He turned to John.

'John Grande,' Laura answered quickly.

'Yes, yes,' Douglas replied and shook hands.

'Well, Laura, you've created quite a storm,' he began. 'Walter Harvey's really worried that you're involved in something dangerous and I heard through the grapevine that the New York Police Department are hoping to question you about an Englishman, something to do with a murder in London.' His eyes hovered towards John as he spoke.

'It's a long story, Jack – the more we find out, the deeper it gets,' she put a hand on John's arm – 'I think you ought to hear our story first.' Douglas nodded and guided them towards a bench.

At the same moment, Weitz stepped out of his cab and walked slowly up the steps of the Lincoln Monument – only yards away from the other three people at the Vietnam Memorial. He looked to his left and right as he walked. He was angry. Grande and the woman had disappeared. He had nothing new to say to Acquilan and it worried him. He stopped halfway up to get his breath. What angered him was the way Cosmo had lured them into the trap. He hated having to react all the time, waiting for the next blow to fall. He was worried that Grande had been found by Cosmo's people. If that were so, it was all over for Kelp and the rest of them.

As Weitz reached the top, he was greeted by Dick Mason. The floor was a mass of cables and lights. They were shooting a commercial for Kelp.

'How's it going?' he asked.

'Fine, fine,' Mason replied, clearly distracted. 'They shoot Ewan walking up the last few steps, he pauses and looks towards the Capitol, then looking at the camera, he walks across to the statue talking about values – American values. At the statue, he pauses and speaks about strong leadership.'

'Sounds great,' Weitz cut in, '. . . great,' glancing at the statue before turning to Mason. 'So, Dick – any problems?'

'Uh, huh,' Mason took Weitz by the arm and guided him towards the corner by a small bookshop. 'I think Senator Wall will mess us up in New York.'

'*What*!' Weitz exclaimed. 'He's going to swing behind Ewan?'

'That's what he said, but he hasn't done it yet.'

'He's our ace in the hole – you said it yourself – the Senior Democrat Senator from New York State coming in behind Ewan, it will kill Carson stone dead.'

'It would, but . . .'

'But what?'

'But Carson ain't dead yet and he's struck back.'

'A deal's a deal.'

'Not in politics. He's had an offer of a better deal.'

'The General Electric plant has 2,000 jobs hanging on a Pentagon contract for air-defence radar – Carson can make it happen for him.'

'That greasy son-of-a-bitch!' Weitz snarled.

'We're still ahead,' Mason continued, 'but Carson's picking up a bit of a sympathy vote – he's still there – it's very tight.'

He pointed to Kelp, who was talking to the director. 'You know there's something else, Bernie.'

'What?'

'Money, Bernie, money – we're running low.'

Weitz rubbed his brow. He knew what Mason meant. The Seattle deal had hit their cash flow, forcing them to raise more money at this stage than they had planned. But the biggest blow was the New York Senator: Carson had delivered what only he as President could and it seemed to be working.

'One other thing, Bernie,' Mason continued, 'well . . .' He chewed his lip. 'There are rumours around about Ewan's marriage – he refuses to have Mary-Lou with him and . . .'

Weitz nodded. Kelp's Achilles' heel was well known to all of them. His wife hated her husband's obsession with the Presidency. She suffered from depression and it was well known in Washington circles that she drank heavily. Kelp's response was to leave her in Washington and only bring her out occasionally.

'I warned him that she was required in New York but he said he couldn't trust her,' Mason admitted.

'Well, he'll have to. Get someone to stay with her.'

'Well, I would be grateful if Victor could talk to him. He listens to Victor. It's beginning to affect us in New York and I've got to straighten it out now. Carson's people are pushing the rumours – we need to kill them fast.'

'I'll see to it.'

'Sure, but if Senator Wall backs Carson . . .'

'Carson lied to the American public,' Weitz snapped, 'Wall's a butthead, we'll just have to start playing hardball with him, that's all.'

'Sure, but if talk of Ewan's marriage, her drinking, the fact they hardly talk – if this gets out, it could wreck everything . . .'

'I told you – I'll speak to Victor and we'll get Mary-Lou up with Ewan by tomorrow night – leave it to me.'

'The money?'

'Like I said,' Weitz spoke slowly, 'I'll fix the problem, but you'd better concentrate on Wall – there's a few skeletons in his cupboard and perhaps he should know that it's time the public saw them. You've got that crap about his girl?'

Mason nodded slowly.

'Use it.'

'But what if . . .'

'Use it!' Weitz said firmly. 'He won't back Carson after that. If he does – well, he's more of a fool than I thought!'

They talked on. Half an hour later Weitz looked at his watch and set off down the steps.

He stopped by the road looking for his car. A cab had just pulled up ten yards away – two men and a woman walked towards it. Weitz gazed in a distracted way at the group and then, turning away, searched the road again for his car. 'Where is my driver?' he muttered.

Laura got into the cab as Jack Douglas held open the door. She was pleased because the brief explanation had been enough to make Douglas decide to go back to his house with them to see if the two parts of the story fitted together. Douglas slid into the seat beside her.

As John walked around the cab, he saw a small man standing ten yards away on the edge of the road. He was wearing glasses but his face was turned so that John could only see half of it.

'I know him,' John thought, as he reached for the door handle and paused. He looked at the man again.

At that moment the man turned his head and looked towards him. John froze, his hand still on the handle.

'Wessells!' he exclaimed.

Weitz was vaguely aware that the man by the cab was staring at him, but he couldn't place him. Yet still the man stared. Weitz strained his eyes, the man was beginning to annoy him now. He stared back. Perhaps there was something

257

about his face, something about the eyes, he thought. 'Looks very familiar,' he muttered to himself, 'Looks like Grande,' Weitz said absent-mindedly as he watched the other man getting into the cab. 'God, yes! *Grande!*' he exclaimed. He moved quickly towards the cab, his heart pounding but before he'd gone more than two steps, it pulled away from the kerb. Frantically he looked up and down the road for another cab. By the time one came, Grande's had disappeared.

'Grande, in Washington?' he said, 'right here . . . I don't believe it.' The girl in the cab with him, he guessed, was Buckley. But why, he wondered, why here? They couldn't have been to the Lincoln Monument, he would have seen them, so it either had to be a walk from the Washington Monument or the Vietnam Memorial. With an older man too. Someone helping them. But who – why?

As his car pulled up and he climbed in, angry, frustrated, but also relieved; at least Cosmo's people hadn't caught them, he thought. He was thankful in his gloom for very small mercies.

'It was him, ten yards away!' John said, staring out of the rear window, as his cab drove on.

'He's not following, is he?' Laura asked.

'No, but it was him – the man Wessells, I'm certain,' John replied.

'Wessells?' Douglas asked.

'I'm sorry,' John answered quickly, 'the man who bought the pictures in London.'

'Ah, did he recognise you?' Douglas continued.

'I think so – I was staring so hard. I shouldn't have done, I know, but it was the shock of seeing him there.'

'I only hope he didn't see you, Jack,' Laura said. 'I'd hate to involve you any more.'

'Oh, I don't think you need worry about me,' Douglas said. 'It just makes it all the more urgent we get this story straightened out.'

'But why would he be there?' Laura asked, expecting no reply. 'Why?'

An hour later, they were in Jack Douglas's study. John had just finished re-telling the story of what had happened to him, but in more detail this time, and for the added benefit of the other man sitting in the corner.

'These paintings,' Joe Schwartz began with an air of cynicism, 'why would anyone – any self-respecting artist – do this? After all, you said this guy Licatta was known as a good painter, so why would he paint over masterpieces? He would have known it was crooked.'

'Well,' John began, 'in short – money. After all, during the war he was considered a dissident by the fascists and was in and out of prison; his property and possessions were forfeited to the state. His last known picture was painted in 1942. He disappeared suddenly after the war. The guy was broke. I expect it was good money, there wasn't anything else.'

Schwartz reached for a box file and smiled, 'It's all guess-work – you don't know for sure that your pictures weren't painted before the war, before Acquilan . . .'

'I do. His work is pretty well recorded,' John snapped. 'Right up until 1942. These were not part of anything he'd ever done before.'

'How can you be sure? You said he was pretty obscure.'

'Yes, but he's become very popular since then – there have been a few books written on him.'

'So you think these pictures have something to do with the fire in the warehouse?' Schwartz asked as he started flicking through the file.

'What's this?' Laura asked, leaning over and lifting up an article headed by a big photograph.

'That's the picture of all of them when they came back from the plane crash,' Schwartz said, without looking up.

'Who's that?' Laura asked, pointing to a man on the left.

'Cosmo, one of the platoon who . . .'

'He's very familiar,' she continued, ignoring Schwartz and looking closely at the picture. By now John was looking over her shoulder.

'This one hasn't really changed,' John said. 'I recognise him as a younger version of the man Wessells, who came to the gallery – the one we saw before, in Washington.'

'No, it can't be him – his name is Weitz!' Schwartz snapped.

'But I saw him . . .'

'Well, must have been someone else,' Schwartz said firmly.

'No, don't you see? It would have made sense to send him under a different name because he would have known about the pictures.' John looked up at Douglas. 'Surely that is evidence that they were involved in a fraud?'

'Well,' Douglas began, 'it's very helpful but it isn't good enough as evidence – they'd never believe you against their war heroes – two successful businessmen and a Senator, who is also a presidential candidate.'

'It's really strange,' Laura murmured again, 'this one here – Cosmo, I think you said – he looks really familiar. Have you got any other pictures of him?'

'No, that's the only one,' Schwartz answered, studying the photograph, 'because he died out there in the warehouse fire though he's buried here in New York.' Laura nodded but continued to stare at the picture.

'Well, there's only one way,' John addressed the other three. 'I'm going to have to find those paintings and establish my story.'

'*Sure!*' Schwartz broke in, 'Acquilan or Kelp will just give you an invitation.' He laughed sarcastically.

'I'm serious. All I need to know is where each of them lives.' Schwartz stared back at him blankly.

'Supposing you got to one of their houses, John – how would you begin?' Laura asked, looking up. 'How would you know where to look and what to look for? I mean, what if someone's already cleaned the pictures? You'd never know.' Even as she asked him, she felt a strange, nagging worry growing about the photograph she had in front of her. The face was so familiar, as though . . . as though . . .

'. . . There are a couple of ways,' John continued, 'When the painting arrived in the gallery, I kept some original paint flakes so I could compare anything I gathered from the paintings that I wasn't certain of. Second, and perhaps most important of all, something I didn't tell you – I marked all of these pictures on the backs underneath the frame in a particular way and I could check for those marks. Chances are, he hasn't noticed them,' he shrugged, 'There is no other way at the moment – it's my story against theirs. Unless I manage to link 1946 with what happened in my gallery, I might as well hand myself over.'

'Look,' Douglas said quietly, leaning forward, 'dealing with Acquilan, or Kelp, is only part of your problem. What about Laura's father?'

'He's dead,' Laura responded, with a firm voice, 'I ought to know – I saw the death certificate. They buried him, or at least his ashes. I accept he may have had something to do with all this but it's too late to be worried about him now.'

'We can't be sure, after all . . .' John began.

'No, he's dead!' she was again definite. 'Don't worry, I know, he's involved in much of this – God knows why – but he's gone. Someone else is responsible for all this now.'

The silence in the room was broken only by the ticking of the clock in the corner. No one made eye contact.

'Well,' Douglas began, 'if your father was there in Italy, you know it would make a difference.'

'But he wasn't. She's right, they're all accounted for,' Schwartz said as he swung around and looked at Douglas.

'But what if they weren't?'

'They were,' Schwartz insisted, reaching back into a file

for the cutting with the picture in it. 'No point in playing kids' games. This guy,' he said, pointing at Grande, 'is on some personal kick of his own. We shouldn't fit our stuff around him.'

He flicked open the file. 'Here – Kelp, Acquilan, Cosmo, Weitz and Morrow.' He jabbed his finger at the picture as he spoke, 'Two dead, Morrow and Cosmo, and three in the USA, all alive.' He passed it across to Jack Douglas.

'No, Joe, give it to Laura.' Schwartz frowned, then handed it over to her. 'Laura,' Douglas continued, 'just look at it again. Which one did you say looked familiar?'

'This one – Cosmo, I think, don't ask me why – just something, but it's difficult . . . the photograph . . . not great, but then something about the eyes,' she looked up at Douglas.

'What do you see?'

Laura stared at Douglas, her eyes wide open.

'Well, Laura?'

'I . . . I can't say.'

'Have another look,' Douglas urged.

Laura looked down at the picture again, 'Dark eyes,' her voice was barely audible, 'always had dark eyes – strange haunted look . . . Yes, it's there, this face . . . but you know, I only really got to know him when he was suffering from cancer . . . he looked drawn . . . it's too difficult.' She shook her head.

'But Mr Douglas,' Schwartz interrupted, 'two bodies – they came home, they're dead, there's no way it could be Cosmo.'

'Stay with me, Joe – let me go with this,' Douglas looked at Laura, 'Well?'

'I guess it could be my father. I never knew him then – as I said, only as an ill old man. There were never any pictures of him in our house.' She looked up. 'But there was one, I recall, in Positano, in his study . . . just him and someone he said he grew up with and was his best buddy . . .' Her chin was up, her eyes blazed, then she looked down at the cutting again. Could it be? She wondered. Those eyes, that shape . . . it could be anyone . . . why couldn't she be sure? After all those years, then she found her father . . . was it him? It would explain so much, she knew, but surely her father was dead now? She'd seen the death certificate. Why should it matter? Why? Why?

'Laura,' Douglas spoke softly, 'Laura, there's something?'

'Yes,' She said almost as though he'd dragged it from her. 'I just can't say for sure. Anyway, if he didn't die in Naples, he's sure as hell dead and buried now. So I'm not so sure what it means.'

'Let me explain,' Douglas said carefully. 'You say Licatta disappeared around the same time and we believe he is linked him to the fake pictures. What if . . .' he glanced at Schwartz as John nodded, 'what if it wasn't Cosmo in that fire but Licatta?'

'But their papers . . . They were . . .' Schwartz spluttered, shaking his head but Jack felt his voice carried less conviction, the words fading before the end.

'Of course!' John's voice startled Laura and she glanced apprehensively at him. 'Kelp or Acquilan would have been the ones to identify the bodies. That could account for D'Ostia's – I mean, Cosmo's – involvement.'

'Precisely,' Douglas smiled, 'but what happened at the warehouse? Something must have gone wrong.'

'I see where you're going, the second box wasn't Cosmo . . . Sounds like a simple switch,' Schwartz admitted.

'Yes, that's it – they switched identities,' Douglas looked from one to the other.

'If that's the case,' John spoke with growing awareness, 'then we know what those diaries contained and why everyone wants them – they tell the whole story.'

'But,' Laura began, 'what the hell have the paintings got to do with it?' Laura stared at John. 'And why doesn't someone use the diaries?'

'The pictures are all about one man – Acquilan – and his obsession. They're the key that your father knew would prise Acquilan into the open and the diaries would do the rest. They would work together as proof,' John looked at Douglas, who nodded.

'Remember, Laura,' began Douglas, 'remember the plane crash, May 10, 1944? How Kelp and the others who were left from the platoon got back to safety? They were given up for lost, yet they arrived back four days later on May 14 and in captured German trucks. The trucks were empty when they arrived. You know, it's always bothered me – they said they'd ambushed them but why would empty trucks have been so far from the front line? There's not even a main road up in those mountains. Unless they had been transporting some-thing too special for just anyone to know about . . . that would account for the fact that they were able to take the trucks – because there probably weren't too many soldiers on them. In fact, in Joe's department of defense report, there was – I recall – a mention by one of them that there were only a handful of officers on the trucks and no ordinary soldiers. Strange, until you realise they might have been transporting valuable loot.'

'Hang on,' Laura said, perplexed, 'the pictures and other things, you're saying those were being transported?'

'Yes,' Douglas answered.

'A private operation? Who for?'

'Who knows, a German general? Your guess is as good as mine,' replied Douglas. 'It happened all over. Hell, I remem-ber reporting on one such case in France.'

'Imagine them coming across this fabulous wealth by accident,' said John, picking up Douglas's theme.

'Yeah, so they stash the goods,' Schwartz continued, 'and drive back. When the Allies overrun the area later, they find some excuse and they move the goods somewhere else.' He smiled. 'It works, Mr Douglas, the chain comes together. A year after the war they meet up, in Naples . . . and something goes wrong, two die in a fire and Cosmo . . .'

'My father?'

'Well, it makes sense,' John began, 'but while we've pieced together a plausible story, Jack, as you said before, the police aren't going to buy it. It's big stuff. Kelp came by his money through theft and fraud – there were two suspicious deaths in Naples as well. They sold many of the items through the black market after the war. We also know, or at least we think we do, why Laura's father was involved – yet it doesn't get me any closer. In a sense, we may know more, but we're still back at square one. I have to find those pictures – or the diaries, if I want to prove the link.'

Douglas nodded.

'Yes,' Laura said in a soft voice. 'Well, at least we're not chasing shadows now, you've got something. You now know where to look – although where that leads is anyone's guess.' She frowned, 'But why was my father still involved?'

'Revenge, Laura,' Douglas replied.

'But Mr Douglas,' interrupted Schwartz, 'we can't print anything – the guy's a war hero – Purple Heart, Congressional Medal of Honor. If we start pissing on his war record, all hell will break loose and we won't have a leg to stand on. It's just a story, that's all. We need to prove some connection – or all the rest is shit!'

John nodded and felt his nerves tighten. Schwartz was right – no pictures, no diaries, no evidence to clear himself. The pictures, the diaries . . . and him. Now he understood. He was the connection. Everything revolved around and depended on him. Only he could solve it.

Douglas glanced at Schwartz, who was now smiling broadly. They were all agreed: there was only one possible course of action – they had to find out who held the paintings:

Acquilan, Kelp or whoever, no time to guess. And they had to find them before the others found John.

In New York John's bewildered uncle sat in a sparsely furnished office.

'You said that I might be able to help my nephew, John,' Ralph Grande began. 'That he was in trouble here in New York.' He straightened up in the worn leather armchair, as the thick-set man with the limp walked from behind the desk to Ralph's left and sat down in front of him. 'I've been in New York for some time now and, apart from changing hotels three times, you've given me no further information about my nephew. I feel like a thief in the night. I wouldn't have come but . . .'

'When we brought you over here, Mr Grande,' the man interrupted, in a thick New York accent, 'we thought you'd meet him but he just disappeared.'

Ralph noticed that his voice, as ever, was calm and yet icy cold. His muscular upper body filled his suit and his neck seemed to tighten in strange spasms. Ralph hadn't liked him from the first but because of his concern for John, he'd overcome his misgivings and agreed when the same man came out to Positano and persuaded him to return to New York with him. The police in Italy had long since stopped bothering him and he hadn't heard from John for many weeks. Worse, he also knew that John now stood accused of murder in London and while not believing any of it, he worried for his safety. Most of all, he felt guilty; after all, he reminded himself continually, it was he who had involved his nephew and he now felt he had to do something, anything, that might help him.

'You see, Mr Grande,' the strange man broke in on Ralph's thoughts, 'your nephew is wanted for murder here, a society lawyer, big in the community – and he needs all our help . . .'

Ralph disliked the use of the word 'our' – it was patronising and assumed his inclusion in their schemes. He straightened himself up and lifted his chin. No, John would never be mixed up with these people. Yet they were right, our – our problem, our – our help. His chin dropped.

'. . . but we've got nowhere chasing after him. Guess we'll just have to adopt some new tactics,' the man continued. The door behind him opened and another man walked in. It was the same young man, Ralph remembered, who had met him on the first night in New York. He whispered something in the older man's ear. Ralph looked out of the window while they spoke, he couldn't hear them and feigned indifference.

His tired eyes moved from the window and looked around the room. Again, his chin held high, he took in the threadbare carpet, old chairs and bare walls. He realised now how much his judgement had been clouded by his concern for John – he should have gone back, should have spoken to the police. Anything would be better than this, he thought.

'The thing is, Mr Grande,' the first man said as he turned to face Ralph, 'we've got a new plan.'

'Yeah,' the young man murmured, smiling through gum-chewing lips.

'You've found John?' Ralph asked, sitting up.

'Not yet,' the first man glanced back at his colleague and then at Ralph. 'But you don't need to worry, we've made contact.'

Ralph started, his mouth forming a question.

'But before you ask, we've got to send a message – you know, something from you direct to him,' the man continued.

'From me?'

'Sure, if we're not going to chase after him, we thought we could get him to come to us. We've got a video camera next door to record a message,' he smiled at Ralph, as though he was addressing a child.

Ralph looked from one to the other; their faces were deadpan masks, no expression. Perhaps they were right. After all, what harm would a video do if it went direct to John?

'Certainly,' he hesitated, 'but I insist we take this up with the police if we don't make contact.' Ralph looked from one to the other as he spoke.

'Sure,' the older man smiled, 'sure, right after, Mr Grande, right after,' he said, patting Ralph on the back, 'but first the video.' He pointed towards the door.

Ralph recoiled from the man's hand. It was bad enough dealing with them, but for them to patronise him as well . . . He shuddered.

The room Ralph walked into was about the same size as the last. By a window to the left of the door was a large old table and chair. On top of the table was a video camera, its dull black, clean lines contrasting with the chipped wooden surface. To his surprise, Ralph noticed that on the other side of the room was an iron bedstead, made up with sheets and blankets and a small cupboard set beside the bed.

The younger of the two men picked up the video camera and held it to his eye. The other walked over to a chair, pulled it out and turned it to face the door. 'Sit down here, Mr Grande,' said one of the men.

Ralph walked slowly over to the chair and sat down. He was handed a card. 'All you have to do is look straight at the camera and read that out.'

Ralph read it slowly. 'John,' someone had written in a juvenile hand, 'I am here in New York, safe and well and hoping to see you. If you're in some kind of trouble I want to help. To make contact, please follow the instructions you'll get after my message.'

'What instructions?' he asked, turning the card over. He was still uncomfortable with all of this but he realised there was nothing else he could do.

'Don't worry, we'll arrange all that. We will film those after your message.' The young man glanced at the other before bending down behind the eye-piece of the video camera again. Ralph read the note twice more. The whole thing took only a few minutes.

'Very good,' the young man spoke for the first time as he lowered the camera; his smile, thin-lipped and far from reassuring, left Ralph feeling even more concerned. He stood up.

'Good,' Ralph said quickly, 'if that's all, then if you'll excuse me, I'll be going.' As he spoke he noticed a familiar-looking suitcase against the bed. 'But why is my suitcase . . .' he began as the older man was walking towards the door.

'Oh, I forgot to tell you – you just moved rooms again.' He gestured with his hand, 'I'm sorry about the furniture, but I think you'll find this a bit more private.'

Ralph looked at the suitcase again and then back at the man, 'I don't understand.'

'Well, it's like this, Mr Grande,' he shrugged, 'it's for your safety. You know, there are some strange people out there and you'll be much safer in here. The john and shower are through there,' he pointed at the door on the far side of the room.

'I didn't ask for another room . . .' Ralph said, trying to walk past him. But his arm was tightly gripped by the older man.

'No, no, Mr Grande – I insist!' The voice was hard.

'I don't understand, surely we should go to the police?'

'Not a good idea. After all, your nephew's now wanted for murder and they just wouldn't understand – for now, the less they know the better. Take my word for it. For your own safety, Mr Grande.' He smiled again and left the room, shutting the door behind him.

Ralph heard the lock click just as the slanting rays of the late afternoon sun sliced through the dirty window and lit up the room. Despite its warmth, he was cold, cold and tired. He noticed that his shadow cast by the sun's rays was stooped – the shadow of an old and very stupid man, he thought. He sat down on the edge of the bed and buried his face in his hands.

'L'tenant!' Munroe stood in the doorway, a big smile on his face, 'you were right.' He walked in, followed by Rutgers. 'Alice van Buren has an apartment – just off Central Park West on 63rd.'

Jasinski nodded.

'Top part of a townhouse – nice. Of course most of them over there have been ruined by office . . .'

'OK, OK, Munroe! Cut the crap! I don't want to buy the place!'

'Sure,' Munroe stiffened, 'as I was saying . . .' he raised an eyebrow before continuing, 'she seemed happy enough for us to look it over. Doesn't even live there – lives just off Sutton Place. Anyway, it's been empty for over a year – she's trying to sell it. She says she let Buckley use it, said she'd been told that a relative of hers had come to stay and she needed the extra room.'

'Did she know anything about who occupied it?' Jasinski asked.

'No,' Rutgers answered for the first time, 'she didn't know or, as she said, didn't care. She said she trusted her friend. The super confirmed that she hadn't been to the place for ages.'

'Anyway,' cut in Munroe as though worried that Rutgers might get the congratulations from Jasinski, 'Grande had been there – the super made him out from two photographs. It seems he'd grown a moustache – but he was still sure it was him – and the woman's description he gave sounded like Buckley.' Jasinski's eyes met those of Detective Sergeant Mackie, sitting just behind him.

'The only thing we found was this,' he held out a piece of paper, 'Top sheet of a pad of paper on the desk by the bed. Someone was writing on the page above. I thought it would be worth seeing if there was anything on it, you know indents, anything.'

'Any point in bringing van Buren in for questioning?' Jasinski asked.

'She's pretty sharp, but I don't think she knows where they've gone. I thought we'd watch her for a while and then bring her in if we needed to.'

'OK, keep an eye on her.' Rutgers and Munroe started to shuffle out as Detective Sergeant Mackie spoke.

'I've overhauled the files. All the information we had, including photographs, descriptions and his medical records. You've now got more on Grande than we have. They're on your desks.'

'One other thing,' Munroe interrupted, stopping by the door, 'that reminds me – funny thing, L'tenant, but I'd laid money on there being only one Brit called Grande in New York. It's a real strange name, but what do you know? Someone else with the same name turned up.'

'Where?' demanded Jasinski.

'The Hilton just called, after we put his name out, said they'd had somebody called Grande staying. No good, though – when I checked it out this morning, it wasn't the guy we were after, just some old guy who . . .'

'What? When was this?' Mackie leaned forward in his chair.

'A week ago, he moved on pretty quick. As I thought, just an old guy.'

'I wonder, Lieutenant, would it be possible to visit the hotel and try and find out some more?' Mackie asked.

'Sure, sure,' Jasinski answered. 'But the man we're looking for is much younger . . .'

'Yes, he is. But he has an uncle. It's a long shot but it's such a coincidence,' Mackie looked through the glass panel, taking out his pipe and filling it with tobacco, 'You see, I spoke to his uncle a while ago and I had a feeling he'd heard from his nephew but I was sure he didn't know then where he was. I even had the Italian police tap his telephone.' He lit his pipe.

'Then if he didn't know where he was, why would he come here?'

'Someone must have brought him here. There were strong emotional ties. Could be nothing,' he shrugged, 'but worth checking, if only to eliminate it.'

Jasinski turned to the two detectives, 'Get Detective Sergeant Mackie down to the Hilton now!'

'Oh, by the way, I'm due to fly back to London tomorrow. While we're gone, I wonder if someone could check on my flight?' Mackie pulled out a crumpled ticket from his battered briefcase.

'Fly back tomorrow – impossible! I need you here,' Jasinski protested.

'Oh aye, if it was up to me but . . .' he shrugged and followed the others out of the office.

Jasinski was more and more comfortable in the company of this quiet, contemplative Scotsman. He'd become a welcome feature during the few weeks he'd been in New York. He'd helped grind some old-fashioned police work into his standard New York detectives. Mackie had gone far beyond his short brief to bring them up to date with all the information from London. Jasinski thought of the District Attorney jumping up and down on the case again. Everyone, from the captain to the whole of the Jewish community, had a view – he needed extra help and Mackie was perfect. As he picked up the telephone, he realised that it was more than just the need for help, he'd actually enjoyed Mackie's company – two old-fashioned cops. He smiled.

At the Hilton Mackie found that the staff hardly remembered the old man. He hadn't stayed long enough – a couple of nights, no forwarding address. Polite, quiet, they said. He didn't pay his own bill. It was paid for in cash by a man who went by the name of Labria. Just as they were giving up, another hotel contacted the office to say that a man called

Grande had been to stay. Same man, same routine. Stayed a few days and then checked out, bill paid for by someone else, in cash. This time at the next hotel, they remembered the person paying for Grande used a walking stick, that he was thick-set. They didn't remember much about Grande himself except he was polite and had a beard.

Mackie was puzzled. He'd spoken enough to Ralph Grande weeks ago to be certain that he'd not known the whereabouts of his nephew. Yet could it be him in New York?

When Mackie returned to the precinct station, a quick call to his office produced the information he sought – confirmation from the Italian police that Ralph Grande had left Italy one week before. Mackie now knew it was the uncle. The Passport Office in London would confirm the passport number. It was like finding a piece for a jigsaw only to realise that no one knew where the rest of the puzzle was.

17

Acquilan

The clouds thickened across the sky, dark, rain-filled, threatening. Like a growth, they spread quickly until the day had all but gone and a strange twilight fell on everything. The increasing wind had a thin edge and in its bosom it carried a distinct brooding growl. The water of the ocean was slashed with white foam and, like whipped and frenzied horses, the waves began to crash against the stone wall of the harbour mole, exploding into the wind. Somewhere, as the growl turned into an intermittent roar, a light flashed again and again. The clouds began to disgorge their rain in sheets as the dark was split by tongues of light that cracked and stabbed.

On a slight hill, across neat, trimmed lawns, stretching back from a small harbour, the mock Georgian façade of a large house stood sharp-edged in the stabbing light. The sudden volume of rain overfilled the gutters and rolled down the face of the house. Ground-floor lights shone in the gloom through the water.

Yet there was one dark window behind which the flashes of light revealed a face and dark eyes calmly surveying the full onslaught over the tip of a lit cigar. Gently, carefully, in slow and almost sensuous movements, the cigar was smoked, the man's face always still.

Since childhood Victor Acquilan had always believed that you shouldn't just *watch* a storm – you had to *feel* it. The dark raw power that lashed its way across the earth was always breathtaking and exhilarating. This one also carried in its heart a sense of foreboding. He felt as though the gathering storm and the growing darkness were a manifestation of his problems. He was so close, so near to his dream and yet so many things now seemed to be going wrong. The diaries, the murders, their failure to find the man Grande, an inquisitive columnist sniffing around his business, writing lies and innuendo – and Cosmo dead. To top it all, his Seattle project had crashed, with losses of up to $50 million, perhaps even more. And all because of a rumour. Added to all this, he knew things in the campaign weren't as good as they should be. They'd kept their momentum going into the South on Super Tuesday but Carson had come back hard and gained New York by the tightest of margins, a desperate boost at the last minute. General Electric's award of a government contract in Senator Wall's home state had worked. Carson had done just enough to hold on among New York democrats. Part of the problem was that the prosecution had failed to prove any connection between Carson and the property company. It was beginning to look like there was nothing – he was even picking up a bit on the sympathy vote. It all depended on the Prosecutor finding something. Whatever happened, California was no formality. Whoever won it would take the nomination. But he also knew there was one home-grown problem: the rumours, now widely reported, that all was not well with Kelp's private life – his wife's depression, her drinking and her absence from the campaign. People were openly speculating that this had been brought on by Kelp's arrogance and his bad treatment of her. It had to stop.

The lights of a car slid across his window, lighting up his face, then another and another. He watched impassively as the limousines passed, leaving him in darkness.

The mess in Seattle had been planned. It was so public, but had Cosmo really been responsible? Acquilan wondered if he was becoming paranoid – did he see Cosmo in everything? So many lines of attack, shadows over everything, and then the realisation that, far from fighting back, he seemed to be simply hanging on by his fingertips.

Minutes passed, then the door on the far side of the room was slowly opened.

'Victor?' Acquilan recognised the voice of Ewan Kelp. He looked towards the door at a figure standing in a wedge of light.

He squinted, 'In here.'

'Christ!' Kelp said as he entered the room. 'It's dark in here, what the hell are you doing sitting in the dark? Where . . .?' Then the lights clicked on. 'Victor, we've got to talk.' Kelp's voice was anxious.

Acquilan moved over to Kelp and away from the window seat.

'Carson's in shit, Victor – deep shit – but we don't seem to be able to bury him,' Kelp complained. 'That son-of-a-bitch Wall – after all, I promised him!'

'He got a big contract, which will secure his re-election. You can only promise,' replied Acquilan sharply.

'Well, what's happened to the damn Prosecutor? Now he's picking up sympathy votes! We are so near, if only . . .'

'No ifs. Let's deal the cards, Ewan,' Acquilan interrupted. 'You and me, we've been together too long to play games. You know the real reason why you lost in New York and only you can put that right. The other stuff you can't help, but this . . .'

'If you mean that crap started by Carson and his goddamn allegations about my marriage . . .' At that moment the door opened and Weitz walked in.

'Here, sit down, Bernie,' Acquilan pointed at the chair next to Kelp. 'When are the others due?'

'A couple of hours, depends on the storm,' Weitz was uneasy.

'Right, we'd better use that time. We got one hell of a fight on our hands and we've come too far to pack it in.'

'I still think we can do it, it was always going to be tight. Three months ago, we'd never have done so well in the South, Carson's backyard,' Weitz began. 'Remember when you declared? No one gave you a cat's chance in hell – then the Prosecutor came along and it all changed. Sure it's tight and we shouldn't kid ourselves, this guy is the most ruthless son-of-a-bitch I've ever come across. He was never going to lie down and die!'

'What do the polls say?' Kelp asked.

'That he's a lying, over-sexed corrupt scumbag. But they also say they're in work and content with their lives. They want him punished but not prosecuted, so he's getting some of the sympathy vote. He's playing it all the way.'

'Plus that goddamned contract!' Kelp muttered.

'It's what presidents do,' Acquilan sighed, 'That's why they get re-elected.'

'I think the money's under control,' Weitz continued. 'Some donors are slowly coming forward, the cash is coming in . . .'

'No thanks to you, Victor! That stupid deal in Seattle has really put the squeeze on us,' Kelp jabbed his finger at his partner.

'It's not a problem,' Acquilan said soothingly, 'I'll just transfer some assets.' He shook his head, 'It's not a problem.' He stubbed his cigar out, 'We've just got to keep our nerve. We had him on the ropes and let him off, you can't do that to a man like Carson.'

'It's not my fault!' Kelp hissed. 'I'd have thought the Prosecutor would have got all he needed by now.'

Acquilan interrupted, 'Ewan, you know why you slumped in New York. As I said earlier, all they needed was a whiff of

OK—

---

scandal and they got it, enough to hurt you. It's your fuckin' private life!' – he exclaimed suddenly – 'Your marriage! Right from the beginning we all knew they'd throw this shit at you. We had it planned though, we weren't going to give them an opportunity, were we? So why didn't you stick to it?'

'I didn't change anything,' Kelp spat his words out. 'It was Mary-Lou, she was getting difficult. It was becoming . . .'

'Yes, but look at this,' Acquilan picked up a pile of papers and dumped them one at a time on the floor in front of Kelp. 'I collected these the day before the poll. Look!'

'SENATOR'S PRIVATE LIFE A SHAM. WHY KELP'S WIFE SAYS NO TO THE CAMPAIGN TRAIL.'

Acquilan glared at Kelp, 'Two days before the polls and this breaks loose. *Christ*, Ewan! I don't give a shit if you want to break up with Mary-Lou, but you can't do it now! We said from the start you had to keep her with you.'

'It's bullshit!' began Kelp defensively.

'Well, where *is* she?' Acquilan raised his eyebrows and snorted as he saw Kelp's face freeze. 'Let's not play games, Ewan – it's too late for that.' He tossed another paper down at Kelp's feet, 'And *that*, what the hell was *that*?' Lying on the floor in front of him was a picture of his wife slumped across the seat of her car, an empty glass in her hand, asleep.

'I know, it was a couple of years ago,' he said softly, 'things were bad, she was drinking. You both know it's better now – she's having treatment. How did they get *that*?'

'You *know* how!' muttered Acquilan.

'Carson – good old President Carson,' said Weitz slowly. 'But how?'

'How many ways can a President get things done?' Acquilan cut in. 'NSA, FBI, CIA, take your pick, Ewan. The real problem is you gave him the chance.'

'But look,' retaliated Kelp, 'it was your crackpot scheme to put pressure on the *Post*. I wasn't happy right from the start, I should have overruled it. Now look, Douglas is digging around my first election in New York and he's even asking what happened to that goddamn paper he used to edit, remember?'

'They've got nothing to go on.' Acquilan's voice was dismissive. 'It was a legitimate purchase.'

'Maybe so, but you fired him back then for no reason and it doesn't look good coming on top of all that crap that Douglas has been writing.'

'Hold on,' Weitz held up a hand. 'Look, let's focus on California, it's still winnable. I just spent some time with Mason and the polls there aren't bad. We're neck and neck. Sure, we had a lead but we can get it back.'

'OK. So what next?' Acquilan asked.

'Well, Dick's got a whole series of photo shoots of Ewan and Mary-Lou lined up. You already know about this, Ewan.' Weitz watched as Kelp nodded. 'And she's not gonna leave your side for the rest of the campaign?' More nodding from Kelp and Weitz sighed, 'We can work Carson and Wall over. I've got some dirt on Wall that should keep him quiet for a while.'

'OK,' Kelp said standing up, 'so what's stopping you coming back on the team?'

'Well, I . . .'

'He can't, at least, not yet,' Acquilan cut in quickly.

'Why not?' Kelp asked. 'Or is this not the most important thing we've ever done? After all, the three of us are the only ones we can trust, so?'

'Sure, but we need to clear something up first.'

'Ah!' Kelp studied Acquilan then Weitz, 'Not by any chance something to do with Cosmo?' He slowly and deliberately walked to the window and stood looking out, his back towards Acquilan. 'You did tell me it was over, didn't you? Only if it is, then why did the police come and see me today?'

Acquilan sat up and stared hard at Weitz.

'Looking for a guy, some Brit,' Kelp continued, 'wanted in connection with a murder. Apparently, they found my name on a pad of paper he'd been using.' Kelp turned to face the other two. 'Seems he'd been some sort of art dealer in London. They said his name was Gramm, or something like that.' He watched Acquilan's jaw muscles tightening. 'You lied to me, Victor. You lied when you said it was all over. It's not, is it? That's the reason you kept Bernie. And that's the reason you won't let him go now.'

For a few seconds their eyes met and held before Kelp turned his head away. 'All these years, and everything we've been through, and you lie. The most goddamn important thing I've ever done. All the shit I've been going through out there, everything I've had to put up with, and you can't even tell me the truth. Tell me this then, is he the one who did the deal on the pictures?'

'Yes, he was,' Weitz responded despondently.

'So what does that bastard want? What's he doing here?'

Acquilan shook his head. 'It isn't what you think, it's not what it seems. There's nothing to worry about, this guy's a loner, he knows nothing. After all, if he did, wouldn't he have done something by now? As I said, you've got nothing to worry about – just leave the guy to us.'

'Well, if he didn't know so much, how did he get my name?' Kelp's teeth were clenched. 'What does he know about me?'

'Nothing that need bother you, Ewan. Just leave him to me!'

'Well, that's just great! Now I've got some lunatic on my tail. Almost anything could happen and you stand here, gazing into space, telling me to leave him to you.' He shook his head. 'I seem to recall you saying that last time and look at the results!' Kelp went to the drinks cabinet and poured himself a Scotch. '*Jesus*, Victor! Of all people, I thought I could rely on you at least.' He gulped back his whisky and slammed the glass down on the table.

'Don't overreact,' Acquilan responded. 'Remember, we all sink or swim together. It's too late to walk away – you should have thought about that all those years ago in Naples. We're going to see this thing through. Cosmo may have started this, but as sure as hell I'm gonna finish!'

'Well,' Weitz said, glancing from one to the other, 'there is a little bit of good news anyway. The boys say they think they've got a fix on that woman from the Network. She's been staying somewhere in Chelsea.'

'And Grande's with her?'

'I don't know, but Pichowski's on it – we'll know soon enough,' Weitz smiled slightly as he spoke.

'Good, Bernie,' Acquilan acknowledged.

'So you see, Victor . . .'

'Don't change the subject. You said something earlier to imply that Cosmo may have started this. But you told me the guy was dead.'

'He is . . . as far as we know.'

'Wait a minute, you said for certain last time. There was no "as far as we know". . .'

'You can never be one hundred per cent, Ewan. You of all people should know that,' Weitz took his glasses off and polished them. 'I warned you both when you decided to start your presidential run. Not only would we waste good money, and we've done that already, but I said it was all Cosmo was waiting for. We should've stopped while we were ahead. I never wanted to do all this. That was a bad call.'

'*So?* What's that supposed to mean?' Kelp flared.

'Goddamn it!' Weitz answered, raising his voice for the first time. 'I know I don't mean anything in your eyes. It's all about you two – it's Bernie this, Bernie that, but you never listen to me.' Weitz leaned his head back and closed his eyes. 'It's like I said, we're in this crap because of this campaign. I don't have any answers. All I know is that this crazy English guy and his girlfriend are out there kicking our ass. Nothing else. I'm working my butt off to get answers. And if I can, I will – but if you'd listened to me . . .'

'Look,' cut in Acquilan, 'we can argue about this all night. We can all say what we should have done, why we shouldn't have done this or that and it won't matter a damn! Sure, it'd make some of us feel better but that's all. Bernie, I know you didn't want this campaign but it was always clear Ewan would go for it from way back. We missed earlier opportunities because Cosmo was out there. You know that even if we hadn't done this, he'd have found his moment to screw us up. We knew that. The problem is he's better than even I believed he could be. I – we – underestimated him. That's our real problem.' He turned towards Kelp. 'It's not lost yet, the plan looks good for California – we'll just have to deal with Carson and Senator Wall. After all, we've got that stuff about Carson's record – in Alabama in the 1970s.'

'What if it backfires?' Kelp was worried.

'We'll have to take that chance, the result is too important to play safe. We need him out of the way and now he's gone too far. If that's his game, don't you think it's time the public knew everything about his past?'

'But that's only part of our problem,' cut in Kelp, 'what about Wall?'

'We'll deal with him – he's a nobody from nowhere without Carson. Get Mary-Lou back with you and we'll fry him!' Weitz replied.

'That goddamn English guy and those diaries and . . .' Kelp paused, 'what a mess!' He poured himself another drink. 'Thank God those paintings were destroyed. You did destroy them, didn't you, Victor?' He waited for an answer but none came. 'You destroyed them like you said you would, didn't you?' his voice rose.

'I never said, "destroy", Ewan,' Acquilan replied. 'If you remember, I said, "get rid of them"!'

'Let's not play games. It all means the same – destroy! You know as well as I do, if those paintings are linked to the diaries, then we're all finished.'

'They won't be.'

'God help me, I don't believe it – you've still got them! My God! It really is over! Might as well give it up now, all wasted.'

'Look, if it makes you feel better, I haven't destroyed them, OK? But no one except you, Bernie and myself knows they exist,' Acquilan said firmly.

'You're mad,' Kelp spluttered. 'What about Cosmo?'

'He's dead.'

'Then this English guy?'

'He can't possibly know about . . .'

'Us? Well, if that's the case, how the fuck's he managed to get hold of my name and put it down on a pad of paper? And what the hell is he doing here anyway? You've never answered that question.'

'If he knew anything, by now, as I said before, he'd have gone to the cops. No, we're OK. Anyway, the pictures are somewhere no one will ever see them but me.'

'This is all madness,' Kelp began, 'it's like being in a goddamn lunatic asylum – I can't believe this is happening.'

'Have I ever steered wrongly before in the last fifty years, Ewan?' Acquilan laid his arm on Kelp's shoulder. 'It's tight, but hell, we've got out of worse scrapes than this together. As Bernie said, we're almost onto this English guy and we'll get on and deal with Wall and Carson. We'll do it – together.' He tried to put his arm around Kelp but he moved away.

'There's little point – it's all over. Everything you promised wouldn't happen has happened. Be honest, Victor, you've no idea what to do. He's beaten you; a dead man's beaten you both. And worse, you don't even know if he's dead, do you? That's how bad it is.'

'It doesn't matter,' Acquilan replied, 'Their plan has gone wrong as well.'

'Don't humour me.'

'The English guy – they've lost him. Without him, they've got nothing.'

'So?'

'Well, we'll just have to get to him first.'

'You're serious? You're not just trying to soft-soap me?'

'Yes, I'm serious.'

'Bernie?'

'Victor's right, Ewan,' Weitz answered, 'we've got a lead on him, we should be able to close . . .'

'Do it quickly,' Kelp snarled, 'I don't want to hear any more about the guy or Cosmo either, just do it. If they get him with the diaries, we're dead.'

Weitz nodded as Kelp stalked out, slamming the door behind him.

'Is he going to make it, Bernie?'

'He'll come through, Victor. He's a lot tougher than any of us give him credit for. And anyway, he's got no choice.'

'It seems none of us has,' Acquilan walked over to his chair and slumped down into it.

'There's more, Victor,' Weitz waited as Acquilan looked up. 'The source I've got in the department tells me some deadbeat English cop is now helping them with their case.'

'Then you knew about the name on the pad?'

'Sure, Victor, but I thought I shouldn't tell Ewan. After all, I reckoned that it was better that he didn't know. That way his reactions would be credible.'

Acquilan was a man who prided himself on his ability to control events. It was the way in which he ran everything, directing, controlling. As he sat in his study listening to Weitz, he began to feel a sensation he hadn't experienced for a long, long time – fear. Despite his outward appearance and soothing words to Kelp earlier on, deep down inside he knew that events were moving beyond his grasp and that he had been out-manoeuvred from the outset. They were on the very edge of the cliff. Ewan had been right and Acquilan knew it; he'd wanted it all and Cosmo had anticipated him. Cosmo had known his inner greed and read him like a book. All those years in search of Cosmo, the pictures and the diaries, and now the hunter had become the hunted.

'So, is that it?' Acquilan looked at Weitz, eyebrows raised.

'Yes and no. When I said we were onto them, that of course was for Ewan's benefit . . .'

'I figured as much.'

'No, Victor, it's only slightly exaggerated. We *are* onto something.'

'Good,' Acquilan nodded. 'What about Washington? I notice you didn't say anything to him about who you think you saw by the memorial.'

'No point.'

'How did Grande get Ewan's name?'

'Maybe he's guessing.'

'Still, if your information's correct, we should know soon.'

'I don't have an exact address but we're working on it.'

'Cosmo's people are out there as well looking for Grande. We've stupidly done what they wanted step by step – now is our chance to get ahead of them.'

Acquilan levered himself out of his chair and walked over to the window. The storm had now cleared, leaving the pale, watery, late-afternoon sun glinting off pools of water, but the wind continued to roar through the trees, peeling the branches back. And down at the little harbour, the waves foamed around the mole, bursting across the stonework. Behind the window, the sun fell across Acquilan's face and he began to feel its warmth, gentle and strangely reassuring.

'You'd better watch that woman, van . . . van . . .'

'van Buren?'

'Yes, if Grande's about to be set up, I want to know! Tell me when you've cornered him or Buckley – there's no deals, their silence is our only safeguard.'

*

'Pete!' exclaimed Parry as Pete Neal walked into his office in the White House. 'Good of you to come.'

'Well, we've got some news, though nothing substantial yet,' Neal began. 'Seems that one of Acquilan's people was buying paintings in London last summer.'

'So?'

'Hear me out,' Neal continued, as he sat down. 'The point is that the man he bought them from is wanted for murder.'

'Coincidence.'

'Maybe. But I haven't finished. He turned up in New York and another man, a lawyer, gets murdered. But the interesting part is that the guy left a note with Kelp's name on it in his hideout.'

'Kelp?' Parry stared at Neal. 'You don't think that he's in touch with Kelp?'

'No,' Neal said quickly, 'but there's some connection and it sounds messy for Kelp. Besides we're looking into his postwar record in 1947 and 1948. Came by a lot of money, not certain how. We're checking.'

'Good.'

'My source in NYPD tells me they want the British cop who's helping to stay, but he's due to go back to London.'

'No problem, I'll make sure the right calls are made to London – he stays,' Parry smiled at Neal. 'Well, it's good there's some real news for once. Carson's struggling, Pete. At this rate he's going to lose California to Kelp.'

'*Jesus*! What about New York? We made it there – that stuff on Kelp was pretty hot!'

'Only temporary, just enough to hang on in New York. Trouble is, they're publicly back together again now and she's told the story about her struggle with the bottle. Says she succeeded, got a lot of sympathy. No, we can't use it again.'

'All his life he's been close to trouble, so he must be a good actor. But this time he's getting desperate – we all are.

California is still winnable but we need Kelp's shine to go –
you're all we've got in that department. Don't let us down,
Pete. We'll play for time, and hope you come up with
something.'

18

Laura's Friends

'It's all fixed,' Laura's voice rang out from the bedroom. John Grande looked up from the table and smiled as she walked over to him. 'The day after tomorrow, at ten o'clock.'

'Good!' He smiled at her and kissed her gently. 'Thank you.' He tapped some papers on the table, 'And thanks for these architect's drawings of Acquilan's house. However did you get them?'

'You don't want to know,' she laughed, 'I pulled in an old favour – an ex-boyfriend – he slipped them to me. It seems they were filed when he bought the house and renovated it.'

'They're exactly what I wanted, better than I'd hoped for,' he purred.

'Good,' she smiled, yet John sensed she was distracted, even worried.

'Problem?'

'No, it's nothing.'

'Come on, no secrets, remember?'

'OK, perhaps this is not the best time to remind you – but well, we're working on your hunch, remember. If you don't find anything, we're all washed up.'

'I know,' John said, staring at the plans again. 'It's going to be tough. I can see he's modified the house: now the question is, where would he put the paintings?' He ran his finger across the drawings. 'Which damn room? Well,' he sighed, 'let's hope it's clearer when we're in.'

'Hope?' Laura raised her eyebrows, 'only hope?'

'Hope will have to do. Just get me in there,' he started folding up the drawings, 'What about someone for the alarms? You said you had someone.'

'Don't worry, that's all in hand,' Laura replied.

'Look, we both know it's a calculated guess, but I don't think he has all that many options. The paintings will have had to have been cleaned very carefully first and to do that, he'd either have to have someone he could trust completely or . . . he would do it himself.'

Laura frowned.

'But that's skilled work. You need years of training.'

'Yes. And that's what he's had.'

'What do you mean?'

'I checked with Maguire in London and he checked in New York with some restorers. Acquilan's known as a collector but he's also spent years learning how to restore paintings. On its own it makes no sense but if you think that for decades he's waited to get hold of these paintings, well . . . I can only guess, but now I know he can do it himself, I am certain the pictures are here.'

'God – anyone that obsessed isn't normal.'

'What's normal? Look at me, running for my life!' he smiled. 'Look at *you*, even worse, *with me*! Anyway, once we're certain of that, there's the little matter of where to hang them. After all, there's no point in storing them – not after what he's been through to get them.'

'But he could have sold them?'

'Perhaps, but I don't think so. He didn't go through this for money – he wants the pictures, as I said before. But he can't tell the world, so that means they won't be hung where anyone can see them.' He glanced down at the plan again.

'I guess it's just a matter of discovering where. Obviously, he'll have a special place, which will be well secured in some way.'

John finished folding the drawings and slipped them into a briefcase. 'No, these paintings will be where they can never be seen by anyone else, you can be sure of that.'

They were both edgy as they prepared to set off for Easthampton. Laura had managed to get access to Acquilan's house. Their cover story was that she was a freelance journalist writing for a magazine called *Interior Art*, which just happened to be her friend Alice van Buren's magazine. She was to interview Acquilan's wife who had, prior to her marriage, been a very successful interior designer. For a period after her marriage she had stopped working but had recently decided to return. With her new business just starting up, she was keen on the publicity. An interview at her home, with pictures of some of the rooms she had recently decorated, was what she had agreed to.

John watched Laura. She had, he now realised, brought new hope to him in all respects. His customary dull ache and emptiness no longer dominated him. With surprise, he had even realised that it had been days since he last lay awake waiting for his dawn memory-rush to begin. Sleep had come, not the fitful sleep he had grown accustomed to, but deep, refreshing sleep. All was due to her. He felt he was drawing closer to her and he sensed she felt the same, but part of him still wanted to keep her at arm's length. He felt guilty for having got her involved and this guilt was compounded when he chided himself for so easily forgetting his wife, Julia, who had died so tragically.

'It's all so pathetically vague,' he said. 'God knows what I would have done without you.' He shut the briefcase and pressed the catches. 'We've come so far and yet the solution is still out of reach. I keep asking myself over and over again,

290

what is his motivation? I mean, he clearly knows how dangerous they are for him. If they become public, they would connect him to his past in Naples. But,' he said in a quiet voice, 'if it is a special room, a private gallery away from the others' sight, it could be anywhere in the house and once I find it,' he sighed, 'once I find it . . .'

'That girl, Ari – you remember, I told you – the one in the bar? Well she's going to help us.'

'Isn't that a bit risky? After all, you hardly know her.'

'No, I've seen her since a couple of times and I like her. She seems pretty straight and she knows a lot of people.'

'Oh, when you described her to me I thought she was . . .'

'What? A hooker?' Laura frowned at him, 'What difference would it make if she was? Like we're much better, about to break into someone's house!'

'OK,' he shrugged, 'OK.'

'Look,' Laura began, the annoyance gone, 'she's going to help on the alarms.'

'What? She's good on alarms?'

'No, not her – but she's got someone.'

'Can we trust her?'

'I don't know,' Laura replied, 'but unless you've got a better plan . . .'

'You're right,' he nodded, 'If there is an alarm, I'll be stuffed. I have to see the paintings. Either that or perhaps I can find some evidence that they were cleaned somewhere in that house.' He walked over to the door and picked up their coats, passing Laura hers. 'I don't need much, I just need to prove this link with the pictures and Cosmo.'

'You mean my father,' Laura reminded him.

'Yes, I'm sorry but I must prove that link with Acquilan and maybe even Kelp – if it exists. It's the only way. Jack Douglas will go to town on this if I can prove the link.'

'Look, John,' Laura began, 'I feel uneasy about why you are

involved. There's too much coincidence. We know you're not just an unlucky bystander, somebody who happened by and ended up selling the pictures simply because your uncle lived near him.'

'I've given up asking the question, why me? I just don't know. If I'm involved, then perhaps this gamble won't pay off. They'll come for me anyway, but if I'm *not* part of it, then at last I'll be free. God only knows but I just can't sit still and wait.'

There was a sharp knock on the door.

'Yo! In there, it's me!'

Laura moved to the door and looked through the spyhole. 'It's Ari,' she hissed, 'You know, from the bar.'

Laura opened the door. Before she knew what was happening, the woman pushed inside and slammed the door behind her.

'Quick!' she said, walking towards the window, 'you've no time, girl.'

'What's all this . . .?' Laura followed her.

'No time, just trust me.'

'But what about the man you said you'd find?'

'Oh that – that's done.' She glanced from Laura to John as she spoke. 'But we got a big problem.'

'I don't understand, what problem?'

'Look,' the girl commanded, as she stared out of the window at the road below. 'There! See those three gettin' out that car?'

Running to the window, they looked out and saw below three men in raincoats climbing out of a large grey Mercedes parked beside the sidewalk.

'Look, you sure are in some serious shit! You didn't tell me it was this bad. All I know is that they're coming for you. I mean, these guys, they're serious!' She glanced out of the window again as her voice trailed away. 'Look, I'm getting the hell out of here! You guys comin' with me?'

'OK, OK!' John said.

'But what about our things?' Laura broke away from John and started to walk towards the bedroom.

'No time, Laura, no time. She's right. Look, everything important to us is here in my briefcase – papers, plans, money. Where to?'

'All right,' Ari opened the door slowly, 'the roof!' She saw Laura's eyes open wide, 'Hey! Don't worry, I know all these blocks; when you work on your back, you always know which way is up.' Motioning with her hand for them to keep quiet, she stuck her head out of the door and listened. Then she led them up the stairs.

As they ran up the next flight of stairs, Ari stopped and again listened. All three of them could now hear steps echoing below them. They moved as quickly and as silently as they could up the next two flights until they came to a battered, metal-skinned door at the very top of the building. The locks on it had long since rusted away and John put his shoulder to it. There was a teeth-jarring screech as it slid open.

Outside the roof, which was bound by a broken, low stone parapet, was windswept and cold. A clothes-line dangled across it. John followed Ari over to one side of the building.

'Christ!' John exclaimed as he looked at the gap between the building next to them and their own. 'It must be nearly twelve foot wide.'

'You don't expect us to jump that, do you?' Laura began.

'Jump? Who said anything about "jump"?' Ari laughed and then, sticking her fingers in her mouth, gave out a piercing whistle. There was a moment's pause before two women emerged from behind some laundry hanging on a line across the other roof. The first woman waved at Ari and then they bent down below the parapet and lifted up a large scaffolding plank. Slowly they swung it round and pushed it across the gap until Ari took hold of the other end.

293

'There! Now,' she faced Laura, 'You lucky I got these girls to get up here with this,' she pointed at the plank, 'now go, hurry up, we got no time to talk.'

John could see Laura's jaw was set, her face white and her eyes staring. She looked frightened.

'God, I hate heights,' she breathed. 'I don't know if . . .'

'Hell! This is as safe as the Brooklyn Bridge, girl,' Ari laughed. 'Anyway, safer than your ass if you don't go across.'

'God help me, what am I doing?' Laura appealed to John. Then she turned and climbed carefully onto the plank.

'Don't look down, Laura,' John's voice was a tense whisper, his arm outstretched as though to hold her but, by the time Laura heard the words, she was a third of the way across. She walked steadily, one foot in front of the other until she reached the far side. Next over was Ari, who flipped off her shoes and moved across as gracefully as a cat, her slim, lithe figure assured, her movements elegant.

'OK!' Ari called to John, who smiled nervously as he climbed onto the parapet. Heights were never something that normally bothered him but the very thought of walking between two buildings which were ten storeys high made his head swim. He was heavier than the others and the board beneath him began to bend as he edged out over the gap. He could hear and sense each end beginning to slide across the parapets as the board sank down. He looked across and saw their faces; they were not looking at him but past him.

'Quick, John, the door!' Laura shouted as she pointed behind him. Over his shoulder, he saw the door beginning to open. He needed no further urging and dived across the last three feet over the parapet. As he flattened himself against the wall he watched the others duck down and could hear the scraping, squeaking sound as the door opened wide.

'The board, Laura, the board!' he whispered.

Laura needed no second telling. She raised herself above the parapet and, with one movement, swept the end of the board off the parapet. It plunged between the two buildings, clattering against the walls on its way down.

'Grande, Mr Grande!' A deep, harsh New York voice barked out. 'Police department, we've got a few questions!' John could hear footsteps and muffled voices.

'Bullshit!' hissed Ari under her breath. 'I know cops and no cop I know drives a Mercedes-Benz!'

Again the voices. John strained to make out their words to each other. '. . . You stay . . . downstairs . . . apartment . . . check it out . . .' There were further footsteps, the door squeaked and scraped open again, then there was silence. Laura was just about to stand up, when John put his hand on her shoulder and held her down. He shook his head and then signalled to the others that he smelt smoke. Ari nodded and cautiously peered over the edge of the parapet, signalling to John and Laura to look as well.

What they saw made their hearts miss a beat. One of the men was sitting with his back to them, on the parapet of the other building twelve feet away, smoking. They crouched back down again.

'We've got to distract him,' John whispered. He noticed that there was a large crack in the brickwork of the parapet and started to pull at a bit of broken brick until it fell out into his hands.

'I'm going to throw this. There's an air or a heating vent the other side of him across the roof,' he hissed. 'I'll signal you when he gets up and on that signal everybody run for the door, as quietly as possible. It's the only way.' He eased his head gently above the parapet. The man was still sitting in exactly the same position, staring into space. John stood up very, very slowly and then, putting the piece of brick in his right hand, he took aim at a metal air vent situated by the door of the other block. God help me, he thought to himself as he threw the piece of brick. It seemed to take an age as it curled through the air – and then there was a metallic crash as

295

it struck the air vent, rattled on the lip, and then slithered on down, the noise echoing out through the vent like a megaphone.

The man jerked his head over towards the door and stood up. His hand reached under his coat as he broke into a run and headed for the vent. At that moment, John waved to the others and they all ran towards a door about twelve metres across the roof. John followed.

He was a few metres away when they heard the man shout.

'Don't stop,' John screamed, 'keep on running!' Just as John was pushing his way through the door, there was a crack and the brickwork above his head splintered and showered down on top of him. His head pounded as he pushed Laura through the door. Her face was white – then another crack and thump as a second bullet struck the wall and they were all inside.

Half running, half jumping, sometimes slithering, they made their way down the flights of steps as quickly as they could, reaching the bottom faster than John or Laura would have thought possible, and ran out through the back door into an alleyway which went between two other apartment blocks at the back. They made their way through the alleyway and eventually out into a small road. There, at the far end, was a brick wall. A red Cadillac was pulled up, half on, half off the sidewalk, its engine running.

'Now who's this?' John shouted at Ari.

'Don't worry!' Ari screamed. She flung open the passenger door. 'Get in – let's go!'

They crammed into the car, and without waiting for the door to close, the driver put his foot down on the accelerator.

John sat uncomfortably wedged between Ari's two friends while Laura, on the far side of the speeding car, was still trying to shut the door.

'Shit!' The fatter of the two women leant across John and poked Ari in the shoulder. 'You can drop us right here.' She sat back, 'I ain't staying with these two – no way! Hell, we nearly got iced – I mean, you never said nothin' 'bout that, Ari. Man, this is heavy shit!' She finished speaking as the car screeched to a halt and they clambered out.

As the car pulled away again, Ari turned around and stared at John before speaking.

'She's right, you'all goin' to get us killed.'

'What about that man you promised?' Laura said calmly.

'He's ready,' she said, glaring at Laura before telling John, 'But the price just went up.'

'What price? How much?' John turned to Laura. 'That's your money, you . . .'

'Don't worry,' she said, laying her hand on his arm. 'How much?'

'Fifteen thousand dollars', Ari replied, 'Seven thousand now, the rest on completion.'

'But that's too much . . . too high,' John responded quietly.

'No problem, you got a choice,' Ari replied. 'Pay, or . . .'

'No, the money's OK, John, and we just can't do it without her help. You said yourself what if it is alarmed and locked.' Laura turned to Ari, 'That's OK, but he'd better be good.'

'And he'd better be worth it,' added John.

'He *will* be,' Ari intoned.

19

Foreign Trouble

Weitz sat at his desk, his arms crossed, head bent, deep in thought.

His hunch had paid off. Not that it made him feel any better. The fact that Pichowski had missed Grande and Buckley at the apartment was a blow but he had at least come up with important information. Following their disappearance, Weitz had instructed Pichowski to check the telephones. There wasn't one in the apartment. So he checked the payphones nearby. The nearest was across the road in a bar. Information about their movement was easy to come by. Buckley had used the telephone in the bar on a couple of occasions.

For once Pichowski had used his initiative and managed to check calls made from that telephone on the evenings she'd been there. As Pichowski had said, it was a long shot, but then, sticking out like a sore thumb from the host of local numbers, was one to Alexandria in Virginia, just down the road from Washington. When the number was checked, it proved to be the worst nightmare Weitz could have had, belonging as it did to Jack Douglas, Kelp's tormentor.

The tapping of his pen speeded up as Weitz reflected on the way Douglas had singled out Kelp's record for analysis recently. Alone among the commentators, he'd eaten away at Kelp's credibility. Buckley's call therefore troubled him. In the midst of all her worries, why would she be calling Douglas? Grande and Douglas working together was bound to increase the sum total of their knowledge. Perhaps, Weitz mused, Grande had even seen the diaries. Weitz stopped tapping his pen at the thought of that and took a sharp breath.

Of course, he realised: Kelp's name on the pad. But was that before or after?

He remembered the three people getting into the cab by the Vietnam Memorial. For a second he froze, and then in a blind panic he reached for his pocket diary and flicked through it very quickly.

The day after the phone call. He slammed his diary down on the desk. It must have been them, he was sure. He could see Grande's face as he stared back. There was also a third, an older figure, although he couldn't recall the face. The thought that he'd been so close to them made his blood run cold.

If only Victor had got rid of the pictures – Ewan was right. Just as Cosmo needed Grande with the diaries, he mused, Grande must need them and the paintings. Yet Weitz knew that time was running out for all of them. Kelp was making a comeback in California, the nomination could be his for the taking – providing nothing else went wrong. Weitz was aware how little room there was for manoeuvre. If Douglas knew what Grande probably now knew, plus his earlier research, he might really be able to damage Kelp.

No one, he reflected, would listen to the allegations made by a murderer. Unless, he thought, his pulse racing, such a person was covered by the credibility of Jack Douglas.

As Weitz realised what that meant, he smiled. It occurred to him that the meeting between Grande and Douglas could be turned to his own advantage. For, while they couldn't find Grande, they now knew he had met Douglas and would probably meet him again at some time. And even if he didn't, he must call in. Grande needed Douglas. Douglas needed Grande because he helped him fill in the gaps. 'All we need,' he said aloud, 'is a tap on Douglas's telephone and someone to watch the house.' Grande's reputation as a murderer could bear an additional dead body, or two – even if one turned out to be Grande himself. But first, Douglas would have to be watched around the clock.

Weitz leaned forward and picked up the telephone. After a couple of rings, Pichowski's unmistakable voice grated at the other end.

'Pichowski,' he said slowly, 'I've got a job for you.'

In a small diner on the outskirts of Easthampton on the edge of Long Island, three people sat staring into their coffee. Through the noise of the clattering plates, the strains of Glen Miller wafted from the juke-box in the far corner. An attractive young black woman shook her head and snorted.

'Goddamn!' Ari exclaimed. 'Sittin' in a greasepot in Whiteville listenin' to this,' she jerked her thumb at the juke-box, 'sure ain't no party I ever wanted to be at.' She addressed the middle-aged man opposite her. 'Yo, Pervis! Whaddya say?' Pervis merely shrugged and drank his coffee.

John Grande looked at the man again. He was stocky with a bald head and a permanently red face. Yet his hands seemed out of place; they were slim, with almost elegant fingers which moved like snakes. This man was his only hope of gaining access to any locked rooms when they entered Acquilan's house. It was all a huge gamble. He shuddered as he thought of the risk.

Matt Pervis, Ari had told him, used to be a safe-cracker. Years spent in and out of prison and away from his family had persuaded him to go straight. He now owned a security company specialising in alarms and locks. There was, she had reassured them, nothing he didn't know about security systems and he had also managed to lay his hands on the photographic equipment John had requested.

'So,' Laura began as she slid into the bench seat next to John, 'It's still on?'

John and Ari smiled, but Pervis remained impassive.

'What time?' he asked.

'Ten o'clock tomorrow.'

'That doesn't leave us much time. I got equipment to prepare and you need to check out the cameras.'

'How much time you wantin', Pervis?' Ari exclaimed.

'Enough to do it properly. What you got to realise is that these things need to run smooth or you foul up. And, anyway, I ain't no actor.'

'Don't worry,' John said quickly, 'as I said, you are my assistant – I'll do the talking.'

'Your plan sounds OK but I've heard better ones that ended up putting me in the slammer before. Let's get this straight – we ain't taking anything, you say?'

'No, just some photographs, of . . .'

'So, if you find what you're looking for,' Pervis continued, 'and that's a fuckin' big "if", mister, you're just going to take pictures?'

'Yes.'

'Well, that's the strangest deal I ever heard. What, you casing the joint?'

'No, just pictures, that's all I need.'

'OK, well as long as I don't break my pledge – I said no more stealing.'

'Now wait a minute,' Laura began, 'you're being paid good money . . .'

'If the plan's shit,' he snapped, 'I walk – don't matter what the money is.'

'Now don't let me down, Pervis – I got a piece o' this ridin' on your ass too,' Ari said, glaring at him.

'I didn't say I wouldn't do it but the plans don't seem so great,' he sounded defensive. 'It's . . . it's complicated. I mean, you don't know where to look and you don't even know what security they got. How you gonna look round a house that size?'

'I don't think I'll need to. After all . . .' John replied, 'the paintings are not for public display. So they must be some-where he can see them but not anywhere obvious. Some sort of hidden gallery – not big but secure.' He opened his briefcase, 'We should go over the house plan again.'

Laura gave his hand a squeeze. He smiled briefly at her.

'OK,' Pervis nodded, 'but if it don't look right, I'll get the hell outta here.'

Ralph Grande put down his book and looked out of the window. There was no horizon, just incredibly tall buildings. Yet he could see the sun reflected and refracted across a thousand skyscraper plate-glass windows. He took his glasses off his nose and gazed out.

He'd been in the same room for what seemed ages. He'd lost count of the days. His food was brought to him by the younger man who, despite Ralph's repeated attempts to engage him in conversation, never spoke. The best he'd extracted was a couple of 'yeahs' and the rest were all grunts. Once the older man came in with his food and told him they'd made contact.

'Now it's all down to your nephew,' Ralph recalled him saying. 'It's in his interests to contact us because . . .'

'Because you're keeping me a prisoner – I'm the bait, am I not?' Ralph had replied. The man smiled briefly before continuing.

'Mr Grande, you're here for your own safety and it's in the interests of your nephew, otherwise we can't help him.' Again the thin smile and without further comment he turned and walked out, locking the door behind him. That had been the last time he'd been in.

No amount of smooth words could alter the fact that Ralph was a prisoner. What was worse, he knew he had been used. They told him that his nephew needed him in New York urgently. Now he felt deeply ashamed at his own naïveté in doing as they had asked. For all he knew, John's life was in jeopardy just because he had interfered. He should have listened to John. He should have stayed out of it in Italy – that would have been best.

He levered himself up from his chair, walked to the side of his bed and switched on the sidelight. He felt very tired; he seemed to sleep so much these days. He finished the glass of wine and put it down. A strange red light from the dying sun bathed his room as he slumped down on the bed. He felt old, every day of his 84 years; old, tired and lost. He lay his head back on the pillow and closed his eyes. In the distance, eight storeys below, he was faintly aware of police sirens and car horns, which merged together as he slipped off to sleep.

'All the fault of D'Ostia, poor John, poor boy . . .' His voice faded away as his breathing became steady.

The light dimmed outside. He didn't hear the key in the lock and his heavy breathing remained unchanged as the door swung open. The younger of the two men walked in and picked up the tray. He stopped and glanced at Ralph Grande as a wheelchair moved through the door. It stopped, half in shadow.

'He's asleep,' the young man said to the old man in the wheelchair. 'This stuff works quickly.' He tapped a bottle he'd just taken from his pocket. The other man made no answer and, after a few more seconds of silence, the wheelchair reversed out, followed by the young man.

'No one but no one works an audience like he does,' Frank Parry told Dan Petrone.

'Amen to that,' Petrone sighed.

They were watching President Carson working the crowded hall, shaking hands and joking with the crowd, applauded all the way.

'But you and me know it'll take more than that,' Petrone continued ruefully. 'Neck and neck with Kelp was not how it was meant to be.'

'It's all down to California now,' Parry sighed, 'and anything Pete can come up with.'

'Has he got anything?'

'I'm not sure, but we'll find out in an hour, we're meeting him at the hotel.'

Frank Parry had a heavy feeling in the pit of his stomach; the campaign was hanging by a thread. Watching the President he realised it was only his immense personal charm and the stable economy that kept his hopes alive – anyone else with his problems would have been dead and buried by now.

Parry also knew that where there was life there was hope. Pete Neal was coming to California to talk about Kelp.

Carson walked towards him, shaking hands, smiling, 'So, Frank,' he said into his left ear, 'what's next?'

'Back to the hotel for that meeting with Pete, Mr President.'

'Oh yes,' Carson turned and waved one more time. Then, surrounded by his secret service agents, he was steered out of the hall.

An hour later the two men, Frank Parry and Dan Petrone, were sitting opposite the President in the campaign HQ.

'Well, Pete'd better have something good,' Carson began. 'So far we don't have anything on Kelp and his vote is holding up.'

'Pete's done some good work so far,' Parry replied.

'Not good enough,' barked Carson. 'I need some real dirt on Kelp.'

'The public are split about it,' Petrone began, cautiously. 'A small majority still believe you about the land deal allegation but that number is falling. The no-smoke-without-fire idea is taking hold.'

'What, so the longer it goes on, the more public opinion will swing against me?' Carson snapped.

'That's about the size of it,' said Parry, nodding slowly. 'But there's more . . .'

'*What?*'

'Well, they're insisting now that they interview you.'

Parry expected an explosion from Carson but nothing happened. He just sat in silence staring at his hands. Petrone shuffled uneasily in his seat. It was minutes before Carson spoke.

'I thought you said you could stall them,' Carson sighed, leaning back in his chair. 'So that's it, I have to perjure myself?'

'Look, we can make it short and sweet. He can only ask you certain questions and we know he hasn't got anything so far, so this is a fishing expedition. You can just block him off.'

Parry watched as Carson visibly shrank.

'It's going to look bad,' Petrone chipped in.

'*So?*' Parry glared at him, 'I don't hear you offer a better way!'

Petrone shook his head.

'Well,' continued Parry, 'we can't stall him any longer.'

'What if Kelp gets hold of this?' Carson sighed. 'He'll use it – I know I would.'

'I don't know,' said Parry, 'there's not much time – he can't refer to it directly. The most he could do is to muck-rake about it. And anyway, we might just be getting somewhere with Pete.'

Carson sat up and shook his head, 'That'd be the day.'

'Well, it's our best shot, play for time, campaign like hell and dig something up on Kelp.'

'Sure,' Petrone said quickly. 'He's right, Kelp's an old loser – you can beat him, it's still there for the taking.'

'Maybe, maybe,' Carson muttered. 'So where the hell is Neal?'

As if on cue, there was a knock on the door and Pete Neal walked in.

Petrone nodded to Parry and left the room.

'So, Pete, what have you got?' Carson asked as Neal sat down.

'We may be onto something . . .'

'Kelp?' Parry asked.

'Yeah,' Neal pulled out some notes from his breast pocket. 'Seems that English guy I said the NYPD were after, well, I think Kelp's people are after him too.'

'Why?' Parry asked, leaning forward.

'I don't know, but I understand they were seen just off East 31st in the Murray Hill area.'

'So?' Carson shrugged dismissively.

'It's only important because the police now think the English guy was there.'

'What, they found him?'

'No, but they were looking.'

'Thanks,' Carson said sarcastically, 'I suppose that's something. Looks like you've got some way to go though on that one, Pete.' He stretched his arms as he walked to the door, 'I'm going to call Dick Barnet at the Pentagon. He needs some decision about the budget.'

'California?' Parry asked.

'Why do you think Dick made the call? $10 billion-worth of benefits to be allocated to the West Coast. I'd call that more impressive than trying to find an English guy in New York.'

Carson paused at the door and looked back at Neal. 'Still, keep us informed, Pete, if you get any closer.'

'What's eating him?' Neal asked, as the door shut behind Carson.

'He thinks you're getting nowhere with Kelp,' Parry replied.

'Look, I think we may be,' Neal began, 'I took a chance and persuaded the Feds to help me. I had a look at Kelp's wartime file. You know, he was involved in a strange accident in Naples in 1946, a year after the war. There was a fire and two men from his old army unit were killed. There was a brief investigation at the time but the file was closed.'

'So?'

'Well, I had the bodies exhumed – the two who died were brought back to New York.'

'What?' Parry exclaimed.

'Relax. No one knows – special job – the Feds do it all the time. They helped.'

'And?'

'One of the bodies was a fake.'

'What d'ya mean, a fake?'

'Oh, it's a real body, but it's not the right body. The man that's missing is a Corporal Cosmo. Dental records don't check.'

'Who's the one . . .?'

'I don't know,' Neal replied, 'but the interesting thing is that Kelp must know about it.'

'We'll never prove anything.'

'No, but that's not why it's interesting. This English guy may be caught up in it, which would be why Kelp wants him.'

'What for?'

'Blackmail?' Neal shrugged. 'Perhaps he has some information on him. Who knows? But if we could get to him before Kelp . . .' his voice trailed away.

'But can you find him?'

'The NYPD are looking everywhere. We should help them.'

'So what do they need?'

'That English cop. You know, the one in New York. Well, he's made a real difference to the investigation. It's a good job we kept him there. But I hear he's about to go back and our guys need him here until it's over.'

'OK, it just needs a call to London,' he tightened his lips. 'Whatever they need . . . just find the guy,' Parry paused. 'There's something else,' Frank Parry began, 'the Mother Superior.'

'Who?' Neal spluttered.

'You know, the old girl who was in charge of the convent hospital.'

'Uh huh, so what?'

'Well, she contacted us again.'

'Why would she do that?' asked Neal.

'Says she was worried she couldn't remember about the child and because the records were destroyed. She's written to all the nuns who are still alive, asking if they remember. Said she would let us know.'

'*Jesus*!' Neal exclaimed, 'What is she doing?'

'Trying to help, I guess.'

'I know that! What I mean is, what if someone remembers?'

'Precisely,' Parry continued, 'that's the point.'

'Too late to stop her?'

'Yes.'

'I guess we can only hope they've all got memories like hers.'

'And that the Haskins woman used a different name.'

'God, yes!'

'Don't say a word to him,' Parry said, jerking his head towards the door.

'No.'

'The truth is, Pete, we need the police to find that guy and find him fast!'

At 9.45 a.m., Laura Buckley turned the car south off the Easthampton road and along a curving drive lined on either side by copper beeches. About half a mile along this drive, the trees stopped and gave way to an expanse of lawn running up to a large Georgian-style house in front of them. With its imposing columned portico facing out onto a sweeping lawn, which dipped into a small harbour and bay beyond, Laura was reminded almost instantly of *The Great Gatsby*. She smiled at the absurdity, despite her nerves.

Pervis whistled as they parked the car. 'Goddamn!' he swore. John was silent, staring in front, too nervous to speak. He didn't dare exchange glances with Laura for fear of giving himself away. For about a minute they were motionless until finally John opened the door and took a deep breath, 'Well, let's go.'

They'd practised what they had to do endlessly the night before in their hotel room. John had run them through one routine after another. He briefed them on where he thought the pictures might be and the sort of things that they had to look for – rooms that were locked, even describing the scenes that the pictures depicted and the style that they were in just in case they hadn't been cleaned: nothing would surprise him. He then ran through the simple camera drills with Matt Pervis: the way to set up the tripod and the lights, the sort of things that any photographer's assistant would have done automatically and which would not bring him any undue attention. John had already told them that they were to somehow find a way of looking around the house first, before Laura started her interview.

As Laura got out of the car and walked past John, he instinctively reached out and held her hand. Surprised, she stared at him for a few seconds before her face relaxed into a smile.

'Sorry,' he whispered, 'this is one hell of an outside chance.'

'Better than waiting for that knock on the door anyway,' she whispered. 'You OK?' she asked Pervis.

'Sure,' Pervis answered, as he hauled a canvas bag from the car. 'We got a job to do, so let's do it.'

'Now remember, we ask to look around first,' John said. 'I'll take the cameras with me when I go round the house.' He turned to Laura, 'When she's finished showing us round, you must start immediately on the interview. If they're not anywhere else,' he said to Pervis, 'then the only place left will be in the cellar. We'll have to create some kind of diversion so I can explore . . .'

They walked up to the door in nervous silence. Only Pervis, more relaxed than the others, whistled softly as he gazed at the front of the house. The other two avoided each other's eyes.

A large, heavy-set butler answered the door. After eyeing them coldly up and down, he stepped back and with the minimum of grace ushered them into the hall.

On the far side of the entrance hall, a large staircase swept away from them, down which, a few minutes later, came the elegant Mrs Acquilan. She didn't seem to walk so much as flow down the stairs. She was tall and easy-limbed and John was struck by the almost perfect balance of her face. With her black hair tied back he found it difficult to guess her age. Her clothes and her face seemed to contradict themselves; her clothes suggested mid-thirties, yet the harder look in her eyes and the determined set of her chin made him think she was probably older. As she approached, hand outstretched, her smile and eyes never left him. Despite his nerves and the charging adrenalin, he found himself smiling back. Then, at the last moment, she turned and faced Laura. The butler in the dark coat announced them as she shook hands slowly with Laura, then she turned briefly to John before glancing at Pervis.

Once the formalities were over, Laura discussed the interview. Mrs Acquilan had already made up her mind where it was to take place and how it was all to work. Her slow Southern voice took them through her plans with calm authority.

Laura asked if they could look over the house first. Mrs Acquilan agreed.

She led them into the drawing room, talking all the while. It was all polished oak flooring, chintz curtains and antique furniture. The pictures on the walls were Post-Impressionist landscapes. Laura exchanged looks with John but he shook his head. Once they'd placed their equipment down near the fireplace, Mrs Acquilan led the way around the rest of the house, clearly flattered by their enthusiasm.

They visited every room, discussing each one animatedly, with Laura taking notes and John checking his camera lens as though sizing up a shot or two. The tour took nearly three-quarters of an hour with no sign of the pictures. John expected this and yet he couldn't help feeling disappointed. As they arrived back downstairs, Laura calmly and in a matter-of-fact way asked if John could photograph one or two of the rooms upstairs as well as a couple downstairs. She explained that they could do the interview while John took the photographs, then they'd finish off with some shots of Mrs Acquilan.

The butler made a noise and shook his head: 'Mr Acquilan said . . .'

'Nonsense, Martin, now see here, you show these two to the rooms they want to photograph,' she smiled at Laura.

The butler hesitated, 'Go on!' she ordered. He nodded slowly and led John and Pervis upstairs.

Carrying their equipment, and to the great annoyance of the butler, they wandered from room to room, as though unable to decide which one would make the best shot. Eventually, John settled on one of the bedrooms nearest to a set of back stairs.

'I'll finish off up here. I'll be about ten minutes.' John began, looking through his camera. 'Could you get the rest set up in the drawing room?' he said to Pervis. 'And don't forget the tripod and lens.'

'Sure,' Pervis answered, his face impassive as though this was the most natural thing in the world and something he did every day.

'The cable and stack for the lights, they should be in the back of the car in that bag,' John said as he turned to the butler. 'I wonder, could you help him while I finish here?' He watched the butler hesitate. 'It would really speed things up.' Again the man hesitated and then nodded.

As soon as the man had followed Pervis down the stairs, John made for the back stairs. Once at the bottom, he turned left into a long corridor, the other end of which came out by the main hall. Opposite him were three doors. He was certain from the plans that one had to lead back into the drawing room. He opened it carefully and peered through the crack. He was right. Shutting it, he pushed on the second, a swing door, and saw that that led through to the kitchen. He could hear women talking and laughing. He let the door swing slowly back and turned to the third. It was covered in green baize; behind it were the stairs to the cellar.

At the bottom of the stairs he found himself in a corridor almost exactly the same length as the one above. The difference was that there were doors on either side. A number of crates were placed at intervals down the corridor. One or two were open and inside were some statues. He quickly tried all the doors, first going down the left-hand side of the corridor and then the right. They were all unlocked and each room seemed to contain a number of boxes, some open, some closed. Alongside these were stacked paintings and books. He checked the paintings in each room rapidly. While they were all valuable, none of them was what he was looking for. He thought it strange that most of them were more valuable than those in the rooms above. The way they were stored puzzled him. There was something reminiscent of *Citizen Kane* about the scene. It reeked of possession for possession's sake.

As he left the last room, his heart sank. He was running out of time and no nearer to finding the pictures. Pulling the plan out from his pocket, he cursed under his breath. As he checked the rooms, he noticed one he hadn't seen before. The door at the bottom of the stairs had swung across and covered another door to the right of the stairs. He pushed it back. Inside, there were a few boxes by the door but beyond, the room was open and at the far end was a long wooden trestle table. He shut the door carefully behind him and walked over to the table. On the table was a box full of paint-stained rags and behind the table and above on two wooden shelves attached to the wall, sat jars of chemicals. He crouched down and looked across the floor at the flakes of paint. His heart began to beat faster as he stood up. As he looked at the table again, there were more paint flakes. He reached into his breast pocket and pulled out a small, clear plastic sample bag, into which he put the bits of paint from the table and the floor. Then, examining the jars of chemicals, he noted down one or two of the compounds. The room seemed smaller and a little more cramped than the others in the cellar on the same side of the corridor. At the far end was a bookcase full of what appeared to be leather-bound books.

How strange, he thought, as he moved from one book to another, all these in a bare workroom. When he attempted to pull out one of the books near the corner of the room he found it was stuck. He tried again to pull another, with the same result. He then examined all the books more closely – all of them in the same area were cut off, leaving a quarter of the backs sticking out on the shelf. Above these, however, there were proper books. He slid one or two books out to check them and did the same on the rack below.

'Of course!' he exclaimed, as he studied his plan again. His pulse was now racing as he frantically searched along the bookshelf. He pushed and pulled at the books in front of him and then, just as he was about to give up in frustration, he pushed at a volume of Longfellow's Collected Poems and it moved in, followed by a click. A section of six books swung slowly down on a hinge. He swallowed hard; he was staring at a keypad with an electronic display with six digits. He was about to press one of the keys when he stopped and remembered the time. He shut the panel and left the room fast.

Once on the floor above, he shut the door gently behind him. He heard voices down the corridor and he walked boldly towards them. Turning the corner, he came face to face with the butler, who was standing at the end of the corridor, his face impassive but his eyes showing his annoyance. Behind him he saw Pervis and beyond that Laura, her face revealing her anxiety.

'Oh, there you are,' Laura spoke quickly as she walked towards him, 'We're ready for that shoot.' She forced a smile as she passed the butler and then raised her eyebrows questioningly. John shook his head gently. 'Are you ready, John?' she asked.

'Just about,' he replied. 'Got a bit lost,' he said and smiled. The butler turned and walked back into the drawing room. John beckoned to Pervis. 'Laura,' he whispered to her as Pervis approached, 'you've got to keep that butler busy.' She nodded and John turned to Pervis as she walked back into the drawing room. 'Look, I think I've found it,' he hissed, 'It's in the cellar through the green baize door, first on the right when you get down the stairs. Inside is a bookcase, press the Longfellow volume and you'll find a keypad. There's our problem. It's an electronic lock and probably alarmed as well.'

'OK,' Pervis nodded. 'Don't worry if you hear the alarm go off. It's all in hand – just leave it to me.' As the butler turned to go into the drawing room, he slipped away down the corridor.

For a few moments John stared at his retreating back and then walked into the drawing room. The minutes ticked by and John had just started taking the first pictures of Mrs Acquilan when the piercing sound of an alarm shattered the silence.

'Martin!' Mrs Acquilan yelled at the butler, 'Where in hell is that coming from?'

The butler shook his head.

'Well, sort it out!' she shrieked at his retreating back while clutching her ears.

Laura stared in abject horror at John, who tried to reassure her by smiling back gently until, a few seconds later, the alarm stopped.

'Thank God!' Mrs Acquilan exclaimed as John glanced nervously towards the door, expecting any second to see the butler dragging Pervis behind him. They carried on taking photographs for a few minutes. Then the butler's footsteps could be heard coming along the corridor.

As the butler came back he looked at John, walked over to Mrs Acquilan, leant down and whispered something in her ear.

'Sure, well, why didn't you do that before?' She waved him away with her hand.

'Where's your assistant?' the butler demanded of John.

'I sent him outside,' John answered quickly. 'I wanted a couple of shots of the front of the building. Ah, this sounds like him.' As John moved towards the door, Laura took up the cue and walked over towards the butler.

'Don't you worry about him,' Mrs Acquilan cut in, 'just make sure it doesn't go off again.'

'Surely the alarm, it couldn't be our assistant – you don't think he . . .' Laura sounded worried.

'Hell, I'm sure he didn't!' Mrs Acquilan interrupted. 'Stop being so damn inquisitive, Martin.' She had just finished speaking, when Pervis appeared round the corner.

'Did you find a good place outside?' Laura asked.

'Sure,' he began, ignoring John and walking over towards Laura. 'Those outside shots are all done,' he announced. Then he took up position behind John.

John waited until the butler had turned away before glancing at Pervis. As their eyes met he inclined his head very slightly and then turned away. Beside Pervis's feet was the camera bag and John walked over and bent down.

'I'm just going to change the lens, I won't be a second.' As he rummaged in the bag, Pervis bent down close to him.

'It's all yours,' Pervis whispered, 'the alarms are all off, just open the door. Make sure you push it shut when you go.'

John returned and made an adjustment to the tripod, intending to take some more photographs. Ten minutes later he started packing his gear up.

'I've got enough, I'm just going to clear up,' he said to Laura. She nodded and carried on with the interview. John handed his camera to Pervis. 'Distract him now,' he whispered.

Pervis turned, 'Hey, could you give me a hand with some of this?' he asked, looking at the butler. John slipped quietly out of the drawing room as the butler walked over to Pervis. Passing through the green baize door, he went down the stairs and opened the door into the room with the bookcase. In front of him the bookcase door was ajar. His pulse quickened.

Taking a deep breath, he stepped inside. A set of lights came on automatically. Around simple white walls hung a variety of paintings lit from the ceiling above. He could see at least one Canaletto and another by Brueghel, but it was then that his eye fell upon six pictures at the far end of the room. Four were hanging up and two were leaning against the wall below them. He whistled softly to himself for one of the paintings was, without question, a Licatta – not just any Licatta, but the one that had been in the gallery all those weeks before. The other was half-cleaned but still identifiable as a Licatta, the cleaned half revealing what looked like a Velázquez. He stood up and looked at the others hanging on the wall above them – he stared wide-eyed as he recognised a Caravaggio and a Caracci. He wasn't so sure about the other two. But when he looked a bit closer he could see that one was by Domenichino and the other a Raphael. All of the four cleaned pictures depicted the Madonna and Child, masterpieces which were lost during the war. Then he whistled softly, 'Incredible.'

Then, with a jolt, he remembered where he was and quickly checked the backs of the paintings. As he dropped the fourth cleaned-up painting back against the wall he smiled. The marks he had made on the back of each of the canvases were still in place. He quickly took photographs of each of them and one or two of the whole gallery. As he finished, he checked his watch. He'd been gone four minutes. He left the room and hurried upstairs. Hardly able to contain himself, he arrived just in time to assist in packing up the equipment. He tried not to catch the others' eyes, unsure whether he would be able to keep his poise. Eventually all three walked down the steps and into the car. Only as Laura drove away did he dare to speak: 'We've got them – all of them on film. We've done it!' His face was flushed and there was a sparkle in his eyes as he spoke. Laura grinned and even Pervis showed enthusiasm for the first time, slapping John on the back, even breaking into a grimace, which was meant to pass for a smile.

Back at the hotel Laura handed over the second part of the money to Pervis and Ari, who had been anxiously waiting for them there. John was surprised at how emotional he felt. After all, he reasoned, they had both been paid. Yet he hugged Ari and thanked her, genuinely sorry to see her go.

'You take care,' Pervis said, patting John on the shoulder, 'these guys play in the major leagues, you'll only get one shot at it.' He half turned and then stopped. 'Just remember, always watch your back.' He smiled and walked away.

'Strange guy,' John said, 'but he certainly knew his job.'

'What you didn't know, John, was that Pervis had a gun on him the whole time.'

'Today?'

'Yes. Said he wasn't going to "go down" again. He insisted . . .'

John felt cold as he watched the car pull away.

'I thought it best not to tell you. After all, we needed him.' John shook his head slowly and smiled.

'Now,' Laura continued, 'you'd better get these pictures to Jack in Alexandria.'

'You know,' John began, 'for the first time I feel as though I'm up with the game. Jack will be able to use this . . .' he tapped the camera with his left hand, 'to convict Acquilan and with him, Kelp. Once we've got them, perhaps our troubles will be over.'

'Maybe, maybe,' Laura said as they put their things in the back of the car, 'let's hope so.'

'What's the matter?' he asked, sliding into the seat beside her.

'Nothing,' she forced a smile. 'I'm on edge, I guess – I just can't see where this will end. You were right, he had the pictures but even having proof of that won't end it . . .' She started the car and drove off.

'There's something else you're not telling me about, isn't there?' he asked, his smile now gone.

'It's nothing to worry you,' she replied.

'Oh, come on, Laura! Surely we shouldn't have secrets now, not after what we've been through together?'

'Look, the thing is, John, you'll have to go to Jack by yourself. I've got something else I have to do. I'll join you afterwards.'

'No.'

'What do you mean, no?'

'You shouldn't – we should stay together!'

'We can't.'

'Well,' John spoke quietly, 'we should do whatever it is together and then both go on to Jack.'

'That,' Laura shook her head, 'would be crazy and you know it. Jack's waiting for your photographs and the quicker he can write his piece, the better.'

'Then come with me. Nothing should be more important, you said so yourself.'

'For you, John, for you. However, there is something I've got to clear up.'

Laura remembered the message her secretary had given her. She hadn't told John that before she left her office, she'd arranged an elaborate system whereby her secretary could pass information to her. The message was simple. There was a video meant for John now in her secretary's possession, which contained a message from John's uncle. What she also hadn't told John, because she didn't want to worry him, was that Pat Danvers had informed her that John's uncle had disappeared from Positano. No one knew where he was.

The last few weeks had left her in no doubt about John's feelings for his uncle – she knew for certain how he would react if he knew that he had disappeared. If it was Acquilan's people, she thought, she could at least protect him from them. She felt a warmth fill her. She realised what happened to John mattered more to her now than anything else. It was not a feeling she had ever had before. And, paradoxically, despite the clear threat she was under, she felt a strange sense of wellbeing.

'I won't be long – I'll be with you later tonight,' she smiled and stroked his cheek.

'Well . . .' He looked at her and frowned. 'I can't see . . .'

'Trust me, John, trust me – it's going to work out.' She surprised herself, the reassuring sound of her words belying the deep anxiety she felt. She knew she was right to take on this new challenge and not to worry John with it. He must clear his name as fast as he could through Douglas. In the meantime, she knew that whether she was there or not didn't matter. There was one thing she could do and that was to try and help his uncle; she didn't know how but she at least had to try.

319

20

A Presidential War

'You see that house just around the headland?' Kelp asked, pointing. Weitz nodded, squinting into the sun's reflection on the sea. 'That used to be our family home in the summer,' Kelp continued, 'That's why I bought this house, for the memories. They were wonderful days.'

The afternoon sun was hot but the gentle sea breeze made it seem cooler. They had come together knowing it would be their last chance to tidy up their plans before moving the campaign HQ to California.

'That's quite a view, Ewan.'

'That's Block Island over there and beyond that Long Island, although it's too far away to see. I used to go out there on my father's yacht.' Kelp laughed in a self-deprecating way. 'Time seemed to stand still in those days – a full house, sailing by day, parties at night,' he sighed.

'My old man worked in the docks, that was the closest I ever came to sailing,' Weitz responded, forcing a smile.

'Well, Bernie, to business,' Kelp said, absent-mindedly, rolling a small stone around in his hand. 'So,' he tossed the stone into the water before turning to walk back to the house, 'has Victor destroyed those paintings?'

Weitz shrugged.

'I assume that means no?'

'I don't know, Ewan – I never asked.'

'Come on, Bernie, we both know. He's never going to, he lied.'

Weitz shrugged again.

'And I'll bet you're no nearer to finding that English guy, are you?'

'We're pretty close . . .' Weitz began.

'That means no as well,' Kelp laid his hand on Weitz's shoulder.

'Look, let's not play games, Bernie. He's still out there, and the diaries too.'

'We don't know, Ewan – we don't even know whether they exist. It's probably a bluff.'

'Don't try to reassure me, Bernie. I'm not a child. Of course, we both know you can't be sure but until then we have to assume he's got them. And if so, God, the guy's a walking time bomb.' He shook his head, 'What a mess.'

'Don't worry, Ewan,' Weitz replied. 'You're nearly there, just concentrate on California. Concentrate on our main problem – Carson. We have to finish him!'

Kelp looked back out to sea, 'Carson's not going to just give up. But if you don't fix this mess, it won't matter what he does or doesn't do – we're finished.'

'Ewan, Bernie!'

They looked up to see the approaching figure of Dick Mason striding across the lawn towards them.

'I think you'll want to hear the latest news, Ewan,' Mason began as he walked up to them. 'A terrorist attack on one of our navy ships.'

'Sunk?' Kelp asked.

'No, badly damaged, about five killed and some injured.'

'Just when we had him on the run,' Weitz moaned. 'This will give him a chance to look strong.'

'You're taking this very calmly, Ewan,' Mason said, looking surprised.

'Sure I am. There's nothing we can do – we'll just have to get behind our guys on this, even support Carson. We'll be crucified if we do anything else,' Kelp answered, his face relaxed.

'This'll help his poll rating,' observed Mason, 'and he's only just behind.'

'It could all change,' Kelp replied. 'It depends how he reacts.'

'And,' Weitz smiled, 'I know the Prosecutor is still chasing him on that land scam. There's a story that he thinks Carson lied. He wants to interview him. I think he'll do it – I'm told the White House is set to agree.'

'Surely now the public will see him as a liar and a cheat? Even this bomb can't stop that!' exclaimed Mason.

'Maybe,' Kelp answered staring out to sea, 'maybe. But whatever else happens, right now we need to ride it all out. I'll just have to grab hold of the son-of-a-bitch. He's not going to break free on this. I'll match him word for word. Perhaps we should demand to know why this ship was so unprepared and why American lives were lost for nothing.' Kelp smiled, 'After all, he's never seen action and that's something the Press might like to think about.'

Weitz and Mason exchanged looks.

'Sure, Ewan, I'll get Donald onto that,' Mason replied. 'I'll see to it straight away.'

'I'll come with you,' said Weitz. 'What about you, Ewan, you coming?'

'No, thank you. I'll just stay here for a while longer.'

Still talking, Weitz and Mason walked off while Kelp continued to gaze out to sea.

'You're not going to take it away from me. I've come too far for all this – the hard way. Whatever it needs, Carson,' he muttered, looking across the bay before turning to walk up to the house.

*

It was late afternoon when Laura's cab pulled up at the hotel. She strode into the lobby, checked in, collected a parcel from the desk and then, with head cast down, walked quickly to the elevator.

As she walked into her room, she realised how tired she was. Only a few hours before her adrenalin had been pumping as the three of them entered Acquilan's house. Even now, hours after the event, she felt a shiver of excitement as she remembered John turning towards her and smiling.

She shut the bedroom door and leaned back, smiling to herself at the memory, then shuddered at the thought of those who wanted him dead. Laura knew how high the stakes were and that others would stop at nothing to kill John. Her breathing grew faster as she felt waves of panic threatening to engulf her.

Taking a deep breath, she walked to the bed and pulled out the video from the envelope. Pushing it into the machine at the end of the bed, she sat down.

The next few minutes created a jumble of emotions for her. Anger, concern, sorrow, fear, but most of all anger. As she played and replayed the tape, the tired face of an old man seemed to grow and fill the room, his soft voice mouthing the words he'd so obviously been given. He looked so bewildered. It was too much for her, she hung her head.

She had never met Ralph Grande but from John's descriptions she knew exactly who the old man was. Who were they, these people? These people who could do this? People who would use a poor old man simply as bait for his nephew?

She noted down the telephone number and instructions given on the tape after Ralph's message then paced up and down the room staring at the phone, building up her courage.

Why John? Why were they still after him? They must

know he didn't have anything. She shook her head in frustration and picked up the receiver. She felt her pulse quicken as the phone connected and started ringing at the other end. It rang and rang. It seemed to Laura as though it would never be answered, then suddenly there was a click, followed by a soft voice.

'Inquiry . . . 777,' she said quickly, just as the video had instructed her. Her voice quavered and she thought it might dry up. The same man she had heard on the tape gave her some directions and a time. He repeated them in a flat monotone and then said, 'Don't be late or we won't be there,' and hung up.

Laura put the telephone down and glanced at her watch. Twenty minutes to get there. She grabbed her briefcase – what was it again? Oh yes, the northeast corner of Washington Square. Then she was in the elevator, her heart pounding. The doors opened and she walked through the lobby to one of the payphones. There she dialled her secretary's cell phone.

'Sal,' she began as the call was answered, 'It's Laura . . .'

'Laura, thank God! Where are you? Everyone's searching for you – this man you're with is dangerous . . .'

'Sal!' The voice at the end fell silent. 'Look, I don't have much time. Take this down.' Laura then gave her secretary the address of the hotel and the room number. 'I want you to do something,' she continued. 'If I don't call you on this number in four hours, give the police the information I've just given you and tell them that they'll find the video cassette in the video and a contact number in my room.'

'This is crazy, Laura. Give it up – you're in great danger!'

'I'm all right, Sal. Just do as I ask and make sure you wait four hours.' She hung up and, grabbing her bag, walked out onto the street and hailed a cab.

Almost exactly twenty minutes later – 5.35 p.m., she noted – her cab pulled up in the northeast corner of the square.

The weather was unusually mild and people still wandered in and out of the Park. The minutes ticked by. She checked her watch again – 5.45. Perhaps they'd seen her . . . Weren't they going to approach her? After all, it was John they were after. Again, her heart started racing.

'Hey, lady!' Laura was startled and turned around. 'Hey, you waitin' for someone?'

In front of her was a pimply teenager, with very greasy hair, on roller blades. He started to circle her, chewing gum. She turned away and glanced up and down the street again. The same boy came to a halt in front of her.

'Get lost!' she told him.

'Hey, did you hear me? I said, you waiting for someone?' He smiled at her, 'Maybe 777?'

'What did you say?' she asked.

He grinned, 'I got somethin' for you, "777". They say you got to go to the southwest corner and you got to be there at 5.50.' He grinned again and, without waiting for her to answer, he skated off and was soon weaving in and out of the pedestrians.

Laura started running – she only had a few minutes.

She just made it to the opposite side of the Park as her watch reached 5.50. She was breathing hard.

'Where . . .?' she said to herself as she stood on the edge of the sidewalk gazing up and down West Fourth Street. At that moment, a black Cadillac pulled up slowly beside her and a young, heavily-built man in a close-fitting suit got out and walked up to her. She couldn't see his eyes because they were shrouded in thick, wrap-around dark glasses.

'Follow me.' He turned almost immediately and walked back towards the car. She knew that this was not the voice she heard on the telephone, it was too sharp. 'Come on, oh yes, 777,' he waited.

'Where to?' she asked.

'Like the man on the phone said, you'll have to get there to find out.'

Laura hesitated, every fibre of her being screamed at her to walk away.

'Look,' the man said, turning back to her. 'Grande was meant to be here, not you! So if you want to play the hero, lady, it's no concern of mine! But if you don't get into this godamn car now, you can say goodbye to his uncle!'

'What guarantees?'

'None – take it or leave it!'

Laura nodded slowly. She'd come too far to turn back. She followed him to where he stood by the passenger door: he opened it and she got in. Before she could say anything he jammed a pair of very dark padded glasses over her eyes. She felt them tighten sharply against her nose and the side of her face as a piece of elastic was flicked into place at the back of her head. They were so dark, she could see little except varying shades of grey out of them. They even had leather patches on both sides to stop any peripheral vision. Her heart pounded, she was suddenly very frightened.

'Keep your hands on your lap, lady, and don't touch the glasses,' he barked.

The next few minutes left her feeling disorientated as they drove through New York. She guessed it must have been five minutes, but she couldn't tell for certain. At first she tried counting the number of left and right turns but soon gave up. After a while they pulled up and she was helped out and led up some steps into a building. She then found herself being pushed into a elevator. Seconds later, she was ushered into a room and forced down into an armchair. She reached up to take the glasses off.

'No, leave them on!' someone else snarled as he pulled her hands away. She sat still. Now the voice she heard was the same as the one on the telephone. She gripped her hands together on her lap.

'Miss Buckley,' the voice began, 'you should never have got involved, you know. It wasn't part of the scheme.'

'Whose scheme?' she asked, turning her head towards the sound of the voice.

'The general scheme,' the man continued. 'If Grande hadn't run away, all this would be over by now.'

'Who do you work for? Acquilan?' she snapped.

'Who?'

'So why am I here? Why have you got John's uncle?'

'Well,' he began, 'you forget that you came freely and for that matter, so did he. You see, I need to talk to Grande, that's all.'

'Kill him more likely.'

'No,' he rasped, only inches from her right ear. 'You're wrong, Miss Buckley. That's a misunderstanding – I've no desire to kill him. I just want to give him something and explain its full significance.'

'You mean the diaries?' No sooner had Laura said that than she regretted it.

'What do you know about the diaries?' he snarled. She heard the creaking floorboards as he started to patrol around her. 'Anyway, I've got something Mr Grande needs. Whatever you think, do you dare take the gamble that I'm lying? You could be condemning him.' Again, the creaking floorboards. 'If the cops get him, they'll put him away for a long time.' His pacing stopped. 'Of course there are those who would like to get rid of him.' Again Laura jumped, this time he was whispering into her left ear. 'His disappearance might solve a lot of problems. Yes, ma'am, a lot of problems. You know that at least.'

Laura swallowed hard and tried to moisten her dry lips. She felt cold metal touch her cheek briefly. It felt like a gun and her throat went dry.

'Who . . .' she coughed, 'who are you? What do you want?' Her words came out as a strangulated whisper.

'You've no need to fear me.' The voice was calmer, softer. 'His uncle came to New York of his own free will. Do you think for one moment we could have kidnapped him?' The man laughed eerily, 'No, he may not like his room but he came here freely!'

Somewhere in the distance sirens wailed.

'Free will!' Laura snorted, 'I guess just like I'm here out of free will?'

'Yes.' His voice was above and behind her now and she could feel that he was leaning on the top of her armchair. 'Nobody forced you. It wasn't supposed to be you. John Grande was meant to be here but you chose to come in his place. You're free to go any time,' he said, his finger running slowly down her neck.

'Well,' Laura hesitated, 'what about these dark glasses, why can't I take them off?' She reached up to brush his hand away but it had gone.

'They're just a precaution.' She swivelled her head, he'd moved to the other side of her. 'What you don't see, you can't describe. Anyway, it's not important – it's enough that I have my reasons.'

'You're trying to make me believe you actually wish John Grande, his uncle and me no harm?'

'Sure . . . why not?'

Laura heard the man walk past her and slowly drag a chair towards her. He sat down heavily.

'So what are you after? You never answered me,' Laura continued.

'It doesn't matter. What's important, what matters, is that I have something to give to Mr Grande, that's all. Surely you can see it will help him understand and even end all of this?' Still his voice was calm and measured.

'What?'

'For him only.'

'It's those diaries, isn't it?' Laura's voice became more emphatic, clearer.

There was no answer.

'Are you working for my father?' she spluttered as she leaned forward. 'Is he really dead?' she continued. '*Is* he?'

'Only you can answer that.'

Perhaps they did have the diaries, she thought. If they did then it would all be over. Was her father really dead? Her emotions were in turmoil. She didn't know whether to feel sad or angry about him. He'd dumped her just like he'd dumped her mother.

'Look, Miss Buckley, there's no point in all of this. Just give me Grande's location and I'll reunite you, all three. Then I won't trouble you again. After all, without my information, Grande is in the dark – he hasn't got a chance.'

Laura was getting more and more aggravated by the way he seemed to patronise her and John and, most of all, she hated his controlled delivery.

'I wouldn't be so sure, if I were you,' she replied.

'Oh, why not?'

'We already know and can prove where the pictures are.'

'You don't say?' His voice, she noticed, had become sharper, the words came out a little faster – not much but enough to make her feel pleased with herself, as though she was perhaps taking control.

'Yes, it'll be enough,' she continued.

'I doubt it, Miss Buckley,' again the controlled voice, 'You know, no one's likely to believe the word of a thief and a murderer and a woman obviously infatuated with him.' She could just make out a gentle mocking laugh that followed his words. 'That's asking a bit much; with Grande's record for murder, somehow I just don't think so.'

Laura straightened up, suddenly determined to wipe the smugness out of his voice.

'They'll believe it all right, they'll believe the oldest and wisest political commentator in the business!' she countered.

'John isn't what you say. When the photos are delivered, that'll be enough. The story will be complete. So, you see,

there is no need for all this. Just let John's uncle and me go –
if, as you say, you want to help.' Laura finished speaking, her
face flushed, straining her ears for his answer. The man made
no reply – he simply got out of his seat and walked slowly past
her.

'I'm forgetting myself, you must be thirsty.' His voice now
came from the far side of the room. Laura didn't reply for, as
her anger slowly subsided, she realised she'd all but told him
where John was. Her temper and self-importance had now
put him in jeopardy.

'Now let me go!' she said quickly.

'Fine,' the man replied, 'we'll just get Grande's uncle,
which should take a few minutes, and then you're free to go.'
He pressed a glass into her hand.

'What is it?'

'Just Seven Up – I'm sorry, it's all I have. Of course, if you
don't . . .'

'No,' her lips felt dry, 'that'll be fine.'

She felt depressed as she spoke. How stupid could anyone
be? To have fallen for such an obvious trick. She gulped the
drink, realising she was thirstier than she had thought.

'OK,' the man continued, 'you will get him to contact me,
won't you?' His voice and manner were still controlled. It
made her feel worse and she sat for a few seconds without
answering.

'It will be up to him,' she said, resting her head on the back
of the chair. She felt tired, so tired. If only John were here
now. She felt giddy . . . the drink, what was in the drink?

'So, will you be joining him in . . . Alexandria, or will you
meet somewhere else?' The man's voice was close and
strangely soft.

'Yes,' she began, tired, so tired, 'Alexandria . . .' Laura
paused. No more answers, she had said too much already.
'No, I don't know.' The glass slipped from her fingers and she
heard it thump against the wooden floorboards.

'What's she saying?'

Another voice – the other man – Laura tried to lift her head. Where? Too heavy. How did he . . .?

'Douglas,' the first man replied, 'he's with Douglas.'

That was the last she heard.

Detective Sergeant Mackie dropped his bag on the floor outside Jasinski's office and walked in. Jasinski was just finishing a telephone call and Mackie sat down by his desk and waited.

As Jasinski talked, Mackie gazed at the office outside. By the precinct standards, it was pretty quiet. Half the desks were empty. He laughed to himself when he remembered how he'd thought the floor was a scene from bedlam when he first arrived. He'd miss it.

'Where you going?' Jasinski's voice broke in on Mackie's thoughts.

'I'm on a flight in two and a half hours,' Mackie answered as he turned round.

'I think not,' Jasinski stood up and smiled, 'you'll be staying a while longer.'

'No, I've been ordered back. I . . .'

'Sure you were, but my captain just told me you been cleared to stay,' Jasinski grinned.

'But only yesterday my chief superintendent insisted I return.'

'Don't worry, it's all cleared – call him.'

'I'd better,' Mackie was puzzled.

He dialled his superintendent's home number. A sleepy voice answered.

'Yes,' Mackie heard the unmistakable tones of his superior.

'It's Mackie, sir, I'm sorry to . . .'

'Oh, you got the message then?'

'Aye, but why?'

'Seems they can't do without you – anyway, you're staying.'

'For how long?'

'As long as it takes.'

'What?'

'Don't ask me why. If it had been left to me, you'd have been back ages ago. Seems someone high up, and I mean high up, wants you to stay, so . . .'

'I'll do what I can . . .'

'You'll have to – just solve the damn case and get home!' The telephone went dead. Mackie put the receiver down and looked at Jasinski, a puzzled expression knotting his eyebrows.

'I know, don't try to understand,' Jasinski laughed. 'My captain says this came from the police commissioner himself.'

Mackie shook his head. 'Well, if I'm going to stay, perhaps you'd let me interview van Buren and the secretary again. I'm sure they're hiding something.'

'Yeah, I was sure van Buren would give us a lead, but . . .'

'Yes, Laura Buckley's covered her tracks well. It's all gone quiet, too quiet.'

'L'tenant!' Rutgers said breathlessly as he burst in, 'look, I think we got her.'

'Who?'

'Buckley.'

'Where?'

'In a hotel off Central Park South.'

'You've picked her up?' Jasinski stared at Rutgers, who hesitated.

'Well, not that we got her . . .'

'So you haven't?'

'No, I mean we got her room – she checked in four hours ago.'

'How do you know?'

'Her secretary just called, gave me the address, even the room number. Said she was very worried and that she was doing something dangerous.'

'Is she still there? Have you checked with the hotel?'

'No, she rushed out soon after she got there and hasn't returned yet.'

'Damn!' Jasinski hit his desk. 'Well, what are you waiting for?'

'There's one more thing, she says there's a tape in the video machine.'

'OK, let's go,' he glanced at Mackie, 'You come with us, too.'

Fifteen minutes later, the hotel manager opened the door to Laura's room. It was empty. Apart from the slightly ruffled corner of the bed where she had sat, there was no sign of occupancy.

'So where's her bag?' Jasinski asked.

'The porter said she didn't have one.'

'Not much here,' said Jasinski as the manager excused himself and left.

'Why did she use a hotel? She must have known we would have got her records from the hotel clerk,' continued Jasinski.

'Well,' Mackie replied, emerging from checking the bathroom, 'she knew we'd been watching her apartment and office, so it had to be a hotel.'

'L'tenant,' Rutgers said as he cupped his hand over the telephone, 'she made a call – they're just checking the number.'

'As I thought,' Mackie nodded at Rutgers.

'Ah!' Jasinski pressed the eject button and a video tape slid out. 'There, just as the woman said.' He pushed it back in and pressed the play button.

At the same time the telephone rang.

'It's the operator,' Rutgers said after a few seconds. He pulled out his pen and wrote a number down and then replaced the receiver.

'Bloody hell!' exclaimed Mackie, as the television screen flickered into life. 'That's Grande's uncle. God help me, look at this!'

21

Para Bellum

Jack Douglas sat in his darkened study, hunched over his keyboard. His fingers moved in a blur as letters streamed onto the computer screen in front of him. The only light came from an anglepoise lamp, its pool of light spilling across his arms and hands. Around his feet in the gloom lay newspaper cuttings and half-open box files. Douglas felt driven, like a young journalist again on the edge of a breaking story, racing against time. He smiled – life had gone full circle.

Behind him, the door into his study creaked open. John Grande stood in the doorway, his eyes gradually becoming accustomed to the gloom. He knew he should feel a sense of relief as he watched Douglas. After all, he kept telling himself, he was close to clearing his name. He reflected on the past months, haunted by the constant fear of capture; and now here in this small room, in the mind of an old man, and bit by bit on the screen, lay all his hopes. Despite that, he couldn't even smile; he just stared at Douglas's back, an empty feeling knotting up inside him.

'That's about it,' Douglas said with a flourish, as he clicked the mouse button. He sat back to watch the printer. 'Never quite sure that I've done it correctly,' he laughed. 'What's the matter?' he asked, catching sight of John's long face. 'You don't look too happy, considering . . .' The printer whirred into action.

'No, it's not that,' John began slowly, 'you must think me immensely ungrateful but . . . it's just that I've been trying to contact Laura, without success.'

'She's pretty smart,' Douglas said, as he stretched across his desk and picked up the first of the printed sheets. 'She'll be OK.' He began to read.

'I know,' John said quickly, 'but she agreed to call this afternoon. I've got a bad feeling about this. God knows why she had to stay in New York. All she said was that she had business there.' He shook his head ruefully, 'Stubborn, far too damn stubborn. It was always going to be dangerous. I can't think why she had to go back.'

Douglas held up the sheets of paper and his wrinkled face broke into a smile.

'Look, let's concentrate on this and, with a bit of luck, it'll all be over soon. Anyway, what can you do now? You'll just have to stop worrying.' He put the papers down on the desk. 'This will do more than anything else to safeguard both of you.' He slid a disk out of the computer and tapped it. 'This goes into the paper tomorrow – I'll take it in first thing.' He switched off the computer.

'I know, I know . . . but . . .'

Douglas could see in his eyes how much Laura had come to mean to him. He placed a hand on John's arm. 'Look, whatever she decided to do was done for your benefit. She knew that we needed to get this written and published – your pictures were the final proof. I'm sure she's OK but if she is in trouble, the longer we take to publish this, the worse it will be for her. The more reason to get this,' he said, tapping the disk, 'into the public domain.'

John agreed, with some reluctance.

'Well,' Douglas said, as he held the article out to John, 'tell me what you think.'

'I hope you're right,' answered John, taking it from him. 'So did you make a mention of the diaries?'

'No,' Douglas's voice was flat, 'but then, there wouldn't have been much point – we don't have them. We don't even know if they exist.'

'What do you mean?' John looked up from the article. 'What about Acquilan? Why would he go to all that trouble to get something which didn't exist?'

Douglas swivelled his chair round to look at John.

'Perhaps they don't know any more than you do. Unless Acquilan or Kelp, or the others knew, or saw they were destroyed, they've got to assume they exist. That's what makes you so dangerous. They have to have assumed that you've got them. What they probably can't understand is why you haven't acted already.'

As John started to read, Douglas tidied up some of the files scattered around his desk and put them into a pile, ready for John to take away with him.

'It's excellent, Jack, really excellent,' said John as he finished. 'I see what you're trying to do . . .' John handed the article back to him before continuing, 'linking Kelp and Acquilan to what happened in 1944 and posing a whole series of questions about the missing pictures, which these photographs will help back up.'

'Good job you took a photograph of one of the paintings next to that newspaper with the date. Have you got it there?'

Douglas smiled briefly as he looked at the picture again, 'Good, the date on the newspaper is clear.' He put them down. 'I wish it were so easy,' he said quietly, 'if it was just about exposure of Kelp and Acquilan, I'd be pretty close. At least this should clear you with the police. However, there's one other question, which has been nagging away at me. Why did you get picked in the first place? That's something I can't deal with in the article. If this was just straight revenge, then why didn't Laura's father try and brief you properly? Your presence in all this wasn't an accident. Someone wants you involved, but why? No, you may soon be in the clear with the police but that doesn't mean you're safe.'

'So, what's it all for then? You're saying I'm dead either way?'

'As I said to you when we first met, this would only be the end of the beginning. Until we find out what your connection with all of this is, we'll never be sure.'

'Great!' John groaned and turned away in frustration.

'Hold on,' Douglas raised a hand, 'we've got to start somewhere.'

'And after that?'

'One fence at a time, John – each one we cross makes the next one easier.' Douglas got up to go to a table in the corner, on which sat an array of bottles and some glasses. He poured them both a whisky. 'You're part of this, the same way that Kelp and Acquilan are – the only problem is we don't know why.' He handed the drink to John.

For a while John had chosen to forget how complex his problem was. He had piled so much hope on this article and had begun to believe it was his passport to freedom. Yet he knew that Douglas was right – there were too many unanswered questions.

The grandfather clock struck midnight as John finished his drink. At least, he thought, in a few hours they would be taking their first positive step. He smiled at Douglas as he handed him his glass.

Mackie gazed up and down the corridor. A 1940s office block in downtown Manhattan. There was a Gothic feel to the place as the tiny number of unbroken light bulbs in the corridor threw strange surreal shadows across the walls. The place was empty, about to be renovated. Dirt-encrusted windows left the building dark and dingy, and the grey footworn carpet only added to the gloom. Ahead, on the left of the corridor, Mackie saw the first of a number of frosted-glass panelled doors, some of them smashed, others still with the remnants of peeled lettering as mementoes of previous tenants. Across the first he read: LEVENE, PAR . . . and BELLU . . . ATTORNEYS AT L . . .

Mackie strained his eyes to make out the missing lettering in each of the names, but soon gave up. Instead, he turned his attention to the flak-jacketed policemen standing either side of the door. Flattened against the wall, their faces tense with expectation, revolvers and shotguns in their hands, they waited for the signal.

Strapped into his flak jacket, Mackie felt absurd, like a turtle temporarily stranded on dry land. It had been simple, he reflected, to trace the number on the video tape, which was the same one the woman had called from the hotel.

He looked back at the faded lettering on the door. Ironic, he thought, as his eyes returned to the tense police officers on either side. 'Bellu— Bellum. Si vis pacem para bellum,' he recounted quietly to himself. 'If you want peace, prepare for war.'

'Go!' Jasinski screamed. Two men stepped forward and, swinging a large tube of heavy metal, crashed it into the door handle and through the lock. They stepped back as men streamed into the room shouting, 'Freeze, police!' A few seconds later someone screamed, 'Room clear!' There was a further crash as another door burst open, followed by 'Room clear!' Jasinski followed and then Mackie.

'Over here, L'tenant!' Rutgers shouted from the office.

On the sofa to the left of the door, lay a woman in her thirties, half-covered by a blanket. Jasinski and Mackie rushed over to her.

'I think that's Buckley!' exclaimed Jasinski. He knelt down beside her and took her pulse. 'Slow, but seems steady. Fitzsimmonds! Call medical back-up.' He was about to say something to Rutgers when there was a shout from the room next door. Both men ran to the source of the noise. They passed through an adjoining door and stopped immediately for there, in what once must have been an old office, was a single metal-framed bed and on it lay an old man in a deep sleep.

'Grande,' Mackie dryly. 'Poor bastard, must have been here for a while.'

'Get the paramedic in here!' Jasinski barked to no one in particular.

'I've given the woman next door a shot,' the paramedic announced as he hurried into the room. He bent down over Ralph Grande, checked his pulse, pushed his eyelids open and flashed a torch into them. 'He's coming round. Another couple of minutes and a cup of strong coffee and he'll be on his feet.' He reached into his bag, took a capsule out and broke it into a small cloth. He waved it under Ralph's nose and the old man coughed. 'As I thought, he'll soon be up and about.'

Mackie walked back into the first room as he eased himself out of his flak jacket and dumped it on the side of the armchair. Laura Buckley was sitting up, her head cradled in her hands.

'So, how are you feeling?' he asked.

Laura looked up. 'Like Rip van Winkle,' she replied, her voice heavy and very sleepy. It was all she could do to stare at Mackie through bleary, bloodshot eyes, 'Did the British take over in New York since I went to sleep?' She let her head fall back into her hands, 'You sure as hell don't sound like one of New York's finest.'

'No, I'm from London.'

At that moment Jasinski came up to them.

'Laura Buckley?' he asked.

'Yes,' she replied slowly.

'You OK?'

'I feel, heavy, slow but . . . I'm alive.'

'Do you know where you are?'

'No, they made me wear dark padded glasses,' she replied.

'Who's they?'

'I don't know, they never said.'

'You must have seen something,' Jasinski frowned. While he was questioning her, Mackie walked over to an armchair a few feet from them; something had caught his eye. Putting on a pair of gloves, he bent down, sliding his hand down one side, and carefully held up a pair of dark glasses.

'Do you know who's in that other room?' Jasinski turned back to Buckley.

'No,' she looked up and across at the other door, 'as I said, I couldn't see anything.'

'Does the name Ralph Grande mean anything to you?' Mackie asked.

She stared back at Jasinski and then at Mackie.

'D'you know him?' Jasinski asked.

'No,' she shook her head, 'that is, not to talk to. I know about him from John . . .' she hesitated.

'John Grande,' continued Jasinski.

Laura nodded.

'Could you at least give us a description of the people who brought you here?'

Her head was in a whirl. Fragments of noises and words buzzed and echoed inside as she tried to understand what had happened – whether what she'd done had been a good thing, or a disaster. John, she knew was in Alexandria, at Jack Douglas's house, or at least he had been. It occurred to her that she had no idea of what time of day, or for that matter, even what day it was. Her watch told her it was 1.30. She looked up, her forehead wrinkled.

'It's 1.30 on Saturday morning,' Mackie said, anticipating her question. 'So, when did you get here?'

'Must have been early evening, Friday. Look, can I have a few minutes?' As she finished speaking, one of the uniformed policemen arrived with a cup of coffee.

'Drink this,' Jasinski said as he handed the polystyrene cup to her. He tapped Mackie on the shoulder and they walked to the far side of the room. 'What do you make of all of this?' he whispered, 'What in hell is she up to?' He spoke in a low monotone. 'That's Grande's uncle in there – you said they were close. Surely if his uncle was in trouble, Grande would come to find out, not her?'

'Perhaps he didn't know about it,' Mackie answered.

'Hey, L'tenant,' Rutgers interrupted, 'the old guy seems okay.'

Laura watched them as she sipped her coffee. The hot drink helped to thin the intense yellow fog that hung around her brain. Her eyes cleared slowly and so too did her senses. Yet her emotions continued in a jumbled state. At first she felt like laughing at the day's events – the absurd charade with the dark glasses, the detached inquisition from behind her ear, the strange noises and shadowy shapes. Then, hard on its heels, came a depression. What was it she had said? She shook her head as she tried to remember. What if they'd got to John already? Had she let too much slip?

'Oh, my God!' she muttered to herself, 'what have I done?' Her head rested in her hands. Did she say enough to put them onto John? Had the police caught them? The tide of apprehension and fear rose again, engulfing her, and then, as though squeezed out by the sheer pressure of it all, tears began to roll down her cheeks. She sat, clenching and unclenching her fists, as she wiped them away. The fear ebbed and instead she felt a sense of helplessness. She had gambled and failed; instead of resolving the problem she had made it worse. What a fool she had been – the arrogance – the conceit. She looked at her watch again, nearly 2 a.m. They'd been gone for hours. She had to do something, but what? Washington, she could go to Washington, but she knew the New York police wouldn't let her go; they'd want to question her about John. She was now their prisoner.

The cold recognition of her predicament washed over Laura. She imagined she'd be charged with some sort of felony. John was on the run with those bastards after him, while she'd be languishing in a New York jail. As the two detectives returned she saw behind them a much older man with a mop of white hair and a sad, rather puffy face. He stared hard at her.

'You Ralph Grande?' Jasinski asked.

'Yes, I am,' he replied.

'Of course,' Laura tried her best to smile at him, 'John told me so much . . .' Her voice trailed away.

'You've seen John?' He held out his hand to her. 'Forgive my appearance,' he said, as Laura took his hand, 'but I am a little disorientated. I don't know how long they've kept me here, days or weeks.'

'Now look,' Jasinski began. 'I want to know what's going on here. You're in deep trouble, ma'am, so either you cooperate or I book you, the choice is yours. So what's it to be?'

'And then what?' Laura asked.

'Well, we'll see. It all depends on what you've got to tell. Oh yeah, and it ain't just us – the British police would like some answers too. But most of all, I want to know where John Grande is now.'

Laura turned her head away. Perhaps, she thought, the best way was to use the police, maybe they could be persuaded to help? If she could get them to believe John's story and her re-telling of it, maybe they would understand about Kelp and the others? Yet, at the same time, she also realised that the very mention of Senator Kelp's name would make them hesitate. After all, he was a powerful and influential figure. She shook her head as she thought about the alternative; to say nothing, to be charged, that would get her nowhere. Besides Jack Douglas would have completed his work by now and handed it over to the *Post*, so that at least part of her story would be corroborated. After all, with the photographs at

Acquilan's house and all the supporting information, they surely must be in the clear? Clearing John's name was the first important step; the next would be to stop Kelp and Acquilan.

'Look,' she began, 'I'll tell you what's happened and where John is.' Mackie and Jasinski exchanged glances. 'But,' she continued, 'you must hear me out in full, no interruptions.'

Jasinski nodded.

'It's a long story.'

'We've got time, but we'd better get this on tape.'

22

Of Mice and Men

The high-pitched, insistent bleeps of the telephone seemed to come from deep inside Acquilan's head as he felt himself dragged back to consciousness. His arms flailed about in a vain attempt to search for the offending noise and gradually his heavy eyelids tugged open.

It had been a long day, followed by a long flight to San Francisco and on arrival at his hotel, the Mark Hopkins, he'd gone straight to his suite with two things on his mind – firstly, he had to check that the deal in Seattle had been closed and secondly, he wanted to read the campaign report. Ten minutes later, with the campaign report spread all around him and propped up by pillows, sleep had claimed him. Not a light nap but a deep sub-human state, beyond dreams, beyond the reach of conscience or concern.

The pressures of the last few weeks – Cosmo, the paintings, his business difficulties in Seattle and the campaign – were the backdrop to his exhaustion.

With the primary in California climaxing over the next few days, all was not well. Instead of being ahead as they planned, the President had closed the gap again. Now they were neck and neck but all the recent running in the polls had been Carson's.

The noise ricocheted around Acquilan's head, breaking up his thoughts. So close . . . nearly there . . . then Grande, on the loose with all that information . . . the window was closing . . . that terrible doubt, the panic . . . Cosmo, Cosmo, Cosmo . . .

Acquilan stared at the ceiling. The light was bright and there was a grinding pain in his head. He laid a hand on his forehead – the noise, he must stop the noise. He stretched out for the telephone. His eyes closed again, sealing his aching brain from the light. Then he pressed the receiver to his ear, just sleep . . .

'What?' Acquilan jerked his eyes open wide and sat up. The torpor lifted, jerked by invisible strings. 'Are you sure, Bernie?' Acquilan asked, grafting the receiver tighter to his right ear. 'You'd better get here right away,' he ordered. 'Where's Pichowski now? Good. Five minutes, Bernie!' He slammed the receiver down, swung himself out of bed and started to dress.

'Four days to go and now this!' he exclaimed, sliding his arm through the newly washed and heavily starched shirt.

Minutes later he was drinking bourbon while reading a five-page fax. In front of him Weitz sat in a large armchair, cradling a glass in two hands, his eyes downcast.

'You're right, Bernie, this is absolute dynamite,' Acquilan's voice was hoarse. 'The main part of our story is here. The convoy, the warehouse, Cosmo and Morrow, Licatta, the deal in London. Jesus! He also says we're involved in the murders in London, Rome and New York. And look here,' he tapped the document with his finger and held it up for Weitz to see, 'it all rests on Grande's say so and his belief that I have the pictures. It's very detailed, more than I expected, but who'll believe a murderer? After all, they can't prove . . .'

'Actually, Victor, there's one other thing,' Weitz began, 'there were some photographs with the piece. Pichowski took them, and the negatives too.'

'*What*? What photographs?' Acquilan's bravado slipped.

'Well, it seems they're of your house on Long Island and your – your special gallery. You know, Victor, the paintings.'

'How the hell did they get in?' Acquilan exclaimed. 'Goddamn it, my wife! She said something before I left about an interior design interview. How dumb can you get? I never thought . . .' Acquilan shook his head. 'But that still won't prove anything.'

'They don't have to – the allegation is enough and it does confirm our involvement, to Grande and now to Douglas.'

'It still doesn't become a testimony which would stand up in court. After all, this is only the say so of a wanted killer against an upright citizen – they'd never convict . . . I know, Bernie, I know what you're going to say. It would be enough to wreck Ewan, even if they never manage to fully prove it,' Acquilan tilted his glass back and drained it.

'Right, Victor?' Weitz sat down heavily. 'At least Pichowski used his brain. Once he'd made the entry he found all the papers on Douglas's desk. He had a fast look through the whole stack of files that was sitting beside the guy's desk and he realised he'd struck gold. He said to me that most of them seemed to contain information about what happened at the end of the war – big box files with old *Time* articles, war records, etc.'

'And Douglas?'

'Upstairs asleep. Pichowski was in and out unseen.'

'Diaries?' Acquilan finished his second drink.

'No, no diaries, Victor, but we didn't . . .'

'Then how . . .'

'There's no question, Victor – Douglas is good, we both know that; better than expected. He must have been close before Grande made contact. What Grande did was to fill in some gaps and then there were the photos of your paintings – Douglas could never have known about them before they met.'

'And the diaries? Surely Grande must have them?'

'Who knows?'

'What about copies of this?' Acquilan flicked the fax with his finger.

'Pichowski took all the disks in the study and then, for good measure, he took the whole damn computer.'

'Good,' Acquilan paused. 'What about Pichowski, is there anything that could connect him with this?'

'No, he wasn't disturbed and he was in and out in ten minutes. The house isn't overlooked at the point where he made his entry. No, he's pretty sure he's in the clear.'

Acquilan nodded and went to pour himself another drink.

'Anyway, Victor, Pichowski was on the ball – he made it look just like a burglary. He even took the television and stereo as well,' Weitz smiled. 'And he arranged to have the house two blocks up burgled half an hour later. Made it look like someone was working the area.'

Acquilan returned to his chair.

'Grande was relying on this to clear his name,' Acquilan said, as he thought of the implications, 'there's no doubt. Without Douglas's information, and the negatives, they'll never put this together again. Where is Grande now?'

'Pichowski wasn't after him – his brief was to find out how much they knew – but when I heard about the photos, I told him to watch the house. And remember, Cosmo must have known the story alone was not enough. He set us up because of that and Grande is the link. He came pretty close tonight, Victor. If this had got out it would be over. But it's not the end. With Grande as the link from London through Rome to New York, Cosmo needs to find him, kill him, plant the information and finish us!'

'And,' Acquilan began, 'without this, Grande will have to get to us now – there is no other way.'

'What are you saying, Victor?'

'He'll soon see we're the bait – his last chance.'

'What about Cosmo?'

'He'll be after Grande.'

'But why?'

'Because it all hinges on Grande and they don't have him, just as you said.'

'Agreed, he's the link. But Cosmo only wants him to link us to the other murders.'

'God!' Acquilan held up his hand, 'I've been a fool. Grande's more than just an accidental link – he's as much a part of this as you and me. Look, that photograph of him, the one Pichowski brought – remember how we both thought he reminded us of someone?'

'Sure.'

'Well, look at it again.'

'I got the file downstairs, I'll have a look when I get down there.'

'Get it!' Acquilan barked.

Ten minutes later, Weitz had returned to Acquilan's room, where they were both studying the photograph of John Grande.

'Just follow me, Bernie. Why would Cosmo just happen to be living next to the guy's uncle? It's as though he's been studying Grande for years. Even Cosmo wouldn't set someone up like that – there are just too many things that could go wrong. No, he's used Grande, knowing it was a risky game. After all, his worst fear must have come true: they lost him just at the minute they were about to strike. But Cosmo was prepared to risk it only because Grande is as much about Cosmo's plan for revenge as we are.'

'I don't follow . . . the guy's too young . . .'

'He's part of our past, Bernie – he *must* be. Cosmo wants us all cooked at the same time, whether Cosmo's dead or not. Grande's part of this great plan and someone's seeing it through for Cosmo.'

'But,' Weitz began, 'that's crazy, Victor, he can't . . .'

'The photograph – that's the point. I know it's a long shot . . . remember the man who set up the deal in Italy for us?'

'Oakley, that British major, Oakley . . .' Weitz frowned. 'I don't get it . . . Grande's not Oakley, he's too young.'

'No, but Oakley was the man behind it all, the man with all the contacts, with the Licattas, everything. He moved all the stolen pieces, everything, through contacts in the black market. You remember we thought he was brilliant? And remember who planned the fire?'

'Sure, and when Morrow got cold feet it was Oakley who helped us get rid of him . . .'

'And Licatta, don't forget him.'

'How could I? I remember Oakley was right about Cosmo as well, said the guy was untrustworthy, but you didn't believe him.'

'I know,' Acquilan looked down, 'there'd been too many killings . . . I thought Cosmo would see sense.'

'Morrow was his best friend.'

'I know.'

'How could I forget? None of us knew how to get any of the shit out of Italy or how to sell it – Oakley did it all. Cold-blooded son-of-a-bitch, I remember. But as I said, Grande's not Oakley. It's not the same name and anyway, we never heard of Oakley again. Jesus, Victor! I mean he's young enough to be the guy's . . .' Weitz stared at Acquilan unable to finish his sentence.

'Son?'

'Son,' Weitz murmured as if in a trance.

'Sure, why not? With Cosmo, anything's possible – the man hates us that much.'

'Look, I had a check run on Grande's background; it says in this file that Grande's father went crazy, lived in an institution. Remember, I told you, he committed suicide?'

'Well, I guess so,' Acquilan answered. He sighed. 'Anyway, for whatever reason, Cosmo doesn't just want us, he wants

Grande too and that gives us a chance. Cosmo has to find him first. Grande can't know any of this. Look at the Douglas article – all the murders are down to us. He must think it's all of us, so . . .'

'So you're saying he'll have to come after us?'

Acquilan nodded.

'Maybe, maybe. It depends on what Douglas writes,' Weitz frowned. 'I wouldn't underestimate the guy. After all, he's kept one step ahead of us and Cosmo the whole time.' He put the file back together, 'One more thing, Victor.'

'What?'

'I've just heard, the Feds dug up the two bodies.'

'What? Morrow and Licatta?'

'Yes, they're bound to know now that one of them isn't Cosmo.'

'Why'd they do it?'

'My contact says the order came from someone at the White House.'

'Carson knows?'

'I guess so. Can't think why otherwise.'

Acquilan sat in silence.

'It's like I've always said, Victor – we can walk from this; we could still get out, leave all of this and go.'

'No, we can't and anyway, even if we did, what'd be the point?' Acquilan smiled, 'At least we know now it'll go to the wire.'

'But we could lose it all!'

'Or win it all. No, we'll just have to wait for them to come.'

'I've got a bad feeling about this, Victor – you're asking us to become bait for Grande and Cosmo.'

'It's all or nothing now, don't you see, Bernie? All or nothing – this is what we have to do. We knew that when we started out.'

Weitz shook his head. He'd never wanted any of this. Acquilan and Kelp's obsession with the Presidency had made them lose their judgment. He shrugged and turned on his heel. As he shut the door behind him, for the first time since they'd teamed up all those years ago, he realised it was now time to make his own plans.

23

Saturday Morning

Six o'clock on a misty morning. John Grande opened the back door to Jack Douglas's house located in a small alleyway concealed from view.

After discussing the article with Jack, he had stayed the night with Joe Schwartz. Now, as arranged, they were going to have an early morning meeting before John went to ground while Jack sorted it all out with the police.

'Jack!' he shouted. No answer. He knew Jack's wife was away and that he was alone. Perhaps he had overslept. He waited for a few seconds and then walked down the corridor to the study.

Inside, the scene of devastation stopped him at the threshold – he felt as though someone had knocked the wind out of him. There were papers and files on the floor and family photographs, which had been on Jack's desk, lay smashed nearby. The far window hung limply on its hinges.

'Jack!' he called again but there was no answer. It was then that he realised something was missing – the computer. Staring at the space it had occupied the night before, he cursed as he searched for Schwartz's box files, which contained all the evidence for the article, but he couldn't find them. Turning, he caught sight of what he at first took to be a pair of carpet slippers poking out from the far side of the desk. Puzzled, he walked tentatively towards them, but to his horror he saw Jack stretched out alongside the desk. His body was crumpled, his head twisted grotesquely to one side and blood stained the carpet.

As John bent down, he was assaulted by waves of nausea and had to fight to get his breath. He applied his fingers to the side of Jack's neck but he knew the answer even before he touched him – there was no pulse. Worse, the head and neck were ice cold, while beneath the shirt, the body was still warm. He gazed at the pale face, overcome by a deep sense of guilt. The man was dead because of him. If Jack had never met him, he'd still be alive – it was all his fault.

'It's over Jack, it's over,' he whispered, tears sliding down his face, 'it's over for you, for us all. I'm sorry, *so* sorry.'

He stayed kneeling beside the body, head bowed, without any sense of time.

Wiping his eyes, he looked around the room, wondering vaguely how it had happened. Remembering the missing box files, he realised the intruders must have been after the information. Everything was missing – the computer, the files, everything of importance. The photos, which had been by the computer, had gone and so, too, had the negatives. No one would believe him now.

And anyway, he thought, who cares? 'God, I'm sorry, Jack,' he whispered, 'it's all my fault. I shouldn't have got you involved. Just like the others, you got in their way. They want me and they're not going to stop at anything until they get me.' He felt empty, his body drained of energy. He looked down at Jack. 'You knew the risks and yet you still went ahead. You're another good man who's come to a violent end because I got too close to you,' he said bitterly. He thought of Laura and panic seized him. Everything was being destroyed by the same men, men who would stop at nothing.

John picked up the telephone, dialled 911 and gave the address. He asked for an ambulance and the police, but refused to give his name, then hung up. Once again he knelt down by Jack, laying a hand on his cold hand and squeezing it.

'It's not your way, Jack, I know, but I'm going to finish this the only way left to me. It wasn't my way either but they forced me down this road. There doesn't seem much to live for – just this, that's all.'

He picked up his briefcase and let himself out the back door and into the small alley. He was in such a hurry that he almost bumped into an elderly woman walking her small terrier; she stifled a scream and stared at him but without a word or a backward look, he brushed past her and was gone.

Laura rubbed her eyes and forehead as she sat back. She rolled her head around to loosen up her neck muscles and let her mane of dark hair hang over the back of the chair.

She provided a sharp contrast to the three men. She still held their eyes easily, her attractive face and clear voice betraying little of the tiredness she felt. Her large eyes were wide open and there was a balance and a certain poise about the way she moved. They, on the other hand, looked hot, unshaven and bleary-eyed as they listened to her unfolding story.

All of them, that is except Ralph Grande. He had sat in on the interview at the request of Mackie because the Scotsman felt their stories would dovetail and he intended to bring him in at the right moment. As a result, Ralph's admiration for the woman in front of him grew by the minute.

It was 6.45 in the morning and Laura knew that they had only to hear the last part about the paintings before the questions would begin. True to their agreement, they had, for the most part, listened in silence. There was the odd question but other than that she'd been able to speak unfettered. Occasionally, she would glance over her shoulder at Ralph

Grande, each time expecting to find him asleep, but he was sitting bolt upright, listening intently. She couldn't explain why, but she found this reassuring. Then it was over. She rested her arms on the table and closed her eyes.

'That's it,' she said, 'that's all.'

Jasinski finished writing his notes and rubbed his eyes. 'That's some story,' he croaked. He reached out for a drink of water and gulped it back. 'I think we'll take a break. Paused at 7.05 a.m.,' he said and stopped the tape recorder. Sweeping up his papers, he pushed his chair back noisily and left the room, followed by Detective Sergeant Mackie and Detective Rutgers.

'So?' Jasinski asked.

'Well,' began Mackie, 'it all sounds pretty far-fetched – a chain of murders linked to John Grande, all carried out by agents of Senator Kelp or this other man.'

'Acquilan,' Rutgers said.

'Aye, thanks,' Mackie continued. 'Of course, it could all be dismissed as a case of paranoia.'

'True,' replied Jasinski.

'Well, that bit about the paintings is pretty credible. There were definitely six that Grande sold at his gallery and it appears there was one that was delayed but eventually sold to the same man. Then there was the shooting on the street in New York, you remember?' Mackie carried on.

'Sure,' Rutgers interrupted his flow, 'but to link Senator Kelp to all of this . . . Look, Mackie, you probably don't know but the guy's a war hero, a Senator and a goddamn presidential candidate as well, for Christ's sake!'

'Have you got the tape, Rutgers?' Jasinski interrupted.

'Yes.'

'Take it outside and have it transcribed, and then get them some coffee in there!' he jerked his thumb in the direction of the interview room. 'Oh yeah, and we'll need to visit this guy Douglas. You'd better call Alexandria – they'll need to be briefed. You see, the problem isn't just Kelp,' Jasinski continued, 'it's Acquilan as well. They're both war heroes, and what's worse, Acquilan is a New York success story. And remember Goldstein, the lawyer?' Mackie nodded. 'Well, guess who else is on that lousy crime commission?'

'Acquilan?' Mackie asked.

'Exactly,' purred Jasinski. 'Even if I wanted to believe this, and I don't see any evidence yet, look what lies ahead if I even start down that road. Rutgers is right, we'd be in deep shit!'

'She still hasn't said where Grande's gone,' Mackie observed.

'She's not going to either, unless we somehow guarantee that he won't be charged. You know I can't do that. The guy's the only suspect we've got, we'll have to take a chance. The District Attorney and the Captain are screaming for some action. There's just not enough to go on.'

'Well, at least we can speak to Douglas and the sooner the better, see if he backs her story up.'

'Sure,' Jasinski said standing up, 'sure.'

Mackie hadn't said as much to Jasinski but he was already convinced that Laura Buckley was telling the truth. He'd believed for some time that Grande was not the murderer but being used. He ran his fingers over his grey stubble.

'Tired?' Jasinski asked.

'Aye . . . I'm too old to do this.'

'You and me both.'

'Well, if we believe what she says,' Mackie continued, 'there would be only one purpose in taking photos of the paintings – to use them to clear his name. The only question is *how*? First, he could try and deal directly with Kelp and Acquilan. But that's fraught with problems. If he doesn't trust them and thinks they're planning to murder him, then he's unlikely to do that. Or he could work with Douglas and write up the evidence, which just might clear his name. Then, of course, he could be telling a pack of lies, having committed the murders – in which case he's gone to ground.'

At that moment Rutgers returned. 'Hey, L'tenant! The guy's dead.'

'Who?' Jasinski asked.

'That columnist – Douglas. I've just been on to Alexandria as you said and they confirmed it – it's just happened.'

'Let's go!' Jasinski stood up. 'Rutgers, bring the old man and Buckley, and get us all on the next flight.'

Ewan Kelp slumped into an armchair in his suite on the seventeenth floor of the Mark Hopkins Hotel. He closed his eyes and was only vaguely aware that Sol Levinson was talking.

'Well, Ewan,' Levinson continued. 'I hate to say it . . .'

'Well, for pity's sake, *don't*, Sol!' interrupted Kelp. 'I think we can all guess what you plan to offload on us. I just don't see how else we could have done it. We're neck and neck with the creep! When we started here we were ahead.' He stopped speaking, leaving the others expecting something else, yet nothing came.

'I still think we peaked too soon, Ewan, but . . .' Levinson began.

'Four days to go and we're in there – that's what counts,' Sam Eadie cut in.

Kelp opened his eyes and sat up in surprise. He smiled briefly at Eadie. Assistance and a positive view were not normally expected from that quarter, so were all the more of a surprise when they came.

'OK, let's look ahead,' began Kelp. 'What have we got?'

'Press conference today at ten, after . . .'

'Hold it, Dick – where's Jim?' Kelp asked.

'He was coming on down with us when something came on his pager. It seemed important so he went back to the campaign press office before joining us. I thought he'd be here by now.'

'Well, I want more detail on that press conference. Where is he?'

Close, so close, Kelp thought – just four more days and he was there. He wasn't even worried about the money, he knew they had some good shots left and they could do it. His belief had grown throughout the campaign despite the setback in New York. They were too close to let it go now. Nothing should stop them. But wait . . . He rubbed his eyes.

'Look, Ewan,' Mason began. 'You're tired, we can . . .'

'No, let's continue. We can't wait for Jim.'

Just then the door opened and in strode Jim Donald.

'Good, at last,' Mason exclaimed as Donald walked in, his lips trembling.

'What's the matter?' asked Mason.

'Jack Douglas of all people has been found dead at his home – murdered!' Donald exclaimed.

There was a sharp intake of breath from the other men.

'How? Who?' Mason spluttered.

'No one knows yet. The body's only just been discovered . . . The police . . .' his voice trailed away.

'He was an institution,' Eadie said. 'It'll be hard to imagine the *Post* without him.'

'Who'd do something like that? *Who?*' Donald spluttered.

'OK, OK, you'd better organise a statement from me,' Kelp interrupted. 'Condolences to his family – an institution, set a high standard in political journalism, he will be greatly missed, you know . . .'

Donald nodded slowly, 'Who could imagine he would be a target?'

'The thing is,' Kelp continued, 'I know we're all meant to feel sorry, even sad, but I don't! He hated me and I hated him – he would have crapped on me as much as he could. While I don't say I'm happy,' he looked around, 'we're better off without him.' He shrugged, 'OK, let's get back to work, we've a campaign to run.'

Donald stared in disbelief at his boss. 'I'll get someone on to your statement,' he said hoarsely.

As he left, Kelp turned to Mason, 'What's up with him?'

'He worked on the *Post* when Douglas was the editor, you remember?'

'Oh, OK . . . So as I said, no more problems from that department – let's get back to work.'

The car pulled up outside Jack Douglas's home in Alexandria at 12.30. Blue and white plastic tape surrounded the entrance to the house and blocked off the sidewalk. A couple of police cars were parked in front of the house, one of them with its lights flashing.

Jasinski got out of the car followed by Mackie, leaving Ralph Grande and Laura Buckley in the car with Rutgers. Minutes later they were inside the study.

'These fingerprints you sent . . .' began Mackie as they entered, 'forensics say they match some of the prints found on a couple of glasses in here.'

'So, what do you think?' Jasinski asked.

'Two possibilities,' the detective continued as he walked over towards them, 'a burglary that went wrong, Douglas comes down – finds them – there's a fight and he's killed.'

'How?'

'Over here,' the detective pointed to one side of the desk. 'He was hit by a hard object, perhaps a pistol butt, and fell. He smashed his left temple on the corner of the desk – must have been killed instantly. As I said, a burglary that went wrong. Whoever it was took the TV, stereo and probably even a computer.'

'What's the problem with that?'

'Timing,' the detective answered, 'The murder took place between 5.30 and 6.30 a.m.'

'So?'

'Well, someone nearby thought they heard the sound of smashing glass at around midnight and about half an hour later another house up the road got hit.'

'Could they have come back afterwards?'

'Maybe, we've got a description of one man leaving here at about 7 a.m. Someone saw him at the back of the alley.'

Jasinski walked towards the smashed window and peered out. As he did so, the detective opened his notebook and read back the description of the man the old woman had seen at 7 a.m., Jasinski turned and exchanged looks with Mackie. They both knew that it was Grande.

'Have you checked out all the calls?' Jasinski asked.

'We're doing that right now.' As the detective finished speaking, a uniformed officer came in and they went into a huddle by the door.

'You know,' said Mackie, 'they're separate crimes.' He joined Jasinski at the window.

'Look,' Jasinski pointed outside onto the path, 'glass – and a lot of it, too.'

'Yes,' Mackie replied. 'I know, this window was broken from the inside.'

'It's the oldest mistake in the book, done for effect.'

'I know what you're thinking,' Jasinski began. 'Grande was here this morning – this is where he came after seeing Buckley. She was right!'

'Well, there's a lot in her story that seems to hang together now.'

Without saying anything else, Jasinski left, only to return a couple of minutes later with Laura Buckley and Ralph Grande in tow.

Laura stopped by the door as her eyes took in the devastation. It was difficult enough to cope with the idea that Jack had been found dead but now she was in the room, the same room in which they had all met only a short while ago . . . She shivered . . . Had they got John?

'Was . . . was John here?' Laura stuttered, her eyes searching Jasinski's face for the truth. She felt a wave of pain rush through her – what if he was dead? It would be all her

fault. She was the one who had given the information away
. . . The room began to spin.

'Catch her!' Jasinski screamed at the detective. The man
caught hold of Laura by the shoulders and then helped
her into a chair by the desk. For a few seconds her head
was bent down between her legs and then she sat up, her
face white.

'I think she should rest – this has been a huge shock,' Ralph
said. He had been full of admiration for Laura through last
night's interrogation; her tough no-nonsense style, her inner
strength.

'No, don't worry, I'll be all right,' she gave him the faintest
of smiles.

'Look Miss Buckley, your boyfriend . . .' Jasinski seemed to
spit the word out as he sat down in front of her, 'is the prime
suspect in a whole bunch of homicides, and now this.'

'No, it wasn't John,' Laura shook her head fiercely as she
spoke.

'I agree, L'tenant, John is not guilty – he's just not
capable . . .' Ralph began, his voice quavering slightly.

'Hold it!' Jasinski barked. 'I think I'll be the judge of that
and I'll ask the questions! Look, you give us a bullshit story
about him and you're not telling us where he is now. If you're
so sure he's in the clear, then why not tell me straight?' He
stared hard at Laura as he spoke, making no effort to disguise
the sneer in his voice.

'But he didn't murder Jack,' she said. 'Why would he? Jack
was helping him.'

'Look, he was seen leaving here earlier this morning after
Douglas was murdered. His fingerprints are everywhere.
What's a cop supposed to believe, your story or the facts?'

'You can call it what you like, but he didn't do it.' She was
sitting upright, her chin thrust forward, her lip quivering
slightly, 'I've no idea where he is now.'

'Last night, Miss Buckley,' Jasinski tried again, 'you told us that Jack Douglas had been researching Kelp and Acquilan.'

'Yes,' Laura breathed, 'Can't you see? He must have been killed to shut him up. Who had the most to lose if he published? It sure as hell wasn't John! Anyway, for all we know he's passed it to the *Post* already. Why do you insist on hounding John? Why can't you help him?'

Jasinski snorted. 'Well, that's it then. One hell of a stroke of luck – this so-called evidence you said would expose Kelp and the others is gone. For that matter, so's your boyfriend.'

'You just can't see it, can you? He was here because Douglas was writing the story – that's why we needed the pictures. He came to give them to Douglas and to complete the story with him. It may sound far-fetched but you can say what you like, it's the truth, and unless you believe it, John Grande is going to be murdered too.'

'Maybe, but what if he didn't have any story? What if, when he got here, Douglas had rumbled him and maybe the whole story put the drop on Grande? So he whacks him,' Jasinski's voice was insistent, provocative. 'That sounds more like it to me!'

'That's nonsense and you know it. I was with him when he took the photos – I was there.'

'Oh yes, the photos,' Jasinski sneered, 'Were you in the room when he took them? How do you know he hadn't taken them before? He's a pretty resourceful guy. Maybe he'd set all this up?'

'Miss Buckley,' Mackie broke in, 'you said in New York there was another man at the meeting you held here that day. You said he had some files – can you remember what his name was?'

'Of course, of course – what a fool I've been!' she replied. 'You're right – Joe Schwartz – he'll have the files, at least he'll confirm my story.' She smiled at Jasinski as if to say, 'Told you so'. 'I don't have his address but I'm sure you'll get it from the *Post*. After that,' she said stepping slightly to her right and staring at Jasinski, 'you'll have to believe me and then . . .'

'Perhaps,' Mackie said, 'perhaps, but we've got to find him first.'

On board Air Force One bound for California, President Carson sat alone for the first time that morning. On his lap was a briefing document on the budget increase for defence. He'd wanted time to read the brief before speaking to his secretary for defense, Dick Barnet. Carson shut the file and placed it on the table in front of him. He had fifteen minutes before the meeting and he closed his eyes. The constant media attention about the Prosecutor's increasing demands had begun to wear him down.

He was also getting worried. The Republican-dominated Congress hadn't reacted in the way he had expected. The Public Prosecutor was clearly carrying out a vendetta against him, but perversely they continued to encourage him. With public opinion against the witch-hunt it was incomprehensible to him why Congress allowed it to continue. All his political life he had only moved when opinion polls showed him the people were in favour. It had been the cornerstone of his political creed, he had made it a science. Being on the wrong side of the polls, he believed, was a one-way ticket to failure. And yet Congress was doing just that. Under his formula, he should have been relaxed, even happy. But what worried him was that his own ratings had also fallen. There were dangerous conflicting signals. While the public were against the Prosecutor, they continued to believe that he had been involved in an illegal land deal when governor. The result of all this was that Kelp was level with him.

'Mr President . . .'

Carson looked up to see Frank Parry standing in front of him.

'Frank?'

'Before you speak with Dick, can I have a few moments?'

'Sure.'

Parry handed Carson a thin file.

'Dick wants much more money for his budget. You were right, Mason didn't come cheap,' he sighed. 'So how's California?'

'Well, I don't know, as you'll see . . .' Parry spoke gently, as he handed Carson some sheets of paper, 'We're making no progress, our early momentum has gone.'

Carson began to read.

'You're going to have to debate with him,' said Parry.

'Why now?' Carson asked, continuing to read.

'Before there wasn't much point but now . . .'

'Now we're desperate,' Carson looked up. 'That it?'

'No. Anyway, just think how Kelp must feel. They thought they had sown up New York,' Parry shrugged.

'Well, these figures don't look great – I should be ahead,' Carson tossed the papers down on the seat next to him. 'What if I screw up?'

'Then it's over. High stakes, but you won't.'

'OK, I guess you're right – I'll do it,' Carson said, shaking his head, 'This paper predicts a late surge for Kelp.' He tossed the sheet of paper onto the table.

'Marginal.'

'But marginal will give him the nomination.'

'Unless something else happens.'

'Like what?'

'Talk to Pete Neal.'

'He's got nothing.'

'Well, there *is* something. Seems that he was right about this Brit. Kelp and Acquilan are after him but it turns out so is someone else. The cops have found the girl who was with him.' Carson listened intently. 'She told them about someone else.'

'Who?'

'They don't know. But whoever it is wants the guy as well. And he's also pretty certain that this links back to some sort of fraud at the end of the war.'

'The guy's a crook?' Carson's eyes lit up.

'Maybe, maybe,' Parry replied. 'Anyway, someone switched the bodies, as I told you. One of his soldiers went missing.'

'Can we use it?'

'No, we'd need to have a reason to exhume the bodies officially . . .'

'You see, just as I said – nothing!'

'Wait, there's Douglas – Jack Douglas.'

'What about him?' Carson was beginning to look annoyed.

'The Brit's linked to his murder, probably even Kelp.'

'We can't use it,' Carson replied. 'Look, I know Pete's got good information but we need more.'

Carson looked out of the window. Down below he could just make out a patchwork quilt of fields through which a large river meandered. It looked strangely peaceful.

'Look, if Kelp's got a past – as you say he has – then find it, otherwise we'll both be looking for new jobs.' He picked up the phone, 'Get me Dick Barnet, Mati.'

Parry picked up his paper and walked back to his seat. Then he slumped down and closed his eyes, pleased with himself for securing the President's agreement for the debate. He still felt confident that they could give him the nomination. As long as the Prosecutor kept drawing a blank on the hitch with Haskins, they were OK. 'Now to get him ready for the debate,' he said out loud.

Ewan Kelp brought the press conference to a close, snapped the folder shut in front of him and turned to Dick Mason, who was standing behind him.

He'd put the problem about the diaries behind him; he knew there was nothing he could do to help and so he'd left it all to Acquilan and Weitz. His whole focus was on winning in California. All that he'd ever wanted was within a finger-tip's grasp and he was damned if he was going to let it go now.

'Nice touch by the way,' Mason congratulated him, as they walked towards the cars. 'Your comment about the Jack Douglas murder was very good, particularly that bit about principled journalists like him who'd always been fair, even though they didn't always agree with you – great under-statement, Ewan,' Mason chuckled. 'Yes, sir! It went down very well.'

'Good,' Kelp opened the car door. 'I'll admit it was easier talking about that son-of-a-bitch than talking to him.' He gave another one of those thin-lipped smiles as he slipped into the car.

'I guess we won't miss his column either,' Mason laughed.

'Amen to that, Dick, amen to that,' Kelp settled back in the car. 'Anyway, what time am I due at the hospital?'

'Eleven-thirty, Ewan. We've got to stop by at the campaign headquarters just before that.'

Kelp sat quietly while Mason talked about the remaining events. Hospital visits, lunch with businessmen, a visit to a housing project and then on down to San Diego for a big veterans' dinner.

'Those figures should be in by now. If what I was hearing before was right, it'll give us a good feel for the next couple of days. I'll pick them up in the office.'

Ten minutes later they were in the campaign headquarters. A young man with short hair, wearing fashionable glasses with small lenses, stepped forward and handed Mason a single piece of paper. As Kelp shook hands with a couple of people nearby, Mason read it through quickly, then looked at Kelp and smiled.

'Ewan, can we have a moment?' He took him by the arm and steered him towards an office to their right. 'Look, Carson's peaked!' He grinned as he handed him the piece of paper. 'This is the summary of the poll of polls and it shows his support is tailing off, his surge has stopped. Now, look at the back of the paper,' he said, turning it over. 'It's one of our private polls and shows he may even be about to lose some crucial support among the white-collar voters.'

Kelp smiled back at him as he skimmed the polls. 'We're not there yet, Dick, but it's the best news we've had for a while.'

Kelp knew that Mason's heart and soul were in this and he'd grown to trust him completely in the last few months. Between him and Weitz they'd put this plan together, even after they'd been knocked back by Senator Wall's unexpected declaration for Carson in New York and then by Carson's resurgence. Mason stayed steady and he and Weitz helped plan their way through it. It was all coming good. He'd been written off by the pollsters and the commentators but he'd hung on and now he was heading to victory.

Kelp patted Mason on the shoulder as he turned to leave the office just as Acquilan appeared with Weitz.

'Victor,' Kelp said, smiling, 'when did you get in? You should have told us.'

'Last night,' Acquilan replied. 'I was tired, thought I'd have a look through the most recent reports. Ewan, have you got a minute?'

'Sure. How long have we got, Dick?'

'Ten, maybe fifteen minutes, Ewan. I'll pick you up at the door.'

Weitz shut the office door behind them.

'You know all about Douglas?' Acquilan began.

'Sure, first thing this morning. Can't say I'm sorry – he'd done so much damage . . . Hold on, Victor, you're not telling me this is anything to do with us?'

'No,' Weitz answered quickly, 'someone else.'

'Good,' Kelp smiled, 'like I said, they did us a favour – the worm was eating away at me. So what's it all about?'

'Pichowski says it was a robbery but the cops think it was something to do with the British guy, Grande.'

'You saying they got together?' asked Kelp. Acquilan nodded, almost absent-mindedly. 'Why? How?'

'Difficult to say,' replied Acquilan, reaching for a cigar. 'One thing's for sure, he's their prime suspect now.'

'*What*? They've given out his name?' Kelp asked.

'The murder is all over the news,' Weitz answered quickly. 'No name or pictures, but he was there and they know it.'

'What if they catch him – can't he talk? After all, if he met Douglas, maybe . . .' Kelp's voice trailed away, as though he was inviting one of them to complete his sentence.

'No, even if he did,' Acquilan's deep voice was firm, 'he still couldn't have anything like enough.'

'What, you mean without the diaries?' Kelp asked.

'Yeah.'

'And he hasn't got them, otherwise he'd have used them by now – is that what you mean?' Acquilan nodded. 'And Cosmo?'

'Like I said, Ewan,' Weitz confirmed. 'He's dead.'

'Last time you said you couldn't be sure,' retorted Kelp.

'That's right, you never can be.'

'What?' Kelp turned on Acquilan. 'Just like those pictures, Victor, the ones you said were destroyed and turned out not to be. I suppose that was also something you weren't too sure about.'

Acquilan shrugged in reply. Kelp glanced at his watch.

'What about money?'

'Back on an even keel. It cost us, though. The Seattle project is OK but I had to sell shares at half the value before the S.O.B. pulled out. Anyway, we've got enough there to see you through.'

'Good, that'll be a weight off Sol's mind.'

'And Bernie's going to stay with you?'

'At last!' Kelp replied. 'And the Brit?'

'Taken care of.'

'If Cosmo's dead, then who wants the Brit dead?'

'I don't know but whoever it is has lost his chance. We're pretty certain we know where he is.'

'Excellent,' Kelp smiled broadly. 'Well, all I've got to do is win.'

'From what I've seen, you're pretty close,' Acquilan smiled. 'All we've dreamed of, Ewan, and you're almost there.'

'Yes, just the debate left – that's worrying enough. Thank God the rest is all over.'

'We're just about to close it down.'

They were interrupted by a knock on the door as Mason arrived to shepherd Kelp out.

'Well,' Weitz began as the door shut behind Kelp. 'It's one thing to reassure Ewan, but we're in deep shit and until we find Grande, this whole thing could blow at any time.'

Acquilan nodded, 'Sure, but as I said, we'll have to change tactics. We're gonna let him come to us.' He looked at Weitz, his face set, eyes unblinking. 'We know that Douglas must have been killed by Cosmo. From what Pichowski tells us, the files he picked up from Douglas's office were a complete life history and, as you said, he and Grande must have put two and two together, including the wartime photograph. Another hour and we'll be able to see for ourselves when Pichowski gets in, but I reckon we should plan for the worst.'

'And Grande's wanted by the police. He could bring them with him.'

'Look, there's only one place for Grande to go now – it's here, not to the cops. And what d'ya think? Don't you suppose that Cosmo's people will follow?'

'If what Pichowski says is correct,' Weitz continued, 'and the photographs Grande took are clear, he knows where the paintings are. Pichowski didn't say anything about having the negatives.'

'Sure, he did. Relax, he's got them. And, more important, Grande needs them – he hasn't got anything without me.'

'So we're just gonna sit still and lure him here?'

'Yes,' Acquilan replied. 'He'll bring Cosmo's people after him. We're gonna set a fly to catch two spiders and then get rid of both.'

Weitz stared at Acquilan. He was worried. He'd always known him as the Ice King. Nothing ever phased him, he never showed his emotion. Weitz knew that Acquilan had always considered it a sign of weakness to be any other way. Yet here, for the first time Weitz could remember, Acquilan was emotional. He'd become obsessed by Cosmo to such an extent that his judgement was suffering.

'This is where Cosmo would want it to be,' Acquilan continued.

'Where?' Weitz asked.

'Think about it! Between now and Tuesday, the timing is perfect – all of us in one place, on the eve of the nomination. At the moment of Kelp's triumph – perfect. He was always theatrical – it's perfect for him.'

'But Cosmo's dead.'

'Maybe, maybe not – it doesn't matter, his plan's alive with someone running it.'

'I think your scheme is full of holes, Victor,' Weitz said. 'So much is left to chance. What if they catch Grande before they get here? We'll be through! Surely now's the time to cut our losses? Let's get the hell out of here – let's tell Ewan the truth, tell him it's all over. He gave it a good shot but if he hangs around we could all be finished.'

'No,' Acquilan replied, 'you haven't forgotten, have you, Bernie? It's all or nothing. Ewan knows that and so do I, and if Cosmo is still alive, he does too.'

Weitz shook his head.

'We're all in this together – we'll all go up together.'

'Maybe, maybe . . . or down,' Weitz replied. 'The difference between us is that you don't realise it's all over. He's won. A gamble like this isn't a plan. Victor, you of all people taught me that! Why, if I'd come up with something like this before, you'd have chewed me off!'

'That was before – it's all changed now. Trust me, I've never got it wrong before.'

'But you never had Cosmo breathing so close down your neck before,' Weitz replied in an exasperated tone. 'He's read us all like a book. Every turn, every scheme. It's got so I don't even trust myself, Victor. Let's get the hell out of here – cut our losses,' he pleaded. 'This isn't your plan any more, it's his.'

'*Bullshit*! What's the matter with you? I can see the loser coming out in you. Don't lose it, Bernie, you know we can do it. Trust me, we can have it all.'

Weitz nodded and replied, 'If you say so, Victor.' Then he turned away.

24

Saturday Night and Sunday Morning

Deep in the Tenderloin district of San Francisco stood a small rundown hotel just off Jones Street. An all-night gas station, a parking lot and a diner were the view from the reception area, beneath whose flicking neon sign shards of peeled paint lay scattered across torn black bags.

'Twenty bucks in advance – each,' the receptionist growled. A cigarette clamped between her teeth, she kept her eyes on the TV screen beside the door. Schwartz put the bills down. She swept them up and tossed the keys across the counter.

'First turning on the left, last two on the right!' she screamed. A dark-haired man poked his head through coloured plastic strips hanging limply across the door behind her. 'Towels!' she ordered.

A minute later John Grande and Joe Schwartz were walking to their rooms, each deep in his own thoughts. Schwartz clutched a box he'd picked up from the Federal Express office in San Francisco.

John felt tired and bewildered. Schwartz's face was set and he made no attempt at conversation. Not only had everything John hoped for been lost but someone who'd become a good friend had been brutally murdered. Here he was again, stumbling around on the trail of those he believed were responsible, yet with only the outline of an idea of what he was going to do. He was certain that Acquilan had either killed Laura or was holding her hostage. The man who murdered Douglas and all the others, he knew, was capable of anything.

The day played through his memory again and again like a videotape. After finding Douglas's body he'd made his way by cab to Joe Schwartz's place. At first Schwartz had wanted to go to Douglas's house himself but John dissuaded him. Instead he made a call to a contact in the police department, who confirmed they were at the house and an inquiry was underway.

John had arrived with no plan, just a desire to destroy those who had wrecked his life and everything around him. He had no idea how to do it, or for that matter where to begin. As his anger subsided, his depression deepened. No money and no plans – they had won. It was here that Schwartz had taken control. He pointed out that Jack's murder left John with only two options: to give himself up to the police and face murder charges, or to make contact with Acquilan.

'They'll all be in San Francisco over the next few days,' Schwartz had said.

'Why?'

'Because of the televised debate between Carson and Kelp. But we'll find out for sure through the paper.'

'But I won't be able to get near them with all that security. And anyway, more importantly, I've no money – I was relying on Laura.'

'Don't worry about that!'

'I don't want to drag you down as well. This is for me to settle.'

'You don't have much choice – I'm in it, with or without you. When they murdered Jack, they made sure of that.'

'All right, suppose we go to San Francisco, the only way for me to settle this is to get either Kelp or Acquilan alone – to obtain some sort of confession – taped. I don't suppose I will get anywhere near him. Jack talked to me about doing it if we needed to – a sort of standby – but I doubt he will see me.'

'He'll see you all right.'

'Why are you so sure?'

'Because he has to kill you.'

John shuddered. His lips went dry. What Schwartz said was true and he had already accepted it, but nonetheless he felt cold at the thought.

'Me or him?'

'That's the way it'll be. He now knows you took those photographs. He knows it all – he must have all the files, everything – that's why he'll meet you.'

'But what about Kelp?'

'You'll have to go after Acquilan and I'll watch Kelp. To do that, we'll need to get into the secure areas at their hotel and the convention centre where they're holding the debate.'

'Not a hope.'

'Don't be so sure,' Schwartz's craggy features broke into a smile for the first time. 'We have passes waiting at the *Post's* press office in downtown San Francisco. I'll pick them up when we get there.'

'What passes?'

'The ones Jack and I got, including one for you.'

'What?'

'Sure, you're his other researcher – Jim Bryant – that's the name he's put you down as. He created you.'

'But how come?'

'Simple, no one asked at the *Post*. We figured there was only an outside chance that you would come up with the proof Acquilan had the pictures, so we had a second plan. The idea was that Mr Douglas would come here with me and maybe you if . . .'

'If I was still alive,' John interrupted.

'Or something,' Schwartz admitted, straight-faced. 'Jack

was due to be one of the panel of journalists who were down to ask the questions at the debate, so it was no big deal. He was determined to finish this – I've never seen him so fired up.'

'He believed my story that much?'

'Sure, he said it was what he'd been writing about all his life – the little guy against the big one. Same story, just a different script,' Schwartz stood up.

'I never knew his whole reputation was riding on my word and your research. He'd have risked all that?'

'Sure. He knew it was dangerous from the start, but that's what made him who he was – of all the people I've ever known he was the best,' he said, shaking his head slowly.

Reaching his room, John sat on the bed and waited. Schwartz had gone to get the press passes. Everything moveable was chained down and even the television was coin-operated. The whole room was dilapidated and the noise from the nearby freeway was a perpetual background. He took off his shoes and lay back on the bed. It wasn't like this in films, he thought. The hero was always resolute, defiant and determined. How could he have been so stupid? He knew there was something wrong with the art deal from the first moment. Yet he had gone ahead with it. His greed had caused all of this.

When Julia had been killed in the car accident, he swore to himself that he would never let himself get close to anyone again. Now, on the run, wanted for murder and with someone trying to kill him, he had broken his own rule and allowed someone else into his life. More than that, he could smell her perfume, feel her warmth. But even now he couldn't bring himself to admit he loved her. That, to John, was a concept reserved only for Julia. Love was a term that brought with it waves of guilt and a deep sense of failure. He couldn't help himself – Laura's company was what he longed for – perhaps Julia would have understood? He shook his head.

It didn't matter now anyway, he thought, his selfishness had done for them all. The only way left open to him was to become like them, hard and ruthless like Acquilan, Kelp and the rest of them. He didn't care any more what happened to him; he just wanted to punish them. Once Joe returned with the passes, they'd then be able to finish the job. That was all he had left – payback. And then what? An empty nothing, a shell, a sham – nothing mattered. He drifted off to sleep.

On board an American Airlines DC9 halfway to New York, Jasinski and Mackie sat in silence. Each had been deep in thought about the latest events they'd witnessed in Alexandria.

'I just wish someone would cut me some slack here,' Jasinski said. 'None of it makes sense.'

'Aye,' replied Mackie. 'The trouble is, it's like a 50-piece jigsaw – we've got the pieces but they all seem to be from a different puzzle. Take Grande Junior, he's behaving like a hit man – dead bodies wherever he goes. Everything around him seems to have a plan, a purpose, but he doesn't. Even the murders, there's nothing to connect them except him.'

'Except him,' Jasinski chipped in.

'Aye him and that woman's concern for him – why, after all, would an intelligent woman like her get mixed up with someone with all his problems, particularly when everything points to him being a murderer? What does she know that makes her stay, even jeopardise her job for him?'

'Beats me,' Jasinski replied. 'The trouble is we seem to have wasted all last night listening to some bullshit story from her. Meanwhile, there's another murder and Grande's directly involved.' He shook his head in disgust. 'Do you think she knew? After all, it could have been an act.'

'You know,' Mackie began. 'Let's look at her story again. If we assume, just for a moment, that Buckley's telling the truth, at least as far as she understands it . . .' He reached absent-mindedly for his pipe.

'Sorry, sir,' the flight attendant bent down, smiling at him with one of those smiles with which they apply with their make-up, 'no smoking allowed.'

'I was only planning to smoke it without tobacco – just like this,' and he placed it in his mouth and sucked it, 'like a baby.' The stewardess's smile fell away and was replaced by a puzzled expression.

'Well . . . I guess,' she searched up and down the aircraft for guidance, 'the rules, well, they – I guess that'll be OK.' She walked away quickly.

'What do you mean – as far as she understands it?' Jasinski asked.

'Simply, that there may be more. What makes you think that hers is a complete jigsaw puzzle?' He sucked at his pipe before continuing, 'She told us a story that takes us from the end of the war right up until today. In her story, Grande is the innocent party – someone has been trying throughout to catch and kill him.'

'Yes, but this whole thing hangs on the belief that what happened in Naples in 1946 was criminal and that the two people who died in the warehouse fire were not the two Americans, but an American and an Italian,' Jasinski understood what Mackie was up to and knew that it was necessary for him to play devil's advocate – the role was easy, he didn't believe Buckley's story anyway.

'Not Cosmo and Morrow,' Mackie said, 'but Morrow and Licatta – you know, the painter.' He flicked over a few more pages of his notebook. 'If that was the case and they were double-crossed, then at least it helps us understand the connection to Grande.'

'If, that's a pretty big "if",' Jasinski retorted.

'Aye, but we've got to start somewhere,' Mackie sucked on his pipe again. 'So Cosmo, or D'Ostia as he's become known, decides to sell the pictures through Grande. It could be coincidence but maybe not. After all, he moved near

Grande's uncle and spent a number of years as his neighbour . . .'

'Well,' interrupted Jasinski, 'Grande was an art dealer, you said it yourself.'

'Yes, but there are lots of dealers in London, or for that matter in Italy, who could have done a good, if not better job. Why him?'

'Coincidence – he just picked him out.'

'Maybe, maybe not.'

'Either way, this story can't be corroborated because Cosmo is dead and buried.'

'True, but let's see where it takes us. Don't forget the editor of the *Post* spoke to Douglas the night before.'

'Look,' Jasinski protested, 'if this guy Cosmo wanted to expose Kelp, and this story about the diaries is true, then why didn't he just publish? Why would Grande need Douglas? And anyway, remember Meyer told us Douglas didn't say very much to him when they spoke.'

'No, he didn't but Grande needed Douglas because of his reputation. Perhaps the diaries alone aren't enough, perhaps he thought they wouldn't be believed, perhaps there's another reason?'

'But I don't buy this Kelp link – the guy's clean and anyway, why would he need to stir up trouble at the start of the primaries? Sure, I grant you, maybe Grande's got someone after him but not Kelp. Grande could've double-crossed someone, maybe a partner of Cosmo's, Cosmo himself, who knows? Then he murders his own partner in the gallery, maybe because he found out. The rest isn't special – the classic story of a man on the run. After all, last seen with his partner, last seen with a lawyer in Rome and now last seen with Douglas, all murdered. Too many coincidences, too many murders, too many times he's there at the wrong moment.'

'Unless he was being set up?'

'Who by? You're not going to tell me it's Kelp!' Jasinski exclaimed.

'No, but what about Cosmo?'

'But you already agreed, the guy's dead.'

'Perhaps, but . . .'

'Perhaps?' Jasinski's voice was harsh.

'All right, probably, but either way it doesn't matter.'

'Huh!' Jasinski snorted. 'I'm surprised at you, it's basic police work. Your answer either dumps a suspect or keeps him in the frame.'

'What if Kelp and this man Acquilan think Grande is dangerous, that this is because they think he has diaries which reveal something from their past? We already believe they know he knew about the pictures being a fraud.'

'How?'

'Let's just assume they do. I understand disguising pictures is difficult enough but repairing a disguised picture would be hard to hide from someone with a trained eye. That puts Grande in real danger because they're going to assume he knows the whole story. Now, if whoever started all this arranged to have the killings ultimately point towards Kelp, then all they would need to do is kill Grande and publish the diaries at the same time, perhaps even with an explanation. It would make it all look like Kelp and Acquilan had tried to catch up with Grande to silence him. They know we would have to follow the most compelling evidence.'

'But according to your story, we should be on to them by now.'

'Ah, that's the key point – we won't be until we find Grande – he is central to this.'

'OK, then why isn't Grande dead?'

'I suspect that's because they lost him. "The best laid plans of mice and men . . ."'

'So, you think they're all looking for him?'

'Perhaps.'

'OK, but what you haven't answered is why Grande, why him? You're not telling me that he was just an innocent bystander?'

'I'm stumped on that one.'

'What?'

'I don't have a clue.'

'Then the guy who kidnapped Buckley and the old guy Grande, who's that? What's his connection?'

'I've no idea. Perhaps something to do with this man Cosmo.'

Jasinski sat staring ahead without further comment for some minutes.

'What do you plan to do with Buckley?' Mackie broke the silence.

'I should charge her.'

'But we're no nearer finding Grande and she's the only one who can help.'

'Sure, but she's not saying – or she doesn't know. Sure, I agree there are serious questions that need further investigation but you've been around long enough to know that if I lay all that on the Captain, I'm finished. There's no way he'd let me continue.' He sat in silence for a moment, 'I agree, Grande holds all the answers. One way or another we've got to get to him, and all we've got that gives us a chance of finding him is her. That don't leave me with much,' Jasinski paused and took a deep breath, 'I guess I'll have to take a chance so when we get to New York we'll put her on a long leash and see where she runs to.'

'What about your captain?'

'Well, the way I see it, this is all I got – Buckley and a goddamn Disney story! So I'd better go with it and see what happens. What d'you think? What would you do if you were Grande?'

Mackie sucked his pipe thoughtfully and then replied, 'I'd

run for it, not away, but to where the person I thought responsible for the murders was.'

'That's what I was hoping you'd say. He'll take after Kelp – she made that clear enough,' he tapped his fingers. 'And that means San Francisco, the debate between the President and Kelp.'

'Quite a gamble.'

'Yeah. And if you had to predict where she'd go?'

'Grande – straight there.'

'Yeah, I guess.'

One row in front Ralph Grande and Laura Buckley at first talked in a desultory manner, avoiding the one shared interest: John. Yet after a while, Ralph carefully and deliberately encouraged her to repeat her story, the relief clear on her face. Throughout, Ralph noticed an intensity in her, her words pouring out at speed. At the end her voice dropped as a sense of foreboding shouldered its way into her thoughts and silenced her.

Laura had banked on getting to Joe Schwartz and talking to him. When they'd found he'd gone she felt finally as though she'd been cast adrift, alone and lost. Looking around the plane – full, it seemed, of smiling, laughing people – deepened her gloom. They were all no doubt anticipating an enjoyable weekend in Manhattan. More laughter, which annoyed her – she hated their display of wellbeing. She wanted to shout, to scream her frustration at them, but instead she sighed and looked at Ralph Grande, vaguely aware that he was speaking to her. His words, she realised, were of John – John as a boy with his mother, John at the villa; his sense of fun, their adventures; his intelligence and gentleness. Then there was more, more about the enjoyment and pride Ralph felt for his nephew and the special relationship which had developed between them. His words seemed to her to linger on John's mother more than perhaps she might have expected and then he spoke about her death. It was as though a chest full of memories locked away for years had been opened briefly.

Through this slow, but gentle interpreter, Laura began to understand John a little better. She learned how the outgoing and amusing man she had never known became, after the death of his wife and child, the quiet, withdrawn one who now seemed to dominate her waking and even her sleeping hours.

'Do you think he's dead?' Ralph asked, almost hesitatingly.

'I don't know, I just don't know,' Laura replied.

'And the ones who held me, the same ones who held you – do you think they killed Jack Douglas?'

'Who knows?' She shook her head. 'The worst part about this is knowing so much about it and being utterly helpless. Because I don't know the full story, the police clearly don't believe a word I've said. Yet I know that Kelp and Acquilan are the key. The trouble is, Jack Douglas had all the files and they're gone. Now he's dead, John's disappeared and Joe Schwartz can't be found. God, what a mess we've made of it!' She smiled in a derisive sort of way. 'I wouldn't mind but it's the knowing and not being able to prove it that hurts most.'

'I've only ever seen this sort of thing on films, it all seems so easy there,' Ralph was saddened by his own sense of uselessness. 'Extracting a confession by subterfuge or some-one believing the heroine against all the odds . . . It didn't take much and then, it was all over.' He closed his eyes. 'I remember going with John to see a film called *Touch of Evil* in London a few years ago. They were giving an Orson Welles season at the Gate Cinema in Notting Hill. Orson Welles was a favourite of John's. I remember him laughing about the scene where the detective Vargas trails Orson Welles and his detective friend, who's wired up to a transmitter as he listens to the confession being squeezed out of Welles. He spent ages telling me about how it was so much easier these days, with little tape recorders strapped to their backs. It's funny but when you think you know somebody, you don't. I never even thought he was interested in that sort of thing . . .'

'How stupid!' Laura interrupted. Ralph stared at her in surprise. 'No, not you, me – I've been very stupid. It makes sense, what he said to me before he left – that if Douglas didn't work out, they'd have to get a confession out of one of them. He didn't say how and I thought it was far-fetched, but now I know what he meant. Let's see, only a few days left before the California Primary – Tuesday, I think. That's right, Kelp will be at his headquarters in San Francisco and I'll just bet Acquilan is around there. I think there's due to be a debate between the two of them.'

'I'm sorry, I don't understand,' Ralph was mystified.

'Look, I think I've just figured out where John will be and for that matter, Schwartz. What a fool I've been. Here I am, about to be charged by the police, on my way back to New York, and John is thousands of miles away in California and there's nothing I can do to help him.'

'They might not charge you if you told them what you've told me.'

'No, there's no point. We both know they wouldn't believe me and even if they did, they'd only use it as an excuse to go and pick him up. No, there's not a chance in hell that I'll be free to do anything. I'll just have to wait – and hope.'

Sunday was a frustrating day for John Grande. With the press pass, Schwartz also brought the news that Kelp was travelling all over the state until late Monday evening. John's heart sank when he heard that, for it meant that he would have to stay put until he returned. He didn't dare go out in case he was recognised. Instead, he stayed in his room and paced up and down.

The late morning sun reflected off the windscreens of cars passing his window as he absent-mindedly counted each one. That he couldn't leave his room until the next day was almost more than he could bear. He felt like a caged lion. With an effort, he turned from the window. Joe Schwartz had told him to write the whole thing down, just in case something went wrong. Pulling some paper towards him, he began.

The moment John turned away from the window, the curtain moved in the room directly across from his. A face stared into John's room before the curtain dropped . . .

Lunch in the Mark Hopkins Hotel coffee shop consisted of a sandwich. Joe Schwartz ate slowly, pausing to record his own thoughts on a notepad. He was aware that the hotel was awash with journalists and security guards but, with his press pass hanging from his neck, he felt reasonably secure although none the less nervous. He'd managed to glean some information about Kelp's movements and discovered that Acquilan was already in the hotel. What had pleased him even more was that he'd managed to find out what rooms they were in. Acquilan was on another floor, away from all the security.

He slipped the notepad into his pocket as he finished his sandwich. Paying the waitress, he left the coffee shop and made his way towards the front entrance, where he stopped by the reception desk. His eyes took in the main elevators, the entrance and then the payphones, which stood in sound-proofed cubicles. He noted down the telephone numbers of two of them, the third being occupied. Inside the cubicle, a man was hunched over the telephone. '. . . So Gene, I've faxed the tribute from Wall and Kelp, they're probably on your desk . . . Ah, good.'

Sam Dunbar, the *Post*'s political correspondent, continued his conversation with Gene Meyer in Washington. In his early forties, grey-haired, pasty-faced and overweight, he was none the less one of the most respected story-getters in the business.

'The problem, Gene, was Carson . . . Damn it! He was in a prayer meeting last night . . . I know – you should see the latest poll ratings . . . Sure, he'll need to pray now. Kelp's in front. Son-of-a-bitch!' he suddenly exclaimed. 'No, not you, Gene. I've just seen someone. You know, that old guy – the one who used to run the library, retired and then you brought back, worked with Jack a few weeks back – you know, Gene . . . That's right, Joe, Joe Schwartz . . . I don't know why he's here. Hang on, I'll speak to him,' Dunbar opened the door.

'Joe!' he shouted as Schwartz disappeared through the entrance.

'I don't know what he's doing here – no, he's gone now . . . He just walked out. I'm sure he heard me, everyone else did,' Dunbar finished the conversation and hurried to the hotel doors. Outside there was no sign of him.

In Washington, as Meyer put the telephone down, a puzzled expression crossed his face. He'd just finished writing his own tribute to Jack Douglas in a double page spread and he was drained. Still numb from the news of Jack's murder, he couldn't understand how a man who had served front-line in the Second World War and as a correspondent in the Korean War could die at the hands of some punk petty thief just for a computer, a television and a stereo. It just didn't make any sense. Meyer felt there had to be another reason. He remembered that Jack had telephoned him the night before, really excited about some article. It was all a little fast and he couldn't remember much about it. Was it just a coincidence?

He was quite surprised when some New York police lieutenant and a couple of detectives had asked him about Jack. He hadn't told them much – everyone seemed to think it was a robbery. But then they asked him about Schwartz. He was really surprised but gave them his address and didn't think much more about it. Schwartz hadn't come to work since then – no word, no message, nothing from him. Then Dunbar said he had seen him.

385

Could it have been Schwartz, Meyer wondered, in San Francisco? Could Dunbar have been right? And what did Schwartz know about Jack's death?

He pressed the intercom and asked his secretary to try Schwartz's home again. A few minutes later she told him there was no answer.

'Give me the list of those eligible for press passes in San Francisco,' he ordered. 'My God!' he exclaimed as he checked the list she brought to him, 'get on to the press office in San Francisco and find out if Joe Schwartz has picked up his press pass,' he asked his secretary. 'Wait!' Meyer remembered Jack Douglas's words the night before he was murdered, 'an English guy on the run'. He read the list again, 'We don't employ a Jim Bryant, do we?'

'I think he's Jack's young assistant.'

'Have I met him?'

'No, no one here has. Jack said he worked from home.'

'Check if the pass has been picked up.'

Ten minutes later his secretary walked into his office. 'Well, both passes were claimed last night,' she said, her voice quizzical. 'Do you want me to contact the police and get the passes stopped?'

'I'll be . . .!' Meyer exclaimed.

'What was that, Gene?'

'Nothing.'

'Do you want me to . . .?' she began again.

'*What*? No, leave it!' He smiled. 'You're up to something, you old loon!' he muttered, 'At least you believed in Jack, when I didn't.'

'What was that?' his secretary asked again.

'Nothing. Look,' Meyer felt a surge of excitement, 'get me all the columns that Jack did for us over the last five months.' Meyer realised that Douglas had really been on to something. He cursed himself for not taking it more seriously. Now Jack was dead and Schwartz was clearly trying to finish what he had started. He shook his head as his lip quivered. 'You were the best, Jack – I just forgot. You were always way ahead of us all. I'm sorry,' Meyer's eyes glistened. 'I owe you, I owe you!'

He wiped his eyes and pushed the button on his intercom.

'Before you start on his columns, check out the next flight to San Francisco and get me on it. Then, when you get his columns, tell Jeff Staed and Will Searcy to get their asses into my office – I've got a job that needs finishing.'

25

Monday

'It turns my stomach . . .' began Kelp, 'to think that went out in my name.' He jabbed his finger at the *Post*, which was spread open on the table, 'That son-of-a-bitch hated me. In the last few months he could have cost me this election.' He snorted derisively, 'To think that crap went out in my name!'

'Ewan,' said Mason, 'after all, the guy was a national hero – a sort of institution.' Mason watched as Kelp shook his head. 'If you hadn't . . . '

'I know, Carson has done the same – you were going to say,' interrupted Kelp. 'It was different for him, though. Douglas didn't hound him.' He screwed the paper up and threw it across the room. 'The guy twisted the truth and pissed all over me from the first moment I was in politics. The only thing I'm sorry about is that he won't have to eat his words when I get this nomination sewn up tomorrow.'

'Amen to that,' Mason replied, breathing a sigh of relief. He desperately wanted to move Kelp on to discuss the eve-of-poll debate between him and Carson.

'Look at it this way, Ewan,' Jim Donald said, cautiously, 'everyone knows you and Douglas didn't see eye to eye.'

'Oh really, you don't say!'

'OK, OK,' Donald replied. 'But knowing that, they'll all

388

think you were more than generous in your praise and that deep down inside you really are a decent guy. Who knows, it could sway some more out there. Dick was right to give the *Post* your tribute. Besides, just think how pissed off Gene Meyer must have been when we gave him this.' He laughed nervously.

'Fine,' interrupted Kelp, 'but I don't have to like it, that's all. Let's move on.'

'About the debate tonight, Ewan . . .' Mason began.

'Sure, let's get down to business,' Kelp's demeanour changed immediately. 'Shoot!' he glanced from Donald to Mason.

'Jim's going to start first with a brief on the press – who's likely to ask what, you know. On the flight back to San Francisco, we'll brief you further on the details of the questions and answers. Remember, Ewan, we're going to try and concentrate on his weak law and order record . . .'

Kelp nodded but his mind drifted. He was angry – angry with Acquilan, whom he still blamed for much of what had gone wrong. The paintings were his worst mistake. His obsession had nearly brought all his hopes crashing down.

Here they were, Kelp thought, with a more and more unpopular President, who was up to his neck in an allegation of land deals as governor. They were within an ace of securing the nomination and yet he was still worrying.

'Damn him!' Kelp swore.

'What?' Donald looked up from his briefing note, surprised.

'Nothing, keep going!' ordered Kelp.

'Sure, well, what we want to do is to take his record as governor and paint a picture of . . .' Donald continued nervously.

Paintings, all because of the paintings! What they needed were the diaries. The paintings were to be the way to prove or disprove whether Cosmo had his diaries. Did they still exist? If so, what did Grande have to do with it all?

'Why doesn't Cosmo publish?' he muttered.

'Sorry, Ewan, what . . .?'

'Nothing, keep going, Jim,' Kelp replied. 'I'm listening.'

Mason and Donald exchanged glances.

'Look, Ewan, something's bothering you; we can take a break if you want,' Mason said.

'No, go on, I'm fine.'

'The momentum is with you, Ewan. All we need to do now is secure at least a draw,' Mason took over from Donald, his voice carrying assurance. 'The way things are now, it's Carson who needs to score well tonight. But we've got one ace left and it's pretty negative. Here, read this,' he handed a couple of sheets over to Kelp.

'You're right, this is negative,' Kelp said as he looked up from the page – and smiled. 'How long have you had this?'

'It's been waiting in the war chest for the critical moment and it's all about timing. When we hit the law and order area, you let him make one of his statements about being hard on crime and then stick him with his record – particularly the early release and re-conviction rate. And . . . this case of Sam Garbenkin – five rapes and a murder he committed after being released early on Carson's policy of early-release incentives. The point is that Carson made a big thing, as you remember, of being tough on re-offenders. He was elected to the White House on his law and order policy – that didn't include incentives for early release. In the last year, re-offending rates have risen by ten per cent.'

'But everyone knows that,' Kelp replied.

'Our research shows they're still not that aware – we need something to get the message across. This case is the one. Garbenkin was only picked up last month.'

'Now you're both sure about this? If any of this is wrong in these Garbenkin details . . .'

'Don't worry, it's all been checked out,' Donald replied. 'And double-checked. It's the final straw – you can talk of his failure and throw this at him! And there's plenty more where this came from.'

Kelp smiled again, 'OK, have this put on some cue cards and I'll keep them on the lectern with me.'

'It really is all here in this article,' Acquilan said, glaring at Weitz. 'Everything that's happened to Grande and a pretty good outline of our problems in Italy. Then it's all about us after that. Look, he's asked leading questions about the gallery murder, the dead Italian lawyer, Goldstein and the super in New York. But there's nothing here about Cosmo setting us up. Douglas didn't write about that.'

'But Douglas wouldn't have known anything about Cosmo, didn't even know Grande was being set up,' Weitz replied. 'He was certainly doing Cosmos' work for him.'

'Not quite – you're forgetting why Grande is involved. The death of Douglas will force Grande to come after us.'

'So?'

'So, we've just got to wait, like I said. Grande has no option – it's us or him. I'd say a pretty straightforward choice, don't you agree?'

'What about Cosmo?'

'If he's still alive . . . More likely someone else is acting on his behalf, but who?' Acquilan looked questioningly at Weitz. 'Cosmo's guys want Grande dead.' Acquilan tapped his pen on the table. 'Either way, my guess is that they killed Douglas because they didn't want the information to come out in a way which could have let Grande off the hook. They want him as much as us, otherwise they'd have let Douglas publish – that would have finished us. Douglas had it all here. But it would have cleared Grande. They must know that with Douglas dead, Grande is left with no option but to come after us. So, we wait and we make sure that the fly finds easy access to the centre of the spider's web.'

391

'That's not so much of a plan, more a suicide note,' Weitz made no effort to disguise his cynicism. He was angry with both Kelp and Acquilan – Kelp for his determination to go ahead with this Presidential run and Acquilan for his obsession with the paintings and with Cosmo. All along he'd had his reservations, all he'd ever wanted was to make money, and now the two of them were throwing it away. Cosmo had baited the whole plan with the six paintings and the promise of diaries, and Acquilan, in his eagerness, had swallowed the whole thing.

Weitz regarded Acquilan and, for the first time, saw to his horror a man staring over the edge. The usual calm mask had slipped enough to reveal someone in turmoil. Weitz knew too well that Acquilan understood the huge nature of this gamble. The only plan he had was to wait. But Weitz had made his mind up that he wasn't prepared to be part of such a gamble. If they went down, he was damned if he was going down with them. The recently opened Swiss bank account would, had anybody known about it, have borne ample testimony to his version of the alternative.

'You with me, Bernie? Well, are you?'

'That's not the question, Victor – the question is how. How, in the space of a few months, we've drifted from calling the shots to becoming the target – waiting for someone else to move. Like I said, yours is one hell of a plan, though I can see that you're right about one thing, for you there's no other way.'

'What do you mean, *you*? It's us, all three of us, we sink or swim together,' Acquilan stared hard at Weitz, 'unless, of course, you've got a better plan, Bernie.'

'I never thought I'd have to say this, Victor, but for once, your plan sucks and you know it. There is another way – we just cut our losses and get the hell out – leave the goddamn pictures, the diaries and all this political shit, and just go! You know, Victor, it would be like the old days. We could start out somewhere else; we'd have enough money, we'd be free.'

'Bernie, if we've been round this once, we've been round it a million times, I'll be dead before I do that,' Acquilan pulled a cigar and a silver clipper from his pocket. 'Survival's not the point,' he said as he clipped the cigar. 'It's winning, that's all, it's winning that matters. If we did run away, we'd spend the rest of our lives running – three losers! What's the point? I'm too old, Ewan's too old, and even you, Bernie . . . No, we're down to the short strokes; now, there's nothing else left.'

'You're OK, Victor. You and Ewan, you've always wanted this,' he moved as though to leave, then stopped and turned back to face Acquilan. 'I'll be honest, Victor – I've had enough. Ewan and you – your obsessions, they're killing me. Everything I've worked for is going down the tubes. No one can accuse me of anything – I've worked my butt off to help and to support you both. I've stayed loyal, I've never said a word in criticism. From Italy onwards, I've always followed your leadership. Well, Victor, for old time's sake, I'll do what I can, but remember this guy Grande's no robot. Both you and Cosmo, or whoever the hell is working for him, you both think you can move him here and move him there and he'll do what he's supposed to do. Well, he's proved that he's got a brain of his own, so don't blame me if this all goes wrong. As I said, you can rely on me and Pichowski, but I hope you think about this again. Christ! Use your brain, Victor – he wants to destroy you and he's close to doing it! If it isn't Grande, it'll be somebody else. Dump it all and run, think about getting the hell out of here.' With that, he turned on his heel and left the room.

Acquilan's pulse was racing. They'd been through too much for him to simply brush Weitz's comments aside. He always thought they were indivisible, that they'd see it all through; so much so, he'd paid little attention to Weitz's words of warning before. This time, however, he knew Weitz was determined and genuinely angry.

'So, you're right, Bernie,' he muttered, 'So what? It was living on the high wire that brought you all your money. You settled down – pah!' But his words were more an attempt to reassure himself; they sounded hollow in the empty room. He reached for the telephone and dialled.

'Pichowski, get in here!' he ordered. 'I'm worried about Bernie.' He put the receiver down and was about to walk into his bedroom when the phone rang again. He picked it up.

'Yes? Sure, put him through!' His face crumpled into a frown.

'Acquilan, who's this . . .?' His frown disappeared, to be replaced by a quizzical smile. 'So tell him, sure I'll be here.' He held onto the receiver after the caller hung up.

There was a knock on the door and Pichowski entered.

'OK, go get Bernie,' Acquilan ordered, putting the receiver down, 'and tell him they just made contact.'

'Who?'

'Never you mind, just get Bernie,' he said, still smiling. As the doors shut behind Pichowski, he said, 'There, Bernie, what did I tell you?'

'That should do it,' Schwartz said as he finished strapping the tape recorder into the small of John Grande's back. 'Can you move and breathe OK?'

'It's a . . . bit uncomfortable but I'll survive.' He caught Schwartz's eye. 'Well, at least long enough to get his confession. After that . . . who cares?'

'Sure, you will and together we'll take the son-of-a-bitch down.' John put his shirt, tie, jacket and raincoat on and Schwartz then fed the microphone through the shirt and up underneath the lapel of his jacket. 'There, now once you switch it on here, it becomes voice-activated. So when you get to him, just hit this button by your belt buckle,' Schwartz pointed down to a switch protruding just above John's belt. 'You look OK. Jack would be proud . . .' He turned away quickly.

'Meant a lot to you, didn't he, Joe?'

'Yeah,' he croaked, 'we went way back. He was one of a kind. He was a newspaper man but, more than that, he was the straightest guy I ever met. Not like some of these college kids today, who go straight through to the big papers still wet behind the ears – he learned his trade through small-town papers. He could smell a story through a false trail until he got to it. Then you'd never shake him. He was living proof that there's no short cut to experience in this game. But now,' he sighed, 'they've all changed. We were both dinosaurs, only he knew it.'

John nodded, 'OK, Joe, let's go through it all just one more time.' Schwartz walked over and sat down on the edge of the bed. 'It's five o'clock now, the TV debates are scheduled for 7.30. According to the plan, we'll both go to the hotel; then I'll wait by the telephones, you'll go on over to the debate and use your pass to get in. Once there, you'll check to see if Acquilan is with Kelp or with Kelp's group and then, whether or not he is, you'll call me.'

'Right,' Schwartz agreed, 'I don't reckon he will be, but just in case. He agreed to meet you in his room.'

'And when you let me know,' John continued, 'I'll wait by the telephone for you to come back and then we'll go to his room.'

'Now remember, I'll call the cops five minutes after you enter and they should take at least five minutes to get there. That means . . .'

'That means I have ten minutes to get the truth out of him. That's not long, Joe. What if I go on in before you come? That should give me an extra ten minutes.'

'No! Look, I said this before and I'll say it again, you gotta wait for me. You can't just go in by yourself.'

'But we won't have the time.'

'We will, there'll be enough. I'll be over just before it gets under way,' Schwartz replied, his voice tense. 'Just follow the plan. Oh yes, you might need this if it goes wrong,' he pulled a Second World War Luger pistol from his pocket. John winced.

'I don't remember you putting that in your baggage.'

'A little insurance policy via Federal Express.'

'I'm not sure.'

'Don't worry, you might not have to,' Schwartz leaned forward and tossed it lightly onto John's lap. John stiffened and looked down at it in horror. 'Last time I used that,' Schwartz began, 'was during the war. It was given to me by a captured German pilot after I'd pulled him out of his burning aircraft just outside Salerno. I used it once – emptied a whole magazine into a German staff officer.'

'Well . . .' John looked at the pistol in his hand.

'D'you know how to cock it?' Schwartz asked.

'Not a clue,' John replied. 'I don't think I . . .'

'Like this,' Schwartz reached for the gun and took it out of John's hand. Cradling the pistol grip in his right hand, he slid his left hand along the top of the breach and pulled it back with thumb and forefinger. 'Now look here, this is the safety catch, which you flick with your thumb – on, off, it's easy.'

'Watch it, that thing might . . .'

Schwartz laughed as John spoke. 'Don't worry,' he said, squeezing the trigger, 'it's still missing one thing.' He reached into his left pocket and produced the magazine. 'Until I've put this in the handle, it's not dangerous.' He put the safety catch back on and slammed the magazine into position. He held it out to John, 'The next time you cock this, it'll put a round in the breach.'

John slipped it into the right-hand pocket of his jacket, pulling his raincoat around it. He self-consciously patted it, 'I wish I'd had a chance to speak to Laura just one more time,' he said wistfully.

Schwartz made no answer but walked quickly over to the door and reached for the light switch.

'Well,' Schwartz laid a hand on John's shoulder as he walked past, 'remember you gotta be by those telephones smack on time and . . .' Schwartz faltered, 'just keep faith and wait, that's all.'

Preoccupied, Grande and Schwartz were oblivious to their surroundings as they walked to their car. Across the parking lot, the dying sun refracted on their windscreen, dazzling them as they started to drive out. Unnoticed, behind them, a black two-door Sedan pulled out and followed them, dipping and bumping across the rough exit road.

'Are you telling me that Jack Douglas was killed by someone working for Kelp?' President Carson gazed at Frank Parry in amazement.

'It looks that way.'

'Then why haven't the police arrested him?'

'They're chasing that British guy, I told you . . .'

'You mean,' said Carson, 'they don't think it's Kelp?'

'No, it's more than that. He's connected with Kelp, they think he's chasing the guy; they think he's here.'

'Why?'

'No one knows.'

'That's great. For a moment there I actually thought you had something,' Carson shook his head. 'Don't try and make me feel better. If that's the best Pete can come up with, then we might as well call it a day.'

'No, I'm serious. The cops are chasing the British guy and it seems he has come here. I've already been on to the Mayor – he'll make sure they get all the help they need from the police here.'

'Look, can we use any of this?'

'Maybe.'

'So?'

'We could start the papers looking at this, like Douglas was.'

'Well, I guess that's a start. Too late for the debate but if we can get them to look at this and publish something, we could save it.'

Carson slumped into his seat, 'That last poll is bad.'

'Well, he's only two points ahead and there are still fifteen per cent undecided.'

'Don't soft soap me – we both know I need something big! First, the Republicans and now Kelp's attacking me for the land deal.'

'The prosecution hasn't got anything.'

'My evidence in two weeks.'

'Won't matter so much if you sew up the nomination here.'

'Sure, but I'm not going to do that.'

'Well,' Parry shrugged, 'Do you want us to go hard on the Kelp story?'

Carson stared at the floor, 'I don't see what option we've got, we're sinking fast.'

'It could backfire if we're wrong.'

'Do it!' Carson's face was lined with worry. 'But cover your tracks . . .'

Parry walked slowly back to his office.

In his heart he knew the Kelp story wouldn't run – that it would take much longer to get someone onto it. For once he was at a loss to see how to damage Kelp sufficiently to secure the nominations. He shut the door of his office and sat down slowly. There was something else he hadn't told Carson. He picked up the telephone – he had to speak to Pete Neal.

'Pete, have you got a moment?' Parry sighed, at least he'd caught him before he left the office. He knew it was better if it leaked out from a Government agency – it would provide more credibility. 'Look, he thinks I should get that stuff on Kelp put out. Can you do it? . . . Good!'

Parry smiled, 'There's more. Remember I told you about that old Mother Superior? You know, the one who . . . sure, *her.* Well, we've just heard from her. She says she's found a nun working in India, well, she remembers . . . No, not him but she remembers Haskins. It's because she was much older than the others, most were teenagers in trouble. Haskins stood out. No, she remembers her very clearly, particularly the name . . . I know – it gets worse. The woman has linked the name Haskins with the report about the reopened investigation . . . yeah, we're in deep shit!' Silence at the other end of the line. 'You know, I'm beginning to feel like the little boy who stuck his finger in the dyke. She did let one big hint slip, kept saying they always needed money. Sure, she's one smart woman. That's a good idea, let's get Abe Roma on the case. They need money. He can sort it out . . . don't worry, I'll see to it.'

Parry knew Abe Roma was a long-trusted confidante of the President, a financial Mr-Fix-it for Carson.

'I'll see if he can offer an inducement . . . I don't know, but if she lets the Prosecutor know, we're finished.'

Laura Buckley and Ralph Grande walked through the arrival hall at San Francisco Airport with their small bags.

Events were moving so fast, Laura had difficulty making sense of it all. Jack was dead and John was on the run and with Joe Schwartz. Only 24 hours before, Laura had been depressed because she was certain the police would arrest her on their return to New York. Instead, the sharp-tongued police lieutenant had let them go. No last-minute demands, no restraints on where she could go – not even, she mused, her passport.

Laura knew what she had to do. She'd planned it in her mind over and over. First, she called Walter Harvey who, typically, wasn't angry, just relieved to hear from her. She was touched by the way he expressed himself yet that made her feel even more guilty for having put him through so much. At a tactical moment in the conversation, she put in her request for two press passes in San Francisco and for a few seconds there was silence. Again he asked her what kind of trouble she was in and again she declined to say anything. But, after the initial hesitation, he agreed.

'The thing is, Laura, we thought you'd been kidnapped, so we informed the police. Everyone here was worried. Why couldn't you at least have let us know?' That question kept echoing in her head. She knew she'd been selfish, but she also knew there had been no other way. Perhaps it could have been different. All those years spent getting to the top, being in charge. Yet here she was now in San Francisco with an old man she'd met only a few days before in the most ridiculous circumstances, searching for a man she still hardly knew but whom she thought she loved. That they were in San Francisco was absurd enough, but as a strange detective unit, made up of an old man and a young woman – hardly the deadly duo.

'We've got about an hour and a half until the debate starts,' she said to Ralph, as they walked towards the cab stand. She hoped above hope that she was right; that John would go after Kelp and try to expose him. She was certain his plan would be Kelp's exposure, and almost certainly at the debate.

They threw their bags into the trunk of a cab.

As it moved away, another car stopped beside a short, stocky man, who had stepped out to the edge of the kerb. He slid into the back seat and they sped off after the first cab. 'That's right, that's them straight ahead,' Detective Munroe ordered. 'Just stay with that cab.'

'They're here,' Jasinski announced as he walked back into the building. 'Munroe's on to them.'

'Good,' Mackie replied.

'Travelling light, one small bag each,' Jasinski announced. 'They're going straight to the debate.'

'Aye, they're not bothered with hotels,' Mackie replied. 'They're after him and she knows Grande will be somewhere near Kelp. Christ knows what he looks like by now.'

There were police around and within the conference centre, and all were working with Jasinski. He had no jurisdiction in

San Francisco but when he returned to New York from Alexandria he'd been called in to see the Commissioner of Police, who had told him that the San Francisco Police Department would give him full support. What had particularly surprised him was that this was before he'd informed anyone that he wanted to go to San Francisco. Now in the office in the conference centre, which had become the security control centre for the debate, the San Francisco Police Department and even the Secret Service were helping.

'Look,' Jasinski whispered to Mackie, holding his arm and steering him to a corner of the office. 'When we left, I checked on Buckley's story. I even had someone find out where the two bodies were buried. They got the remains out and ran dental checks – guess what?'

'What?' Mackie exclaimed. 'Don't tell me she was right, one of them isn't the one on the record.'

'That's right,' he smiled, 'something else though – one of my people found out that someone else had just done the same thing. They said it was the Feds but one of them is thought to be working for the National Security Advisor.'

'NSA?'

'Yes. They would normally never be involved in anything like this – but it answers something. You see, I couldn't figure out why we've been given a free hand all of a sudden and so much co-operation here in San Francisco. Even the Secret Service is involved.'

'And that explains why my commander in London told me he was ordered to let me remain here – it wasn't what he wanted.'

'Someone big is tracking us and wants results.'

'Who?'

'Well, the NSA means only one person.'

'The President?'

'Sure, must be what this is about. After all, Kelp is his opponent.'

'Politicians!' Mackie groaned.

'Sure,' Jasinski shrugged. 'Let's go.' He gathered others in the room around him. 'Everyone's briefed, no one's to move in without my word. I've got that much agreement from the San Francisco police although they're in overall control.' He turned and walked out of the office.

'Good,' Mackie said as he caught up with Jasinski, 'they've got to be on a long lead if we're going to get Grande or else it'll all be for nothing.' Mackie glanced at Jasinski, 'If this goes wrong, retirement beckons pretty smartish for us both. I'm not a gambling man but I guess these two old cops are down to their kecks.'

Jasinski laughed, 'OK, let's do it!'

26

Monday Evening

John Grande felt uncomfortable as he perched on a stool at the bar. The hidden tape recorder kept digging into the small of his back when he moved. He glanced occasionally at a TV in the corner as he sipped slowly and distractedly at his beer.

There were a few people scattered around the room and some, like John, were sitting at the bar. Although he looked at the screen, he was only vaguely aware that political commentators were discussing the debate between the candidates. He hadn't the slightest interest in what they had to say but continued to watch, knowing the moment the two protagonists took the stage would be his cue to move to the payphones in the hotel lobby and wait for Joe's call, as arranged, to confirm whether Acquilan was in the hall or not. He knew Schwartz was worried that the meeting might be a set-up. Acquilan had to be there at the hotel for the plan to work.

The hands of the clock crept towards the starting time of the debate and, as they did, John felt a strange calm descend upon him. His pulse had steadied and he was surprised how detached he felt. He turned his head away from the TV, feeling slightly light-headed, as though he was somewhere else simply watching from a distant place. His mind kept wandering back to every wrong turn, every dead face. He felt responsible for them all. Most of all, Laura's face swam in and out of focus. Was she alive? Where was she? His own selfish motives had dragged people in, often fatally. Their blood was on his hands.

John waited quietly, unconcerned about what would happen to him. He wanted to bring it to a close – one way or the other, it no longer seemed important how he did it.

He tipped his drink back and slid the empty glass away from him. He felt the Luger, cold and heavy in his jacket pocket. Its presence brought him back to reality with a rush. He looked towards the television – a football game. God, someone had changed channels! He sat up, his pulse racing. The barman had disappeared. Leaning over the bar, he searched frantically for the remote control. Again, no luck.

'It's gone time!' he realised in horror. John looked at the clock, 'Seven-thirty-two, what was I doing?' He hurried from the bar, afraid he'd missed Joe's call.

Joe Schwartz breathed a sigh of relief as he walked past security at the entrance. He'd known from the outset that there was a strong chance his press pass would have been cancelled. With only twenty minutes to go, Joe positioned himself to the right-hand side of the stage. He already knew that Kelp would be on the same side and he began scanning the seats, his eyes darting from one to the other. In the centre, between the stage and the main body of the hall, a long table with big microphones awaited the independent journalists, who would ask questions of each candidate. He watched as they moved to their seats, sat down and started shuffling papers. The seats were now filling up in the auditorium but he couldn't see Acquilan. He half expected to see him sitting with Mason, Levinson, Donald and the other members of Kelp's campaign team – but there was no sign of him. There were now only five minutes to go. He walked across to Levinson, who was sitting on a seat on the edge by the aisle.

'Hey,' he began, 'Joe Schwartz, *Washington Post*.' He flashed his pass.

'How'ya doin?' Levinson glanced at him and then his pass. 'You got the wrong man – you don't want me, you want Jim Donald just up there, aisle six.'

'No, it's not him I want,' Schwartz said. 'I'm after Victor Acquilan.'

This time there was no smile. 'As I said, you've got to speak to Jim Donald.'

'No, you don't understand. Acquilan promised to talk to me here just after this was all over,' Schwartz lied as he glanced up and down the row of seats, his pulse pounding.

'He's not here. And I also happen to know he doesn't give interviews, so if you want to speak to someone,' Levinson turned away from Schwartz and pointed down the row of seats, 'speak to him.'

Schwartz gritted his teeth as he walked away from Levinson. He wanted to be sure, so he decided to wait for Kelp's entrance, his eyes meanwhile scanning the lobby, returning involuntarily to where Mason, Levinson and Donald sat. Their blank faces made him angry as he thought of Jack Douglas. But he knew he had to hide his emotions or he'd give it all away.

At that moment the candidates were announced and the audience started applauding. Schwartz looked carefully up and down the rows of faces one more time.

'Got to be sure,' he told himself. He listened impassively as the President and Kelp were introduced and the first question was asked. Only when he was certain he couldn't see Acquilan did he start to move towards the entrance and the payphones. The aisle was full of journalists, photographers and camera crews and he made slow progress. The candidates were well into their first answers when he pushed open the door and walked out.

Across the other side of the hall, Laura Buckley forced her

405

way through a group of photographers and stood still just in front of them. She felt more and more depressed. She'd been in the hall for fifteen minutes and hadn't seen either Joe Schwartz or John. She hadn't expected there to be so many people and was beginning to wonder whether she was likely to see them even if they were in the hall. As the applause began, her shoulders sank and she decided to return to the entrance. She had just squeezed past the last of the photographers when she felt, rather than saw, a figure standing in front of her. She knew before she even looked at his face that it was Walter Harvey.

'Laura,' he whispered, 'what . . .?' She held her fingers to her lips and shook her head. He held onto her arm.

'Wait, we must talk,' he insisted. 'You owe me that at least.' He reached down and grasped the pass hanging round her neck between his thumb and forefinger and shook it slightly, 'You promised,' he whispered.

He was right of course, but she couldn't explain to him now. She hesitated and it was just at that point her eye caught some movement on the far side of the hall, someone walking towards the rear. Someone was leaving? Strange, she thought – the debate had only just started. She looked across and could just make out from behind a grey-haired man. Somehow he seemed familiar. Her heart leapt.

'Joe Schwartz!' she exclaimed.

'What?' asked Walter Harvey.

'Sorry, Walter, I've just got to go,' she whispered back at him.

'Laura,' he held onto her arm, 'what's happening?' He looked at her with such concerned eyes that she stopped for a moment.

'Walter, I just can't explain – I'm in something big. Look, you'll just have to trust me, please. I must go.' She gave him a weak smile and, twisting away, shook her arm free of his hand.

'Laura,' he appealed. But she was gone. 'Take care . . . just take care.'

John stood by the telephone and waited. He stared at his paper, his heart pounding. Perhaps he had missed the call? What then? 'Ring! Ring!' he repeated to himself. 'For God's sake, ring!' A man with a limp walked towards the telephones and made as though to enter the cubicle directly ahead of him. John quickly stepped in front of him and picked up the receiver as if about to make a call while sliding his finger across the bar on the top and holding it down. He knew that this was the telephone he expected Joe to ring him on. The idea that it might have been engaged had not occurred to either of them and he breathed a sigh of relief as the man walked past him and into the next cubicle. Through the Perspex canopy, his eyes seemed to go straight through John before he turned away. At that moment, the telephone rang.

Lieutenant Jasinski watched Laura Buckley make her way towards the rear of the hall. He nodded to Munroe in the far corner and then followed her. Outside, a couple of San Francisco police detectives waited with Detective Sergeant Mackie. Jasinski had observed the encounter with Harvey and her sudden departure.

'OK, where is she now?' Jasinski spoke into his lapel mike as he pushed open the door of the lobby.

'She's looking around the entrance lobby,' Munroe's voice crackled in his earpiece. 'Wait! She's . . . she's going towards an old man, just walking away from the telephones.'

'Don't get too near,' Jasinski cautioned.

'Joe!' Laura shouted across the lobby. 'Joe, it's me, Laura Buckley!' She walked quickly towards Schwartz. At first he looked startled. As soon as he recognised her, he broke into a smile.

'Jeez! What are you doing here?' He stopped walking as she rushed over. 'I mean, we both – that is John and me – thought you were dead!'

Laura grabbed hold of his arm, 'John's OK? Where is he, Joe? I've got to see him!'

Schwartz hesitated before replying. 'You by yourself?'

'Of course. Well, that is, I've got John's uncle with me – they kidnapped him.'

'Acquilan and Kelp?'

'Must have been, who else?'

People were coming and going, it was time to move. 'I've got to get to the Mark Hopkins,' he replied.

'Is that where John is?'

'Maybe . . . I only came to check that Acquilan was here with Kelp and the others. He wasn't . . .' He hesitated again. 'You ain't wired or anything, are you?'

'No!' she looked startled.

'OK. Well, John's waiting for me and we're going to confront him. He's probably at the hotel now. I don't have much time to . . .' he stopped.

'What is it, Joe?'

'I just realised, they were all there – Mason, Levinson, Donald, everyone, everyone except . . .'

'What's the matter, Joe?'

'Got to make another call,' he insisted and moved quickly back towards the telephones. She watched as he dialled frantically. No answer. He dialled again. No answer.

'The fool!' he muttered, emerging from the booth.

'Why? What's happening, Joe?' Laura grabbed him. 'For Christ's sake, Joe, let me into the picture – tell me!'

'I hope I'm wrong but I've just realised two other faces were missing from the line-up.'

'Who?'

'Weitz and that man Pichowski,' he began to hurry past her towards the door as he spoke.

'So?' She chased after him.

'Don't you see, that means that they're up there too, all three of them – it's a trap!'

'What do you mean? You said he was waiting for you.'

'He's meant to.'

'So call him!'

'He's not there – he's gone,' Schwartz stopped speaking, his craggy features strained, his mouth tight. 'He was meant to wait by the phone till I got there just in case I turned out to be wrong and Acquilan showed up . . .'

'But that doesn't mean . . .' she began.

'Yes, it does! He's going to do it alone. He doesn't seem to care about taking chances; he just goes on blaming himself.'

'Look, I've got a cab by the door with his uncle in it. If we leave now, we might just get there. Let's go!'

They rushed out of the door and jumped into the waiting cab.

John put the receiver down. The thick-set man with the limp whom John had seen in the next cubicle was still talking and kept glancing at him every few seconds. 'Wait by the phone' had been Schwartz's last words as he dropped him off. But John had no intention of waiting. He knew now that Acquilan was not at the debate. He had to assume he was in his room but if not, he'd have to return there anyway at some point.

Time to move. He walked towards the elevator doors and waited. He made certain his pass with its big red P was visible and he even forced himself to smile at the nearby guard. The man stared back impassively, his heavy jowls moving up and down as he chewed gum. John found himself nervously fingering the cold metal barrel of the Luger.

An electronic bell sounded and the elevator doors slid open. Then, as he stepped in, he was vaguely aware of the sound of a phone ringing. He remembered Schwartz's words

409

and felt a pang of guilt. His eyes fell on two men standing in front of the telephones. He recognised one of them as the man who'd been in the next cubicle. They were staring at him but when he made eye contact, they turned away.

'You got a problem, fella?' the guard growled.

'Sorry' – should he walk away? Then the hiss as the door started to shut. The door opened again, 'No problem, just . . .' The telephone rang again. 'I was just, distracted.' He stepped quickly into the elevator as the doors closed and, pressing the button, he felt the elevator rise.

Cocooned in the metal cylinder, he was strangely calm. Then all too soon, the doors slid open. Cautiously he stepped out into a long hotel corridor with rooms on either side. No security, which struck him as strange at first, but then he remembered Schwartz explaining that Acquilan was not on the official floor.

He counted the room numbers as he went along the corridor. All was quiet – he was alone with his thoughts.

His lips were dry and his heart pounded. What should he do when he got there? Knock? Demand entrance? He touched the cold metal gun for reassurance. He stopped and faced one of the doors. He cast his eyes up and down the corridor, then checking his watch, he swallowed hard. He took a pace forward and reached out, about to knock, then stopped. Pushing the Luger out of his pocket and remembering Schwartz's instructions, he cocked it. He felt the back part lift up, there was a heavy click and then he let it go. He stared at the pistol for a few seconds before sliding it back into his overcoat pocket. Again he checked the empty corridor and reached out to knock, then again he stopped. He noticed that above the door handle in the computer key slot was the entry card. He pulled it out and turned it over in his fingers before pushing it down in the slot. As a green light flashed, he swallowed hard and put his right hand onto the door handle.

Inside, the room was darker than the corridor and his eyes took a couple of seconds to accustom themselves to the gloom.

'Ah, Mr Grande . . .' A voice sounded to his right.

John stepped forward and turned, startled. The television was on in the corner of a large room. The overhead lights were dimmed and as John shut the door behind him, he saw a large man with thick grey hair and a heavy-set face sitting behind a dining-room table, on which had been spread a white cloth.

'Do come in, I've been expecting you.'

John reached up to his belt buckle and pressed the button at the back to start the recording. He then slipped his right hand down into his pocket as he moved towards the front of the desk.

'I take it you're Acquilan?'

'That's right, you've found him.' Acquilan smiled. 'Do take a seat,' he pointed at an upright dining-room chair just in front of the desk. 'You'll forgive me,' he said turning back towards the television, 'only I must finish watching this.'

John remained standing while he looked around the room. Two wing-back chairs and two large silk-covered sofas positioned at one end of the room round a coffee table, the cloth-covered dining-room table with Acquilan behind it at the other. Just beyond Acquilan, there was a door ajar but whatever was behind it was in pitch darkness. A sixth sense told John something wasn't quite right about the arrangement of the furniture. It was as though the table had been moved to cover the corner of the room just in front of the half-open door. It all pointed to the fact that he'd been expected. All these arrangements, the man was well ahead of him. But Acquilan's demeanour was so calm as he watched the television it seemed hard to believe that he'd been hunting John all these months. John grasped the handle of the Luger more tightly, his hand sweating.

'Well . . .' Kelp's voice rang out from the television 'we've heard many times about the President's tough stance on crime. Yet talk is cheap. You see, when I tried to push my mandatory Life for Rapists Bill through the Senate ten years ago, when he was there, I got no support from him.' Acquilan's eyes were focused on the television and John followed them as the cameras cut to the audience applauding Kelp's words.

'And . . .' Kelp's dry voice continued, 'as President, one of his first acts was the early-release programme. This led in his own home state to the early release of Sam Garbenkin, a previously convicted rapist and arsonist, who then went out and raped and murdered Louise Schweik and four others – only days after he was released.' Again the audience reaction. 'Wrong, Mr President, wrong, and someone else, as usual, has to pick up the pieces.' Some of the audience started to cheer and clap, others booed as Kelp finished unfolding the story. 'Now you've cancelled the programme, but how many other Garbenkins were there before you did that? The difference between us is I would never have started it.' Laughter followed the applause. The camera cut to President Carson, who looked straight ahead, unmoved.

'Well,' Acquilan said, as he aimed the remote at the TV and switched it off, 'that should wrap up the nomination.' He turned and looked at John, 'Not going to sit down?'

'No, I'll stand.'

'OK,' Acquilan shrugged. 'Suit yourself.' His face was expressionless. 'You know, Mr Grande, you should never have got involved.'

'I don't recall having the choice,' John shot back.

'Oh yes, you did. You should have ignored the damaged picture. You see, I know about that, too – you should have let it go as it was.'

'Oh, and I suppose you and your thugs wouldn't have murdered my partner as a result?'

'You just don't get it, do you? A smart guy like you and you still don't get it.' Acquilan smiled as he spoke, 'His murder had nothing to do with me.'

'Nor, I suppose, the lawyer in Rome or the lawyer in New York – just accidents, fortuitous accidents, I suppose.'

'Perhaps, but nothing to do with me. Though I grant you that the evidence probably points this way. The thing is, you've been used.'

'Yes, by you.'

'No, by someone else.'

'Who?'

'Cosmo.'

'Cosmo?'

'Oh yes, I forgot. You'd use his other name. Let me see, let me see – D'Ostia, that was the guy's name,' he laughed. 'What a screwball name!'

John was taken aback. All the questions he wanted to ask, the logical excuses he'd expected – it was not meant to be like this.

'The final contact I had with him was last summer in Positano,' John replied defensively. 'He sold some pictures to me which, you cannot deny, your people wanted to buy. But that wasn't enough, was it? You had to murder my partner to try and make it look like me!' John's face flushed as he gripped the pistol handle in his pocket. 'And besides,' he continued, 'D'Ostia has been dead for months.'

'Maybe, or maybe not. But you were still part of his plan.'

'What plan?'

'His plan to get even.'

'You're mad – you're just covering yourself. The fact is that you tried to kill me from the outset and managed to murder others, and you've been after some diaries, even though I've never seen the damn things and I doubt they even exist.'

'You're right there, I did want the diaries. I still do, if they exist. But you're as important as they are.' Acquilan picked up a cigar which had been lying on the table and lit it. 'Over

413

the last few months, Cosmo has set us both up. Oh, I know all the evidence points to us, but through you. You're a walking confession and he wants you dead as much as he wants Kelp ruined and me destroyed. We're all part of the same game.'

John felt numb. Was the man telling the truth or not? Did he know he was being taped? Surely it couldn't be true? But that picture hadn't been damaged by accident – Maguire had confirmed as much – it had been done before it even went in the case. Then there was the way he was drawn along the trail bit by bit – he never could reason why.

'This is all nonsense,' John stiffened. 'I hardly know the man apart from the pictures, and that was months ago. He'd have no reason to kill me. You, however, are a different story, everything points to you. First the pictures, then the diaries; you wanted them both desperately enough to kill for them. No one goes to the trouble of cleaning paintings up and creating a private gallery around them if they just wanted to get rid of incriminating evidence. No, you wanted them, you wanted them badly, and you got them – I know all about it.'

'Sure, you're right, I do want them. I want them because they are mine. These,' he picked up the photographs of the paintings, 'they're just photographs of restored pictures. Could be anywhere, could be owned by anyone. Where's your proof?'

'Not just any pictures, everyone in the art world knows they've been missing since the war.'

'Sure,' Acquilan nodded, 'but where are they?'

'With you, of course.'

'Where does it say that?'

'There are a number of witnesses, they'll all testify.'

'You meant the small-time security guy and that black hooker. I think not – we'll be seeing to them.'

John felt a cold chill run down his spine. 'You bastard!' he exclaimed and took a pace forward, then stopped when he found himself staring down the long thin barrel of an automatic pistol.

'Only those who meddle and who shouldn't. I never started this, but I'm sure as hell going to finish it.'

'Like Douglas and Laura Buckley?'

'Well, for what it's worth, I hated that self-righteous bastard but I didn't have anything to do with his murder.' Acquilan shook his head. 'I can't pretend I'm sorry, though.'

'Easily said. Your people must have done it.'

'No, you don't know the whole story. You've only got yourself to blame for Douglas. He was all your fault – you ought to have known better. You should never have got the guy involved, nor the others. All of this is because of you. If you hadn't decided to play "detective" we wouldn't be here now. And as for Buckley, again for a bright guy, you sure are dumb. Why should I know what's happened to her?'

At that moment the phone rang. John started at its shrill tone. Acquilan checked his watch and then picked it up.

'Bernie? Good! All the boys in place? And Pichowski? Good! When the other two come up, give me five minutes and alert the cops. See you later.' He put the receiver down.

Downstairs, Bernie Weitz shut his cell phone and opened his briefcase. Inside were his passport, air ticket and cash. Shutting his briefcase, he closed his eyes. In five minutes, he would have discharged his last obligation to Kelp and Acquilan. He sat back and waited.

'Looks like we're going to have company, Mr Grande, and that's good because I was getting tired of this conversation,' Acquilan laughed.

He was right, John thought, they were all dead because of him. There was an empty feeling in the pit of his stomach as he thought of Laura and the others.

'No, sir,' Acquilan mused, puffing at his cigar. 'You might look like him, but sure as hell that's where it ends.'

'Who?'

'You really don't know, do you? The man we used to know as Major Oakley.' John frowned and Acquilan smiled. 'Your father.'

John's eyes were wide open, 'My father?'

'All of this and you still don't know. He was the one who was with us in Naples. Planned the whole customs scam with the pictures and everything else. Got Licatta to paint over them and got us the best prices for the gold at the time. He had one of the coldest, most calculating brains I ever came across. He was brilliant.' Acquilan opened a file on his desk and pointed to a black and white picture: 'There.' He shoved it across the table.

John looked down. He knew at once. A young man in military uniform stared back at him. It was a picture he'd seen a hundred times before.

'Oakley, but who's Oakley? My name is . . .'

'It was obviously a fake name! Once the deal was done, he just disappeared. I never saw him again. That was one ruthless, bastard!' he exclaimed.

'But why?'

'Cosmo? It was your father who planned to get rid of Morrow and Cosmo,' he laughed. 'More for the rest of us, he said. He reckoned they'd blab.'

'Why?'

'Because Cosmo and Morrow wanted out when we knocked off Licatta – another part of your father's plan. Like I said, cool, really cool.'

John remained gazing at the picture. All of this, his partner Richard Patrick, the lawyer in Rome, Goldstein . . . the list went on . . . all of this because his father had helped in their plan. John's hand tightened again in frustration on the gun. The realisation that he'd been tossed around and used because of something his father did made his anger rise.

'Sins of the father, eh, Mr Grande?' Acquilan laughed. 'And of course, it was your father who . . .'

They were interrupted by a sharp rap on the door.

'Move back to the wall,' spat Acquilan. 'Whatever you do, don't move suddenly. Remember, this gun is on you at all times.'

Another rap.

'Laundry!' A muted voice from the other side of the announced. 'It's open,' Acquilan replied and slid the gun underneath the desk.

The door opened and a man in a white coat stood with a suit on a hanger covered with polythene in one hand and a box in the other.

'Where do you want them?'

'Put them on the chair over there,' Acquilan replied, inclining his head in the direction of the wing-back chair.

The man shut the door and limped over towards the chair. As he did so, Acquilan pulled the gun out from his lap and pointed it at the man. 'Now,' Acquilan ordered, 'keep your hands where I can see them and walk over to the front of the table.'

The man's hand stopped at the front of his white jacket.

'Don't even think about it. As I said, over here – and quickly!' Acquilan barked the orders out.

The man's face was impassive. As he got closer, John recognised him as the man who'd been downstairs by the telephones. He had a heavy-set face, lined with a dark stubble.

'That'll do,' Acquilan said. 'Now, who the hell are you?'

'The name is Morrow. Perhaps you remember my father, Corporal Morrow . . .?' He shot the words out in a low voice. The colour drained from Acquilan's face and his lips tightened.

'Pichowski!' he shouted, inclining his head towards the door behind him, 'Pichowski, get in here!'

'Well, Mr . . .' Acquilan waited as the door behind him opened, '. . . Morrow, I should have guessed, it needed two memories to pursue the vendetta the way you both have. Well, it's all going to be over now.'

John was watching the door, expecting to see Pichowski but instead, to his surprise, the man who came through the door was young and heavily built. In his right hand he carried an automatic pistol with a long dark silencer attached. John shuddered as he saw what was in his left hand – a thin switch blade, which was covered in blood. The man stood behind Acquilan and brought the pistol up behind his ear as Acquilan finished speaking.

'Sure it is, Mr Acquilan, it's over now for all of you,' the young man said. 'Put your gun down on the desk or I'll leave your brains there instead.'

Acquilan slowly lowered his gun onto the desk. 'Where is . . .?' he began.

'Pichowski?' the young man interrupted, and his lips curled into a smile as he raised the knife in his left and flourished it in front of Acquilan's nose. 'Why, he's gone ahead of you, down there,' he jerked the knife point down towards the floor.

The older man quickly reached into his jacket and pulled out another pistol. From his pocket he took out a silencer and fitted it onto the front of the barrel.

'Put the knife away!' Morrow ordered. 'Weitz?' He looked at the young man.

'Not in there, Pa,' he answered as he folded the blade back and slipped it into his pocket.

'OK,' Morrow waved his gun at John, 'you deal with him.'

'Wait!' John shouted, 'Wait, surely I've got nothing to do with all this?'

'Nothing?' Morrow sneered. 'Your father was with this creep,' he jabbed the gun at Acquilan. 'They double-crossed my father and Cosmo, and murdered my father and the painter Licatta. Nothing to do with this?' he spat. 'Oh no, well, we'll have the greatest pleasure in finishing this after fifty years of waiting. Maybe we can't get your father but you're more than good enough.'

John had used the few seconds while Morrow was talking

to raise the Luger slightly in his pocket so that it pointed, he hoped and prayed, in the direction of the man ahead of him. As Morrow finished speaking, he squeezed the trigger.

There was a deafening crash as the gun went off. It kicked back into his hand and twisted him around. Almost at the same moment another gun went off and John felt as though he had been punched in the left shoulder, followed by a painful burning sensation like a red hot poker being pushed through him. He fell heavily on to his right side, winded, and lay gasping for breath, everything around him blurred.

Morrow jumped as John's gun went off and at the same moment his son fired his. Morrow watched horrified as his son pitched backwards and fell against the door, crumpling onto the floor. Shaking, he pointed his gun purposefully at John's head but before he could pull the trigger, there was a loud crash from another gun. Jerking his head round, Morrow stared at Acquilan, his mouth opening and closing before he fell to the floor.

As John fought to get his breath back and his vision cleared, he could see Acquilan turning the pistol, smoke oozing from its barrel, towards him.

'Now, Mr Grande, your turn . . .'

'Police! Nobody move!' someone screamed. Then it was all a confusion of men and guns.

John lay still, the pain sweeping over him in waves. He was drifting into unconsciousness when someone turned him over. Again, that burning sensation.

'Stay still!' a voice barked at him. A hand roamed over him and through his pockets. 'L'tenant! This one's hit and he's got some goddamn cannon on him! Blown a hole through his jacket.'

John tried to sit up as a medic knelt beside him. The man put an arm round him and helped him into a sitting position. He took some large scissors out of his bag and started cutting off the sleeve of John's jacket.

'. . . Sure, all of them . . .' John could hear Acquilan's voice, 'threatened me. That one tried to shoot me, missed and must have hit his partner.' John could see he was pointing in his direction. He wanted to shout out that it was all lies, but he just couldn't find the strength. His eyes closed.

'Ah, at last John Grande!'

John was surprised to hear a Scots accent and he nodded, opening his eyes.

'Are you badly hurt?'

'Yes, it hurts like hell . . .' John's voice was barely a whisper. 'What on earth . . . ?'

'Remember me? Detective Sergeant Mackie, Crime Squad?'

Even in his present state, John could see the almost comic absurdity of the situation. Here in San Francisco, surrounded by heavily armed policemen screaming out commands, and the first person to speak to him was a soft-spoken Scot from the Crime Squad in London. Despite the pain, he smiled. His smile was cut short as the medic, having removed half his jacket, began probing the wound.

'Aagh! Careful!' John screamed.

'You're lucky,' the medic replied in a matter-of-fact voice. 'It's passed clean through; a flesh wound that hasn't hit any major blood vessels.' He started to dress and patch up the wound.

Mackie watched John grimace as the dressing was applied. It seemed so long ago and a whole world away since he'd last spoken to him. So much had changed, even he had changed. Now it was all over. The hunt had ended.

'He's lying,' John struggled to be heard, but his voice was no more than a whisper, 'He who was going to kill me . . .' He gave up the struggle and lay quiet.

'Another one in here, L'tenant!' A voice screamed out from the room beyond the covered table.

'An awful lot of bodies to explain, Mr Grande,' Mackie said. 'You seem to be followed everywhere by dead bodies.

What are you doing here? You say you weren't trying to kill him? And if you weren't trying to kill him, why do you need a Luger?'

'Trying to prove that he'd set me up for all the murders you mentioned . . .' John breathed.

'Well, it's just your word against his. It doesn't look good.'

'Maybe not, but if you check the small of my back, I think you'll find that'll help explain it all – a tape recorder.'

Mackie slipped his hand behind John's back. 'You taped everything?' he asked.

John grimaced again as the last part of the strapping was applied to his wound.

Mackie stood up and beckoned to Jasinski. 'He recorded their meeting.'

'Smart guy!' Jasinski exclaimed under his breath.

'Maintains Acquilan set out to kill him . . .' Mackie continued.

'Well, if that's all on tape, he's home free.'

'Detective Sergeant Mackie here tells me you were wired,' Jasinski spoke as he knelt down.

'Yes.'

'Well, let's hope for your sake, there's something on that tape. Right now, things don't look too good for you. Acquilan there,' – Jasinski waved his hand towards Acquilan, who was now sitting in a wing-back chair on the far side of the room – 'he's a very influential guy and he says you came in with the other two and threatened him. Now the way I see it, this is his room and it doesn't look like you were invited. You not only threatened him – he says you blew that young guy over there away. And your partner here,' Jasinski pointed to Morrow, who was now being carried out on a stretcher, 'was shot in self-defence. You've also got to explain what you were doing with a World War Two unlicensed gun. It doesn't look like you came in peace, Grande, and you're wanted on two continents for murder. Your story had better be good.'

421

John was helped to his feet. Jasinski unbuttoned the front of his shirt and, lifting it and what was left of the jacket up above his head, he unstrapped the tape recorder. The pull of the sticky tape on his skin caused John to exhale in pain but it was over in a matter of seconds. John thought he caught the faintest trace of a smile as Jasinski and Mackie looked at each other briefly.

'You OK?' Jasinski asked, tapping the tape machine up and down in his hand. John nodded in reply. He was feeling weak but stable. 'Well, we'll go out by the back door,' Jasinski continued. 'Take Grande first, I want another word with Mr Acquilan, and then we'll follow.' Jasinski held the tape between his thumb and forefinger. 'We'll be down in a few minutes.'

Mackie smiled and walked over to the door with Grande and Detective Munroe.

Ralph Grande sat quietly, as immobile as a statue. His eyes were fixed on the elevator doors. Laura, sitting next to him, reached across and squeezed his hands a couple of times. Outwardly, it looked as though she was attempting to reassure an old and clearly tired man, but it was as much to calm herself. Joe Schwartz paced up and down, a cigarette clamped between his teeth.

They had made it to the hotel, but the police had caught them at the entrance. Schwartz realised there was no alternative but to tell them where he thought John was. They were held downstairs while the police took over.

To the right of the elevator, there was a wide corridor, which ended in double fire doors opening onto the parking lot behind. Separating a small lounge where Laura sat was a low screen. Schwartz, meanwhile, had stopped pacing up and down and was deep in conversation with Gene Meyer, who had just arrived. The uniformed police officer stood just behind Ralph while another police officer was behind Meyer and Schwartz.

'Do you think he's all right?' Ralph was anxious.

Laura made no answer, her pulse was racing fast and she was again overcome by waves of panic. She didn't trust herself to speak as her mouth and throat were dry. All she could manage was to squeeze Ralph's hand. He didn't ask again.

Laura focused on the elevator doors. She was no longer concerned that she'd led the police to John but rather that the police should have got to him in time. She was scared. It wasn't fear for her own wellbeing, but of John being taken from her at this last moment. In just a few months, her whole life had been turned upside-down. Here she was, a fugitive in police custody, unconcerned that a successful career in broad-casting was over, but worrying about the wellbeing of a strange English murder suspect.

The elevator bell sounded and the doors slid open. Laura and Ralph immediately stiffened; Schwartz and Meyer stopped talking. An overweight man in a raincoat stepped out.

'Sam, over here!' Meyer called out.

'It's no good, Gene,' Sam Dunbar began. 'I can't wait up there, they've sealed the whole floor off.'

'What's happening?'

'Nothing much to go on yet. There's been a shooting – it's gonna be a while before the bodies come down.'

At the word 'bodies', Laura stood up and walked quickly towards the group.

'What about John Grande, was he . . .' She pushed herself past the others and stood facing Dunbar. She couldn't bring herself to finish her sentence.

'I don't know,' Dunbar shrugged.

At that moment, the elevator bell sounded again and everyone spun towards the door. As she caught sight of John, Laura rushed forward. Startled, she stopped as she saw his ripped shirt and jacket, and his arm in a sling. Blood was just starting to stain the pad on his left shoulder and she was shocked to see how pale his face was, his eyes bloodshot and glazed. John didn't see her at first, he just stared straight ahead.

'John!' Laura tried to shout, but her voice was hoarse and came out as a loud whisper. 'John!' This time it carried more force. She stepped forward again, her arms outstretched as he turned towards her.

'Laura? My God!' he whispered. 'It's you – you're alive!' Was he seeing a ghost? The uniformed police officer in the group immediately stepped between them but Detective Sergeant Mackie gestured to him and he backed off. Laura was about to embrace John when she remembered the arm. She looked up and they kissed.

'Thank God!' she whispered. 'Thank God! I thought . . . We all thought . . . Thank God!' She smiled up at him but, seeing his shoulder, her expression instantly changed.

'I thought, when I hadn't heard from you, that they'd killed you. I never believed I'd see you again,' John said, a weak smile crossing his mouth like a shadow. He bent down and kissed her head, inhaling the scent of her hair as he closed his eyes.

Schwartz came into view, smiling broadly. John managed to smile back faintly. Then, for the first time, to his surprise he saw his uncle. 'My God! What are you doing here?'

'It's a long story, John. I'm just relieved to see you,' Ralph's round face was broken by his broad smile.

'What happened?' Laura asked as Ralph came up beside her.

'I was set up from the first, not only as a means of destroying Kelp, Acquilan and others, but also because my father, using a false name, had been in Naples and worked with Acquilan to get rid of Morrow and D'Ostia – Cosmo – in 1946. He was as bad as the rest and I was to be killed as the final act of revenge.' John frowned and cast his eyes down, 'The son of a man who helped murder someone else.'

'It isn't so!' Ralph protested.

'It's the truth. Knowing that, everything else seems to fit into place.'

'No, no! You don't understand, you're not – you weren't involved,' Ralph began, 'I should have told you before . . . I didn't know about my brother's links with Acquilan but they shouldn't have tried to kill you. You're not . . .' The bell on the elevator sounded again as the doors opened.

'Bring those three with us,' Rutgers said, pointing to Ralph, Laura and Schwartz. 'OK, let's go.'

Jasinski then emerged, preceded by a couple of police officers and Acquilan.

'Kelp's finished, Sam!' shouted Meyer, who had heard everything. 'You follow this, I'm going to that goddamn celebration party. Here's some news that should kill it.' He smiled. 'This one's for you, Jack,' he said at the top of his voice before vanishing down the steps.

Acquilan turned and stared at Meyer as he heard those words and the whole group stopped.

'Let's get out of here, for Christ's sake!' ordered Jasinski. 'Come on, Munroe, let's go.'

At that moment there was a dull thump and Acquilan pitched backwards into the open elevator. For an instant everyone was motionless, then Jasinski and the others grabbed frantically for their guns screaming, 'Get down!'

Ralph found himself looking through a gap in the screen to see, ten feet away, an old man in a wheelchair. He recognised the eyes almost immediately and then saw the gun in his right hand as it pointed towards John.

'No!' Ralph shouted to his nephew, who looked up just as Ralph grabbed him. In John's weakened state, Ralph's weight was enough to knock him over. At the same time, there was a second thump and almost immediately the sound of guns going off. That was when the screaming started as the cordite thickened the air.

425

Six seconds and it was all over. A strange and uneasy quiet descended on them. Then the shouting exploded again. Behind the screen, an old man in a wheelchair lay dead, his head lolling back over the seat, a gun on his lap. In the background, the elevator doors opened and shut relentlessly on Acquilan's lifeless legs.

John lay groaning on the ground, his face contorted in pain, his eyes blurred.

'Quick!' screamed Laura. 'He's been hit, someone, he's been hit!'

'It's my shoulder, I landed on it!' John hissed. As Detective Sergeant Mackie helped him to sit up, he noticed Ralph lying curled up, gasping for breath. Blood was visible on the old man's shirt. Mackie turned him over gently. His eyes were open but, when he coughed, blood bubbled up onto his lips.

Laura turned towards the man in the wheelchair. Before she even looked, she instinctively knew what she would see. Her first glance confirmed her worst fears – it was the thin body of her father.

She choked for a few seconds, unable to catch her breath. Then, oblivious to the noise all around her, she stood up. She felt as though someone had pumped ice through her veins. She tried moving her legs but they felt too heavy at first and they wouldn't respond. With superhuman will, she forced one foot in front of the other, staring ahead at the body of her father as she slowly walked towards him. By the time she reached him he was surrounded by police.

'Can I come through?' she asked, her voice barely more than a whisper.

'No, ma'am,' a uniformed police officer answered, barring her way.

'But you don't understand, he's my father.'

'What was that?'

'He,' she said in a much louder voice, 'he's my father.'

Her voice suddenly silenced everyone around the body and

they parted. She walked over to him, she could feel all their eyes burning into her as she did so. She bent down and took hold of his hand – it was still warm.

'Why? Why? Why?' she whispered. The father she had searched for most of her life, whom she had only so recently found, was the instrument of so much death, driven by so much hate. The tears started to flow as she moved his arm back onto his lap.

'Did you say this was your father?'

Laura turned and through her tears she found herself staring at Jasinski. She nodded.

'Over here!' another police officer shouted. Jasinski turned and walked back to Mackie. Wiping away her tears, Laura looked at Detective Sergeant Mackie, who was talking to Jasinski. 'The old man's been hit,' she heard. She went quickly to where John was now sitting up next to his uncle.

'Look, John,' Ralph struggled with the words, red flecks of foam bubbling up into the corner of his mouth, his words no more than a whisper. 'Listen to me . . .'

'Don't, Uncle Ralph, preserve your strength,' John urged.

'No,' Ralph breathed. 'I must, I should have . . . years ago . . . Your mother, I loved her . . .' There was a cough followed by another long pause as Ralph's eyes closed. 'You weren't his son . . . you were mine . . . we knew it was wrong . . . but,' his eyes opened, 'I always loved your mother and you . . . I'm so sorry . . .' His eyes closed again and there was a series of retching coughs. This time blood bubbled out of the corner of his mouth. 'It was wrong . . . she shouldn't . . . I should have told you . . . I'm so sorry. You're my son and . . . I'm so proud of you . . .' The blood had spread down his shirt as a medic arrived.

Dazed, John stared at him in disbelief. Then, taking his hand, he shouted, 'Do something, help him!' He pushed some hair back from Ralph's face. 'It's going to be all right,' he soothed, pressing his hand.

'No . . . John, I feel so cold, so cold . . .' He was slipping away; John could feel his hand slacken.

The medic was shouting as equipment arrived. He grabbed an oxygen mask and was about to put it over Ralph's face, but the eyes had closed. He placed his finger on the side of Ralph's neck, then turning to John, he shook his head gently. At that moment Laura knelt down beside John, putting her arm around him and feeling his body shake in spasms.

Laura looked away, her eyes full of tears. Through a haze she could see people crowded around her father. She felt cold and dirty.

'All that hate,' she muttered, 'all that hate . . .' She turned to John, whose white face was screwed up in anguish.

Detective Sergeant Mackie looked at Jasinski.

'He's dead,' he said and bowed his head. All his years in the police and he was unprepared for this vision of hell. 'We failed, we were just too late.'

Jasinski nodded. Mackie looked across at the wheelchair. 'What about *him?*'

'Dead too,' Jasinski answered, 'but I found these.' He held up a set of old exercise books and opened the first one.

'*1944*' was written across the top of the page. He flicked through the pages. 'They're diaries, all of them. I guess these were what they were all after. And look, they're written by a man called Kelp,' he snorted. 'I know one Senator who's just struck out!'

Laura helped John to his feet and held him, wiping his eyes.

'I never knew my father,' he said, 'or at least the man I thought was my father at all. It was always him I really loved.'

'It's ironic,' he said with bitterness. 'I always wished he was my father . . . the one thing I secretly wanted.' He took a deep breath before turning to Laura, 'And you, Laura, are you all right?'

'I guess as OK as anyone can be who finds the man she idolised was responsible for so much suffering.' She rested her head on his shoulder. 'Thank God it's over, John, the long nightmare is over for us both.'

Around them the police were sealing off the area. Across the foyer Weitz picked up his briefcase. Quickly and quietly he made for the entrance. 'You see, Victor, you just can't have it all,' he murmured.

Outside he hailed a cab. As it pulled away, the driver half-turned his head.

'You see that debate, mister?' Weitz nodded. 'That guy Kelp don't look bad – he certainly burned Carson. Hey, I think he'll do it. Whad'ya think?'

Weitz made no answer.

Letter from the Capital – Gene Meyer (Editor)

This will be the last time this column appears. Some of you reading it will be surprised to see it at all. With the death of Jack Douglas you may have assumed you had already seen the last of it. But as editor of the *Post* I wanted to write the final important farewell to a man I was proud to call my friend, my mentor and a wonderful American.

Two days ago Senator Kelp ended his campaign for the Democratic nomination. When I say 'ended', in fact it was ended for him. His connection with Victor Acquilan, a successful businessman who was killed in a shooting in San Francisco, is now under FBI investigation. It is my understanding that a number of missing paintings, stolen from Italy during the War, have been found in Mr. Acquilan's possession. Furthermore, a string of murders, in which it is believed Mr. Acquilan had become involved, are also now being investigated. In other words, a whole corrupt political and criminal ring has been broken up. The very Presidency was under threat and had it not been for Jack Douglas, assisted by Joe Schwartz – also, I must say, employed by the *Post* – none of this would have come to light. Jack's persistence, regardless of what others thought, was responsible for this successful operation.

From World War Two through Korea, right to today, Jack never stopped. The most acute journalistic brain I ever worked with, Jack was simply the best. He made a career of rooting out lies and corruption and he wasn't biased. Some of you will recall Jack was the first to call for an investigation into President Carson's land purchase scandal when he was Governor of Kentucky. That investigation has, this week, been unexpectedly dropped due to lack of evidence.

We'll all miss you, Jack, but more than that, so will the rest of this great country of ours. You were simply the best.

DIARY

Strange doings at the White House. After the surprise decision to drop the land scandal investigation, the President has had a new lease of life. So why, we ask, is he going to break off his re-election campaign to visit India for two days? It's even rumoured that just before he leaves India, he will personally hand over a six-figure donation to a project in Calcutta run by the Catholic Church for homeless children. The donor is none other than Abe Roma, the controversial and wealthy supporter of the Carson campaign and a personal friend of the President. The project is run by nuns and the Mother Superior said that she was surprised and delighted that the President had taken such a close personal interest in the project. He's not stopping there, she says that he intends to support it in the future as well.

Sure is a long way, and a lot of money, just to get the Catholic vote!